PRAISE FOR KATHLEEN WINTER AND *ANNABEL*

"A poignant and powerful first novel." — *Montreal Gazette*

"Dramatic, thematically rich . . . [with] skillful prose . . . An impressive first novel." — *Quill & Quire*

"A mesmerizing combination of crisp language, deep empathy for her well-wrought characters, and a world-savvy wisdom . . . [Winter] shows us the humanity that overrides gender and age, and the basic human traits and desires that unite us all."
— *The Telegram*

"A compelling novel, rich in character and scene."
— *Edmonton Journal*

"Winter possesses a rare blend of lyrical brilliance, descriptive power, and psychological and philosophical insight. [*Annabel* is] a compelling, gracefully written novel about mixed gender that sheds insight as surely as it rejects sensationalism. This book announces the arrival of a major writer."
— *Kirkus Reviews* (starred review)

"This is a remarkable first novel, an accomplished debut by an exciting new voice with a confident, mature style."
— *Daily Express*

"An unforgettable novel of struggles, personal and inter-personal, and Winter's empathetic voices does them justice in a way that connects reader to story. Destined to be one of the biggest novels out of Newfoundland this year, this is a story of isolation and a communication breakdown that breaks a family down, and breaks the reader down along with them." — *Telegram*

"A sprawling book filled with musical prose." — *The Walrus*

Annabel

KATHLEEN WINTER

ANANSI

Hardcover edition first published in 2010 by House of Anansi Press Inc.

This edition published in 2013 by
House of Anansi Press Inc.
110 Spadina Avenue, Suite 801
Toronto, ON, M5V 2K4
Tel. 416-363-4343
Fax 416-363-1017
www.houseofanansi.com

Distributed in Canada by
HarperCollins Canada Ltd.
1995 Markham Road
Scarborough, ON, M1B 5M8
Toll free tel. 1-800-387-0117

All of the events in this book are fictitious, and any resemblance to actual persons, living or dead, is purely coincidental.

House of Anansi Press is committed to protecting our natural environment. As part of our efforts, the interior of this book is printed on paper that contains 30% post-consumer recycled fibres, is acid-free, and is processed chlorine-free.

17 16 15 14 13   2 3 4 5 6

Library and Archives Canada Cataloguing in Publication

Winter, Kathleen
Annabel / Kathleen Winter.

Issued also in electronic format.

ISBN: 978-1-77089-334-4

I. Title.

PS8595.I618A65 2013   C813'.54   C2012-906449-1

Jacket design: Bill Douglas
Text design and typesetting: Sari Naworynski

We acknowledge for their financial support of our publishing program the Canada Council for the Arts, the Ontario Arts Council, and the Government of Canada through the Canada Book Fund.

Printed and bound in Canada

To my mother and father

*Annabel, Annabel, where did you go? I've looked high
and I've looked low.
I've looked low and I've looked high . . .*
— Kat Goldman

*Different though the sexes are, they inter-mix.
In every human being a vacillation from one sex to the
other takes place, and often it is only the clothes that
keep the male or female likeness, while underneath
the sex is the very opposite of what it is above.*
— Virginia Woolf

Prologue

"**P**APA!"

The blind man in the canoe is dreaming.

Why would a white caribou come down to Beaver River, where the woodland herd lives? Why would she leave the Arctic tundra, where light blazes incandescent, to haunt these shadows? Why would any caribou leave her herd to walk, solitary, thousands of miles? The herd is comfort. The herd is a fabric you can't cut or tear, passing over the land. If you could see the herd from the sky, if you were a falcon or a king eider, it would appear like softly floating gauze over the face of the snow, no more substantial than a cloud. "We are soft," the herd whispers. "We have no top teeth. We do not tear flesh. We do not tear at any part of life. We are gentleness itself. Why would any of us break from the herd? Break,

1

apart, separate, these are hard words. The only reason any of us would become one, and not part of the herd, is if she were lost."

The canoe, floating in a steady pool at the deep middle, has black, calm water around it, with froth floating on top from the foam around and above and below. The white caribou stands still, in a patch of sunlight between black tree trunks, staring at the man and the girl inside the vessel. The moss beneath the caribou's hooves is white and appears made of the same substance as the animal, whose outlines are barely there, considering the light above and below it. It could have been poured from light itself and made of light, as if Graham Montague and his daughter had dreamed it into being.

"Papa?" Annabel stands up in the boat. She has been told, from the time before she could walk, not to do this, but she does it. For a moment the canoe stays still, then the girl outstretches her arms towards the enchantment, this caribou that now, she sees, wears a mantle of glittering frost around its shoulders and magnificent chest. In fact there are sparkles of frost throughout its white coat, and she cannot believe her father is both blind and asleep. She cannot believe life would be so unfair that a man could miss such a sight, and she stretches out her hands, which are long, and which her father has loved, and for whose practical industry and fruition he has laboured and hoped, and the canoe capsizes in the river's calm, deep heart. It flips easily, in an instant. The gun goes down, the provisions float or go down according to their lightness and the waterfastness of their packaging.

Graham Montague has never had to swim, and he does not know how, and neither does Annabel, his daughter.

PART ONE

1

New World

WAYNE BLAKE WAS BORN at the beginning of March, during the first signs of spring breakup of the ice — a time of great importance to Labradorians who hunted ducks for food — and he was born, like most children in that place in 1968, surrounded by women his mother had known all her married life: Joan Martin, Eliza Goudie, and Thomasina Baikie. Women who knew how to ice-fish and sew caribou hide moccasins and stack wood in a pile that would not fall down in the months when their husbands walked the traplines. Women who would know, during any normal birth, exactly what was required.

The village of Croydon Harbour, on the southeast Labrador coast, has that magnetic earth all Labrador shares. You sense a striation, a pulse, as the land drinks light and emits a vibration. Sometimes you can see it with your naked eye, stripes of light coming off the land. Not every traveller senses it, but those who do keep looking for it in other places, and they find it nowhere but desert and mesa. A traveller can come from New York and feel it. Explorers, teachers, people who know good hot coffee and densely printed newspapers but who want something more fundamental, an injection of New World in their blood. Real New World, not a myth that has led to highways and more highways and the low, radioactive buildings that offer pancakes and hamburgers and gasoline on those highways. A traveller can come to Labrador and feel its magnetic energy or not feel it. There has to be a question in the person. The visitor has to be an open circuit, available to the power coming off the land, and not everybody is. And it is the same with a person born in Labrador. Some know, from birth, that their homeland has a respiratory system, that it pulls energy from rock and mountain and water and gravitational activity beyond earth, and that it breathes energy in return. And others don't know it.

Wayne was born, in bathwater, in the house of his parents, Treadway and Jacinta Blake. Treadway belonged to Labrador but Jacinta did not. Treadway had kept the traplines of his father and he was magnetized to the rocks, whereas Jacinta had come from St. John's when she was eighteen to teach in the little school in Croydon Harbour, because she thought, before she met Treadway, that it would be an adventure, and that it would enable her to teach in a St. John's school once she had three or four years of experience behind her.

"I would eat a lunch of bread and jam every day," Joan Martin told Eliza and Thomasina as Jacinta went through her fiercest labour pains in the bathtub. Every woman in Croydon Harbour spoke at one time or another of how she might enjoy living on her own. The women indulged in this dream when their husbands had been home from their traplines too long. "I would not need any supper except a couple of boiled eggs, and I'd read a magazine in bed every single night."

"I'd wear the same clothes for a week," Eliza said. "My blue wool pants and grey shirt with my nightie stuffed under them. I would never take off my nightie from September till June. And I would get a cat instead of our dogs, and I would save up for a piano."

The women did not wish away their husbands out of animosity — it was just that the unendurable winters were all about hauling wood and saving every last piece of marrow and longing for the intimacy they imagined would exist when their husbands came home, all the while knowing the intimacy would always be imaginary. Then came brief blasts of summer, when fireweed and pitcher plants and bog sundews burst open and gave the air one puff, one tantalizing scented breath that signalled life could now begin, but it did not begin. The plants were carnivorous. That moment of summer contained desire and fruition and death all in one ravenous gulp, and the women did not jump in. They waited for the moment of summer to expand around them, to expand enough to contain women's lives, and it never did.

When Jacinta was not groaning with the mind-stopping agony of having her pelvic bones wrenched apart by the baby that was coming, she too indulged in the dream. "I don't believe I'd stay here at all," she told her friends as she poured scalding coffee from the small enamel pot, her belly as big as a young seal under her blue apron covered in tiny white flowers. "I'd move back to Monkstown Road and if I couldn't get a job teaching I'd get my old job back at the Duckworth Laundry, washing white linen for the Newfoundland Hotel."

Thomasina was the only woman who did not indulge. She had not had a father, and she regarded her husband, Graham Montague, with great respect. She had not got over the fact that he could fix anything, that he did not let the house grow cold, that he was the last man to leave for his traplines and the first to come home to her, that he was blind and needed her, or that he had given her Annabel, a red-haired daughter whom she called my bliss and my bee, and who helped her father navigate his canoe now that she was eleven years old and had a head on her as level and judicious as Thomasina's own. Graham was out now, as were all the hunters in Croydon Harbour, on the river in his white canoe, and Annabel was with him. She rode the bow and told him where to steer, though he knew every movement he needed to make with his paddle before Annabel told him, since before she was born he had travelled the river by listening and could hear every stone and ice pan and stretch of whitewater. He told her stories in the canoe, and her favourite was a true story about the white caribou that had joined the woodland herd and that her father had encountered only once, as a boy, before he had the accident that blinded him. Annabel looked for the white caribou on every trip, and when Thomasina told her it might not be alive any more, or it might have gone back to its Arctic tribe, her husband turned his face towards her and silently warned her not to stop their daughter from dreaming.

As her baby's head crowned, Jacinta's bathroom brimmed with snow light. Razor clam shells on her windowsill glowed white, and so did the tiles, the porcelain, the shirts of the women and their skin, and whiteness pulsed through her sheer curtains so that the baby's hair and face became a focal point of saturated colour in the white room; goldy brown hair, red face, black little eyelashes, and a red mouth.

Down the hall from Jacinta's birthing room, her kitchen puckered and jounced with wood heat. Treadway dropped caribou cakes into spitting pork fat, scalded his teabag, and cut a two-inch-thick chunk of partridgeberry loaf. He had no intention of lollygagging in the house during the birth — he was here for his dinner and would slice through Beaver River again in an hour in his white canoe. His hat was white and so were his sealskin coat

and canvas pants and his boots. This was how generations of Labrador men had hunted in the spring.

A duck could not tell a white hunter's canoe from
an ice pan. The canoe, with the hunter reclining in it,
slid dangerously through the black water, silently slowing
near the flock, whether the flock flew high overhead or
rested their fat bellies on the water's skin. Treadway lived
for the whiteness and the silence. He could not see with
his ears as Graham Montague could, but he could hear,
if he emptied himself of all desire, the trickle of spring
melt deep inland. He could inhale the medicinal shock
of Labrador tea plants with their leathery leaves and
orange, furry undersides, and watch the ways of flight
of the ducks, ways that were numerous and that told a
hunter what to do. Dips and turns and degrees of speed
and hesitation told him exactly when to raise his gun and
when to hide it. Their markings were written on the sky
as plain as day, and Treadway understood completely
how Graham Montague could hit ducks accurately even
though he was blind, for he had himself noticed the con-
stant mathematical relationship between the ducks' position and the hollow, sweeping sounds their wings made, a
different sound for each kind of turning, and their voices
that cracked the silence of the land. The movements of
the ducks were the white hunter's calligraphy.

This was a kind of message younger people had lost,
but Treadway was attuned to every line and nuance. There
were words for each movement of a duck, and Treadway

had learned all of the words from his father. People five years younger than he knew only half the words, but Treadway knew them all, in his speech and in his body. This was how he lived, by the nuances of wild birds over land and water, and by the footprints and marks of branches in snow on his trapline, and the part of him that understood these languages detested time in houses. Clocks ticked, and doilies sat on furniture, and stagnant air rushed into his pores and suffocated him. It was not air at all, but suffocating gauze crammed with dust motes, and it was always too warm. If the women dreaming of life without their husbands could know how he felt, they would not imagine themselves single with such gaiety. Treadway did not tell this to other men, laughing over broken buns of hot bread and pots of coffee, but he dreamed it nonetheless. He dreamed living his life over again, like the life of his great-uncle Gaetan Joseph, who had not married but who had owned a tiny hut one hundred miles along the trapline, equipped with hard bread, flour, split peas, tea, a table made out of a spruce stump with two hundred rings, a seal-hide daybed, and a tin stove. Treadway would have read and meditated and trapped his animals and cured pelts and studied. Gaetan Joseph had studied Plutarch and Aristotle and Pascal's *Pensées*, and Treadway had some of his old books in his own trapper's hut, and he had others besides that he read deep into the nights when he was blessed with the solitude of his trapline. A lot of trappers did this. They left home, they trapped, and they meditated and studied. Treadway was one of them, a man who studied not just words but pathways of wild creatures, pulsations of the northern lights, trajectories of the stars. But he did not know how to study women, or understand the bonds of family life, or achieve any kind of real happiness indoors. There were times he wished he had never been seduced by the pretty nightgowns Jacinta wore, made of such blowy, insubstantial ribbons and net that they would not have enough strength to hold the smallest ouananiche. The closest thing to these nightgowns in his world outdoors was the fizz of light that hung in a veil around the Pleiades. He had a Bible in his trapper's library, and he remembered his wife's loveliness when he read the lines Who can bind the sweet influence of the Pleiades, or loose the bands of Orion? He read these lines on his hard daybed when he had been away from her for months, and they made him remember her loveliness. But did he ever tell her this? He did not.

Home from the trapline, recovered from all loneliness, Treadway loved his wife because he had promised he would. But the centre of the wilderness called him, and he loved that centre more than any promise. That wild centre was a state of mind, but it had a geographical point as well. The point was in an unnamed lake. Canadian mapmakers had named the lake but the people who inhabited the Labrador interior had given it a different name, a name that remains a secret. From a whirlpool in the centre of that lake, river water flows in two directions. It flows southeast down to the Beaver River and through Hamilton Inlet and past Croydon Harbour into the North Atlantic, and another current flows northwest from the centre, to Ungava Bay. The whirling centre was the birthplace of seasons and smelt and caribou herds and deep knowledge that a person could not touch in domesticity. Treadway left this place at the end of the trapping season and faithfully came back to his house, which he had willingly built when he was twenty, but he considered the house to belong to his wife, while the place where waters changed direction belonged to him, and would belong to any son he had.

And now the head of his and Jacinta's first baby glittered beautifully in the white bathroom without his witnessing it, and so did the shoulders, the belly with its cord, the penis, thighs, knees, and toes. Thomasina hooked a plug of slime out of the baby's mouth with her pinky, slicked her big hand over face, belly, buttocks like butter over one of her hot loaves, and slipped the baby back to its mother. It was as the baby latched on to Jacinta's breast that Thomasina caught sight of something slight, flower-like; one testicle had not descended, but there was something else. She waited the eternal instant that women wait when a horror jumps out at them. It is an instant that men do not use for waiting, an instant that opens a door to life or death. Women look through the opening because something might be alive in there. What Thomasina knew, as she looked through the opening this time, was that something can go wrong, not just with the child in front of you, another woman's child, but with your own child, at any time, no matter how much you love it.

Thomasina bent over Jacinta and the baby in a midwife's fashion, a ministering arc, and wrapped a blanket around the child, a cotton blanket that had been washed many times. She did not believe in putting anything new or synthetic next to a newborn's skin. As she adjusted the blanket she quietly moved the one little testicle and saw that the baby also had labia and a vagina. This she took in as Treadway, in another room, threw his teabag in the garbage, as he gave his crust to the dog and clicked shut the front door, as he went out on the last perfect duck hunt of his days, and she let Treadway go. Thomasina asked Eliza and Joan to get the warm towels for Jacinta. She herself handed Jacinta the thick pad to soak up the postpartum blood, and helped her into the terrycloth robe that Jacinta would wear for the next few days.

Then she said, "I'm going to ask the others to leave, if it's all right with you. We have something to talk about."

2

Beaver River

HAD WAYNE NOT BEEN BORN IN 1968 in a place where caribou moss spreads in a white-green carpet, and where smoke plumes from houses, and where gold sand is so remote no crowds gather — the sand is a lonely stretch under the northern lights — things might have gone differently. Treadway was not an unkind man. His neighbours said he would give you the shirt off his back — and if that shirt had not been full of sweat from hauling wood and skinning animals and auguring ice, he might indeed have done so. He was a soft-hearted man when it came to anyone he felt was less practically talented than himself, and this covered a lot of people. He would help a man split wood, build a house, or cut a hole in the right place in the ice, not to show off his superior skills but to save the man time. He did these things out of pure helpfulness, with kindness thrown in.

Pure kindness he saved for his dogs. On one hunting trip he had accidentally shot the eye of his old English setter, a mild-mannered dog whose jaw quivered with tenderness around any bird Treadway asked it to carry. Treadway had ended the trip although it meant he would have to launch it again later, at considerable expense in provisions and time, in order to have enough duck in store for the winter. He had carried the dog a hundred miles on his sled and paid Hans Nilsson the veterinarian a hundred dollars to get up in the middle of the night and tend to the wound, and when Hans told him the dog had to lose the eye, Treadway cried because it was his fault, and he did not eat again himself until the dog could eat, not even when Jacinta fried meat cakes with knobs of pure white pork fat and juniper berries in them. He believed sight to be something the dog loved, valued, and even enjoyed, and it hurt him deeply that he had ruined the dog's ability to practise the talent for which bird dogs are born. He kept the dog though it could no longer hunt, and no one in Treadway's ancestry had ever kept a dog that was just a pet, until the dog grew old. Only when the dog grew so arthritic it could not walk without pain did Treadway consent to have it put down, and on that day he walked to the river and stared at the water for more than an hour, thinking about not just how he had failed his dog but how he could be a better man all around if he paid more attention to every detail and let nothing pass that was off-kilter.

After he lost that dog, Treadway hauled and skinned and sweated, and, in his own way, he loved. He loved Jacinta because she was decent and kind to him; the last thing he wanted to do was to hurt her. He played games with her in the part of the season when he lived at home, games she liked, such as cribbage, which she had taught him when they were first married. He had to force himself to do it, to take his mind off the way he planned to sharpen the runners on his sled or condition the jaws of his traps with seal oil, but he did tear himself away from these things so that when he was with her, she would not feel that his mind was far away. He felt a tenderness that was, in part, a feeling of being sorry for her, for she had to stay indoors and lead a gentle life unconnected with all that was great and wild, and he did not see how she could enjoy this. He knew, during the crib games and the times they ate intimately together over the lamplit table, that she would have liked something more, but he did not know what it was. He did not know it was the city she came from, it was rain on the slate roofs of the shops on Water Street in that city, it was a man who would read poetry and philosophy but not keep it from her, who would lay the book right there on the table, beside the bread and the fragments of roast duck leg and the wine, and would talk about it with her.

Days after the birth, in the manner of secrets held from the world of husbands, Treadway had not been told the truth about his child. Jacinta examined her baby with gentle fingertips when Treadway was not in the room, and when he was, or when neighbours visited with bake-apple tarts and partridgeberry cake and hot caribou stew baked under a thick crust with gravy bubbling out of the knife holes, she gazed on her child with the full power of her concentration, and nothing could break that gaze. Neighbours walked and talked around her, and it was as if she were underwater and they were not, and this did not seem too different from the way it normally was with a new mother and her child. No one expected her to come up with idle conversation.

It was Thomasina who took care of the linguistics. Thomasina who, by miracles of deflection, managed to leave unspoken the first thing spoken of any newborn. To Treadway she appeared the most sensible of his wife's friends.

"Eliza Goudie," he had once told Jacinta, "spends far too much money on white sandals and those dresses out of the catalogue, the ones covered in blisters."

"Seersucker."

"And white sandals. Things that are not practical to wear in this climate." And he could not get over the fact that Joan Martin had forbidden her husband to pile wood near their house so she could plant some kind of fancy tulip that should grow only in a botanical garden somewhere.

"Emperor," said Jacinta. "Those are Emperor tulips."

It was a testament to Thomasina's powers that she

managed to stay eight days in Treadway's house without his protesting. Not even Jacinta's mother had been able to do that, when she was alive. Treadway did not ban a person outright, but he had an ability to give off such a chilled and hostile response to any guest who overstayed her welcome that no guest, not even the most impermeable, could stand it. He was a man who did not want strangers to observe his routine, not that there was anything remarkable about his habits. He simply liked to inhabit his house, when he had to inhabit it, and go about his ordinary pathways in it without being looked at or talked to, except by his own wife, who did not appear to him to mind it when he ignored the fact that she was there.

"If I didn't say anything to him," Jacinta sometimes told Joan and Eliza, "I think he could go a whole year without speaking to anyone but his dogs." She said this, though she felt disloyal, when she got caught up in the women's derisive talk about husbands in general. And because they knew things like this about him, Joan and Eliza had an air about them, one Treadway could detect, of faint amusement towards him, and he could not tolerate them in the house, so when he was home, they hardly ever came. But because she had more gravity than they did, and because she did nothing for herself and everything for Jacinta and the baby, Thomasina was able to stay the eight days without Treadway's disapproval, even though it meant the only time he had alone with his wife was the half-hour before sleep.

"Everything all right?" he asked Jacinta on the eighth day, his huge, comforting paw heating her belly down into her skin, her fat, her womb and ovarian tubes and ovaries, down into the small of her back. She did not tell her friends about his calm heat, or about the deep trust she had in his ability to create a secure home. There were a lot of instabilities in Eliza's home. Her husband drank, and she was forever falling in love with someone — this year it was her children's new geography teacher, a man ten years younger than Eliza, who had come from Vermont and lived in an apartment in the local wildlife officer's basement. Eliza's infatuations were always one-sided, but they powered her in a way her real life did not, and as a result her own house always felt uninhabited by her, and her children and husband walked around lost in it. Joan was less susceptible to falling in love, but her husband was not. All of Croydon Harbour knew he had an Innu wife in the interior, and that while Joan had no children, his other wife had three daughters and a son.

"Everything's perfect." Jacinta never lied to Treadway. He ate steel-cut oatmeal every morning for breakfast, with salt on it. His underclothes were of ewe's wool. When they made love, she climaxed every time, and when she did, he knew. If she were bone tired he stroked her forehead and her hair until she fell asleep. If he did anything that irked her, like drape filthy socks on the bedspread, she asked him not to do it and he did not mind. She agreed with him about Eliza's impractical sandals but disagreed with him about the Emperor tulips. "It won't hurt Harold Martin," she said, "to pile and cut his wood at the bottom of the fence so she can get some enjoyment," and Treadway did not argue with her or take it as an insult against husbands.

But about their own newborn baby, Jacinta did lie.

Siamese twins had been on the news, joined so tightly at the skull doctors the world over had despaired, and the mother — Jacinta had watched her on television — had loved those babies, and had decided, fiercely, that it didn't matter if they were joined. She would bring them both up in the world just like that, no matter what, and Jacinta had not felt sorry for her. She knew better than to feel sorry for anyone. It was one of the things she had learned. Feeling sorry for a person was no help to them at all. People should get on with things. Privately she thought the woman would come to her senses one day and allow the babies to die.

But when you are the mother, you take it in stride. You take albino hair in stride, when you are the mother. When you are the mother, not someone watching that mother, you take odd-coloured eyes in stride. You take a missing hand in stride, and the same with Down syndrome, and spina bifida, and water on the brain. You would take wings in stride, or one lung outside the body, or a missing tongue. The penis and the one little testicle and the labia and vagina were like this for Jacinta. Baby Wayne slept in his cradle under his green quilt and white blanket. His black belly button stuck out, and Jacinta cleaned it with an alcohol swab, waiting for it to fall off. She played with his little red feet, and felt close to him when he crammed her breast in his mouth and sucked while raising his eyes slowly, slowly across her collarbone, across the ceiling, gazing at Thomasina or the stove or the cat, back again to her collarbone, then up, up, till he found her eyes and locked on, and that was a kind of flying, flying through the northern lights or a Chagall night sky, with a little white goat to give a blessing. There was blessing everywhere between Jacinta and this baby, and there were times when she completely forgot what it was about him that she was hiding from her husband.

"Everything," she told Treadway, "is all right," and she believed that this was about to become true.

"All I need," she had said earlier to Thomasina, "is a little more time, and everything will become clear. Everything will straighten itself out. The baby will, in some way we still have to learn about, be just fine."

Treadway persisted. "Baby's healthy?" Jacinta knew he never spoke idly, and he was not speaking idly now, and he was asking her for an honest answer. But what was the most honest answer?

"Yes." She tried this in a normal voice but it came out as a whisper. The strength of her voice, her real tone, which was a tone of plainness, like rain, which Treadway loved but had not told her he loved, did not inhabit the whisper. She wished she could go back and say yes again. Heat still radiated from Treadway's hand deep into her belly.

"He's a big baby," Treadway said, and the heat stopped.

Jacinta wanted to blurt, "Why do you say he? Are you waiting for me to confess?" But she did not. She said yes, louder than normal this time because she did not want another whisper to betray her. Her yes was a shout in their quiet room. Their bedroom was always quiet. Treadway liked a place of repose, a tranquil sleep with a white bedspread and no radio music or clutter, and so did she. She lay there waiting for his hand to heat her belly again, but it did not. Had he moved it away consciously? Treadway was a man whose warmth always heated her unless an argument stood between them.

In the morning Jacinta told Thomasina, "I went stiff as a hare. What are we going to do?"

Any time fortune came to Thomasina — acceptance of her grass baskets by the crafts commission, the flowering of a Persian rose in this zone where no one could grow any rose, not even the hardy John Cabot climber — she knew happiness was only one side of the coin and the coin was forever turning. She had been single until she was well past thirty, when Graham Montague had told her he didn't care that she had a curved spine and felt old — he wanted to marry her if she would marry him. Annabel had been born the following year and Thomasina had every reason to be happy, but instead she held her heart at the same level she had always held it, because she did not trust extremes of feeling. Now she told Jacinta, as they spread jam on toast thinly, the way they both liked it, so gold shone through, "We will love this baby of yours and Treadway's exactly as it was born."

"Will other people love it?"

"That baby is all right the way it is. There's enough room in this world."

This was how Thomasina saw it, and it was what Jacinta needed to hear.

For days after the birth Treadway knew there was a secret, and it was only a matter of opening his attention in a way he was used to doing out on the land before the truth about the baby came to him. He did not need to investigate with his hands or move close when no one was looking. In the wilderness when he opened his attention, it was a spiritual opening, a way of seeing with your whole being, and it helped him see birds and caribou and fish that were invisible to anyone who was not hunting and had not opened their second eyes. He felt the secret in the house exactly as he felt the presence of a white ptarmigan behind him in the snow, and he understood the secret's details, its identity, as easily as he would know the bird was a white ptarmigan before he turned around and saw it. He knew his baby had both a boy's and a girl's identity, and he knew a decision had to be made.

Where had their baby come from? There was no relative in the past, no story to which Treadway might turn. There was only the fact of which sex organ was the most obvious, which one it would be most practical to recognize, the easiest life for all concerned. For if there was one thing Treadway Blake considered with every step, it was how a decision of his affected not just himself but everyone. He understood privacy but he could not understand practical selfishness. Every part of him knew it was physically connected to every part of everyone else on this coast, and not just to people but to the sky, and the land, and the stars. He was both Scottish and Inuit, and he was nothing if not fair. To him the land was a universal loaf of bread, every part nourishing and meant for everyone.

It never once occurred to Treadway to do the thing that lay in the hearts of Jacinta and Thomasina: to let his baby live the way it had been born. That, in his mind, would not have been a decision. It would have been indecision, and it would have caused harm. He did not want to imagine the harm it would cause. He was not an imagining man. He saw deeply into things but he had no desire to entertain possibility that had not yet manifested. He wanted to know what was, not what might be. So he refused to imagine the harm in store for a child who was neither a son nor a daughter but both. He filled a bag with bread, meat, and tea and went outdoors. He went without his gun and walked to a height of land from where he could consider the eagles and foxes and let them teach him the path of most practical wisdom.

Thomasina worked in his kitchen those first eight mornings, kneading touton dough, soaking beans, wringing diapers, and administering to the mother, because without company Jacinta would have wandered off in a drift of worry. Everything Treadway refused to imagine, Jacinta imagined in detail enough for the two of them. Whereas he struck out on his own to decide how to erase the frightening ambiguity in their child, she envisioned living with it as it was. She imagined her daughter beautiful and grown up, in a scarlet satin gown, her male characteristics held secret under the clothing for a time when she might need a warrior's strength and a man's potent aggression. Then she imagined her son as a talented, mythical hunter, his breasts strapped in a concealing vest, his clothes the green of striding forward, his heart the heart of a woman who could secretly direct his path in the ways of intuition and psychological insight. Whenever she imagined her child, grown up without interference from a judgemental world, she imagined its male and female halves as complementing each other, and as being secretly, almost magically powerful. It was the growing up part she did not want to imagine. The social part, the going to school in Labrador part, the jeering part, the what will we tell everyone part, the part that asks how will we give this child so much love it will know no harm from the cruel reactions of people who do not want to understand.

Thomasina brought Jacinta back from these thoughts with her wholehearted company. She kept the kitchen going, the fire crackling, the hum and heat of normal life throbbing, and the undercurrent of her seemingly ordinary, homey activities was one of open acceptance. Jacinta could feel, when Thomasina took the child and held it so she could eat or go to the toilet or rest on the daybed for half an hour, that Thomasina believed the child's difference was a strange blessing that had to be protected. That it was a jeopardized advantage, even a power. Thomasina hid this undercurrent behind business so apparently normal that even the most vigilant opponent of enchantment would not perceive it was there. When Treadway came in from his trip to the height of land, Thomasina was boiling partridgeberries and sugar, and the kitchen was full of their bloody, mossy tang that smells and tastes more of regret than of sweetness.

When he finally spoke, Treadway caused no drama. He sat at the table stirring his tea for a long time. Thomasina was in a state of something akin to prayer, but not as helpless. Bearing the situation up, sitting with it.

As Treadway regarded his blue Royal Albert saucer, Thomasina saw he knew what had been going on with the baby whom Jacinta nursed on the daybed by the stove under a crocheted blanket.

"Since neither of you is going to make a decision one way or the other," he said, "I'm going to make it. He's going to be a boy. I'm going to call him Wayne, after his grandfather."

Jacinta continued to nurse the baby. A look of relief

crossed her face. Not at his decision but at his acknowl-
edgement that their baby had been born the way it had.
Thomasina stood up, looked at Treadway, and said, "Be
careful."

"We'll get the doctor in," Treadway said, "and we'll
see."

After Treadway had spoken, there was a holy lull in the
house in which Treadway and Jacinta cared for each other
and for the baby alone, with no one to look on or advise and
with few words of their own. Treadway moved Jacinta's
hair tenderly to behind her shoulder so he could see the
child nurse, and at no time did he examine the child or
treat it critically. She could see he loved it. There was nothing wrong with the child other than its ambiguous sex. It
nursed and cooed and slept, and its skin was dewy and
cool, and when the kitchen grew too hot, its parents let the
fire die down in the stove so that the child's cheeks would
not have red spots, and if it grew too cool they wrapped
the baby securely. Treadway sat and rocked it, and he sang
to it as well. His singing was one of the beautiful things
women other than Jacinta did not know about. He sang
his own songs, songs he improvised after his time alone in
the wild, as well as ancient Labrador songs passed down
by generations of trappers and nomads and hunters who
have heard caribou speak. The baby loved this; it began a
life of waking to warmth and song and colour and drifting
into dreams threaded with parent song.

After a fortnight Treadway left to go hunting. It was one of the last days you could go white hunting. When the ice melted to a certain degree, when whiteness in the natural world decreased by a margin every hunter knew by an inner system of measurement, white hunting was no longer done. Not because it had become ineffectual — ice still existed in large pockets around the shore, and a hunter could stay well hidden — but because it was unfair; migratory birds were returning in larger numbers to nest, and many had young or needed to keep their eggs warm. The birds' travels were hunting journeys, short flights to find food for their young, and the Labrador hunters knew what was at stake. The next year's hunting was at stake, but so was the livelihood of the flock, and the hunters respected that intrinsically, apart from any vested interest of their own.

So on this day, close to the end of the hunting season, Treadway left his family at home, and so did the other men of Croydon Harbour. And so did Thomasina's daughter, Annabel, and husband, Graham Montague, to navigate the Beaver River in a white canoe.

3

Thomasina Outside the Church

THOMASINA DID NOT GO INSIDE the church at the funeral of her own husband, Graham, and daughter, Annabel, because outside was where the blue butterfly was, darting in and out of the reeds that stuck up out of the snow in the sunny corner facing the sea. Thomasina stood at this corner, a corner small and southerly and windowless, leaning against the clapboard with her face closed and upturned to the sun. Jacinta had not tried to get her to come inside. But everyone else said Thomasina had become temporarily insane, for how else could you explain a woman who did not want to take comfort in red and blue glass candle holders full of light, in stained glass windows with the apostle Mark talking to a brown dove, in the Book of Common Prayer and its order for the burial of the dead, in the gathering of the community, the solemnity of the eight pallbearers, the two coffins made of boards that Graham Montague had hand-planed, intending a bureau for his wife?

Thomasina did not put on a black dress. She did not wear a black hat or even a Sunday hat of green or lavender felt with a satin band. She wore her ordinary coat, a blue wool coat with flat buttons that had belonged to her mother, and she wore ordinary clothes underneath it: a grey and green dress that had no waistband, for she hated waistbands, and no sleeves, for she liked a dress you could work in and not be encumbered by seams or small openings and eyelets and finicky fastenings. She liked a dress you could pull over your head and forget about.

The inside of the church was something she could not stand that day. She liked to sing inside it on other days, and was part of the small choir, and wore the same choir robes as everyone else. But today she could not go in. She did not want to contain her thoughts about Graham and Annabel inside the walls, which shut out the light this spring day, and which smelled of old wooden pews and the fragrant paper of ancient prayer books and the soap and perfume of people who had washed themselves clean enough to come to a religious ritual. She could not bear to have the lives of her husband and daughter reduced to this ritual when out here the sun and air were boundless, and insects had begun to inhabit the place again after the long winter, and there was, even though Graham and Annabel had drowned, glad birdsong. This was the litany she wanted to hear. She could not understand it, but she wanted to hear it, and she would not hear it if she went inside.

Through the church walls she could hear what was inside if she leaned back and touched the boards — there was a low murmur, a strain of sad music from the pedal organ Wilhelmina Simpson had brought in from Boston and on which she would soon play "Christ the Lord Is Risen Today," as Easter Sunday would be early this year, the moon almost full now and March not yet ended. The people inside that church did not realize that Thomasina would be able to sing resurrection anthems when Easter came. They did not know that her idea of resurrection was different from that of the Church, as were her ideas of Christ, of light, of immortality and holiness. Christ, for Thomasina, was not so much a person as an opening in the grass, a patch of sun, a warm spot in the loneliness. She had never been a person who respected stained glass or altars. That butterfly's small early wings were her stained glass. That patch of earth, peeping through the melting snow, was her altar. Her mother had not called her Thomasina for nothing. "If you were a boy," her mother had said when she was young, "I was going to call you Doubting Thomas, after the disciple who wanted to see Christ's nail marks with his own eyes. But you were a girl. So I called you Doubting Thomasina."

After the funeral, at which Wilhelmina Simpson played Bach's "Sheep May Safely Graze," the hymn she played at every funeral, the people walked down the hill to the cemetery, and the gravediggers, Simon Montague and Harold Pierson, lowered the coffins into the graves, and Thomasina watched the part of the procession visible from her sunlit corner. She stood there, the wind blowing her coat, a faintly ominous vision, a figure who had stepped out of the bounds of what was normal for people in this place. Those who stole a look in her direction felt someone should do something, someone should go to her, put an arm around her and guide her into the group; after all, they were supposed to be mourning with her. They thought someone should do this, but nobody did. When the handfuls of earth had been thrown into the graves, the crowd walked up to the tiny community hall across the road from the church, and they walked the way they had descended, along the east and north walls, not the south and west walls at whose corner Thomasina stood — all except Jacinta, who handed the baby to Treadway.

"Go in and get a sandwich and tea," she told Treadway. "Talk to Harold Pierson about shovelling the ice off Thomasina's roof before it slides off in a sheet and kills her."

Jacinta picked her way through last year's thistles. Snow filtered into her ankle-boots as she stood beside Thomasina, raising her face to the sun as Thomasina did, leaning against the church wall inches from where a spider with white stripes made an iridescent web. Not many spots trapped this kind of warmth in Croydon Harbour.

Jacinta saw the blue butterfly — a small moth really; a mud-puddle moth, but pretty, and pale blue like the spring sky — and she knew what Thomasina was doing. Jacinta did not think her crazy, and she did not try to draw her to the reception or to move her from this moment of peace. Women did not get many moments like this in their lives, sun beating on their eyelids in a hidden corner and no one asking them for anything. No one asking them to find the salt, or wait for a man who might come home in three months but who might not. Women of Croydon Harbour knew what was expected of them at all times, and they did it, and the men were expected to do things too, and they did these, and there was no time left.

Jacinta closed her eyes long enough for tiredness to drain out of them. Not all the tiredness, but some of it. A spoonful of tiredness out of each eye. If only a person could stay like this as long as she needed; if only the sun could stay, and the wind not come up, and obligations not line the road.

All Thomasina wanted to do now was go home. Not to talk to well-wishers. Not to intercept casserole dishes full of cabbage rolls and moose sausage and Rice-A-Roni with ground caribou meat. Who would eat it? What Thomasina would eat, if she ate anything, was milk lunch biscuits and tea. The wind changed and the moment of peace in the sun was gone; the two women were chilled. Thomasina walked towards her house and Jacinta walked with her. They did not talk but went together into the kitchen, a plain kitchen, clean, with nothing but a tea canister on the counter. Thomasina boiled the kettle and put out biscuits and she and Jacinta sat there and were silent until Thomasina said, "What are you going to do about that baby?"

"Treadway wants him to live as a boy."

"What do you want?"

"I don't know how to argue with him. He'd say what I'm thinking makes no sense."

"No sense?" In the years of her marriage to Graham Montague, that was a thing of which Graham had never accused Thomasina. "What are you thinking?"

"I'm thinking maybe if we just waited everything would change."

"It might."

"But everything keeps shifting in my imagination. Other things. Completely different things. The baby's ears. Or his face. I think, what if those or other things changed? I don't want anything to change. I don't want to do anything to the baby. I don't want to make any mistakes."

"You want to do everything right the first time? Is that what makes sense to Treadway?"

"I don't know."

"If sense is a partridge in the willows, you have to follow it. You don't know where it's leading. Do you call that baby a she?"

"No."

"Have you tried?"

"Not out loud."

"She might want to hear it. She might want to hear you call her 'My little daughter.'"

"Thomasina." Jacinta laid down her mug with the queen of diamonds on it. "I'm sorry you lost Annabel."

Thomasina drank her tea. She smoothed the plastic tablecloth, which had permanent creases. She said, "You want to be careful what you let Treadway have done to that baby."

There was a mirror on the wall and Jacinta could see both their faces in it. She realized that of the two, her own had no strength left, while Thomasina's held reserves. She had walked here thinking she would comfort the other woman, but Thomasina did not need comforting.

"If a stranger came here now," Jacinta said, "they would guess I was the one who had lost a man and a daughter."

"You won't lose Treadway unless you want to lose him. Treadway is a husband for life."

"I know."

"But it looks to me like I'm not the only one who has lost a daughter."

"I've always felt," Jacinta said, "that daughter is a beautiful word."

The first thing Thomasina did when the funeral was over was rid the house of food she disliked. Venison sausages, large roasts of moose, seabirds Graham had caught in his net. These things filled a third of her freezer and were what Graham had wanted for his suppers, and she had not minded cooking them for him. Half the time he had cooked for himself. Theirs had not been a marriage of sharply defined roles. Men of the cove generally were kings outside their houses — kings of the grounds and sheds and fences — and the women were queens of inner rooms and painted sills and pelmets and carpet cleaners. Thomasina and Graham had come and gone as they pleased, each one knowing how to use a knife for cleaning fish or cutting bread, how to sweep a floor, how to mend a gate or clean the chimney. Thomasina had a grain of sense, men of the cove said, and she walked about in brown cardigans with her hair tidy but not styled. She did not own a pair of shoes in which she could not walk ten miles over rough ground.

Unlike Eliza Goudie in her seersucker and white sandals, unlike Joan Martin with her bulb-planting tool for her Emperor tulips, Thomasina would not fall apart at the loss of her husband. Though they complained about their husbands, the first two would have looked at a dripping tap, a leaky ceiling, a tree fallen on the property as insurmountable difficulties over which they had no control. They were the kind of women of whom the Apostles had written that it was necessary to help from a safe distance. They had not, during their marriages, held any part of themselves in reserve. They joked, when they got together, of how easy their lives would become if they did not have to cook for the men, but if these women ever lost their husbands, they would themselves be as lost as orphaned whitecoat seals.

Thomasina was no whitecoat; she was a fierce grey and silver grown-up who had held her entire self in reserve for a day such as this. Jacinta she felt, lay somewhere between those other women and herself: self-containment was half-formed in Jacinta; she had depths of judgement to which she could turn but did not fully trust them. She had surrendered part but not all of herself to the wisdom of her husband. Jacinta, Thomasina felt, would never be wholly at ease with any decision about which she and Treadway had differing ideas. Thomasina and Graham had married late. Perhaps that was why each never thought to question the judgement of the other. Thomasina had never questioned Graham's blind hunting or his taking Annabel out in the white canoe or any other boat, and he had not questioned Thomasina when she went on her own journeys alone or with Annabel into the interior, which no other white women did. Danger faced Graham and Thomasina and their child equally at every turn, as did discovery, and this was something each faced for himself or herself. In her misfortune, Thomasina did not blame Graham.

None of the townspeople knew the extent of Thomasina's grieving because she did not fall apart in front of them. Nor did she fall apart alone in her house. She sat on the daybed under a small window that looked over the backyard and the inlet and stared for half an hour the morning after the drowning of Graham and Annabel, and she did the same that evening, and the next morning as well. She sat on the daybed because that spot was an in-between place, not a living room or kitchen where scenes of family life had played out. This was a passage in which everyone moved and was unfathomable, which was how Thomasina saw people. She was not a person who froze someone's character in her mind, calling this one egotistical and that one not nearly confident enough and another one truthful or untruthful. To Thomasina people were rivers, always ready to move from one state of being into another. It was not fair, she felt, to treat people as if they were finished beings. Everyone was always becoming and unbecoming. It was unbearable to her that she had lost Annabel and Graham, but she had borne unbearable things, and she knew how to keep going. She had her own way of saying goodbye to her lost beloved, and she said it in private. Then she went about the business of being around for those who were living. Especially, she decided, for that little baby of Jacinta's, Wayne, whom no one wanted to call a daughter.

4

Phalometer

JACINTA LEFT PILOT OBED WILSON on the tarmac and walked in the hospital entrance as if she were taking her child for a routine weighing and measuring with the public health nurse. She walked down the first-floor corridor to the back exit, saw it would not open without setting off an alarm, walked to a side entrance where the cafeteria workers went to have their smoke breaks, opened that door, which faced a deserted lot full of expired thistle and St. John's wort, and ran. She ran to the chain-link fence that surrounded the hospital and stopped when she got to its interlocking wire, which rose eight feet, as if women were always trying to escape with their babies. Beyond the fence was a ditch, then waste ground: rubble and corrugated pipes where men had dug to lay a new drainage system around the hospital. There were errant snowflakes, and no colour save for brown, white, grey, and a green so dark it might as well have been black. In the woods, Jacinta knew, if she managed to find a way around the fence, she would find Innu tents, fragrant with boughs and woodsmoke and steam swirling from sugared tea, the men hunting and the women plucking geese and digging firepits to singe the pinfeathers. Grandfathers rested on their bough beds and the children played outdoors with duck and goose bills and bones and claws, making puppets out of whatever parts of the bird did not get eaten. Once Jacinta had wandered into a camp like this when she was berry picking, and there had been a mother and small baby in one tent, and that baby had had something wrong with him.

He had been born with a genetic anomaly but his mother had held him and sung to him, a lullaby in Innu-aimun, and no one had tried to take that baby to the Goose Bay General Hospital and maim him or administer some kind of death by surgery. No one had found fault with him at all. His family had cared for him as he had been born. The encampment had been at Mud Lake, where a little schoolhouse stood for the children and you could go only by helicopter in spring because the ice was too thick for boats but too thin for sleds. Jacinta had canoed to the place and had felt afraid of its isolation but comforted by its womb-like softness and enclosure. But she had gone in berry season: a warm, golden day when the sun from the whole summer remained, soaked into every berry and leaf. You could get the wrong idea about a place in the fall, before the snow. You could get the idea that it would always welcome you. If Jacinta found her way back there now, frost lying in the seams of the land, who would welcome her? The Innu had given her tea and bread that day, but she would need more than that now.

Jacinta had always been a person prone to bolting, strongly tempted to escape when overwhelmed. She imagined herself running to the desert of New Mexico and finding an uninhabited dwelling. She imagined going back to St. John's and living in a tiny bed-sitter and cooking a mash of oats and sweet carrots for her baby. But she was thirty-four, not twenty, and knew that beyond the romance of an escape, beyond the first euphoric flight, there was a second day that brought a return of ordinary burdens, the burdens you thought you had fled. Now, with her baby, she stood at the chain-link fence and hated that there was no opening, no place for her and her baby to run. She sat on the ground and picked pieces of lambkill and made them into the kind of tiny corsage she had made of clover in her childhood. She kissed her baby's head and sang to him the same Innu lullaby she had heard in the tent. At least that little baby and her own would hear the same song.

At a window of the hospital, on the third floor, stood a blur, a nurse looking out. Jacinta heard Obed Wilson's helicopter lift off and fade. If that nurse hadn't noticed Jacinta she could have sat on the ground until hell froze over and no one would have known where she or her baby had gone. The lullaby had the kind of tune everyone thinks they've heard before but can't remember where. A tune like that floats in the air all the time and now and then you catch it.

"You like the tune, baby?" Jacinta kissed Wayne's nose. He looked at her and trusted her with his black eyes that were changing into another colour. "Nothing about you is the way it's going to be," Jacinta told him. "Nothing about you will stay the same." The nurse came out the exit Jacinta had found. She was short, with black hair, around thirty. She stepped over the mud and snow seams and thistles in her white shoes pricked with a hundred breathing holes.

"Are you all right?"

Jacinta looked only at her baby.

"I'm Tana. Are you here for her three-month needle?"

"No."

"Are you okay? Do you want me to take her? Do you want to come in for a cup of coffee while we get her signed in?"

Jacinta got up and walked with Tana away from the chain-link fence, away from the land that had nothing on it but weeds and stones and drainage pipes. It was not beautiful, but it had space and an undefined air. Everyone was trying to define everything so carefully, Jacinta felt; they wanted to annihilate all questions. As they got close to the door she felt the walls of the hospital lean forward and close in, and she stopped.

"What are you here for today?" Tana asked. She sounded as if she had to come out onto this waste ground every day and round up bolting mothers. "What's your name? Which doctor do you have to see?"

"Dr. Simon Ho."

"The surgeon?"

Jacinta stood on a little pile of rubble and thistles, and Tana put an arm around her. "Do you want me to come with you?"

"I don't know."

"I can come."

"Okay."

Jacinta let Tana bring her along a hallway that had blue footprints leading north and yellow ones facing south. They went through the X-ray section and down a warren of narrow corridors where ancient women and men lay with no one attending them, their toothless mouths open, then through an orange door where there were colours again and a smell of coffee and toast, and brightly lit information desks.

"What's your last name?" Tana asked, as if she and Jacinta shared a confidence against the world.

"Blake."

"Wait here and I'll go see you won't have to wait in the waiting room." Tana went behind the information desk and spoke to the woman working there, who lifted her glasses and looked across the lobby at Jacinta. Tana flipped through file cards, picked up a phone and spoke for a few seconds, then came back out of the booth, brought Jacinta to the cafeteria and bought her a coffee, then showed her into a small waiting room with armchairs in it. "I can go," she said, "or I can wait here with you. Would you like me to wait here with you?"

Jacinta looked at the square green stone in Tana's ring. It was a dull stone. Jacinta liked this better than a stone that glittered.

"Dr. Ho has you booked for ten thirty," Tana said. "The good thing about him is that he does only three surgeries a day, one in the morning and two in the afternoon, so you never have to wait."

Jacinta looked at a *Pediatrics Today* magazine lying on a table. On its cover was a photograph of a baby with tubes coming out of its nose, arms, and head. Why did hospitals think people coming in with their babies wanted to look at magazines like that? A tiny television hung tilted on a metal arm near the ceiling, and a newscaster proclaimed that forty-seven Chinese coal miners had been suffocated in an explosion earlier in the day. There was footage of their families screaming and banging at the gate of the mine, which officials had locked for their own protection. The wall under the television had a dent in it, and Jacinta wondered if someone had kicked it. A door opened that she had not noticed and a nurse in gelatinous lipstick called, "Jacinta Blake?" in a voice too loud. Tana put her hand on Jacinta's shoulder, and her hand was so warm Jacinta did not want it to leave her. But she had to follow the other nurse. Tana's voice had calmed her. Voices were like that. You could lose or save a life with the sound of a voice. White corridors, windows, big silver and white room, Dr. Simon Ho next to four trolleys full of shelves, implements laid out on white cloths. Jacinta noticed the seriousness of Dr. Ho. She liked that he looked at her steadily, that he was young and slim and not aggressive.

Blades glittered on the trolleys, and she thought how Treadway would like to get his hands on some of those for fish and seals and skinning porcupine and stripping bark and just having on him for any event that might need a strange two-pronged blade with a graceful curve, or a stainless steel razor-edged file with a nice fat handle. It occurred to her to steal one, though Jacinta had not stolen a thing in her life.

The parents' waiting room was beyond a side door and it had comfortable couches in it and a painting on the wall of an old mill and weeping willows and some ducks, but Jacinta did not want to go in there. "I'll stay with my baby."

The nurse did not like this but Dr. Ho watched Jacinta respectfully and said she could stay in the operating room. The nurse tried to take the baby.

"I want to see. What exactly are you planning?"

"The point," the doctor said, "is to create a believable masculine anatomy. You can lay him on the operating table yourself if you like. I'll show you the exact procedure. We will show you how to wash your hands and arms and you can wear a mask and you can watch until the point where we do the surgery itself, if you think you can stand it."

Jacinta realized the nurse was chewing gum.

"What do you mean by believable?"

"I mean we try to make the baby comfortable as a male in his own mind, and in the minds of other people who are in his life now or will be in the future."

The nurse chewed as if she intended to grind her teeth to powder.

"I liked the other nurse," Jacinta said. "Not this one."

"This nurse's name is Alma Williams," Dr. Ho said softly.

"She's chewing gum. Her voice is jarring and I don't like her. I liked the other nurse. The one who showed me here. She came all the way out to the back of the hospital to ask if I was okay. She bought me a coffee. She has warm hands. I like her and I want her instead of that one. I really don't want this nurse in here when I could have the nice one. I like the look of you and that you're serious, and I think you will be honest with me, but if that nurse stays here I am going out and taking my baby with me, because I don't like her."

"Alma, can you please ring the third floor and have them send Tana down here, and then be kind enough to abide by Mrs. Blake's request?"

"It's a pretty strange request."

"Thank you, Alma."

"Seeing as how I am a registered pediatric nurse." Alma said the word *pediatric* as if she were about to define it to a kindergarten class.

"It's all right, Alma."

"Whereas Tana is —"

"I appreciate you fetching her, Alma."

Alma left Jacinta and her baby and the doctor alone in the room, and that was when Jacinta handed Wayne to him. She felt that in Dr. Ho's presence any thought, any fear or wish, was understandable. He would not dismiss her.

"You think," she said, "a child's sex needs to be believable. You think my child — the way he is now, the way she is — is unbelievable? Like something in a science fiction horror movie? And you want to make her believable. Like a real human."

"We want to give him a chance. As soon as possible after the birth."

"Have you done it before?"

"True hermaphroditism happens, Mrs. Blake, once in eighty-three thousand births. I haven't done this before. But what we are doing today is the normal medical response."

"Normal?"

"And I think it's the most compassionate one. We try to decide the true sex of the child."

"The true one and not the false one."

"We use this phalometer." He picked up a tiny silver bar from the trolley. It had black numbers on it.

"It's a tiny ruler."

"It is. See?" He pointed to a mark three-quarters of the way down the phalometer. "If the penis reaches or exceeds this length, we consider it a real penis. If it doesn't meet this measurement, it is considered a clitoris."

Jacinta strained to read the tiny marks. "One point five centimetres?"

"That's right."

"What happens if it's less than that?"

"When a phallus is less than one point five centimetres, give or take seven hundredths of a centimetre —"

"Seven hundredths?"

"Yes. When it's less than that, we remove the presentation of male aspects and later, during adolescence, we sculpt the female aspects."

"What if it's right in the middle? Right straight, smack dab down the precise centre? One point five centimetres with no seven hundredths."

"Then we make an educated guess. We do endocrinological tests but really, in a newborn, as far as endocrinology goes, we're making a best estimate. Penis size at birth is the primary criterion for assigning a gender."

"Measure her, then."

Dr. Ho took Wayne from her arms so gently she thought he must love babies, even if he did merciless things to them. He must have bad dreams. He must wake up in the middle of the night just before the part of the dream where he cuts the baby. His wife, if he has one, must have to get up and give him brandy. But maybe not. Maybe he didn't care. Maybe he only looked like he cared.

Tana, the first nurse, came into the operating room. Tana cared. Anyone could see that about her.

"The phallus . . ." Dr. Ho said. He pulled Wayne's penis.

"What the hell are you doing?"

"And it is a phallus, it is —"

"He has to stretch it gently," Tana said, "to measure the length. He can't measure it if it's contracted."

"He's hurting her!"

"No. See? She's not crying."

"It is the necessary length . . ." Dr. Ho showed her the gauge. "It barely grazes one and a half centimetres."

"I can't even see the numbers. They're so tiny."

"This baby can be raised as male."

Jacinta was silent. Then, quietly: "That's what his father wants."

5

Christening

TREADWAY WAS SHORT and not handsome, whereas Jacinta had a long neck and tendrils of hair that curled when damp, and a graceful waist, and long, capable, dancerly limbs. She had accepted him because she felt no attraction to men who knew they looked good, men who were tall and knowing, who looked at a woman with a mirthful challenge in their eye that said, I can get any woman I want, but I'm giving you a chance at the moment. Men like this had fallen for Jacinta and had asked her to marry them, but she had waited for Treadway, who was not five feet nine, who was shy, who had to be prompted to go to a dance or enter the log-cutting contest during the winter festival. Once he was dancing, he danced well, riding the music like a kayak, and if he entered a log-cutting contest he cut fewer logs than the winner but he cut them neater and better. She liked the way he appeared hesitant about good fortune, as if he had not been expecting it. She liked the way he chose a good coat and wore it for five years and then chose another one similar to it. She liked the blackness of his hair, and the clean smell of his skin, and the fact that he would never treat her with deceit. She liked loving a man with whom other women were unlikely to fall in love, because she did not want to waste her heart worrying about unfaithfulness in a husband. She had witnessed enough of that between her father and mother.

Still, Jacinta missed the city she grew up in. What she missed most was the Majestic Cinema on Henry Street. It was true that she held clear in her mind the other pleasures of St. John's: pyramids of oranges in Stokes Market; the slate roofs and chimney pots shining with rain and descending down, down from Lemarchant Road to the harbour; the fact that you could walk outside and see people you knew at any time, in the middle of their real lives; street life; children playing skipping rope; Emma Rhodenizer's black cat, Spritzer, between her geranium and her lace curtains on the corner of Gower and Cathedral streets; and the steeples everywhere. All these things Jacinta held in an accessible place within herself; they were her most tangible memories. Even the pigeons who lived in the O of Bowring's department store — she saw their purple necks, their iridescent collars of indigo, their movements fluid yet full of muscular jumps and starts — belonged to her still in Croydon Harbour. Monochromatic Croydon Harbour, where to see colour you had to learn to find red hiding deep inside green, orange hiding in blue. In the city the colour, the life, came shouting out. Human life. In Croydon Harbour human life came second to the life of the big land, and no one seemed to mind. No one minded being an extra in the land's story.

But among Jacinta's memories of St. John's, the cinema reigned. She had loved the red velvet rope that cordoned off the balcony, and the gold-painted pillars swirling with plaster curls, leaves, and Roman faces, with four lions at the top. Though it was only gilt paint and you could see the plaster where the paint had chipped, she had loved it. She had loved the red velvet curtain, and the fact that there was a guest book on a slender pedestal in the lobby, with a pen tied to a gold cord. She had loved the tall rectangular wagons with huge, delicate wheels that the ice cream and popcorn boys wheeled in slowly before the show, and she had loved the show, from the moment its light flickered behind the closed curtain, through every letter and comma of the title and credits, through the searing drama, lit from the side and the back and the front with floodlights that created planes of light and areas of shadowed mystery, and she had loved staring up close at the faces, the gestures, the emotions of the stars onscreen who had no idea that she, Jacinta Hayden, was there.

In Croydon Harbour there was nowhere you could go to get out of the brightness of a winter day or a glaring summer day. There was nowhere you could sit in the shadows, hidden and secret, with your dreams. And if you ran out of dreams or you lost them, there was no silver screen to find them for you again or to whisper you in the direction of new ones. You were on your own in Croydon Harbour. In the realm of imagination you were left to your own devices, and this was what most people in Croydon Harbour wanted. This was why they came here, if they came from other places such as Scotland and England and even America; they came to leave behind the collective dreams of an old world and they came to glory in their own footprints on land that had been travelled only by aboriginal peoples and the wild caribou. And if you were one of the Innu or Inuit in those days, you had no need of cinema. Cinema was one of the white man's illusions to compensate for his blindness. A white man, for instance, had no idea of the life within stones. Imagine that.

But Jacinta craved the cinema. If she had to list the things she had lost when she made Labrador her home, the Majestic on Henry Street would have been at the top. Not the building, which outside was covered in ordinary blue clapboard and had small wooden windows, but the inside, elevated to Roman glory, and the screen, where the unanswered cries of the heart could live for a while in an element that understood them.

When you came out of the Majestic and walked down Henry Street — one of the steep, friendly hills of St. John's that open out onto Duckworth and onto the steps that lead to Water Street and the harbour, filled with trawlers and cargo boats and sailboats and men stacking pallets of melons and loading crates of wine — the city looked like a place where dreams would come true. You smelled fresh tar that workers were rolling on the roof of Bowring's, and smoke from the wine-dipped cigar of a man on his way to the lawyers' office, and the faint sweetness from melons that had fallen and smacked open on the ground near the boats, and perfume from a woman who had just disappeared around the corner where the newspaper seller sat on his bag in the sun eating his sandwich of hot sausage and onion. You felt young — you were young, because you were not yet eighteen and had not yet gone to Labrador to work, and had not yet met the man you would love but who would never understand the greatest part of your soul, the part that lived on such wisps of romance and faded when they were taken away.

You had not yet thought about how the romance that resided in each of these elements — the melons, the perfume, the rich man with the cigar, the poor man and his newspapers — did not live on its own but must come together with the others in order to exist. The romance was in the whole picture, and each of its parts was only one lonely story, and the story was often sad and without any comfort or answers or poetry or sense, or love.

Now Jacinta sat in her kitchen in Croydon Harbour holding her baby, Wayne. Instead of longing for her youth, the cinema, and the street life she used to know, she found herself bereft of the old wistfulness, and its absence was harder to bear than its existence. When there was another world to remember, a lost world, she could imagine visiting it again. She could imagine the comfort of being there for a week, then coming back to face her real life. But now her real life, her baby's real life, had turned into something she did not know how to face. There was no ice-cream wagon, no music, no usher leading the way with a flashlight to the best remaining seat.

Jacinta was of two minds about Wayne's christening at St. Mark's Anglican Church in Croydon Harbour. A church, in her mind, was not what it claimed to be. Its beauty for her lay not in the meaning prescribed by the Apostles' Creed or the liturgy, or in the banners of red, gold, and blue made by the Anglican Women's Association proclaiming HE IS WITH US. The beauty of the building lay in its space and architecture, and Jacinta felt this beauty existed more fully at the great cathedral in St. John's than it did in this little community church, although she tried to evoke it here by straining her imagination to its fullest limit.

The St. John's cathedral had gargoyles, a crypt, magnificent windows brought to Newfoundland from England in barrels of molasses so the glass would not break. The windows had white lambs against sapphire skies, Egyp-

tian goddesses in the guise of Christian icons of woman-
hood, pilgrims with staffs and scarlet robes straight out
of the Torah and tarot, doves of hope and ravens of doom
and heralds with golden trumpets. The pulpit's eagle,
towering over the congregation with its brooding stare
and ravenous beak, had scared her when, as a child, she
had gone for the blessing of the animals with her Aunt
Myrtle, or placed hay in the crèche at Christmas with the
other children, or smelled the Easter lilies, whose perfume
mingled with the shade and atmosphere of the great stone
walls to create a chalice in which each child sat in wonder
like a small, bright, plump bee sucking mysterious nectar,
intoxicating and unnerving and powerful.

In Croydon Harbour the eagle on the pulpit had been
carved of pine by her husband's father, and it had the
smooth planes and lines of Inuit stone carvings, which to
Jacinta looked open and closed at the same time. She could
not get into those lines, into the myth and anger and spiritual flight and story of that Croydon Harbour eagle, and
she did not like to look at it. It was golden, for the pine
was unfinished, and this too seemed un-eagle-like to her,
benevolent and untrue, not like the texture of her life.

Jacinta knew Treadway did not look at the Croydon
Harbour eagle the way she did. He saw other things in it,
things that had to do with his travels over the land, things
he and Graham Montague and the other men of the cove,
and many of the women, recognized as their own spirit,
made of the energy that came off the land. There was

an energy in the English eagle and another energy altogether in the Labrador eagle. They were so different that everyone knew — Treadway knew, and Jacinta knew in a different way — that the pine eagle did not belong in an Anglican church at all. But it was here, and so were the spruce-wood pews, and the plain windows, and the wooden nave, and the ordinary house carpet, and the glass jugs of flowers from patches of ground descended from the tender but incongruous gardens planted by Moravian missionaries along this coast in the early nineteen hundreds. There were pansies, poppies, and English daisies, flowers that the cliffs and seas and raging skies dwarfed but that the hearts of the first German and Scottish women had needed in order not to break upon the Labrador stones. This whole religion, Jacinta thought — and Treadway knew without thought — depended on people more than people depended on it. You didn't need it unless you did not have the land in your heart; the land was its own god.

The minister's name was Julian Taft — such an English name. He had a square little face, and his body, hidden under his white robe, had no curves. The thought popped into Jacinta's mind, He is made of wood. He is a little wooden minister. Part of her was glad he could not see into her heart. He did not know her baby's secret, just as he did not know the secrets of anyone in Croydon Harbour. He could not see into the past, nor could he see into the future. He did not know her baby had undergone an operation at the hospital in Goose Bay, or that Jacinta's friend Eliza would begin her affair with the geography teacher after the next community garden party, or that he himself would fall in love with the same Eliza in a couple of years' time, after the geography teacher had temporarily moved to Assumption High on the Burin Peninsula. So it stood to reason, Jacinta hoped and prayed, that the little wooden minister would not see into the present either. She wondered at his purple scarf, the gold thread in the cloth, the stiffness of him, the royalty of the textiles and the perpendicular drape of them.

But now here they were, she and Treadway and the baby Wayne, and the whole little community gathered, somehow believing in the minister's ability to bless them. Jacinta wanted there to be a different church: a yellow house with blue sills and an open door. She wanted a big woman to own the house, to be inside it. A woman who would not turn to page 254 of the Book of Common Prayer and recite, "Dearly beloved, forasmuch as all men are conceived and born in sin . . ." What kind of words were these to start off a baby's life? She knew Treadway had no part in the words, yet he was here. Everyone in the harbour was here, light from the windows falling on their heads and darkness inside the church making everything but the lit-up sides and tops of their faces invisible. It was dark in here, and the minister was made of wood, and sunlight blazed and could blind you outside the open door, where freedom lay so bright and frightening.

After the service, Jacinta, Treadway, the uncles and aunts, and Thomasina moved to the font, and Reverend Taft asked the parents to name the child.

"Wayne," Treadway said.

It's the last moment, Jacinta thought, of my daughter's existence. She looked at the door. Where was her little girl in a sunlit dress? Run to me, quick! But the door was empty. Jacinta closed her eyes and spoke to Isis in the cathedral window in St. John's. Not Mary. Isis, whose son, Horus, was both child and falcon.

"I baptize you" — Julian Taft took cold water and drew a cross on the baby's forehead — "Wayne Blake."

Thomasina stood behind Julian Taft in her choir robe, her breast grazing his shoulder, her breath in his ear, and whispered.

Julian Taft knew how to keep his lips motionless and his voice so low only Thomasina could discern it. He concealed his real voice from the people with great skill. "What did you say?"

With skill greater than his, Thomasina whispered, "Annabel," so low he could not hear. Thomasina believed there was power in a name.

The name Annabel settled on the child as quietly as pollen alongside the one bestowed by Treadway.

PART TWO

PART TWO

6

Meat Cakes

THOMASINA AND TREADWAY BOTH, from the beginning, treated Wayne as a person, not a baby. Jacinta took Wayne in his carriage to have toast with Thomasina on her little back deck. While Jacinta dipped the toast in milk and fed it to Wayne, Thomasina showed him the difference between coltsfoot and dandelion. She put quartz in his hand and let him hold it glittering in the sun, then a piece of labradorite.

"See," Thomasina told him, "you can see trees and the sky in that one. Water too, and the northern lights."

"I feel," Jacinta said, "summer hasn't come at all. I'm always afraid someone will know."

Wayne's carriage stood in the coltsfoot. It had a tough canvas hood with green and white stripes that reminded

Jacinta of the canopy over Lar's Fruit Mart at the bottom of Barters Hill in St. John's.

"Why would they know?"

"The garden party was torture." Jacinta had taken the baby to the All Saints garden party and shown him off among the picnic cloths and hams and lemonade on the grass. "I was terrified the whole time that someone would plainly see."

"Was it that bad?"

"I thought for certain someone was going to peek down real close at him and say, 'Oh, but that's a little girl, Jacinta! Didn't you and Treadway know?'"

"But nobody did."

"No. Eliza Goudie and Grace Montague acted the way they would over any normal baby. Even Kate Davis found no fault."

Kate Davis had no children of her own and had been the nursing administrator at Goose Bay General Hospital until she retired, and she knew everything there was to know about medical conditions. Kate Davis had come up to Jacinta at the tea table and said in her grating, bossy tone, "Well, that looks like a healthy child," and Wayne looked back at her the way he looked at all strangers, with a direct gaze that said, I have not been badly treated yet, and so even you are to be trusted.

"You get used to something unusual when you're the one it happens to," Jacinta told Thomasina. "If Wayne had two heads I'd get used to that in a few months, and

I would wonder why anyone would want to change him. There's something good to be said for any circumstance. That's the way I see it."

But it was not, she knew, the way others saw things, and it was not the way Jacinta herself would have seen them had another woman in the cove had a baby who was a hermaphrodite. Sometimes you had to be who you were and endure what happened to you, and to you alone, before you could understand the first thing about it. So the fact that Wayne had ever been a girl as well as a boy was hidden and never spoken of, and no one in Croydon Harbour knew except his parents and Thomasina.

In Wayne's second summer, Jacinta let Thomasina baby-sit him while she did laundry and helped Treadway peel staves for a new fence. Thomasina showed Wayne how you can hear hundreds of black caterpillars munching nettles; if you put your head down close their munching is the loudest noise on a summer day.

"See, Annabel? Every single one of those munchers turns into a red admiral butterfly." Wayne thought she was calling him Amble. He thought Amble was Thomasina's own special word for him, like the way Jacinta called him Lassiebun because he loved bread and molasses, and the way Treadway called him Littleman when they were making balls of sinew in Treadway's shed.

Treadway had been careful to take Wayne down to the shed earlier than he would have taken a girl. He took Wayne to parts of the house that were men's parts: the basement, with its twelve-inch nails hung with bone saws and horseshoe frames, and the side room where he stretched and dried hides; the shed with its snowmobile and axes and makings of sled runners and fenceposts and its back section for hanging game. He took him there not with affection, for it was an effort to take a child that young into his work spaces, and normally he would have waited until a son was four or five before he trained him in the ways of how to become a man. But with this child Treadway did not want to take a chance. He treated the child seriously and told him with a grim face how to cut hide and shave wood and use the right screwdriver head for the right job, so that by the time Wayne approached kindergarten he would know more about these things than any other boy in the cove.

When Wayne had all his baby teeth, Thomasina gave him cold oranges cut in pieces and rose-petal rhubarb jam on bread with the plate on his knee. He ate on her floorboards, which were of juniper that Graham Montague had cut and shipped from Lewisporte. In the early fall nights he looked through a telescope Thomasina had ordered out of the catalogue. It was a Polar Star 140X telescope, a student model that magnified the constellations by ten.

When he was five, Thomasina showed him how to connect the stars. The constellations were stories in the sky, she told him. Orion was a hunter who had a dog, just like Treadway. The Seven Sisters had lost their youngest sister, Merope, who fell to earth.

"Where did she fall?" asked Wayne.

"I don't know. Look, there is Cygnus." Thomasina drew it for him on paper.

"A duck?"

"A swan. In St. John's, where your mother is from, they have swans. You can feed them cherries and seeds."

"Swans like cherries?"

"They love cherries. Your mother told me she used to feed them a handful of cherries on Christmas Day when she was a little girl. Glacé cherries, the kind you put in a Christmas cake. See how Cygnus is at the edge of the sky. He's getting ready to hide for the winter. But in China he's not a swan. He's a bridge."

"Like the one they're going to build at North West River?" There was always talk of bridges in that part of Labrador, where people had been getting over rivers and marshes for hundreds of years using skid runners, flat-bottomed boats, canoes, even a cable car.

"The Chinese bridge is made of magpies."

"What are they?"

"Magpies are birds, Annabel. There are two lovers, Niu Lang and Zhi Nu. They are on opposite sides of a river. They belong together, but no one sees this but the magpies. The magpies fly over the river and make a bridge with their wings."

"Draw me that!"

"Maybe you can draw that yourself." She gave him her pencil. "You'll need to draw on your own when you go to school, and read too."

"I have new jeans and a bookbag. My mom says I can still come visit you after school."

"I have to tell your mom something, Annabel. But I'm going to tell you first. I'm going to school too."

"You're coming to school?"

"I'm going to teachers' college."

"What's that?"

"You go there and you learn how to be a teacher. I'm going for four years, and then after that I might travel. I always wanted to see the world. When my husband was alive, we kept saying we would go and we never did it. I'm going to sell my house, Annabel. There's a family with a little girl coming here from Deer Lake. Her dad goes back and forth working in Quebec. The Michelins. They are going to buy my house."

"Are you coming back?"

"If I can get a job at the school here, after I'm done with my courses and my travelling, I'll come back."

"Will you live back here?" Wayne liked Thomasina's house.

"I'll think about that then. I'll send you postcards with pictures of interesting things in all the countries I go to."

"China?"

"Maybe not that far."

"You could see the magpie bridge."

"That bridge is in the sky, Annabel. It's not real. There's no photograph of it."

"I forget my address."

"Your address is Box 43."

"You better call me Wayne on the postcards."

"Yes, that way the post office will know for sure they are for you."

"I told Dad you were calling me Amble and he said he didn't like it."

"Don't worry. I'll only call you Annabel when there's no one else around."

When Thomasina had gone, Wayne made snowshoe twine and knife bindings with his father and ate meat cakes at the table of his parents, the fisheries report and the weather blaring continually out of both the radio and the television on the kitchen counter. Fly-catching tape hung from the ceiling with bluebottles on it, moving their legs but not their wings. A strange tension persisted when Wayne and his mother and father were together, Treadway asking questions like, "So, Wayne, have you gone down in the basement lately to check how our catgut is drying?"

The child knew that a grim, matter-of-fact attitude was required of him by his father, and he learned how to exhibit such an attitude, and he did not mind it because it was the way things were, but it was not his authentic self.

His authentic self loved to fold paper in half and cut out elaborate bilaterally symmetrical shapes: curlicues, geometrics, architectural planes that bore elaborate sills at the bottom and came to luxurious apexes. Some of the shapes had thin parts any five-year-old might snip off by accident, but Wayne was coordinated and meticulous. He cut slowly and carefully, and his mother saved his work in a binder and bought him safety scissors that she allowed him to keep in his room, where he cut at night for fifteen minutes after he had brushed his teeth, before Treadway shouted, "Get those lights off."

For Wayne, Croydon Harbour and all that was in it had a curious division between haven and exposure. The roads were dirt and there was dust, and this felt raw. The birches, in comparison, felt incredibly soft, their shadows a cool, sizzling green that quenched the parched burning of the roads. Loud engines of trucks and Ski-Doos played against the tinkling of the juncos that made their nests in the ground. A swoop and whisper of wings, then the gun crack. The love he felt for his father, then the cold precision with which Treadway taught him how to perform tasks like scraping rust off traps with the point of a blade. Golden tea under a swirl of steam on the trapline, then walking for miles with no rest until blisters formed on his ankles. When they arrived at the hunting tilt, his father treated them with a mixture of tallow from the haunch of a caribou and black spruce turpentine, which Treadway had collected on the end of his hunting knife after cutting a blister in the trunk of a tree. Treadway administered the ointment silently. He did not say, "You should have told me it hurt before now."

When they got home and Jacinta saw the wounds, Wayne heard her hiss, "Were you trying to wait until his skin was shredded to the bone? And did he eat? Look at his little breastbone and shoulder blades. They have a mind to poke through his skin. And he has a cough."

It was true. Treadway could walk for twenty miles through minus-twenty-degree weather and not mind it. He wore wool next to his skin and his body was compact and dense, his core curled into itself. There were nights when he slept in the open, wrapped in a sleeping bag lined with caribou hide, and in the morning he awoke invigorated by the wild, cold air and starlight. He had not made Wayne sleep out in the open, but there were nights when he did not bother to stoke the stove in his hunting tilt because he himself did not need it stoked, and the air inside the tilt grew damp as well as cold, from their breath and the condensed vapour from their own bodies, and by the time they arrived home Wayne had a racking cough that sounded like a high groan when he breathed in. His mother kept him home from school and boiled water in her big kettle all day to make steam in the house, and bundled him up in his father's chair, and together they ate toast and listened to the radio.

The first and second postcards from Thomasina came together, from the south of France: one had Picasso's *Les Demoiselles d'Avignon* on it, because Thomasina was staying in a hotel in Avignon.

"I had to take a break from teachers' college, Wayne,"

Thomasina wrote. "It is so boring. We have to study statistics. I would much rather study people and history. I think you could graduate without even knowing where all the countries are. I decided to do two semesters at a time and travel between. This is where Picasso found his models for the famous painting on the card."

Treadway, on his way in and out of the kitchen with armloads of spruce, asked, "What kind of postcard is that to send a child?" He picked it up and studied it. "Naked women?"

"It's Picasso," Jacinta said.

"Are they even women? What are they wearing on their faces?"

"What are statistics, Dad?"

"Statistics, son, are facts. Facts connected with numbers. For example, the population of Croydon Harbour is 217. You add or lose a number here or there for a death or a birth, but give or take a half a dozen numbers you know where you stand. There are more interesting questions in science, but it wouldn't hurt Thomasina Baikie to stay in one place and learn a statistic or two."

The second postcard was a photograph of the Pont d'Avignon.

"This bridge was built in the eleven hundreds," Thomasina wrote. "There's only part of it left, but imagine it standing that long. It's not the magpie bridge, Wayne, but wings still helped build it. Angel wings. There was a boy about your age. I forget his name but angels told him to build the bridge. He was able to lift massive stones, and he built it. There's a famous song about this bridge — maybe you'll learn it one day in French class."

"What is that woman trying to put in Wayne's head?" Treadway was covered in spruce shavings. A layer of cold, sweet air from outdoors clung to him.

"Maybe you should put those away," Jacinta told Wayne. "Do you want a tin?" She gave him a Peek Freans shortbread tin and Wayne put Thomasina's cards in it.

"Thomasina is liable to run out of money and get stuck in one of those places," Treadway said. "Some people have an awfully funny way of going on."

7

Elizaveta Kirilovna

WAYNE LOVED SYMMETRY, and so he loved grade three when his teacher taught about three-dimensional geometric shapes. One night while Jacinta was bottling rhubarb he asked her, "Have we got any of those wire things with paper on them that you close garbage bags with?"

"Twist ties?"

"You close garbage bags with them."

Jacinta was fishing Mason jar lids out of her pot with a pair of tongs. "Look in the garbage-bag box."

"Have we got any bread that isn't homemade?"

"Your dad's." Treadway used store-bought bread for his toast every night at nine o'clock.

"I only need a couple of slices."

"Behind the bologna." Jacinta was waiting for the

lids to pop down on two dozen jars. She liked it when the lids popped. She liked the definite, abrupt sound that meant no one in her family would get botulism. She liked the shiny jars on the counter, shoulder to shoulder. The accomplishment of it. Treadway might get lost out on the trapline. If he did, there would be jars of food. She filled and arranged the jars and washed the rhubarb pot and put away the sugar and cloves and the extra raisins. By the time she looked at Wayne he was sitting on the living room floor surrounded by decahedrons and cubes and hexagonal globes all the way from Treadway's *Reader's Digest* stack to the television set. Wayne had peeled the twist ties down to the wire. Then he had taken the bread and kneaded pieces into little balls of putty and connected the wires to each other using the putty. The shapes were fragile and powerful.

"Those are beautiful."

"Miss told us to use toothpicks and modelling clay. But I don't have any modelling clay. And we never have toothpicks."

"Those are something else." Jacinta knelt and looked at the shapes. They were from another world. The skies. "They remind me of planets. And orbits. And stars. And the lines connecting the stars to make constellations. How did you think of using twist ties and bread?"

"That's how Gracie Watts eats her bread at lunchtime. She picks it off her sandwich. She makes gnomes and dogs. You can make anything. When she eats her carrots, she does this other great thing. Her mom gives her carrot slices. She pops the pale orange middle out so there's only the bright orange ring left, with a hole in it."

"What," Treadway said when he came in from his shed and saw the celestial, symmetrical living room floor, "in the name of God?"

"It's homework, Treadway," Jacinta said. "Science."

"Math, Mommy. It's math, not science."

"If that's math" — Treadway picked his bread bag off the floor; it was nine now, and all that was left in the bag was a heel-end — "those teachers at that school need to have their heads examined."

The World Aquatic Championships came on television and Wayne watched them with Jacinta. He saw synchronized swimming for the first time. The Russian team turned into a lily. The lily turned inside out and became a decahedron. The hats of the Russian swimmers had starbursts of sequins at the crown, and they were turquoise. The suits were of Arabian paisley. Wayne was transfixed.

"Mom. They're making patterns. With their own bodies."

"I had a friend who did that," Jacinta said. "In St. John's. Nothing like that though. Eleanor Furneaux."

Wayne looked at his hands, his legs, and wished he had more than two of them. He couldn't get over the Russian team. It was glorious. Much more glorious than the English or the U.S. or the Canadian teams. The Russian team had a symmetry that went beyond what Wayne had imagined possible. He dreamed about it that night, and the next day he asked his mother what they had been swimming in.

"What kind of place was it?" He wanted to go there.

"What do you mean?"

"The water. It was the same colour as their hats. What kind of water was that?"

"It was a swimming pool. Is that what you mean?" There was no swimming pool anywhere near Croydon Harbour.

"Where did they get a pool like that?"

"Pools like that are all over the world, Wayne."

Highlights from the championships were televised over two weekends. Wayne watched the semi-finals and the finals. He noticed the details of the suits, the choices of music. Every departure from perfection on the part of the swimmers, he pointed out, even if he was alone in the room with the television.

When Treadway came in and sat down with his tea and sandwich, Wayne asked him, "Where is their music coming from?" He had been wondering about that for some time. There was no band anywhere visible at the side of the pool. Yet the routines included trumpets, pianos, drums, and all kinds of musical instruments, and even voices.

"What do you want to watch that for?"

"Dad. Where are they getting the music?" The music was loud and it surrounded the swimmers like the water did, and it echoed.

"Well, they just have it for the performance."

"But where is it?"

"Somewhere in the wings. Wayne, hockey is what you want to watch."

"How do they know where to put their arms next? How do they know how to do everything exactly the same, Dad?"

"They count," Jacinta stood in the doorway. "It's all choreographed."

"That explains everything," Treadway said with his mouth full.

"What's choreographed?" Wayne asked. "I like graphs." He was doing graphs in school. He coloured his in with stripes and tiny dots and different shades of pencil. His teacher had written on his report card that it would be good if he could finish his work more quickly.

"They practise for months," Jacinta said. "Years. Choreographed means someone thinks of all the moves and writes them down and the swimmers practise those moves over and over again. And when they're underwater, they count."

"Oh! So if water gets in their ears or they can't hear the music, it doesn't matter?"

"Right. They count and they all come up at the same moment, and everything is identical, and everything matches up perfectly."

"Well, their time would be better spent," Treadway

said, "if they went to secretarial school and learned how to do shorthand."

"It's a pattern the whole time, isn't it, Mommy?"

"It is. It's an intricate pattern."

"Who decides it? Who choreographs?"

"They have different choreographers. I'm not sure. But for her solo routine when we were fourteen, Eleanor Furneaux had to choreograph her own piece."

"Solo?" Treadway said. "I thought the whole point was to make a fool of yourself with eight or ten other people all doing exactly the same thing. You can't be synchronized if you're by yourself. Imagine synchronizing your watch to the right time if it was the only watch in the world." He got up and put his cup and saucer in the sink and went to the bathroom. He did not close the bathroom door and they heard him pee, then hawk and spit into the toilet.

At night in bed Treadway lay on his back beside his wife. He did not try to begin lovemaking but left that to her. It was one of the things Jacinta loved about her husband, especially now that her hormone levels had changed. She had taken Eliza Goudie's advice and sent to Eaton's for three satin slips with lace boleros. She had bought herself three good brassieres, and wore one each night because it lifted her breasts as if to make a present of them. Eliza had told her to say, out loud, alone, through the day, "I am incredibly sexy." It wasn't hormones alone, Eliza said, that dampened a woman's sex drive. It was not the balding of her husband or the thickening of his belly. It was the woman's abandonment of her own body. "If you aren't going to take Valium," Eliza had told her, "at least buy yourself some beautiful undergarments and negligées and talk yourself into being the most desirable woman your husband has ever known."

"Skaters have men," Treadway said.

"Skaters?"

"Olympic skaters. There are men."

"Figure skaters?"

"Even if they are like — what's his name?"

"Toller Cranston."

"Yeah. And they're not all like him. There are normal figure skaters."

"But Toller Cranston is the best."

"That's a matter of personal opinion. Did he win the gold medal? What I'm saying is, even if Wayne picked skating to go crazy over. But no. He picks the one sport anywhere, in the entire world, that you have to be a girl to perform. There are no boys in synchronized swimming, right?"

"I hadn't thought of it."

"Just cast your mind."

"I'm not sure."

In his own bed Wayne looked at the broken ceiling tile, which he knew had only 209 holes in it instead of the 224 in all the others, a fact he had discerned the time he had croup when he was seven and had to stay in bed nine days. He lay picturing the swimsuit of Elizaveta Kirilovna, the soloist for the Russian team. It was the first time he had wished he lived somewhere other than Croydon Harbour. All over the world, his mother had told him, there were swimming pools. Even in St. John's.

"Mom?" he asked Jacinta in the morning. He was trying out the difference between Mom and Mommy. His mother was scrubbing hardened soap out of her English porcelain soap dish. "Where is your friend Eleanor Furneaux now?"

"I think she's in Brampton, Ontario."

"What is she doing?"

"I think she married a man who makes tires."

"But what is she doing?"

"I don't know."

"Is she still synchronized swimming?"

Jacinta dried the ridges. Her soap dish was one of the few things she had left of her mother's. "She'll be in her forties now, Wayne. Like me."

Wayne cut around his yolk. If you did the right thing with the tip of your knife you could eat the white and leave the yolk a perfect circle. "But does she go synchronized swimming sometimes?"

"She might still be interested in it. She might help coach or something."

"Do you have to be young to synchronized swim?"

"You don't have to be. But a lot of things like that are based partly on beauty. And youth."

"Elizaveta Kirilovna is beautiful, isn't she, Mommy?"

They had shared a can of lime drink in wineglasses and watched the Russian soloist together over a bowl of ripple chips. Elizaveta Kirilovna had chosen Rimsky-Korsakov's Scheherazade. It had sounded like snow that floats before a storm. Wayne had listened carefully to the commentator's descriptions of what Elizaveta Kirilovna had choreographed. The commentator labelled and broke down the magic poetry of her routine, naming the parts with names and numbers Wayne liked so much he wrote them in the margins of page 176 of the Labrador phone book. Deckwork eight. Pretzel tuck two. Right left right left eggbeater eight. Move diagonally. Tub two. Front flutter twist. Sailboat. Flowerpot. Vertical spin.

"Yes, Wayne, she's beautiful. If you're not going to eat that yolk don't let your father see it. Here." Jacinta scraped it into the bowl in which she kept kitchen scraps for Treadway's dogs and covered it with a piece of toast crust.

"I wish I was her."

Jacinta put the bowl on the counter and stood with her back to him. "You can't go wishing that, Wayne."

"But I do. I wish it. I would be so good at that. If we had a pool. Maybe we could get a pool. Some people have pools in their backyards. They have them in the catalogue. How do they get the water so blue?"

"They cost fifteen hundred dollars. And they're not practical in Labrador. They're hardly practical anywhere in Canada. Two months of the year. Then the winter destroys them. It destroys them, Wayne."

"Do they put blue dye in it?"

"They have to put a lot of chlorine in it."

"If I was Elizaveta Kirilovna I'd get an orange suit. Bright orange. And a gold cap. I really like orange and gold. And I'd like to do that eggbeater thing. That looks great. I could do that here, in the river, in summer. Mom?"

"What, Wayne?"

"Would it be all right if I got a really nice bathing suit that was orange, the same shape as Elizaveta Kirilovna's, instead of swimming trunks?"

"No."

"It wouldn't?"

"No, Wayne."

"Boys don't wear them?"

"They could, if people would let them."

"But people won't?"

"No."

"Even if I wore it when no one was looking?"

"I don't know about that, Wayne. I don't think so."

"Would you let me?" He gave her a fierce little look that broke her heart. "I know Dad wouldn't let me. But would you? You understand, don't you, Mommy? About how amazing Elizaveta Kirilovna is? I could be like her."

"Wayne, your dad was asking me about that. He doesn't think there are any boy synchronized swimmers."

"Maybe there are some and we just haven't seen them on TV yet. Maybe the boys are on another channel."

"Your dad doesn't think so."

"But he doesn't know for sure."

"He's pretty sure."

"But just because Dad hasn't seen them doesn't mean there aren't any."

"That's true."

"There're lots of things Dad hasn't seen, but that doesn't mean they don't exist. He's never seen a giraffe. He's never seen a hippopotamus. He's never seen Bobby Orr in person. He's never seen the Entire State Building."

"Empire."

"Has he?"

"It's the Empire State Building, Wayne."

"Is it?"

"Yes."

"Could we get me a bathing suit like Elizaveta Kirilov-na's and not tell Dad?"

"I don't think so."

"Does that mean maybe?"

"I don't think so, Wayne."

"Even if I really, really, really, really want one and don't mention it to him at all and he never finds out and I use my own money?"

"I don't know if I can be complicit in a thing like that, Wayne."

"What's complicit?"

Jacinta put the lid back on the jar of Skippy peanut butter. "Complicit is when you agree to something in secret and hide it from another person."

"Is it always bad?"

"It could be, if you hide something important from someone you love."

"But it could be good too?"

"It could be something you do to save your life."

"Could it be in between?"

"This is giving me a headache, Wayne."

"Could it be when you hide something important from someone you love to sort of save your life in a way?"

"Wayne."

"Because I really, really, really, really, really, really —"

"Stop it."

"— want a bathing suit like Elizaveta Kirilovna's. More than anything else in the world."

"I've got something" — Treadway stood in the kitchen doorway draining his cup — "you might like to see."

"What, Dad?"

Treadway put his cup in the sink and went mysteriously out of the room. "If you want to come, come."

"But what is it?"

But Treadway would not tell. He had a way of enticing Wayne out of the house, into the woods, with unexplained beckonings. One time it was to fish smelt on the ice at Bear Island. Another time it was to see his cousin Lockyer tar the joints in a dory. Wayne knew that whatever it was this time would be outdoors, hot and windy. He knew it would take a long time. He knew that before it was over he would be wishing he had not come. Still, there was something irresistible about the way Treadway started on a mission. There was, along with the mystery of it, an intangible promise that Treadway would love and approve of Wayne if he came. By the end of most such outings, that promise had turned into disappointment. Maybe this time it would be different.

"Dad, where are we going?"

Treadway drove the truck past the Hudson's Bay store, which was the westernmost building in the settlement, and into the woods to where began the road everyone called the trans-Labrador highway, though it was only half built and was, for the most part, a one-way dirt track. Dust rose, and no matter how tightly Wayne rolled his window, dust got into the truck, past his shut lips and eyes and into his tears and his teeth. He hated it.

"Are we going to the Penashues' tent?"

The Innu had tents in the bush all along this road. They had used the route long before anyone thought of starting a road. Treadway was not the one who had brought Wayne to the Penashues' tent. Jacinta and Joan Martin had walked there with him to drink tea with Lucy Penashue. The women had given Wayne black tea boiled on a tin stove and bread that Lucy had kneaded and lain on the stove and torn.

"No." The truck lurched.

Wayne wanted a glass of water but did not tell his father he was thirsty. "Did you bring any fly-dope, Dad?"

He touched behind an ear and his finger was covered in blood crust.

"DEET."

Wayne got the DEET out of the glove compartment and rubbed some behind his ears, on his neck, around his hairline, and into his hair. He hated its stink.

"Want some, Dad?"

"We're here now."

The truck swerved into a huge cul-de-sac, a place in the road where men with backhoes were digging dirt out of the side of a hill and heaping it along the road for the grader. This road had to be rebuilt after every winter. One day, said the politicians in Newfoundland, it would cross Labrador into Quebec with two full lanes, and even farther ahead in their crystal balls they saw it paved, so no one would have to spend the summer rebuilding it again. But now flies and heat and dust made the men sweaty and filthy. They sat high in their machines and swigged water out of plastic bottles, and they ate bologna-and-mustard sandwiches that had earth handprints on the bread. It was noon, and the men were happy to see a kid, and they joked with Treadway about putting the kid on the job. Treadway was a man who, though silent in his town, laughed and joked with the road builders and with any men in a group. He was a man who was made to be part of a team working hard with dogs on the ice or machines in the dirt. An easiness came over him. He did not have to think about what to say. It was not one man talking here, but the pack. What one man said could easily have been said by another. They threw their voices back and forth in the sun like baseball players fooling around with the ball. Summers were short in Labrador, and there were not many days a man could fool around with his friends in his shirtsleeves and feel sweat all over his body.

"Hey," said Clement Brake, "Treadway. Is the kid ready?"

Treadway nodded and sat on a clump of lambkill and took a pack of Wrigley's Doublemint gum out of his pocket and offered a stick to Wayne.

"Ready for what, Dad?"

"Sit down, son. That synchronized swimming you're so fond of? Wait till you see this."

Wayne sat beside his dad. The men got their backhoes in gear. They lurched out of their hollows and moved to the centre of the packed dirt.

"Hey," shouted Clement Brake to Otis Watts, "Mister Music, please!"

"Right on," yelled Otis, and he put Creedence Clearwater Revival on bust up in the cab. The backhoes lined up.

"What are they doing, Dad?"

Treadway chewed his gum. "Pay attention, son." The backhoes lifted their arms. They tilted their shovels to the right, then to the left. They lowered their arms and raised them again. Wayne realized this was supposed to be in time to the music. The music was ahead of them, but that did not stop them. Half a beat behind the music the backhoes turned full circle, backed up, and lifted their arms up and down maniacally. Treadway chewed with his mouth open and stared appreciatively at the men. Wayne saw that he was half smiling in a way he had never seen his dad smile. His dad looked at him. Wayne realized he was supposed to smile back and he tried, but it was torture. He had grit in his eyes and he hated the backhoes. The song ended seconds before the machines stopped. Wayne saw the men's teeth in their brown faces through the glass of each cab. They were so proud they couldn't speak. Treadway waved at Otis, who had taken the lead. It was a high-five kind of wave, the kind Wayne never knew was coming.

"Well, son? Did you like it?"

Wayne knew he had to say "yeah" but he could not say it. He watched the crinkles around his dad's eyes go away. His dad was chewing a toothpick now.

"You didn't like it."

Wayne could not protest this.

"The boys have been practising it all week. They're pretty good too. I thought you'd like that. I got them to put on a special performance just for us." He leant forward. "Go up and tell Otis you liked it."

"Dad."

"Just say you thought the boys did a good job. Come on."

"I don't want to."

"Just come with me, then, while I say it." Treadway

pulled Wayne up by an elbow. Wayne followed him to Otis's rig.

"Well, Otis, my son didn't want to tell you this himself, but you know what he told me?"

"Dad."

"He told me you've done an excellent choreographing job on that backhoe ballet."

Otis threw down a banana and Wayne tried to catch it but it fell in the dirt. It had been bruised and now it was dusty too. Wayne picked it up and held it all the way back home. When he got home, he put it on the kitchen table and went to his room and waited until he heard his dad click the back door, then he slid the Eaton's catalogue from under his bed and found the bathing suits. There were only two pages, and Wayne had circled the best suit of all. The others were plain: raspberry with a cream stripe, green with a yellow gusset, a lot of blue. Wayne had circled a flame orange suit with a necklace of oval sequins the colour of the eyes in a peacock feather: emerald and copper sulphate. The suit was twenty-six dollars, and he had saved up nineteen.

8

Wally Michelin

JACINTA DID NOT LISTEN TO commercial stations or to talk shows where people called in about the politics of the day, the state of potholes, or ailments of their houseplants. She kept it tuned to a station that played Chopin and Tchaikovsky and Schubert.

"I know it's not real company," she told Wayne, "but the radio is something. It's a comforting voice that lets you know you're not entirely alone in the world. I need that."

All children, she thought as she watched him, could be either girl or boy, their cheeks flushed, their hair damp tendrils. Wayne looked at her so trustingly she badly wanted to sit beside him, to look at him and honestly explain everything that had happened to him from birth. At nine, she thought, a child has a capacity for truth. By age ten the child has lengthened and opened out from babyhood, from childishness, and there is a directness there that adults don't have. You could look in Wayne's eyes and say anything true, no matter how difficult, and those eyes would meet yours and they would take it in with a scientific beauty that was like Schubert's music.

Treadway had said he liked classical music when he and Jacinta were first married. And he had. He had felt that the radio graced the rooms in his house. He had liked the way music floated from one room to another through an open door. But Jacinta had it on all the time, and Treadway longed for silence as well. And in his house there was no silence. There was always that radio. Now he thought of it as an incessant banging on pianos and operatic foolishness, and it irritated him. But he did not ask her to turn it off. Treadway had his outside world, his magnificent wilderness, and he could go out in it any time it pleased him, and he also had restraint.

Because Treadway was not a man who could reach out to his wife, and because Jacinta had her own inner world, her memories of the city, and her tormented wish for a world in which her child did not have to be confined to something smaller than who he was, the two of them grew separate throughout Wayne's childhood. Each grew more silent outwardly and more self-sufficient, but lonesome inwardly. From the outside they looked the way many middle-aged couples do. Both were models of sensible good behaviour. Treadway was considered such a good husband that many of Jacinta's friends wished they had married someone like him instead of being fooled by wit, grace, passion, or a handsome face. Their own husbands did not bring in as much wood as Treadway did before he went away on his trapline. They did not come back home as early or as faithfully. They did not work so carefully on their skins and furs as he did, and therefore their work did not bring in as much money, and the money it did bring, they did not spend as honourably on their household needs, but bought cigarettes and brandy and beer. That their own husbands talked to them, and took them dancing, and were intimate with them in fun-loving and coded ways known only between the members of each couple was something the other women took for granted. They did not realize that Treadway and Jacinta had moved away from each other, though outwardly each held the golden thread that looked like a marriage.

For her part, Jacinta thought her loneliness her own fault. If she had been a wife who had not been brought up outside Labrador, she thought, perhaps she would have been more content to live in isolation under her own roof. So she suppressed her loneliness, and it resided in her heart along with the suppressed certainty she felt that, while Wayne was being brought up as a young boy, part of him was as feminine as she was. On days when Wayne was home sick from school, she played word games with him, and they sang and drew pictures of funny, random things together: trousers with spots, flying umbrellas, circus dogs they had read about in books, the pyramids of fruit Jacinta remembered in the shop windows of her childhood.

"Can we get Thomasina's tin out?" Wayne asked when they had made pages of drawings. "I want to look at the bridges."

Thomasina had sent a card showing a drawing of the old London Bridge. "They didn't plan this one at all," she wrote. "They just kept adding on a new section when they got around to it. It was so heavy the river had to fight to get around the pillars. It pushed through the arches so fast people crashed into the bridge in their boats."

Many of the bridges on Thomasina's postcards were incomplete. They had been destroyed by centuries or had vanished altogether and existed now only in the frail form of drawings on the postcards. Jacinta liked this. The fragments reassured her. Her own life felt full of incomplete pieces. She remembered the Bible story where Christ gathered fragments of crusts, small pieces of fish, and somehow made them whole again, enough to feed thousands. She liked thinking about the fragments more than she liked the story of the eventual miracle. There was something sacred about the fragments, about hunger, about unfinished bridges or bridges that had crumbled. She did not like the postcard that showed a Stone Age bridge in Somerset in England, where Neolithic men had dragged massive slabs onto boulders that still stood. There was something brutal about their permanence that made her feel afraid, and she wished Thomasina had not sent that card.

"Where's the one from Turkey?" Jacinta loved that the broken Turkish arch was the oldest stone arch left standing in the world.

But the bridge Wayne loved was Italian. It was Florence's Ponte Vecchio. "I didn't know a bridge could have buildings on it, and shops full of gold." He loved how there were people in the buildings right on the bridge, with light in the windows that reflected on the water. He had not known you could live on a bridge, but Thomasina wrote that you could.

"I want to live on a bridge like that," Wayne told his mother. "I want to hang a fishing line out the window and catch a fish."

"There was music on the Ponte Vecchio," Thomasina had written. "I gave the violin player some coins and he played something he said he had composed."

Jacinta sat in Treadway's armchair with Wayne and they read to each other from copies of A. A. Milne and Lewis Carroll that Jacinta had brought to Labrador in the last corner of her trunk. To Jacinta all of this felt like what it must mean to have a daughter, but she kept this feeling pooled within herself, and she did not know what would cause the most harm: to let that pool become a free-flowing stream or to starve it of water gradually, so that one day it might dry completely.

In grade five Wayne became silent until spoken to because that was the way he learned to act with his father. His teachers relied on him to pull the string that displayed the world map, and to clean the filter on the tank that held the neon fish and fire newts. They did not know he did not like cleaning the filter, and if they knew he read novels inside his open math book they said nothing, because he did his homework and managed to get seventies on his tests. They did not know he adored a girl in the first row named Wally Michelin and would have done anything in this world to be her friend.

Wally Michelin had been born on the third of June, which was why her mother had named her after Wallis Simpson, whom Edward VIII had married on that date after renouncing his throne. Wally Michelin had announced this in kindergarten, when the teacher, Miss Davey, asked her where she got her name, and she had said it proudly, her hair black and her face the colour of cream with freckles all over it, and high walking boots on her like something out of an American catalogue. Wally Michelin had stomped through kindergarten and grades one and two with a certainty Wayne found fascinating. The day she got Coke-bottle glasses with black rims, such glasses immediately became a cool thing, not a thing to be laughed at. When she broke her arm falling off the slide in the playground, she had more signatures on her cast than anyone in Croydon Harbour had seen on a cast before. Her father had taken her on a trip to Quebec, and every time they stopped for pie all the waitresses and truckers signed it, and one of the signatures was in rainbow ink. Wally was the first one in the class to get mumps, chicken pox, and measles, and the only one to get whooping cough, which could kill you. She had a first cousin who lived in Boston, and her bologna sandwiches were always Maple Leaf brand. She was the champion marble player of Croydon Harbour Elementary and had an oversized green dragon and a rare black orange flare. Wayne was in love with her from the moment he heard her crumbly voice. So in love he wished he could become her. If there was a way he could make himself into a ghost without a body — a shadow — or transparent like the lures his father used to catch Arctic char, he would have done it. He would have transformed into his father's lure, slipped under Wally Michelin's divinely freckled skin, and lived inside her, looking through her eyes.

There was nothing pretty about Wally Michelin, but nobody noticed this for a long time. To Wayne it was apparent that nothing could make Wally doubt her own self, not even the advent of Donna Palliser.

Donna Palliser came to the school in the middle of grade five. She took one look around her and decided who had to be taken out and who could stay. She had a slow way of turning her head and giving a poisonous look to anyone she was taking out. Sometimes the look alone took the person out and that person retreated to the background, and sometimes Donna Palliser had to take action, which she did in the playground when none of the teachers was looking. She did not have a strong body; she bullied mentally, not physically, and the first and most important person she wanted to take down was Wally Michelin, who had been queen before Donna got there, and whom Donna could see was the kind of queen who ruled by natural nobility and not by cunning or cruelty or clever resolve. Wally was easy to take down because she did not care if she was queen or not. Wally was not going to move. The other girls would move. The other girls would swear allegiance to the new queen, and there would be a ranking order, and no one would care about Wally's green dragon or orange flare, which they had genuinely admired. They would care about Hush Puppies crepe-soled Mary Jane shoes instead, and angora boleros, and having a ballpoint pen with pink ink, and Sweet Honesty perfume ordered from the Avon catalogue.

When Donna had been in town one month, she had a housewarming party and gave out invitations from the Details and Designs Emporium in Goose Bay. She gave invitations to everyone when Miss Davey was looking, but at recess time she told certain girls that they were not invited. All the boys were invited, but she was uninviting certain girls. She uninvited Gracie Watts, who wore the same wool sweater every day, and she uninvited Agatha and Marina Groves, the red-headed twins who were too fat to get through the door on the school bus and had to be brought to school in their father's truck, and she uninvited Wally Michelin, telling her that her mother said she could invite only eighteen people and Wally was number nineteen.

Wayne did not even put his invitation in his bookbag. It was pink with YOU ARE INVITED embossed on the front, and it had scalloped edges. He slid it into his desk, and when the bell rang, he threw it in the garbage.

The party was in three days, and by the second day the girls in the class had reconciled themselves to the idea that it was all right that they had been invited and Gracie, the Groves twins, and Wally had not. They told each other, and themselves, that Gracie, the twins, and Wally did not care, and that anyone who cared had been invited, so it was all right. The whole class talked about Donna Palliser's party, even the boys, because she told them her parents would not be in the rec room where the party was. The parents would be upstairs and were leaving Donna in charge, and there was going to be punch, which Donna said would have some real champagne in it from the back of her parents' liquor cabinet.

Wayne had no intention of going to that party, but on the evening itself Treadway took him to the Hudson's Bay store to get mousetraps. They were standing by the shelf discovering there was only one real mousetrap left when Roland Shiwack came up the aisle with his son Brent and picked up some number-two sandpaper and a couple of cans of WD-40.

"Hey, Treadway, how are things?"

"Dad." Brent was in a hurry to get to the party and drink the punch.

"Pretty good." Treadway looked disgustedly at the sticky mousetraps that were in plentiful supply. The mouse would stick to such a trap for twenty seconds and then you would never catch that mouse again.

"You got mice."

"I don't have mice. I'd like to make sure I don't have them in the future, and I don't want to have to get a cat."

Treadway disliked cats. He disliked himself for implying to Roland that he might get one. He disliked Roland. The reason he disliked Roland was that Roland was a Knight of Columbus, and every time he saw Treadway he gave Treadway the secret sign, which Treadway knew but pretended he did not know. Graham Montague, who was not Catholic either, had showed it to him one night after a few beers, having learned it from God knows what traitor, but Treadway was damned if he was going to let Roland Shiwack know that. It irked him that Roland did it every time, that he never let up, that Roland had some kind of childish obsession.

"You can have one of our cats," Roland said heartily. He was a pleasant, friendly man who had no idea Treadway felt the way he did. "Melba's got a dozen of them in the basement. Our cat had kittens again."

"Dad," Brent said. "I'm gonna be late."

"He's going to a party," Roland told Treadway.

"I see."

"Wayne must be going to the same one. Over at Pallisers."

"Yes, he is."

"No, I'm not, Dad."

Treadway ignored his son. "It's probably time, then, to go home and get ready." And he turned away from the Shiwacks.

"I'm not going to that party," Wayne said in the truck.

"Why not?"

"It's a stupid party. Some stupid thing with these really bad invitations. The new girl. I don't want to go to that."

"Are the other boys going?"

"I don't know."

"How come you don't know?"

"What?"

"How come, son, you don't know what the other boys are doing?"

"I just don't. They can do what they want, Dad."

"Boys, in Labrador, Wayne, are like a wolf pack. We've got to be like members of the dog family. We've got to know what each other is doing. That's how you survive."

"Well I guess they're going. But I don't know if they want to or not."

"If they're going, son, it doesn't matter what they want. It's a question of order."

"I'll work in the basement. I'll work on the catgut."

Wayne did not mind working on the catgut. Catgut was its name but it was really caribou sinew. You took the stomach of the animal, you dried it, then, using a home-made knife with an extremely thin blade, you sliced it in a spiral into a long, thin string, useful for many things in the bush and on the water. Wayne liked the meditative slice of the knife through the sinew. He liked the colour of the sinew, and he took pride in cutting it just the right width for both slightness and strength.

"There's a time for catgut, Wayne, and there's a time for parties. Tonight you need to go to that party. Even if you don't like it. You'll thank me one day."

Jacinta was in the kitchen rolling pastry and spreading caribou paste on it with knobs of fat on top and covering it and cutting it into pies for Treadway to take down the river. She made one pie for Wayne, and on Wayne's pie she shaped the knobs of fat into a heart. No one knew this, as more pastry covered it up. Wayne did not know it, and Treadway especially did not. She did this with the mustard on Wayne's school-lunch sandwiches as well, but with words. She wrote subliminal messages to her son, messages that he would eat. She wrote "Beloved Son" and "Be brave." She wrote them to give her child secret sustenance. Once she wrote "Daughter," but she could not bring herself to put that sandwich in Wayne's lunch box. What if the sandwich fell open and the word was still legible and someone read it? So she ate the daughter sandwich herself.

Whenever Treadway and Wayne came in the house arguing, her chest tightened and she tried to stop herself from interfering. She tried to let the argument play out. The argument was always the same. It was always the same argument in any one of a thousand disguises. The one about how to act like a real boy. The hardest part of it for her was knowing that Wayne had no idea his father stood against his own son out of fear.

While Wayne was still in grade five, he started to get books out of the school library and read them in class while eating chips or hickory sticks in a surreptitious way he had developed. His regular teacher, Miss Davey, never noticed. But one day the class had a substitute teacher, Mr. Henry, who observed the class carefully. Wayne flattened a bag of roast chicken chips inside his desk with the heel of his hand. He had bitten a tiny hole in the bag to let air out. A bag of chips lasted a lot longer when its contents were crushed to a powder that you licked, one coating at a time, off your finger. The substitute teacher smelled like the strong brown soap on a rope Wayne's aunt had sent Treadway one Christmas. The soap was the shape of a stretched egg and had sand in it. The smell made Wayne's stomach lurch. He was on page 174 of *The Railway Children* and reaching for some chip dust when a wave of the soap came over him, like the time his mom permed her hair at the sink and ended up crying. Wayne realized Mr. Henry could plainly see *The Railway*

Children tucked into his math book, but it was not *The Railway Children* Mr. Henry wanted to discuss.

"Do you realize," he said, loud as an actor, "how fattening potato chips are?" At the word *fattening* his teeth smiled but his tongue coiled like an eel. Wayne pushed his chip bag deep inside his desk but kept his hand in there too. There was chip dust all over his finger.

"Fattening," Mr. Henry said again. "You don't want to get fat, do you?"

Donna Palliser and the girls who had joined her club laughed. The boys did not. Brent Shiwack stabbed holes outlining the island of Newfoundland in his desk with a compass.

"Do you," persisted Mr. Henry, his perfume overpowering, "want to become fat?" The girls in Donna Palliser's club waited, and Wayne felt caught in their world in a way the other boys were not. Something about Mr. Henry was caught in the girl world as well, but Wayne did not know what it was. He did not like the way Mr. Henry and the girls all looked at him. This uneasiness followed him all day.

Ice hung on the wool of his mittens, and though students were forbidden to leave clothes on the radiator in the cloakroom, everyone did it. Things got burnt. Wayne told Mr. Henry he had to go to the washroom, but what he wanted was to get away from the soap and rescue his mitts. He was shoving them in his coat sleeve when Mr. Henry came in. Wayne felt that Mr. Henry was not going to get mad at him about the mittens. He felt that Mr. Henry had something else in mind, and he was right.

"Did you need to get away by yourself?" Mr. Henry's voice was softer than it should have been. Wayne wanted to run out of the cloakroom, but it was small and narrow, and he would have had to run right under Mr. Henry's armpit. He stayed by the tiny window, which was frosted over. Hardly any daylight came into the cloakroom. There was one bulb, and its light was yellow. There was a smell of wet wool, sock sweat, and now the soap Wayne had wanted to get away from. Mr. Henry moved close to Wayne and rested a finger on his jawbone and drew a line along Wayne's face, up to his ear and exquisitely, painfully, ever so lightly, around the back of Wayne's ear, where no one had touched him before. The skin was so sensitive Wayne was scared it might break. Flowers were bursting open between his legs, but the flowers were ugly flowers that he did not like. He had no room to back up. Behind him was the radiator. If he touched it, it would burn right through his shirt. As it was he could smell the cotton getting hot, like it did when his mother ironed his shirts. Didn't Mr. Henry have to go back to the class? Where did everyone think he was?

"I just wanted to get something out of my coat pocket."

"I need to get away by myself sometimes too." Mr. Henry took hold of a piece of Wayne's hair, which Wayne vowed to cut as soon as he got home, if he ever got home out of this, if Mr. Henry did not take all the grade five coats off their hooks and smother him. The teacher held the lock of Wayne's hair the way Wayne's mother held knobs of cold shortening with flour streaming down as she tenderly made pastry, using only her fingertips so as not to heat the silky mixture, then he let it go.

"If you ever need someone to talk to, about special things, things you don't want anyone to know" — Mr. Henry's voice was so low it was deadly, as if he were saying Wayne could murder someone and tell Mr. Henry about it and Mr. Henry would help him conceal the crime — "you can come to me."

The bell rang, and it was so loud and shrill it made Wayne's heart jump twice, and the corridor outside was filled with everyone yelling and clanging lockers open. The smell of chicken pies — the cheap kind in frozen boxes heated at 425 degrees for forty minutes — wafted around the doorpost, and the moment of Mr. Henry's tenderness was, luckily for Wayne, finished. Mr. Henry spun on his shoe and barrelled towards the staff room without even saying goodbye to the boy he wanted. Wayne knew Mr. Henry wanted him. He didn't know how, exactly, but he knew it had to do with appetite, and he avoided being alone with that man again. No matter what Mr. Henry did to meet Wayne alone, Wayne was a step ahead, even if he had to run. So he escaped from Mr. Henry, but he could not escape from the fact that a man had wanted him, and that his body had responded to that man with a secret desire of its own. An exquisite stirring, unwanted, involuntary, mysterious. A child of eleven awakens to sexual ecstasy and keeps it to himself, and thinks for a brief time that he, or she, is the only one in the world to whom this has happened. For a little while Wayne's ecstasy remained hidden, like the bulb of any bloom, underground.

"It's like Dad is mad at me all the time." Wayne sat on the tall stool at the kitchen counter, talking to his mother while she cut onions. "How come?"

"He's not mad at you."

"He is."

"He's probably just tired. He wants the best for you. All fathers want the best for their children. He just wants to give you the skills you need to have a good life. He wants his son to be happy."

"He is mad. I can tell by his voice."

"Your father doesn't raise his voice." This was true. Treadway's mother and father had screamed at each other throughout his childhood, and he had told Jacinta early in their marriage that he would not yell, and he did not want her to yell.

"It all comes out one way or another," Jacinta told her sister later on the phone, but her sister was in a Mount Pearl subdivision and could not help her.

Treadway had no idea how to deal with tension. His

house was as quiet as he had vowed it would be, but inner yelling was new to him, and when it began, he left the house and went in his boat to the island, or down his trapline.

9

Lettuce Sandwich

THERE WAS A WAY YOU COULD WALK nonchalantly past Wally Michelin's picket gate and make it seem you were on your way to the shortcut everyone used to get to the Hudson's Bay store. Wayne wished he could go through Wally's gate and knock on her door, but he could not. He wished he could pick pearly everlasting growing in the rocks, wrap the stems in long grass, and stick the bouquet in her letterbox anonymously, though in a way that she would instantly recognize as being from him only, but he could not do that either. He walked past her gate without glancing at it, and felt like a complete idiot.

A red water gun hung in the Hudson's Bay store window. He had outgrown water guns. A plastic radio did not interest him either. Everything in the window looked as if it had sat there too long. It looked as if the things had been sent to Labrador because people in other places had no use for them. It was one of the things his mother complained about.

"They have blueberries," she said, "in quarter-pint tubs for two dollars, when we pick our own five-gallon buckets a hundred feet from our own back steps."

The blueberries in the store were twice the size of the local ones and were nearly rotten. And the store had no fresh milk. Jacinta was the only person Wayne had ever heard mention this. In Labrador you drank tea black, with sugar. The store never ran out of sugar.

On Wayne's fifth day of walking nonchalantly past her house, Wally Michelin came out.

"Do you want a lettuce sandwich?"

Wayne had never heard of making a sandwich that contained only lettuce.

"It's really good with a can of Sprite. I always make one when my mom's out selling Avon."

Wayne remembered the house from when Thomasina Baikie had owned it. Now it was different. Wally's father had put in big kitchen windows through which the light of Hamilton Inlet spilled, and it was in this light that Wally placed four slices of Holsum bread. With a spatula she scraped Miracle Whip on the bread, where it sank into the white holes.

"The most important thing is the mayonnaise."

"My mom waterproofs bread with margarine."

"I never heard of waterproofing bread."

She tore curls of lettuce from an iceberg head, shredded them, and scattered them on the bread, then shook salt. Wayne expected the sandwich to be tasteless. He thought it would taste as if someone had forgotten the luncheon meat.

Wally bit. "See?"

The lettuce tasted green, crisp, cold. Part of him felt that only a deprived person would think lettuce on its own tasted exciting. But it did, and this gave him a new sense that you could strip things down more than his parents had done; a thing like lettuce could sustain you. All the worries his father had, a man's efforts for the survival of himself and his family, were they too elaborate?

His mother was elaborate as well. Here, in Wally Michelin's empty house, without her parents, without meat, and in the blazing light from which his own house turned away, Wayne felt an excitement he could not name.

After the lettuce sandwich Wayne and Wally became friends. Wayne loved Wally in the way that children can love each other only in that flickering window when they no longer play with toys but are not fully sexual. Her mother and father left Wally alone in the house often, because she was intelligent and they trusted her. She was allowed to make tea, and she made it with maple syrup from Quebec. They drank it sitting on cushions stacked on the deck facing the bright south and the mountains. The space let them talk about things that required vision, and they did not go inside to watch *Bewitched* or *Jeopardy*.

"You have to have a goal." Wally was as certain about her vision as she had been about lettuce sandwiches. This startled Wayne, whose parents concerned themselves with what he was beginning to see as only a segment of life. The kitchen: his mother, her pans of fried liver, heart, little shoulder chops of caribou, and the other animals his father hunted — was that all? There was always what Jacinta called beautiful music: Brahms, Chopin. But the music came in to them through the radio, and there was no portal back out through which his mother could leave the realm of the ordinary. Wayne knew Jacinta had come from another world, that she remembered an elsewhere, but she was here now. She was staying here and the radio music could visit her, but she could not escape. She could not go out to meet it. And his father's life was small in a different way. Treadway loved the wilderness, but Treadway's wilderness did not call to Wayne. It did not seduce him and he did not wish he could spend more time in it than he did. Wally Michelin had a different world to go to, and Wayne felt it here, in the sun, on the deck of her house.

"If you don't have a goal" — their backs touched the wall, which was hot though there were patches of snow — "you might as well blindfold yourself and see where you end up."

Wally Michelin's father spent his trucker's wages on building supplies every chance he got, and he had covered the walls with terracotta stucco no one else in Croydon Harbour had. It retained heat like clay. Treadway had not approved.

"That's going to crumble inside five winters," he'd said, as Gerald Michelin and his visiting brothers-in-law had applied the mud with graceful trowels. But it had not crumbled, and Wayne had heard Jacinta tell Eliza Goudie she envied the way Ann Michelin's pots of geraniums splashed red against it like an Italian villa.

"I've got a goal." Wally gave Wayne a stack of Oreos. The Michelins ate brand-name groceries. Wayne was used to food procured from raw materials.

"What?"

"To sing in German."

"Like Lydia Coombs?"

"I wrote her a letter and guess what. Lydia Coombs wrote me back. And she sent me a present. An important present. Want to see it?"

Lydia Coombs had come to Croydon Harbour Elementary on a national tour of outpost schools, to show children the life and work of a real opera singer. Lydia Coombs had told them that, when she was ten years old in her town on the north shore of the St. Lawrence River in Quebec, one of the nuns, Sister Angelica, had told the class to run away. She had told them that if she, Sister Angelica, had run away in time, she could have gone to Vienna and made a life there for herself as a professional contralto. She told the class this in secret. Run away, before it's too late. When the mother superior was outdoors milking the school's cow every morning at eleven, too far away to hear, Sister Angelica had sung Schubert for the children. "It became normal for us to hear Schubert," Lydia Coombs said, "and nothing in my whole life has ever been as beautiful as that voice, and I promised myself I would run away and learn to sing like that." Then Lydia Coombs had sung something for Wayne and Wally's class.

"What was that German thing she sang?" Wayne asked now.

"It wasn't German," Wally said. "It was a French poem by Jean Racine, and Gabriel Fauré composed the music."

Wayne could not imagine anyone else in his class remembering this. After Lydia Coombs had sung for them the recess bell had rung. Donna Palliser had leaned against the wall licking syrup out of her Cherry Blossom until she held an empty cup of chocolate with the bare cherry in it. She nibbled the walls of the cup and popped the cherry on its chocolate disc into her mouth while the other girls repaired hopscotch lines and Bruce McLean and Mark Thevenet scuffed the ground looking for Export A butts with enough tobacco in them to light. Lydia Coombs might as well have spoken to them about dentistry or responsible government.

"You copied her address off the board."

"Yeah."

"What did your letter say?"

"That I'd like her to send me a copy of the poem by Racine. And she did. She sent this too." Wally showed him an envelope of strange limp paper, unlike anything in the stationery section at the Hudson's Bay store. In it was Lydia Coombs's letter, written in black ink, and a creamy booklet.

"This is the sheet music of Fauré's score." Wally held it carefully. The notes, staff, title, and price in francs were marked in a lovely, mysterious script. There were music sheets in school, but they had been copied on an ancient Gestetner, and the notes were sparse on a bare ground of paper: one junco's tracks on snow. These sheets were covered in grace notes, sixteenth notes, sharps, flats, and accidentals; not the tracks of one lonely bird but the song notes of that bird in a glorious meeting of its sisters, friends, and cousins.

"Wow."

"I have to study it every night in bed. Some night a tiny part is going to make sense, and then that part will grow, and one day I'll understand it all."

Wally's mother did not listen to music the way Wayne's mother did. There was no musical instrument in Wally's house. How would she learn the piece? How would she learn anything? Wayne felt dismayed. He had met no one who had such a goal, and felt disturbed by Wally's confidence in something that seemed to him destined to die.

"I remember one part," Wally said, and she hummed the notes. "If I study the notes really hard, I'm going to find it on the paper, and then I'll know where I am."

Through grade six, Wayne and Wally remained friends, and while Treadway wished Wayne would befriend a boy, he did not act. He hoped the friendship with Wally would end on its own. But when he watched Wayne and Wally meet in the mornings and walk to school, he did not like it.

"Dad."

"What, son?" Treadway had asked Wayne to help him tidy old strings and cabbage leaves in the shed. Treadway hung his cabbages from their thick necks with the same nylon string he used to make his woodcutting snowshoes, which were more temporary and rougher than the trapping shoes he made of sinew. He grew between fifty and seventy-five cabbages each year, depending on the weather and the cabbage moth, and he hung these over the barrels of partridgeberries and blueberries, which froze, and which each had a cup lying on top for pies and jam. The outer leaves of the cabbages wrinkled and froze, and in spring you had to clear up old leaves that had fallen all over the floor.

"You know those logs over the creek?"

"Yes."

"Can I have them?"

"What do you want those for?"

"I don't want to take them. I want to put better wood over them. The wood that's over them now is rotting."

"That's because I don't bring firewood out of that part of the woods anymore. You can't keep bringing wood from the same place or you'll have no woods. I should have hauled up those logs last year."

"But could you leave them there and could I have them? I want to make a place."

"You want to make a fort over the creek."

"I guess. Yeah."

"A hideout."

"Kind of."

"We had hideouts. We used to spend the whole summer in them."

"Did you?" Wayne liked it when his father remembered being young.

"Did we ever. We ate and slept in them. Me and Danny Fortescue and Jim Baikie and a gang of other lads. But why would you want to have your fort over the creek? You want a hideout in the woods, not out in the open."

"I think it would be really great over the water."

"I suppose a lot of forts did have approaches by water. You could see the enemy coming that way, by boat."

Wayne had not been thinking of enemies. "Can I use that wood in the corner?"

"I was going to use that to repair the shed." Treadway assessed the pile. "But I suppose you could have some of it. That creek is not very wide. But have you got a clue how you're going to build a fort over it?"

Wayne had something in mind. He did not know if he

could explain it to his father. "It has a cover. Like a roof. But spaces to look through."

"I don't mean the top," Treadway said. "The top is airy-fairy. You can stick any kind of top on it. What I'm talking about is the foundation. How are you going to make the base? That's what you have to think of first."

"That's why I asked you about the logs that are already there. Could we just put some boards over those?"

"That's just a log skid. You're only going over that once in a blue moon with a sled. The logs are slippery and half rotten. That's no good for a fort. For a fort you want something that goes down into the creek bed."

"Dad, I don't need anything like that. I just need a small place."

Treadway did not untangle any more strings. He took a pencil out of his pocket, found a package of soldering wire that had no writing on the back, and drew Wayne a diagram. He drew two concentric circles.

"This is how the Romans did it. You can't be thinking about the thing from the top down. This is a cofferdam. They drove a circle of piles deep into the riverbed. Then another circle inside it. Then they filled the outer ring with a kind of clay."

"Dad."

"Real waterproof stuff. Then, the water trapped inside, in the inner circle, they got slaves with buckets to bail it out. People died. They got crushed. But they emptied that inner circle. They made a dry spot right in the middle of the riverbed. They built the central pier of a bridge or section of a bridge in that."

"Dad, I just want to make something really easy."

"There is nothing really easy, Wayne. Not in this life. Not if it's any good. I'm telling you, if you want to make any kind of structure over that creek, even a small creek like that, you need to think about the river bottom. Measure it and study it. If you don't do that, your bridge is going to fall, with you in it. What kind of a father would let that happen to his son?"

"Dad, the creek has only got, like, eight inches of water in it."

"What I'm saying is, Wayne, you've got to study what's below that eight inches of water. Is it mud? Is it stone? Is it sand? Is it going to be gouged out by the current? You've got to know what you're building on. If you do that, if you study it real good, mind, you can have that wood, son. I'll help you get started. We can start on it this afternoon if you want."

Wayne wanted the wood but he was not sure he wanted his father to help him make a bridge over the creek. "Will we finish cleaning up the cabbages?"

"That's what your mother calls them. Cabbages. Instead of cabbage. That's one way you can tell she wasn't born in Labrador."

Wayne knew his father was right. Anyone from Labrador called vegetables by their single name. Cabbage. Turnip. Carrot. No matter how many individual specimens, you spoke of them as one entity. He realized Treadway thought about people in the same way. Men, to him, were all one man.

The outer cabbage leaves insulated the inner parts, which Wayne's mother rationed until mid-June, two weeks away, when there would be fresh turnip greens and dandelion. The cabbages hung hard and cold and knocked Wayne's head when his mother sent him to get berries out of the barrels, and that hurt. You had to smack the berries with the cup, then they rolled apart, clicking like cold marbles. The shed was dark. You felt your way to the produce. The food transformed once Jacinta boiled it in the kitchen: its colours and flavours burst alive as if the wood fire were the heat of the sun, which Treadway said it was, indirectly. A lot of Labrador was like that. Dull and frozen and in the dark one minute; bursting with sour and sweet and red and green when you did something with it. Labrador was a place where the human touch meant everything.

"What you really want over that creek," Treadway said in the kitchen, "is a simple cantilever." He tore the top flap off the cornflakes box and raised his pencil stub.

"Dad, it doesn't have to be anything complicated."

"That way you won't have to deal with the creek bottom. See?" He showed Wayne a diagram. "You anchor each end to a couple of bases on the riverbank and they meet in the middle."

"But there's a crack in the middle. It'll fall down."

"It won't. The end pieces are going to anchor it. I have some cement and some rebar and some old bolts from Graham Montague's wharf. What we need to do is each get a shovel and start digging foundations for the posts."

"Dad, I don't want to get a shovel. I have math homework."

"What kind of math homework?"

"Measuring triangles. We have to find out the lengths of the missing pieces."

"Perfect. Get your math homework out and we'll incorporate it into our construction project."

"Dad."

"Come on, it'll be fun."

It was a Saturday and on Saturdays Jacinta made bread, so they were all in the kitchen most of the day. The radio was on. There was rain against the windows and some steam, and the family felt happy. By the time Jacinta had kneaded six loaves and set them to rise twice, the table was covered in drawings. Treadway was concentrating on the bridge as if it was his own, and Wayne liked making fair copies of the diagrams with a six-inch metal ruler and a carpenter's pencil Treadway had sharpened with a razor. He liked the flat, chunky width of the pencil.

"Can I keep this pencil, Dad?"

"Yes, son, you can have it."

In the morning Treadway took him to the creek to haul up the old logs and dig holes and build forms for the posts. He showed Wayne how to use a pickaxe and how to mix cement. Wayne liked the sound cement made when you had it wet, when you mixed it with the shovel: a sluicing, slicing sound that meant you were making something big. His father showed him how to mix stones into the cement, and how to place the rebar inside the forms. It took three weekends of this before they had four support posts ready.

"When is it going to be done, Dad? School is over. Me and Wally want to use the bridge and all we've got done is the posts."

"You and Wally Michelin?"

"Yes. We really want to use the bridge."

"I thought you were going to play on the bridge with some boys, Wayne. Brent Shiwack and some of the other lads."

"No! I want to go on it with Wally."

"I was thinking we should construct the bridge so you can remove a section if you don't want the other team to be able to cross it. That is an old, old tactic used in wartime for millennia."

"Dad. I want to be on the bridge with Wally Michelin. We're not going to have wars. And all we've got done is the posts. It's taking way too long."

"Your posts are everything, Wayne. The foundations of anything are the thing itself. Now we've got them done, the rest is easy. We fit the boards, we clamp them, and we have it done. If there was a heavy load passing over we would jack the two sections apart and compress them. I mean a really heavy load, like a train."

Treadway had always constructed things more solidly than necessary. His sled was heavier than the sled of any other trapper in the harbour, which made it harder to haul, but it would never come apart. Wayne could see that this bridge was like Treadway's other projects. It was sturdy and built to last, like Treadway himself. The bridge was four feet wide and ten feet across, and Wayne had to admit he could do just about anything to that bridge and it would not collapse.

"But what am I going to do for sides?"

"You have to design them. Get your pencil out. You can put any kind of sides you want on that. Here, we'll put three posts along each side and you can attach whatever you want to those posts. You can use wood or wire or rope or whatever you want."

"I want it covered. I want it so me and Wally can see out but no one can see in. I'm going to ask Mom for some curtains."

"Curtains?"

"Yeah, Mom has stuff she was going to give me."

"Drapes?" Treadway asked Jacinta when Wayne had gone to bed. "China? A carpet?"

"It's just old material I never got around to using." The brocade had lain on a shelf since before Wayne's birth. Its thread glowed on a matte background. "Wayne thought it looked royal and old-fashioned."

"We never had anything like that in our forts. We used ours for storing things we didn't want our mothers to see."

"Would you rather he had beer and ammunition?"

Treadway took his socks off. He was always peeling his socks off and leaving them inside out on the floor. "We didn't have cake. We didn't have cups with flowers on them."

"It's only a few cracked mugs."

Treadway held a judgement in his body. He moved his body with unnecessary precision, his face rigid with purpose. He became unreachable but his body spoke, and Jacinta hated this. She wanted words to come out of his mouth but they came out of his bones. His bones said, You may be lenient or blind, but I am neither.

Wally Michelin and Wayne created a temporary cover for the bridge out of rope and blankets and a waterproof tarp. The bridge was not the same as the snow forts Wayne had made. Snow forts were all about construction. At no time were they complete. Once you had carved a mound and fitted it with windows and an entrance, you connected it, by tunnel, to a new mound; an endless, interconnected complex of frozen interiors infused with quiet blue light. You were underneath the snow, whereas on the bridge you were suspended over the water of the creek. Wally brought her music and practised singing her scales, while Wayne brought paper and drew designs for other kinds of walls and latticework and coverings for the bridge itself. He brought Thomasina's postcards in their Peek Freans shortbread tin and studied the bridges of London, Edinburgh, Paris, and Florence. The bridges had the same symmetry he loved in synchronized swimming. Wayne looked at their arches and interlacings and copied them on paper.

Wally Michelin had a little radio and she listened to music on it continually, then sang what she had just heard. "It's a way of training your memory. You listen to something just one time, then you copy it. You have to remember every note."

"But how do you know you got it right?"

"It's like hunting for new kinds of wild mushrooms. My dad says you have to peel your senses. You don't let anything get in the way or you'll die."

"But you won't die if you don't get the music right."

"But I am going to get it right."

"But if you didn't you wouldn't die."

"If you were on a concert stage and you sang the wrong note, it would be dying. I'm going to do my dying right now, before anyone can hear it except us."

Wally stole her brother Tyrone's xylophone and brought it onto the bridge. "Play six notes. Then I'm going to sing them, and you tell me if I sang them right. Then we'll do twelve notes, and then sixteen."

"I don't know myself which are the right ones. By the time you start singing them I forget what they were."

"I'll bring my mother's tape recorder and play them into the tape, then we'll have a record."

Wayne told his father he wanted to make the top of his bridge like the Ponte Vecchio. "I like the way things are going on in it all the time. People aren't just going across it. They have shops full of gold. They stay on it and they play music."

"All you need to do to make arches, son, is join and brace those posts. Then you cover them with Masonite, or some of that corrugated fibreglass I've got left over from the greenhouse. Put that on the roof and the light will still shine in. Come on." He found two hammers and a box of screws and showed Wayne how to use a drill and set the screws straight. He made a big compass out of string and an old broom and got Wayne to draw his arches on the Masonite, then he showed him how to cut with a jigsaw.

"It looks just right, Dad. It looks like the bridge on Thomasina's card."

"It looks pretty good, son. Not what I'd put on top of that base if I were doing it, but it's what you wanted."

"It is, Dad, it's great. Can we borrow your big extension cord?"

"Why do you want that?"

"To put lights up."

Wayne strung Christmas lights along the arches. He read reclining on boughs and cushions while Wally Michelin did her voice exercises and wrote in her diary.

They ate lettuce sandwiches with cans of Sprite. Every time Wally learned a new bar of Fauré's "Cantique de Jean Racine" she underlined it in green ballpoint. Wayne was amazed at how slowly but certainly the green lines grew. Wally's diary was green; she had ordered it from Avon and it had a tiny key. When she wrote in it under the lights or sang as Wayne drew his designs, the bridge took on the enchantment of an airborne caravan, something out of a dream.

Treadway watched and did not like the look of the whole thing.

"We never sang in our forts. We didn't read," he told Jacinta.

"You read John Donne in your hunting cabin. You read Poe and Stevenson." All the trappers read by a flame for a chapter, a poem, two at the most, before they dropped, dead tired. "You read Pascal's *Pensées*."

Treadway went to bed at nine thirty. But Wally Michelin's singing kept him awake. He endured this until he looked at the clock and saw it was nearly midnight. He got himself a glass of water. The window was open and he stood listening, then he rinsed his glass and went in the living room, where Jacinta was gathering the front of a rabbit-nose slipper with her long needle.

Jacinta had been listening too. "She's a good singer."

"Why do we let him stay up all hours of the night with that girl?"

A rabbit-nose was harder to sew than the moccasins

Jacinta had learned to make when she first came to Labrador. A rabbit-nose has a series of tiny gathers, and it is hard to get the tension of both slippers identical. Jacinta would have stayed up until three in the morning if Treadway had not minded. He always woke when she came to bed, and couldn't get back to sleep.

"But it's summer," Jacinta said.

"I know what season it is." Treadway grimly considered the carpet. He knew it was summer. He had not at any age wished to stay up past midnight talking to a girl. If his wife could not see there was something wrong with it, he saw no point in explaining.

Jacinta had challenged him in the past and had lost. The Florentine bridge over the creek struck her as lovely, and she wished she could go lie down on it with the children.

"If that was happening next door," Treadway said, "I'd wonder what kind of parents would let a boy and a girl spend half the night alone outside together."

"They're in grade six."

"They're done grade six. I'm surprised Ann and Gerald Michelin let her stay out. If I was her father I'd be over here by nine and I would take my daughter home."

"Wayne?" The moon had come out and Wally Michelin lay on the bridge floor watching it through one of the spandrels.

"What?"

"Remember what Mr. Ollerhead said about the moon?"

"I remember his shirt." Mr. Ollerhead had worn a shirt of pink and silver stripes. He had brought his guitar to school.

"He said if you look at the moon long enough, you'll find out something."

"Like what?"

"He never said."

Mr. Ollerhead had broken the hearts of girls in his class, Wayne knew. He didn't mean to break them, and he didn't know he had broken them, but he couldn't help it.

"Do you like Mr. Ollerhead?" Wayne asked.

"As a teacher?"

"No. I mean, do you like him?"

"You mean do I kiss my pillow and pretend it's him like Gracie Watts?"

"Yeah."

"No. When I'm singing, I'm singing for someone. I don't know who it is yet, but it's not Mr. Ollerhead."

10

Alto

"ROLAND SHIWACK," Treadway told Wayne, "has a boatload of shrimp that need peeling."

Wayne was stirring Carnation into his hot chocolate. Treadway did not believe in buying canned milk, or any milk, because it was insanely expensive in Labrador, and no one used it in tea. If you needed milk, Davina Thevenet had six goats and would trade you as much milk as you wanted for fenceposts or a couple of bales of hay. Was it the can of milk Treadway was looking so grim about now? Jacinta restricted herself to buying two cans a week, out of consideration for her husband's disapproval. When Treadway disapproved of anything, Wayne felt his own chest tense up. If it wasn't the milk, what was it?

"Can you do it for him?"

"Peel shrimp?"

"He'll pay eight dollars."

"I was going to work on something else today."

"With Wally Michelin?" It was late for his father to be in the kitchen. Had Treadway been waiting for him?

Wayne did not want to admit that Wally was teaching him the alto harmony for Fauré's song, or that he was copying postcards from Thomasina into a Hilroy exercise book like the ones they used in kindergarten — half ruled and half unruled.

Treadway ate a piece of bread spread thick with duck jelly and stirred five cubes of sugar into his tea. His hands were black from filing his chainsaw. Nothing Treadway could have said would have matched the disparaging crush of his silence.

"I could do the shrimp," Wayne said finally. He knew his father did not like Roland Shiwack.

"You do remember how?"

The family had eaten shrimp lots of times. You snapped the head, slit the shell with your thumbnail, unzipped it, and eased the fan off the tail. You didn't want to lose meat. You reamed the black thread from its groove and rinsed the meat in cold water.

"There's a lot more than what we did here," Treadway warned. "A boatload will keep you busy for the good part of a day."

"Okay."

"Bring a feed bag. And bring some shells home for my compost." Roland Shiwack did not have a garden, which was another reason Treadway held him in low esteem.

"Okay. Dad?" His father was looking under the sink for SOS pads to scour his hands. What the SOS pads did not clean, Treadway would scrape off with a knife. He did not answer his son. This was not unusual, but Wayne felt he had done some indescribable wrong. He felt ashamed and did not know why. He feared he would not peel the shrimp correctly, that Roland Shiwack, of all people, would tell Treadway that Wayne had torn off too many tails, or dropped heads in the cleaned meat, or taken eight hours to do what should have been completed in five. There were so many ways Wayne could fail. He did not have to ask his father why Roland's own son, Brent, could not do the job. Brent had gone to army cadet camp in New Brunswick. At least Treadway did not encourage Wayne to do that.

"Yes, son?"

"If Wally comes over, tell her I'll be back after supper and we can go on the bridge then."

Roland Shiwack had set up a chair under the aspen in his backyard. He equipped Wayne with two barrels of cooked shrimp, one of cold brine for rinsing, a hose connected to the outside tap, and eight five-gallon buckets to put the peeled shrimp in. Wayne was glad of the aspen. The shrimp were so plentiful, with their tiny black eyes, that when he closed his own eyes he saw versions of them made of pale green light. He enjoyed peeling them for the first half-hour. There was finality in zipping off their brittle coats, and he liked the firmness of the meat, and even ate a few. Mrs. Shiwack brought him cold lemonade, which he held in a briny hand that had shards of pink armour and feelers stuck all over it. The lemonade had the sourness he liked. He did not like it too sweet. What was the point of a lemon if you couldn't salivate and pucker? After an hour the shrimp were tiresome, and in the afternoon Wayne felt grateful for a rain squall that broke the monotony. When Mrs. Shiwack asked him if he'd like to come in and watch *The Price Is Right* until the rain stopped, he told her he didn't mind the rain.

In the rain, Treadway walked with his chainsaw towards the bridge. He took the brocade down and folded it to lay beside Jacinta's mending pile. He did not mean to destroy anything. He wanted to dismantle what he saw as a deterrent to his son's normal development. It was no good to have an obsession that made you sedentary as a child when you should be walking, working, travelling by foot over the land, fishing, hunting, learning what the wilderness had to teach a young person. If Wayne dropped his habit of lolling around this bridge with that girl, Treadway told himself, he would enjoy the summer the way a boy should. It wasn't even a bridge: it was not what Treadway had envisioned as he and Wayne built the base of it. The base was covered now in curtain material, flowers, papers everywhere, crayons, and trinkets. Wayne and Wally had brought out gilt chain and tassels, so every part of the bridge inside was decorated like some sort of carnival tent. Treadway hated it. You could not see its structure; the plain bones of the thing were gone. Fraped up, Treadway called that. The way some women dressed when they went to a garden party, with bits of draped extra material hanging everywhere so you could hardly recognize who you were talking to.

Treadway pulled off the coverings and decorations. Some were tied with knots he had to cut. Why couldn't the boy tie sensible knots instead of getting twine and ribbon of all kinds snarled in such inefficient tangles? Why had he not used the knots Treadway had taught him? When this has blown over, Treadway decided, I'm going to reteach him real knots and get him out of the habit of generating such a fraped-up, convoluted, disorganized mess.

He picked up the Hilroy exercise book and looked at Wayne's sketches. There was a picture of the Pont d'Avignon, and beside it a diagram of two intersecting circles with one smaller circle high in the middle. On other pages were more designs linked to sketches of other bridges. Wayne had been copying the geometry of arches from the great bridge builders of the world. The rain kept up. Treadway sat on Wayne's bridge with the sketchbook and wondered if he had done the wrong thing. But he had already taken down the corrugated fibreglass ceiling.

Other papers were getting wet. Where was the lid for that
tin with Thomasina Baikie's postcards in it? There was
Wally Michelin's green diary, its key tied to the lock with
red thread. What was in that? Treadway sat with it. He
had no intention of opening it but the impulse came over
him. Before his sense of honour intervened he had leafed
open a dozen pages. A gust of wind blew papers into the
river. Treadway tried to gather everything. He shoved
the diary into a box and got to work with his chainsaw in
the rain. He had begun the job of dismantling this thing
now. If he were making a mistake, he would make up
for it in some other way. He would go down to Nansen
Melville's place right after he took down the last two-by-
four and get that dog for Wayne. The pups would be six
weeks old next Tuesday, Nansen had said. Time enough
for them to be taken from their mother.

From the two-by-fours Treadway carefully removed
each screw. He saved them in a jar and stacked the wood
near the shed so he and Wayne could make something
else later. It would make a nice big doghouse, for a start.
When he had stacked the wood, he gathered the box of
papers and other rubble and brought it into the house.
There were twenty yards of good string there, ruined. He
threw it in the woodstove along with papers the rain had
torn. He went out to bring in the curtain material he had
laid on the step beside teacups whose glaze had cracked.

Jacinta came to the gate. Onions hung from her hand.
Why had she bought onions, he wondered, when their

own were nearly ready in the garden? Why was everyone so inefficient?

"What are you doing?" Jacinta put the onions on the ground and lifted her brocade. It was plain what he was doing, so Treadway did not answer. He watched her pick up the cups and wrap them in the brocade. He went back in the kitchen, thinking she would follow him, but she did not come in. He went out to the step but she was not in the garden, and the bag of onions lay on the ground.

Anytime Treadway had done anything against her wishes, Jacinta had told him how she felt. She had respected him but had told him her position. There was no end to the useful things Wayne could make out of the screws and two-by-fours salvaged from that bridge, Treadway told himself. He would go down to Nansen Melville's right now and pay Nansen for that thoroughbred pup. A hunting dog, not a pet.

"You have a fine husband, if you compare him to all the dishonest men in the world," Eliza Goudie said. "There's a lot to be said for a modest, honest man." This was a new point of view for Eliza. She had finally allowed her doctor to prescribe her an antidepressant medication, and had become a different person.

"You were hardly depressed before," Jacinta said. "You were euphoric a lot of the time."

"That was my problem. I was so euphoric I couldn't sit still. Now I'm much more balanced."

Jacinta's friendships in Croydon Harbour were coloured by the fact that she had come from St. John's, though she had been here ten years. They were also coloured by her nature, which, like Treadway's, was reclusive. It was unusual for her to come down the hill, as she had now done, knock on Eliza's door, and tell her friend she was ready to leave her husband. She could not say the real reason was that Treadway refused to let Wayne act like a girl. Nobody understood except Thomasina, and Thomasina was in London. Her last postcard said she loved London and did not want to leave it. There was enough theatre that you could go to a different play every night of the year and not see the same thing twice. Shakespeare, Oscar Wilde, Agatha Christie, and young writers no one outside London knew yet. Thomasina loved all of it, and she was staying in a hostel so she could stay longer and see all the plays she wanted.

So Jacinta fled to Eliza Goudie. Of all Jacinta's Labrador friends, Eliza was the one who confessed the most. She had told Jacinta everything about Edward, her own husband, and had explained her affair with Tony Ollerhead, the geography teacher, in vivid detail. Things Jacinta had not wanted to know, she now knew, such as the colour of Tony Ollerhead's underpants — warm chocolate brown — and the fact that they fitted his body tightly, unlike Edward's plaid boxers. Mr. Ollerhead wore Old Spice, and had a fine trail of silky hair leading from his navel to his pubic bone; hair that turned gold in candlelight.

Jacinta had heard all about this while she was trying to seal two dozen jars of partridgeberry jam.

"If I remember correctly," Jacinta said after she had left Treadway and the bag of onions, "you weren't too fussy about honest husbands a month ago. You could have taken honest husbands to the edge of Shag Rock and pushed them off."

At this point Eliza would have come to her senses, Jacinta thought, had she not been drugged. They would have laughed until tears came, and that was what friends were for. Jacinta had not indulged as much as her other friends had in talking about the folly of husbands, but she had done it at times when the pressure became great. She had not expected Eliza to defend Treadway. But then, she had not confessed her whole story.

"He doesn't even try to understand beauty."

"Since when did you expect him to?"

"I can create my own romance. But Wayne is only a child. How could Treadway stamp out such a sweet thing?" She had told Eliza the bridge was gone, but it didn't seem such a big deal, somehow, when she told it. It did not seem like what it was to her: a kind of annihilation by Treadway of some part of his own child's soul.

"Treadway is a woodsman and a trapper," Eliza said. "He is a good provider. He has never let you down, and he never will. You could go off on your own for ten years and come home and Treadway Blake would take you back. No matter what, you can always rely on him."

"I don't think he'd take me back. I think he'd find another woman after three months. I think I'm completely replaceable."

"You're not. And I'll tell you why. Treadway Blake is an intelligent man, and he knows a fantastic woman when he sees one, and he adores you."

"If I adored someone I would tell them, in plain English."

"Well he's not going to, because that's not his strength, and you should be used to that by now. Go to the doctor and get some Valium. It has changed my whole life. I love my husband. I've finally seen him from a proper perspective."

"You mean you no longer feel like throwing up every time he walks in the house?"

"No. As a matter of fact, our sex life is phenomenal. I sent away for three garter belts for myself and two black jockstraps for Edward out of this catalogue I got from Montreal. You should go through it. I leap into bed with my husband. Leap, I'm telling you. I don't know how he put up with me before. It's all part of his basic goodness. And your husband is basically good too. I wish you could see it, for your sake. Go to your doctor and get the Valium. I promise you, you won't regret it. I leap into the bed."

Jacinta, despite her wishes, envisioned Eliza leaping into bed, highly elevated and in a kind of supernatural slow motion, in her garter belt, and Edward waiting for her clad only in his garment from Montreal. It was not a pretty sight, and Jacinta wished, not for the first time, that she were more honest with her friends. She wished she could tell Eliza to stop taking the drug that skewed the truth for the sake of convenience. She wished she had told all her friends, the day Wayne was born, that he had been born a hermaphrodite. She wished she had not locked the secret inside her, where it clamoured to get out. Treadway would have just had to deal with it. The beautiful bridge would still be up, with her child on it, singing and drawing with his best friend, a girl. Her child would not have to come home this evening to find the bridge had disappeared.

"Why does Treadway have no idea that he has no right to destroy someone else's possession?"

But her friend was unmoved. "The property is Treadway's. It's on Treadway's land, and a man's land belongs to no one but himself."

Jacinta thought of all the times she had listened to Eliza. No matter how outrageous Eliza's reasoning, Jacinta had tried to understand it. Even now Jacinta did not argue about the Valium, though she felt Eliza's new outlook was a chemically induced illusion. This is my problem, Jacinta thought. I am dishonest. I never tell the truth about anything important. And as a result, there is an ocean inside me of unexpressed truth. My face is a mask, and I have murdered my own daughter.

Roland Shiwack gave Wayne his eight dollars, and Wayne walked home feeling the bills in his pocket. He could buy supplies for the bridge: some Caramel Log bars, and Cheezies, and a couple of cans of Sprite. It would be great if he and Wally had some art supplies they could leave there instead of bringing them back and forth from home. There was a spyglass in the Eaton's catalogue. He could save up for it and use it to watch the constellations. He could lie on his bridge and find the magpie bridge in the sky. He could save up for a new sketchbook.

There were dragonflies, ladybugs, and strange, flat bugs whose copper-coloured carapaces glittered amazingly. If you had a spyglass you could watch the secret life of the creek and take scientific notes or make accurate sketches. Yes, he would put money aside, and see what other work he could get, and buy the spyglass. If he saved his whole eight dollars and forgot about the junk food, he'd need only seven more days' work from Roland Shiwack. And Wally could contribute too. She helped Gertie Slab with her grade four homework for three dollars an hour, and she babysat.

The great thing about walking home with eight dollars in your pocket was that you could imagine spending it, over and over, on a whole bunch of different things you might want, and it was fun to envision all of them.

By the time Wayne had walked up the hill he had spent the money, in his mind, on Caramel Logs, on the spyglass, and on things for other people. There was an Italian cheese grater his mother wanted but would not send for from the catalogue. She had a grater but it was ugly. The Italian one grated hard and soft cheeses. The top had a knob that fit snugly in your hand, and it would never rust. And there was a tool in the Hudson's Bay store that his father looked at every time he went in. It was a long iron bar, called a pince-monseigneur, that you could use to lever just about any heavy object from one place to another. Treadway had used an ordinary crowbar to move all the boulders from the front yard except one, a piece of pink granite near his mother's old-fashioned roses. That granite needed the pince-monseigneur, but Treadway did not want to spend thirty-five dollars on something he considered a toy.

I could surprise him, Wayne decided as he approached home. I could put it on layaway and carry it home and let Dad find it propped against the shed door.

Wayne saw the neatly stacked two-by-fours and did not realize where they had come from. He saw the jar of screws and did not recognize those either. He walked into the house, looked around, and wondered where everyone was. His father was not home, and neither was his mother, and there was no cooking, which was unusual, because at five o'clock there was always something sizzling in the cast iron pan or cooking in the boiler. So he went outside and looked around the back, and then he knew the two-by-fours were from his bridge, and he knew it had not been destroyed by an animal or by wind or by anything accidental. He ran inside and saw the string, untangled and carefully wound, hanging on a chair. He went out the back door and looked at the creek with its naked posts that he and his father had taken weeks to pour and set. The creek frilled around reeds and stones. The creek was not thinking of him. It had left him alone.

Treadway walked into the house carrying a mandarin orange box that held a golden Lab puppy on a piece of brocade from the bridge. He laid the box by the wood-stove, and Wayne knew what he had done.

Wayne had never felt two such conflicting feelings in his body: devotion for the puppy, who whimpered and tried to peer over the side of the box, and an utter, bereft betrayal. Treadway looked at Wayne for a second, then at the puppy. The puppy was a safe place to look. You could look at the puppy all day and your feelings could sink into the puppy, and the puppy would not reproach you.

Wayne could not ask Treadway about the bridge, and Treadway said nothing. It was five o'clock, and Jacinta came in the door with a bag from Eliza. It contained a hot loaf. Eliza had rubbed the crust with butter until it glittered and cracked. Jacinta laid it on the table. She got butter out, and a tin of oysters, and corned beef, and some mustard, and an onion which she sliced thin, and some milk and pickled beet, and she opened the tins and sliced the corned beef, and no one mentioned the puppy.

Wayne went upstairs and looked out his window, where he could see the back corner of Wally's house, and he guessed he would have to go down in the morning and see her. He could not believe his father had gone out and found a puppy to make up for what he had destroyed. It gave Wayne a new insight into the character of his father, one he regretted knowing with all his heart. It would have been better, he thought, if his father had just done what he wanted to do and not tried to pay for it. It was the paying, with a live puppy, that Wayne found unforgivable.

At six in the morning Wally Michelin knocked on the back door and Treadway opened it, his kipper with Keen's mustard steaming on the table. He thought Wally looked like a strong little person on his step, her hair making her face narrower, her pale skin and thousand freckles. She was starting to grow tall and she was bony; her shoulder blades stuck out, and she marched around with her head a little bit forward like someone forever ducking raindrops. She had watched him dismantle the bridge from her bathroom window and had come for the most important thing in it.

"It's twelve pages. The paper is yellow."

"I don't remember it." Treadway was honestly mystified. He remembered his son's Hilroy scribbler. He had saved that. It sat now on the chair visitors used. Wally's green diary was under it and she took it, and looked around to see if her "Cantique de Jean Racine" was sticking out from under the TV guide or wedged behind the toaster.

"It was with this." She held up her diary, which still had its key. "Did you read my diary?"

Treadway had searched for what she might have written about Wayne. He hated himself for doing it, especially when most of the parts he read were about music. They were about the northern lights; how she had sung to them and they had sung back to her; and about how she had found out the name of something that happened to her but did not happen to any of the friends she had asked, including Wayne. It was called phantom music: some people heard music replayed inside their heads, every note accurately. It could be something they had heard before, on the radio or somewhere, or it could be music no one had ever heard. It happened when Wally was tired, especially if she was in a vehicle or if something near her were moving, like the creek under the bridge.

The phantom music had first happened to her on the school bus trip to Pinhorn Wilderness Camp, on their way home, after the bus had stopped at Mary Brown's Fried Chicken in Goose Bay and continued on the road to Croydon Harbour. Sometimes she could catch a tiny fragment and pull it until the rest unrolled in her mind, but usually she had no control over the phantom music. She loved it and wished she could hear it always. Treadway had read all of this.

Any parent can scan any piece of writing, even writing done in an unfamiliar hand, and quickly discern the name of his own child, and Treadway had done this. Wayne had brought hot chocolate to the bridge. Wayne had sung melody for Wally so she could try out harmonies. Wayne read while she practised writing treble clefs, half notes, whole notes, eighth and sixteenth notes, flats, naturals, rests, and accidentals. Wayne was copying triangles from Thomasina's postcard of Andrea Palladio's bridge over the Cismone. None of this was what a normal Labrador son would do, but none of it frightened Treadway until the part of Wally's diary that detailed Wayne's recurring dream.

"Wayne dreamed he was a girl again last night," Wally had written beneath a list of supplies. String. Oreos. A shoebox. Scissors. The foot out of an old pair of panty-hose. A cup of cold bacon fat with sunflower seeds in it.

"If you saw my diary, you saw my music," Wally said.

"There might have been some pieces of wet paper. I didn't think they looked like music."

"Can I see them?"

"I threw them out."

"I need to look in your garbage."

"They're burnt." Treadway never threw paper in the garbage. He threw it in the stove. He did not like filling garbage bags with anything you could burn.

He felt sorry about the music, but he did not say so.

11

Old Love

J ACINTA AND TREADWAY WERE POLITE with each other
during the shortening days after Treadway took down
Wayne's bridge. Jacinta made the bed the way Treadway
liked it; Treadway wanted no air to touch his feet, and
Jacinta could not sleep unless her feet breathed through
an opening in the blankets. She no longer woke him when
he snored, and he picked up and washed teacups she left
in the grass. The politeness was unbearable. They avoided
touching each other, careful as strangers on a train. But
there was one thing they had always done, and they did
not stop doing it now, because to stop would have been to
acknowledge their marriage had broken, and they were
not able to acknowledge this. The thing was that when
each took a bath, at the end of the bath the other took
the sponge that hung on the shower head, soaped it with

a cake of Ivory, and lathered the other person's shoulders and back. They had never thought of this as an expression of love. It was something they had started early in their days together, and now it continued. They had always done it without speaking. The silence was nothing new.

A family can go on for years without the love that once bound it together, like a lovely old wall that stays standing long after rain has crumbled the mortar. Where was Jacinta going to go? Back to St. John's? She berated herself for not having the courage. It is amazing how small things keep you anchored in a place — the cake of soap on its little mat with rubber suckers, the moulded plastic shower stall. The bathroom cabinet with Aspirins in it, and blue razors, and Tiger Balm. The plastic runner to stop dirty tracks on the cream-coloured hall carpet. The television with its rabbit ears and its reruns of *Bewitched* and *Get Smart* that give you something predictable at four thirty every weekday. None of these things were what Jacinta loved, or even liked, but she could count on them, and she could not count on what might happen if she left Treadway and went back to St. John's, especially if she took Wayne with her. The thing that had prevented her from running out of Goose Bay Hospital when Wayne had gone for his baby surgery existed in her now, larger and stronger than it had been then. Material things were important. Her slippers. Her sewing basket with sinew in it and needles with the right-sized eye for sewing leather. The cribbage board and the deck of cards that had a toreador swirling his glorious cloak in the bullfighting ring. Any of these things, Jacinta knew, she could find for less than two dollars apiece in St. John's, or in any other place in North America to which she might escape.

But was there a place where she could live with truth instead of lies? *Truth or Consequences* was another TV show. She could relate to that title. You told the truth or you lived with consequences like these. If you held back truth you couldn't win. You swallowed truth and it went sour in your belly and poisoned you slowly.

There was a pale green pill Wayne cut in half with the small, heavy knife his mother used to peel potatoes. There were two white capsules full of powder, which he knew was also white since he had broken one to find out. Finally there were two tiny, flat yellow pills that his mother, when he had asked, had told him were to prevent dizziness.

"Am I a diabetic?" Kevin Slab was diabetic, and he had pills, but his were orange.

"No."

"Do I have leukemia?" In grade four Joey Penashue had got leukemia and lost his hair.

"No."

"Do I have a brain tumour?" Last year Stevie White, who had sat two seats in front of Wayne, developed a brain tumour and died.

"No." Jacinta sounded more impatient than she wanted to.

"Which ones can I stop taking when I start taking the new ones in grade seven?"

They had been through this before. He liked to get it straight, Jacinta believed, as this was the only aspect of the pills about which he was certain.

"You can stop taking the white ones. But then you will take four yellow ones instead of two, and you might have to have a needle."

"But we won't know if I need a needle until Dr. Toumishey examines me."

"It might not be Dr. Toumishey. It might be a doctor you haven't met."

"Will it be Dr. Hedgehog?"

The specialist was always changing. Once it had been a Dr. Edgecombe, who had wanted to examine Wayne's throat using an extra-wide tongue depressor that looked as if it were made of sandpaper. Wayne wouldn't open his mouth, and Dr. Edgecombe had told Jacinta to pin his arms and pinch his nose so he couldn't breathe. "He'll open up then," Dr. Edgecombe had said. Wayne had been six.

"No. Dr. Edgecombe has gone back to St. John's."

"Maybe this time I won't need a needle."

"I wish you could just wait and see."

"If you had to take a needle you'd like to know about it first."

"That's true."

"Will I have to take another needle after the first one?"

"You might."

"If I knew how many then I would know when it was over."

"I know. We would know where we stood."

"Me. Not we." This was new. Now that Wayne was twelve he demanded accuracy, and justice.

"You're right. You. You would know where you stood."

"What if I have to have four needles?"

"You might. You might need more than four. But you might not have to have any. We won't know until the doctor examines you."

"Remember that time we went, Mom? Remember the sign on the glass?" A card posted on the receptionist's cage had said, PLEASE TELL US IF YOU LEAVE WITHOUT BEING SEEN. Wayne had looked at it for a long time. He had been eight. He had looked carefully at all the people in the waiting room, then he had said, "Mommy, do invisible people come in here?"

"Yes," Jacinta had said. "There has been a parade of them since we came in."

"How do you know?"

"Can't you see their wet footprints all over the floor? And they have measles."

"How do you know that?"

"I read it in the paper. An epidemic of measles is affecting the invisible community of Goose Bay and the Labrador Straits."

Wayne had giggled. "Mommy, what does the sign really mean?" he had asked, and she had told him.

"But you were right to wonder," Jacinta had said. "It is grammatically confusing." That day the specialist had prescribed the first yellow pills.

"Is what I have," Wayne said now, "called something?" He did not like to have an ailment for which there was no word. He had never heard of anyone in his class having a nameless medical condition. Even the things that killed you had a name. He had not gone to Stevie White's funeral, but his class had had that day off school, and Mr. White had taken his car through the Techni-Tone Car Wash in Goose Bay, and Stevie's sisters and aunts had decorated it with six hundred Kleenex carnations, and Stevie's coffin had been shiny black with white and pink satin inside and a picture of the Last Supper.

"If I had a brain tumour, would you tell me?"

Jacinta knew this was the last of his questions. It was always the last one, and she always answered it the same way. "You don't have a brain tumour. I promise you that."

"Mom?"

"What?"

"My feet are peeling."

"Stop worrying about everything."

"In bed. I felt them. The skin was peeling off. I pulled an edge and it came off in sheets."

"Wait a couple of days and if it doesn't get any better you can remind me about it."

"Mom. That's what you always say about everything."

"You might already know this." Treadway's voice was half lost under the noise of his chainsaw. He was limbing the last log.

"What?" Wayne supposed his father wanted to tell him how to tie the rope that kept the logs on the sled. His father had ways of doing knots that had to be obeyed according to the task. The acrid gasoline fumes got up Wayne's nose. He liked that. He liked the wood-sap smell, the physical lifting, the noise. His father was happy when Wayne helped him hoist wood. Wood hauling began on cold mornings when the first frost entered the ground, just before school started in the fall. You got to make a fire and boil tea and eat Vienna sausages out of the can with homemade bread and margarine.

"The facts of life," Treadway hollered.

"It's okay, Dad."

"What?"

"It's okay."

Treadway shut off the engine. He was not glad of the silence. Their shouts hung over the caribou moss, in the spaces between spruce. "Get those blasty boughs and make a base."

The circle of rocks was the one they had used last fall. All Treadway had to do was move two that had fallen out of the circle. They had brought birch rinds and back issues of the *Labradorian*, and Treadway handed Wayne his lighter. "You probably hear the facts of life in school. But a father likes to tell them straight.

To make sure his son doesn't get the wrong end of the stick."

"Dad, it's okay. You don't have to go into it. Honest." This was not entirely true. Wayne had pieced together certain things, but there were gaps in the process as he understood it.

Treadway lit the sticks. They inhaled the sugary smoke. They were sweaty from hauling wood and they peeled their coveralls down and sat on cushions of frozen caribou moss in their undershirts. Crumbled lichen and needles and sap lay on their collarbones and shoulders.

"I'll just get it over with," Treadway said, "and I will have dispatched that part of my duty. Your mother reminded me."

"Dad."

"And she's right. So you probably notice sometimes now, when you wake up, you might have, you know, wetness in the bed."

"What?"

"You might have thought you wet the bed. You might be worried about it."

"Dad. I don't wet the bed."

"It happens to all boys."

"It doesn't happen to me."

"So it's just ejaculation and you shouldn't worry about it. The next thing is you probably noticed you get an erection sometimes."

"Dad."

"That's what they call a hard-on."

"Dad!"

"But the real name is an erection, and it's nothing to be embarrassed about. No one can tell."

"Dad, stop it."

"You might think they can but they can't. It can happen any time, not just when you're thinking about a girl."

"Okay, Dad. I get it." Wayne stared at berries that had rolled under the caribou moss. He heard the hiss of torn tin and a broken vacuum seal as his father pulled the ringtop on the Vienna sausage can. He smelled the meat and the brine. He'd had an erection only once. He had not been thinking about a girl. His father handed him the can and he ate three sausages with his fingers while his father buttered some bread. There had been other feelings, deeper and more hungry than an erection.

"You must have noticed changes in your body."

"My feet are peeling," Wayne said, "and I get a stomach ache."

"Your feet?"

"Yeah."

"What do you mean?"

"The skin comes off."

"Take your boots off."

Wayne took his boots off and sank his bare feet in the caribou moss. "The bottoms."

Treadway picked up his son's foot. "Does it hurt?"

"No."

"Did you ask your mother about it?"

"She told me to tell her if it doesn't go away. She always says that."

"Maybe she knows. I never heard of it. But I have to finish telling you this." Treadway sighed. He did not like being sidetracked.

"Dad, it's okay."

"I know you think you know everything about the facts of life. And maybe you do. And if you do, it won't hurt you to hear them again. But maybe there's one or two facts you have wrong, and if there are, I'm going to tell you the right ones. That's all. There's no big deal. But you have to know the real story. And then I won't mention it any more. Okay?"

"Okay."

"So when you get married, you sleep in the same bed with a woman. Women have a vagina. When a man and a wife are in bed together, the penis fits into the vagina. It might not seem like that could happen, but it can. It fits in there. And that's when the seed of the man, inside the penis, comes out and goes into the woman's body. And that's how the embryo of a baby is formed, and of course the baby grows in her belly, and then nine months later, it is born."

Wayne had not known this. He didn't know what he had known. Brent Shiwack had saved his hot dog wiener from lunch one day, and had wiggled it through the fly of his jeans at Gracie Slab while everyone was drawing isosceles triangles, and had panted with his tongue out. Davina White up in grade nine had gotten pregnant, and some people said she was a slut but others said no, it happens to the ones who aren't sluts. Davina White came to the schoolyard with her baby in a stroller at lunch-time to eat bags of chips and drink Pepsi with her friends, and when lunch was over she walked with her baby back down the hill, and Wayne felt sorry for her. Some people said Davina shouldn't be allowed to come to the school-yard because her baby might make other girls want to have a baby too.

Treadway had dispatched his duty but he felt extremely awkward and wished he had waited, as his own father had done, until he and his son happened upon the mating of caribou in the herd. It had been beautiful, in slow motion, snowflakes falling on the creatures, and Treadway had instantly understood nearly everything there was to know about male and female intimacy, the mechanics of it. His father had not had to talk about marriage beds or body parts. He had not had to use the word *embryo*, or any other clinical word. But Jacinta had wanted him to bring up the subject. He felt he had not done the job decently. He had made it seem unnatural. And he had not been able to stop looking at his son's body and seeing things he did not want to admit. His son looked like a girl. He talked like a girl, his hair was like a girl's, and so were his throat and chest. When they had peeled down the tops of their overalls, Treadway had seen that his son had breast buds, small and tender through his undershirt, and it had shocked him. He wondered if Wayne had noticed them himself, or if any of the boys at school had teased him about it. The buds were very small, but they were present. What if they grew larger? What was wrong with the doctors?

He carefully folded the bread bag they had used and tucked it into the empty Vienna sausage can with the used teabags, and he wrapped it all in leftover birch rind and put the package in his knapsack. Wayne got on the back of the Ski-Doo behind him and hung on to the passenger handle for dear life, because there were a lot of bumps and it often felt like if he didn't hang on using all his muscle power, a bump would fling him onto the trail and his father might not notice until he got home. That's how loud the engine was, and how relentless its momentum, on the woods trail. They had a good load of wood, enough to heat the house for two weeks. Half a dozen more loads like this and they would be done, and Treadway could go on his trapline.

Some boys went with their fathers. They just left school to go on the trapline, and no one said anything. Wayne dreaded the day when Treadway would suggest he do this. Wayne was looking forward to school. Thomasina Baikie was coming back. She had sent her last postcard from Wales. On the front was Thomas Telford's iron bridge over the Menai Strait.

"It broke a world record," Thomasina wrote, "for the longest suspension bridge in the world. I love it here so much, Wayne, that I'm finishing my last two classes at Harlow. In September I'll be coming back to Croydon Harbour to teach. I'll be teaching grades seven, eight and nine." Wayne was going into grade seven. He was excited about having Thomasina for a teacher. He loved new pencils and rulers and exercise books, and he liked being at home in the nights, in his room, studying and sketching and listening to music.

But his father could go miles without rest or food, and Treadway did not mind what Wayne saw as monotony: miles upon miles of spruce woods, a heavy packsack, and your footprints sinking through a hard crust of snow, and the death of the beautiful animals.

In bed Wayne thought about what his father had said. He imagined a man and a woman in their pyjamas, lying side by side in their marriage bed. The man fell asleep. So did the woman. While they were asleep, the man's penis somehow reached out of his pyjama pants. It found its way, something like Brent Shiwack's wiener, over towards the woman. She must have been wearing a short night-dress, not a long one like his mother's, or loose pyjama pants. Anyway, somehow the penis, which must have had a sense of direction and an ability to explore on its own, got through the woman's clothes and nosed its way into her vagina. This amazed Wayne. He had not known that such a thing happened, but he did feel there was something powerful and slightly sinister about penises, so he believed his father. The funny thing was that even though this whole story — the facts of life according to Treadway — depended on involuntary activities of body parts unbeknownst to their sleeping owners, the knowledge of it excited the low, aching hunger in Wayne's belly. He lay in bed and touched his own penis. It did not respond, but the place behind it, underneath it, buried in his body between his legs, did respond. If he touched the skin underneath his testicle and rubbed it, it made the hunger clamour and grow wild. He pressed and pushed a little, and he thought of penises going into vaginas while he did so, and in a couple of minutes the hunger between his legs opened its mouth and devoured a shuddering, delicious and joyful series of electric jolts that delighted his whole body.

Treadway went to bed early and dreamed of a baby fox caught in his trap. He wanted to save the fox because it was too young for its skin to be of any value, and it had soft paws and looked at him with pleading eyes.

While Treadway slept, Jacinta cleaned the surfaces in the house. Treadway had not told her about his father-and-son talk but she knew he had done it as she asked, because he always did what she asked if she asked him in a particular way. A way that said she was counting on him to provide a basic husbandly service she could not do herself. She knew he had carried out the father-and-son talk, and she could tell he was disturbed about it in some profound way he did not want to talk about. Whenever Treadway was emotionally tired, he went to bed even earlier than usual, using sleep like a kind of temporary, convenient death.

Jacinta swept the floors and wiped the counters, then got a bucket of red-hot water with Pine-Sol in it and a mop, and scoured the kitchen floor and hallway. She dumped the water down the toilet and filled the bucket again, then put rubber gloves on and took a rag and a scrubbing brush and got down on her knees on an old flat cushion and washed every speck of dirt out of the corners and off the baseboards, then she washed the stairs by hand, and polished the toaster and the fridge, and washed the fingerprints off the walls near all the light switches and off the doors near the doorknobs and off the telephone. She went outside and then came in again to smell with a fresh nose how clean the house smelled, and then she got in bed beside sleeping Treadway and thought how good it would be when he went on his trapline, how there would be fewer footprints to clean.

PART THREE

12

General Electric

WHEN THOMASINA RETURNED TO Croydon Harbour, she rented a room in the Guest House, the big white house built by Moravian missionaries and bought by Sir Wilfred Grenfell's society to rent to new teachers and doctors. Thomasina did not intend to build again. She was past building, or sending down roots, or planning into the deep future. Approaching fifty, she knew there is a deep future in one's life for only so long, then there is no deep future. There is a cliff, you drop off it, and your life comes to an end, and hopefully it has been a life in which you touched other lives with some sort of constructive tenderness.

Wayne's grade seven classmates were not sure what to make of their new teacher. Some of their parents had a few things to say about Thomasina Baikie around the dinner table. How she had gone off gallivanting, after her husband, Graham Montague, had drowned with their little red-haired daughter. She did not look now the way she had looked before. Her hair had turned salt-and-pepper and she had cut it, and she wore wire glasses and jeans. You got the feeling something radical could happen with her around.

"What is she doing living in that place?" Brent Shiwack said at recess time. "My dad says she must be nuts to pay rent there. It's only for visitors."

In class Thomasina did not speak to her students as if they were children, and she did not single Wayne out.

"When you were all babies," she said, "my husband died."

Wayne knew this. He remembered the photograph of Graham Montague that had sat on her sideboard.

"I wanted to see the world, and he said that was all right with him, just wait a year. But it never happened. And then he died."

The class did not know what to make of this.

"You don't say died," Donna Palliser whispered. "You say passed away." There was an uncomfortable feeling in the room. Those who did not smirk tried to look respectful. A man had died.

"So now I can go wherever I want." Thomasina handed them each a blue stone on a piece of elastic. Each stone bore a painted eye that looked out with severity. Wayne felt wary of the eye. The girls tied theirs onto their wrists and the boys laid them on their desks. The eyes had come from Greece. Thomasina showed them a clay lantern that was nothing but a bowl that fit in your hand, and you filled it with olive oil and lit a piece of wick that floated in the oil, and that was how you had light. Using the projector with clacking, whirring sprockets whose sound Wayne loved, she showed them a Greek dance in which everyone did steps that looked easy but were not.

"Why do we have to watch this, Miss?" Brent Shiwack said. "It's queer."

Wayne saw the dance as an elaborate knot but would not say so out loud. It was like the knots his father made in traps and bowlines. Wayne saw it as an interesting mathematical pattern, and wished he could trace its lines with his body.

"How come you don't live in a normal house, Miss?" Brent Shiwack asked. "How come you live in the Guest House?"

"I used to live here in a normal house. I used to live in the house the Michelins live in now." Everyone looked at Wally Michelin. Wally shrunk in her desk. "It's a nice house. It's a beautiful house for the Michelins. But if I was there I'd look out the windows and see my husband, Graham, coming past the fence with a bucket of water for his horse. I'd see my daughter, Annabel. I'd smell the rain on her clothes. She used to sneak up from behind and hug me. Her breath was like cold petals."

When Thomasina spoke the name Annabel, Wayne realized this had been the name she called him years ago.

He had thought the name was Amble, which was a nonsense name, he realized now, but when he was small it had been like any other nickname. But it wasn't Amble. It was Annabel. Why had Thomasina called him that?

Everyone talked about the new teacher at recess. Teachers didn't tell you about the cold breath of their dead daughters. They didn't give you stone eyes. Wayne was glad Thomasina had not told the class she had known him when he was younger, or that she had sent him postcards with bridges on them from all the places she had travelled.

Thomasina waited for Wayne to speak to her. He spoke as he fed the newts in the class aquarium while she corrected math reviews. The recess bell had rung and everyone was yelling past the windows. There were crows in the yard, and frost in the asters.

"I made a bridge." Wayne's voice came out faint, as if he were trying to talk to Thomasina through layers of old paper. "I got all your postcards and I made my own bridge." He did not tell her Treadway had helped him build it, or that his father had later taken it down.

"You did?"

"It was like the one in Florence. The one the Germans didn't destroy in the Second World War."

"Ponte Vecchio."

"It was great. Me and Wally Michelin had it going all summer. It's gone now but we had lights on it and everything. I have all my postcards in a tin."

Thomasina had been watching Donna Palliser and her clique. She had noticed undercurrents normal for a grade seven class; she had learned at Harlow to watch for them, and she had her own insight. Thomasina had always had insight. Graham Montague had called it second sight, but she knew it was not that. It was simply stepping back from a scene and letting its layers reveal themselves. She did not have to step back far or wait long to see below the surface of the life of Wayne Blake.

"It was Annabel you called me, wasn't it? When I was little."

Thomasina saw that the child she had secretly named Annabel, in memory of her own lost daughter, had become graceful and mysterious. She saw how he sat at the back of the class, quietly unrolling the big map or reading library books stuck inside his textbooks. She saw how he walked at the edges of the corridors, the gym, the schoolyard. He had no idea of the circumstances that had surrounded his birth, yet a thoughtfulness lay in his eyes that the other children, save for Wally Michelin, did not have. It was the spirit a poet might have, or a scientist, or anyone who sees the world not as he or she has been told to see it, with things named and labelled. Wayne Annabel, as she called him in her mind now, saw everything as if it had newly appeared. He looked at each thing as if he had never seen it before: chalk, a map of Argentina, or grasses collected in science class, or the steps of the Greek dance she had tried to introduce. When Wayne Blake walked, he floated. He was Wayne, she saw now, and he was Annabel. He was both at the same time, but he did not know this.

"I'm sorry about that, Wayne," she told him now. "I should have called you the name your father gave you. I didn't think clearly enough. I should have kept my sorrows about Annabel to myself."

"Your daughter who drowned. You were calling me after her?"

"I should have kept it to myself."

"You must have been really sad. You only called me that when we were by ourselves, remember? You can still do that if you want. I don't mind."

"You're kind, Wayne. Very kind."

In the evenings Thomasina prepared her classes in her kitchen, which was normally shared with whoever rented the other rooms in the Guest House, but no one else was here now. She did not close the blinds, though every woman in Croydon Harbour closed the curtains at dusk. Thomasina had nothing to hide. The Guest House kitchen was white and modern, with a Formica table and a General Electric stove, and it contained the bare necessities. It had counters that she kept spotless, as it did not take long to wipe up a few toast crumbs after herself or clean the drop left by the back of her teaspoon. There was a small washing machine in an alcove but no dryer, and she laid her clean wet clothes on the radiators under the kitchen windows, so they would dry as she worked.

On her table was a stack of pictures with heavy outlines: archers, lyres, winged sandals, golden apples of the
Hesperides. Normally she would not give grade sevens
colouring sheets, but these were to make booklets about
the Greek deities, and she had found the pictures in an
Athenian museum. They were informative in a way that
would tell a good part of each god's story without words.
Some of her students could read marks on a trail wind-
ing through eighty miles of wilderness but they were not
good readers of English textbooks. Each student would
be responsible for researching one persona: Artemis,
Hera, Dionysus, Aphrodite, Apollo, Hermes, Demeter,
Ceres. There was a deity to represent every human character, and Thomasina had found them all in her class,
though the students did not know it, from the control and
manipulation of Artemis reflected in Donna Palliser to
the musical Euterpe in Wally Michelin and the presence
of a descendant of the child of Hermes and Aphrodite,
Hermaphroditus, in Wayne Blake.

Thomasina did not venerate Greek religion over the
Protestant Christianity of the settlers in Croydon Harbour, or over the aboriginal stories her dead husband,
Graham Montague, had known. She saw all tradition as
metaphorical. It was, in her mind, all about story, character, psyche. She would not drum any religion into her
students. They would see, she knew, through dogma of
any kind. What interested Thomasina in Greek studies
was that there was no pretense that the gods had lived.

Everyone knew they represented the character in all of us. She would not tell her class this but intended only to let them enjoy playing roles they normally hid. Donna Palliser, for example, concealed from adults the way she led and ranked the girls. Wally Michelin had gone so far underground with her music that only the most intuitive person could spy it. Wayne Blake had no idea there was a girl, fully formed, curled inside his body.

To colour the illustrations Thomasina had artist-quality pencils. The Greek dance recording featured drum music she had bought from street musicians in Athens. A small man had played a bellows-like instrument she was eager for her students to hear, since it sounded like the button accordions their fathers and grandfathers played when they came home from the trapline.

She took her trousers and cardigans off the radiators and put them away, and made toast with homemade strawberry jam. She had stewed the berries whole. There was no place in Croydon Harbour to get strawberries. They were a soft berry, a summer berry, and Croydon Harbour did not have a summer long enough to include them. Thomasina had brought these frozen, insulated in newspapers, in her suitcase on the plane along with her tape recorder, her music, her few clothes, Pears soap, a ten-pound bag of coffee beans, and a small grinder. Could you not make a life for yourself any way you wanted, and in any place?

No man in Croydon Harbour would knock on the door of a woman not his wife on a moonlit night unless it was to inform her that her husband had perished, or unless he was a doctor come to save her life or the life of her child. But the night he saw that Wayne's homework consisted of colouring a picture of Hermaphroditus — a young man with gladiator's arms and a beard and a woman's breasts and hips — Treadway felt he had no choice but to knock at the Guest House door and ask Thomasina Baikie what in the name of God she thought she was up to. If there was anything Treadway could not stand, it was someone who was sneaky or underhanded, and who used a back door as a way to get around his wishes.

He stood on the Guest House veranda and rapped his knuckles insistently until Thomasina appeared under her porch light. Anyone in town could see him there and see who he was, and that he was not in a good mood. He was so angry he had ceased to be aware that this might be a spectacle, but Thomasina had not, and she stepped back and pleaded with him to come in out of the night, which was beautiful. Orion had appeared from his summer sleep, and northern lights rippled green and pink at the edge of the sky. There was frost, and the sweet, decayed smell of floating twigs and caribou moss that always meant the partridgeberries were ripe in some places and it was time for the men to go on the trapline. This was Treadway's problem. Just as he was preparing to leave his homestead for months, Thomasina Baikie seemed to be aiming to have Wayne's whole school study in plain view a subject that should by anyone's reckoning remain well covered up. On the trapline, stealth was everything. Treadway was an expert in staying upwind of fox, mink, and bear. His own livelihood and that of his family depended on it. You did not go out in plain view and announce your presence, your secrets, your private life. You did not let a wild animal know you harboured fear. Treadway was able to hold a secret like no other. Now, in Thomasina's hallway by the door to her kitchen, he stood, his fear swallowed and hidden so deep there was no direct way for him to speak it, so he became indirect.

One time, and one time only, before Jacinta had come to the harbour and before Graham Montague had decided he wanted a woman, there had been a dance, and Thomasina had been in Treadway's arms a good two hours. They were both quiet, solitary people, and each had wondered what it could be that other couples spoke into each other's ears, laughing, underneath the band. There had been a sedateness to their dance, and they had thought about each other afterwards, but when Treadway sent his sister to ask Thomasina to go to the next dance with him, she had declined. Now, all these years later, they remembered the touch of each other's body, and there was a tension between them because they were alone. This story could have been told of any woman and any man in the cove. In a small community the whole world dances in one another's arms on one June night or another. Treadway should not have come.

"Are you all right?" Thomasina asked him. Treadway didn't look all right. He was suddenly shy as well as angry, so she said, "Do you want to sit down?" He did not answer, only looked at the floor, so she brought him to the kitchen. He had not been in this house before. The house did not really belong to Croydon Harbour, and everyone knew enough about its story that they felt no need to go in. There was a distance about it, taller than the settlers' houses, imposing, as if the people who built it and who dwelt in it thought they knew better than the settlers.

This was what all houses built by missionaries must be like, Treadway thought now, no matter where they were in the world. The Moravian missionaries' wives had built drills and terraces all around the sides and back of this house and had grown crops no Labrador settler in his right mind would plant. Parsley and sugar snap peas and summer savory, cucumbers and frilly European lettuces, even tomatoes. They had tried to turn their handkerchief-sized piece of Labrador into a little piece of Europe, and had almost succeeded, using cloches and cold frames and other tender and intricate devices. They had grown sweet peas, for goodness' sake — a flower that grew into a pod that had no culinary function — and had tied them to six-foot-high stakes with pieces of ribbon. It had worked for as long as the Moravian women were present and vigilant.

When the Grenfell missionaries took over, they had put an end to herbs and sweet peas. The men tended the gardens, with what Treadway considered a trifle more good sense than the Moravian women had. The men had put in carrot, cabbage, beet, and potato, but then they had gone and brought in a cow, reasoning that a local supply of milk would give greater health to Labrador babies. A cow, in Labrador. You might as well put a cow on the North Pole and expect it to live. Again, with hot water bottles and blankets and God knew what other foolishness, the Grenfell missionaries managed to keep the cow and its daughter alive for five or six years, but then the brutal grandeur of the real Labrador took over. They didn't call this place the big land for nothing. It was big in a way that people who came in either respected and followed or disdained at their peril. You could live like a king in Labrador if you knew how to be subservient to the land, and if you did not know how, you would die like a fool, and many had done. What Thomasina was doing in this guest house, Treadway did not know. She had started out sensibly enough, as a Labrador woman who knew how the big land breathed, but something — Treadway reckoned it was the death of her husband and daughter — had caused her to forget, and act like a stranger.

"The windows are painted shut," he said. No one living in a normal house in Croydon Harbour would have been able to stand this.

"I hadn't noticed."

"It's unhealthy."

"I don't have a wood stove like you."

He had a screwdriver in his shirt pocket, and he started chipping away at the painted seam. "Have you got a thin-bladed knife?"

Thomasina opened the cutlery drawer and hunted through knives and forks the Grenfell Society had put there. They were not the quality you would buy for yourself, but she found him a knife. He slit the paint, and the knife slipped, and he stuck his bloody finger in his mouth and sat down.

He couldn't say a word to her about Greek gods with breasts and beards. He might as well have tried to bring up the subject of his own nakedness. "This," he said, "is an awfully bare room." He saw a bottle of Scotch on her shelf and Thomasina took it down and poured them each a glass. When they had drunk a second glass, she asked him, "Does Jacinta know you're here?"

"It's likely by now that she does. It's the homework I'm here about. Wayne's homework. It's — God, Thomasina. What — I don't know if you're trying to give him some kind of hint or what . . ."

"You don't want him to have any idea of who he is."

"Have you got some kind of chip on your shoulder?"

"What?"

"Some kind of mental problem that came from losing your own family?"

"If you look at the school board curriculum you'll

see everything I'm teaching is in there. I didn't make the curriculum up. And I didn't make Greek mythology up either. It happens to be in the school program, and your son is in my class."

"Right. Don't — just . . ."

"Are you ever going to tell him?"

"I'm not. Why should I? No. I'll tell you something, Thomasina Baikie. It's all right for some people to go around psychologizing, but the rest of us have to live in the real world. Wayne has to live in the real world. I would prefer it if you didn't go giving him colouring books with half-men, half-women in them. To me that's interfering. It's more than interfering."

"He isn't like the other boys."

"It's interfering in a big way."

"Can you see it?"

"I don't believe — no. What . . ."

"You hope you can't. He's not like them at all, Treadway."

"Who says so? Is — has anyone said a word to him at that school? Has Roland Shiwack's son said something?"

"I was thinking I might say something."

"The hell you will."

"I was thinking I might tell him my version of the way things were at his birth."

"Why would you do that?"

"Because his hair is soft. He has two tiny breast buds. And no Adam's apple to speak of at all."

Treadway was taken aback by this. He had seen Wayne's breast buds the day he had tried to tell his son the facts of life. But he had hoped no one else had noticed. Treadway had to go on his trapline now. He had come here to clue things up, not to open new questions he had no time to answer. He put his glass on Thomasina's table and walked back out under Orion, who glittered brightly, except for the dying red star that marked the hunter's left foot.

13

Spin the Bottle

WAYNE HAD GOT USED TO HIS feet peeling. He decided there must be a lot of layers of skin on the bottoms of everyone's feet, because a layer of his came off every day and it didn't hurt. It didn't seem to matter, and he did not mention it to his mother again. Seven layers, eight, ten. The layers must be growing at the same rate at which they are peeling, he reasoned. He monitored the other new thing about his body: the ache in his abdomen. It was like the pulled muscle he once got doing sit-ups in gym, only this was deeper inside and did not hurt as much. He figured he would let this go away on its own along with the peeling, which was the more interesting condition of the two in his mind, so long as his feet did not bleed.

Wally had not come to see Wayne since Treadway destroyed her music. Wayne missed her like crazy and wanted to show her his diagrams of Thomas Telford's bridge and tell her about his peeling feet. But he did not have the guts to go and get her or tell her he was sorry for what his father had done. He felt it was his fault, and he did not know how to make her forgive him.

By the time school started, Wally Michelin had turned into a stranger to Wayne. She was taller and skinnier. No one but Wayne seemed to remember that from grades one to six she had been strong, brave, and independent. It was as if she were an awkward new girl. She did not possess one article of clothing from the catalogue, and she kept her hair in two ponytails with elastic bands. By the first day of grade seven Donna Palliser was the undisputed queen of the class, and no one remembered the time before Donna, when everyone had loved Wally.

Donna Palliser's parties had grown more numerous and elaborate each year. At her Hallowe'en party her mother had decorated the house with bats and cobwebs. Donna had come to the door to greet each guest with a plate of shortbread cookies shaped like severed thumbs and fingers with red icing. There was a haunted house on the mantel, with diabolical laughter coming out of it. Donna had Remembrance Day parties, Christmas parties, New Year's Eve parties, Valentine's Day parties, Easter parties, and Summer Holiday Eve parties, and if there was a lull between these she had sleepovers for selected girls and pizza parties for both girls and boys. Throughout grades five and six she had these parties and had not invited Wally Michelin, the Groves twins, or Gracie Watts, who continued to wear the same wool sweater every day, and Wayne had not told his father about the parties so had managed to avoid them. But in grade seven Donna Palliser changed her definition of a party, and her new tactics entrapped him.

For the first party of grade seven, which Donna called her Junior High Fete, Donna invited those she usually left out. Wayne saw Donna hand an invitation to Wally Michelin at recess, and he hoped she would not go. Anyone could see Donna had something planned for the unpopular people. He vowed not to go, and threw his invitation in the cafeteria garbage. Gracie Watts saw him do it and came over.

"Donna Palliser told Tweedledum and Tweedledee you're trying to decide which one of them you want to go out with." Wally Michelin and Wayne were the only students who did not call the Groves twins Tweedledum and Tweedledee.

"I'm not going."

"She told them you want to French kiss both of them and then decide."

"Fat chance."

"Donna will tell everyone that proves you're a fairy."

"I'm not kissing the twins."

"French kissing. You should say you can't pick either of them because you want to go with Wally Michelin."

"I don't want to go with anyone."

"But everyone knows you want to go out with her."

Wayne felt sick. He loved Wally Michelin the way he loved constellations, or leaves, or king eider ducks.

"Wally Michelin is going to the party. Everyone is. And you have to go with someone or you'll have to French kiss Tweedledum and Tweedledee." Gracie took an Oh Henry bar out of her lunch bag, started biting the peanuts off it, and left him beside the garbage can.

Donna Palliser's mother had laid out a cut-glass bowl of Cheezies and a matching punch bowl with cups on hooks. There was a plate of toothpicks stuck with Vienna sausages and bread-and-butter pickles, and there was orange Jell-O made with Carnation milk and shredded coconut. The party was in the rec room. There was a bar, a pool table, and a corner chest bulging with stuffed animals.

The Pallisers' rec room had a dartboard and a hockey table, the kind where you shift handles to make the players dart around. There was a shelf with a copper Aladdin's lamp on it, a set of ruby shot glasses, and a scrimshaw hunting horn. The ceiling was stucco with silver flecks. The Pallisers had a beagle, and the beagle blocked the bottom stair leading up to the kitchen. It had an orange rubber ball in its mouth, slimy and bitten to show rubber the colour of the Vienna sausages.

Brent Shiwack and the other boys took turns smoking Rothmans and sticking them out the window. The girls gathered around the punch bowl. Donna had put rum in it. The bar had Tia Maria, Baileys Irish Cream, crème de menthe, and some almond liqueur no one had ever opened, that Donna said was made by monks. Donna had floated a tub of pink ice cream in the punch. The boys argued about who was better: Pink Floyd and Jimi Hendrix or CCR. Wayne was on Pink Floyd's side, but that was not what he listened to at home. He listened to "Across the Universe" by the Beatles, and "Song Without Words" by Tchaikovsky, and late-night radio.

There was a downstairs toilet, a tiny cubicle with a bolt on its door, and that was where you went for spin the bottle if the bottle pointed at you or if you had spun it. Donna announced it was time for Casey Kasem's top forty, and "The Tide Is High" came on, and all the girls sang in falsetto with Donna doing the harmony. Carol Rich went in the cubicle with Archie Broomfield and they came out in fifteen seconds. Bruce McLean went in with Donna, and Mark Thevenet started counting on his second hand.

"Whoa," he said as they came out. Donna's hair was all over her face and their heads dipped as if ducking a shower of confetti. "You guys took six minutes!"

The bottle was an old wine bottle with Hungarian writing on it, and it knew where to point. It put Chad White in the cubicle with Ashley Chalk, and it pointed at couples as if it had intelligence. It did not put a popular girl with an unpopular boy, and it never put a popular boy with a girl who wasn't pretty. It did not point at

Wayne or the Groves twins or Wally Michelin or Gracie Watts at all for a long time. Gracie had new clothes on tonight, a pair of pants no one had seen. They were elephant pants like the popular girls wore, but Gracie did not look like a popular girl in them. She looked like an unpopular girl in a popular girl's pants. She looked as if she didn't own them. The rest of her was the same as usual: bony wrists and a nylon cardigan and a ten-karat gold signet ring. The other girls wore lip gloss and scarves and earrings. Ashley Chalk had a new silk headband every day; Gracie Watts wore elastic bands that broke her hair. Wayne suddenly knew this was who the bottle would choose for him, and it did. Donna Palliser might have planned something for him and the Groves twins, but the bottle had Gracie Watts in mind. The bottle cared about no one's plan but its own. Wayne was prepared to go in the cubicle with Gracie Watts if he had to. He did not have to kiss her.

But in the cubicle she stood waiting. "I've kissed lots of people."

Had kissing been going on among his classmates all the time? Was he the only one who had no clue? Had people been kissing each other behind the school Dumpster where they smoked? But Gracie Watts didn't smoke. She got eighties and nineties.

"Lots?"

"I've been kissing since I was four."

"Four?"

"I kissed Duncan McQueen in his father's garage when I was four, and I kissed Brent Shiwack in the woods when I was only seven."

"Brent Shiwack?"

"I kissed Kevin Stacey in his backyard tent hundreds of times, when I was eleven."

"I haven't kissed that many people."

"Have you kissed anyone?"

"I don't want to kiss people. I don't want to go out with people."

"Do you fall in love with boys?" She stood close and he was interested in her lips, but not in kissing them. He was interested in how the two peaks at the top were so sharp and the scoop in the middle had freckles in it, three, like stars behind the Mealy Mountains. He wanted to get a nice sharp pencil and draw that part of her lips. He got the idea she didn't want him to kiss her at all, not really. He got the idea she wanted someone to talk to.

A great hoot went up, and Mark Thevenet called out, "Seven minutes!" Gracie and Wayne went back to their places in the circle.

"This is from Key West." Donna wrapped a sarong around her head and put a glass ball on the floor where the bottle had spun. "You're going to tell me your dreams, and I'm going to interpret them."

"That's only a weight for a fishing net," Mark Thevenet said.

"You have no imagination. I'm an excellent dream

interpreter. I learned how to do it from a kit I got for my birthday when I lived in Riverside, New Brunswick."

"I'll go," Wally said. It was the first interest she had shown in anything at the party.

"You'll have to wait your turn. The ball is telling me Tweedledee has to go first, and then Wayne Blake, and then Tweedledum. We're going to split up Tweedledee and Tweedledum for once in their lives. That's what the ball wants."

"Fuck," said Brent Shiwack. "I need a smoke."

"Which one of you is Tweedledee?"

"Does it matter?" Brent asked.

"Who here knows which twin is which?"

"Everyone knows," Wally Michelin said quietly. "Except you. Their names are Agatha and Marina. Agatha is shyer than Marina but she smiles more. She wants to be a travel agent. Marina makes things. She makes jewellery out of old copper pipes. Agatha and Marina aren't identical. We all know that. How come you don't?"

"Which one," Donna stared Wally down, "is Tweedledee? That's all I want to know. And which one is Tweedledum? Can you tell me that?"

"No," Wally said. "I can't. Because Tweedledum and Tweedledee aren't their names. They don't correspond to one or the other. Those are names people call the twins as a unit."

"Does anybody else here think there's anything wrong with that?"

Wayne said, "I think the twins probably like it better if you use their real names."

"Do you?" Donna looked at the twins, who sat with their chins buried in the collars that peeped out of their cardigans. Both wore necklaces Marina had made. Everyone waited. Agatha directed one of her shy little smiles at the loops on the carpet.

"Do you mind us," Donna said in a louder voice, as if the twins could not hear, "calling you a friendly nickname like Tweedledum or Tweedledee?"

"We don't care," Marina said.

"See?" Donna gave Wally a great big smile. "They don't care. Why should you care if they don't care themselves? Who made you the great authority? Come over, both Tweedles. Tweedledum, tell us the dream you had last night and I'll interpret it. I might even be able to tell your future."

Wally sat apart. The rest of the group nudged closer to Donna and her glass fishing weight.

"I didn't have any dream," said Agatha.

"Close your eyes." Donna put on a wavery, occult voice. "Try to remember."

"I know I didn't have one because I didn't sleep very good last night."

"But surely you dreamt between your moments of wakefulness. Think back. We can only work with material you provide. We can't cheat."

"Maybe you could go on to someone else."

"Do you ever have flying dreams?"

"I love those. But I never had one last night."

"What happens in your flying dreams?"

"I move my hands at first, real fast."

"Do it for us."

Agatha flapped her hands. Everyone laughed.

"Then what?"

"Then I flap my whole arms."

"And do you fly?"

"It takes a long time."

"I dare say it does."

"After I flap my hands, and then my arms, I start to float, then I'm up over the street. I'm over the houses and the telephone poles. Sometimes I look down and there's a gull flying lower than me."

"That must be amazing. Is Tweedledee ever up there with you?"

"No. When I fly in my dreams, I don't have a twin. It feels strange."

"I guess it is strange. Four hundred pounds floating over Croydon Harbour. I hope none of us is ever down on the road if you decide to fall. Do you ever fall?"

"No."

"That's good. Do you weigh four hundred pounds?"

"The nurse measures us in kilograms. We're on a reduced carbohydrate diet. We have to have gall bladder surgery."

"So my interpretation of your flying dream is this. Which one are you again? Are you Tweedledum?

"I don't know."

"We'll say you are. You're alone. You're weightless. You've had your gall bladder surgery but one of you has died. It must be the other one. It must be Tweedledee. When are you supposed to have the surgery?"

"Next August," Agatha said, near tears.

"Stop it," Wally Michelin said. "Give it up, Donna. Agatha, don't worry about it. Donna Palliser can't tell the future just because she's wearing a stupid bathing suit wrap around her head and looking at a fishing ball. Donna Palliser is an idiot."

"We'll reserve judgement on the death. Maybe there isn't going to be a death. I never said it was for sure. Let's do Wayne's dream."

Wayne knew Donna Palliser could not see into the glass ball. He knew she was in the business, tonight, of being cruel. He did not like to see Agatha Groves made fun of and did not mind giving Donna Palliser a change of topic. "I dreamed I was a girl," he said. "I could see my sweater. It was a green sweater with glimmery buttons, like light changing underwater. I looked at my sandals and they were white. I was walking by a river. I tried to see my face in the river but I couldn't. No one was with me. I tried to run with the river. I picked one peak of water and ran beside it and I thought it was the same peak. But then I wasn't sure. I didn't realize I was a girl in the dream until I woke up. While I was waking up I remembered I'm a boy, and I was surprised for a minute, until I remembered that's what I always am when I'm awake."

Donna Palliser rubbed the glass ball and her mouth twisted. She rubbed it until Wally Michelin kicked it and shattered it against the wall. Donna picked a handful of shards off the carpet and flung them back at Wally, and one of the shards flew in Wally's mouth and stuck in her throat, and there was blood coming out from between her lips and it dripped on her blouse, and she was terrified. She could breathe but she couldn't talk, and the only sound she made was loud, constricted panting through her nose. Even Donna Palliser knew she had to call a grown-up.

Donna ran upstairs and brought her mother down and they called an ambulance, and Wally Michelin went to Goose Bay and a doctor took the glass out of her throat, but it had lacerated one of her vocal cords. There was a lot of parental interrogating, and a policewoman even came in from Goose Bay and asked everyone separately and in groups to explain what had happened. In the end all the grown-ups wanted to believe this was a tragic outcome where no one was to be singled out for blame. The grown-ups wanted to avoid blame at all costs, and agreed this could have happened in any group of young people. It was unfortunate and terrible and everyone had had a part to play, and they would hopefully never find themselves in such a situation again, and they could at least take comfort in the fact no one had been blinded, or killed.

Wally came back to school a week later. Wayne wanted someone to tell him she would still be able to sing, to study the "Cantique de Jean Racine" if someone could find it for her, to go away to Vienna and become an opera singer like Lydia Coombs. But no one mentioned Wally's singing, and Wayne had to think hard to remember if anyone but he had known of her singing plans, and he realized he might be the only one Wally had told. He couldn't catch her eye, and she did not wait for him in the hall at recess or lunch. He got the idea he was the only one who remembered about her singing, and he got the idea she somehow hated him for this, and would hate him forever until he forgot what he knew about her.

This was all in his imagination but he felt it as strongly as if she had written a placard and come to his window at night and held it up: "Get lost, and forget about my singing. Forget anything you ever thought you knew about me."

14

Dr. Lioukras

WAYNE WAS PASSABLY GOOD at parts of gym class, but not at soccer or basketball, which required quick connection. Brent Shiwack and the other boys had radar that let them know the instant one needed to pass a ball. There they were, in the right place, before the ball. In basketball their hands looked to Wayne like some kind of ocean anemones with invisible suckers that drew a ball in and made it stick. Brent stuck a hand in the air, and no matter which way the ball had been headed, it changed trajectory and was attracted to his hand. The ball was not attracted to Wayne's hand. Still, his was not the last name called if teams were chosen. The last was Boyd Fowlow, who couldn't see the ball because his mother had written Miss Baikie a note saying he was not allowed to wear his glasses in gym.

Wayne managed to avoid outright disgrace because of his competence in individual sports. He was not a fast sprinter and could not pull himself up by the arms on the chin-up bars. But he could run distances because he ran steadily, which was not glorious but it meant he did not let down his team. He could do a pretty good long jump, though not a high jump, and he liked pole vaulting and, for some reason no one could explain, beat just about everyone else at it. His father said it was too bad they had pole vaulting only once a year, on sports day.

"I like the part after you get halfway up," Wayne told Thomasina Baikie. He sat on the edge of the gym stage, kicking his sneakers against the wall. "You take off in a kind of slow motion, and you feel like you go way higher than you thought you would."

"Does it hurt now?"

Wayne nodded. His stomach ache had given him sharp pains while everyone else was doing cool-down laps. Now it was lunchtime and the others had gone to the cafeteria. He put his hands under his sweatshirt and laid them on his abdomen because their warmth felt good.

"I'm going to go get a heating pad and sit you down in the staff room for a few minutes."

They went in the staff room and Thomasina got him the pad and gave him strong tea with sugar in it. He did not want to eat his potted-meat sandwich or his jam cookies.

"Here?" Thomasina touched his stomach. "Or here?" She placed her hand over his abdomen.

"Yeah. Right there. It's kind of swollen."

"How long has it been like that?"

"It started when my feet started peeling."

"Your feet?"

"At the end of the summer. The skin on my feet peels off. It doesn't hurt. It's just weird. The stomach aching started around then too."

"Can I see your belly?" His abdomen protruded. She put her hand on it and it was full of fluid, but she did not call the school nurse. The nurse did not know what Thomasina knew. That Wayne had a womb, and that it was acting up.

"Does your mother know about the pain?"

"I told her I had a stomach ache."

"Has she seen it?"

"No." He had not let anyone see or touch his body since the swelling. Thomasina looked at the little nubs on his chest and looked away again.

"When was the last time you went for a checkup with the doctor in Goose Bay?"

"Dr. Lioukras or Dr. Giashuddin?" His specialists were always changing. They came to Labrador for two-year positions, then moved to Toronto or Boston.

"Whichever one you saw last."

"I saw them both. Dr. Lioukras gave me my new pills and Dr. Giashuddin did something else, but I had to be put to sleep."

"When?"

"Just when summer started."

"And you weren't swollen then."

"No. And my feet weren't peeling."

Thomasina thought at first that she could not bear to bring up the subject of Wayne's chest. She felt to do so might crush him. He must have noticed it himself. Had no one helped him understand anything about what was happening to his body? Did he look at other boys and try to imagine their chests were no different from his? Thomasina saw there was no one in the staff room or in the hallway beyond the door.

"Wayne, it looks to me like we have to go see about the swelling. Do you think there's swelling on your chest as well?"

Tears blipped over Wayne's bottom lids. He had lain in his bathwater and sunk just enough to see if the small nubbins would make islands, and they had.

Thomasina put her strong hand on his shoulder. She did not have a feminine little voice like other teachers in the school, and Wayne was glad. She did not gush at him about his few tears. She was listening to him. She listened to his whole story, spoken and unspoken. She could hear parts of the story he did not know about. He sensed this, though he did not fully understand it. He trusted her. When she said, "Let's phone your mother and get you to the doctor and find out what is happening here so you won't have to worry any more," Thomasina was angrier than she had been in a long time. A child's worry was not like an adult's. It gnawed deep, and was so unnecessary. Why did people not realize children could withstand the truth? Why did adults insist on filling children with the deceptions their own parents had laid on them, when surely they remembered how it had felt to lie in bed and cry over fears no one had bothered to help you face.

Thomasina got Mr. Stack to cover for her in health class. When she called Wayne's house from the staff room phone, there was no answer. Treadway was at the back end of the garden scraping rust off his traps and rubbing seal fat on them, and Jacinta was at the Hudson's Bay store, walking up and down the cleaning products aisle, looking for a bar of Sunlight to wash Treadway's socks before he went on the trapline. Wayne sat on the couch next to the coat rack with his hands up his shirt, warming his belly.

"How much does it hurt, on a scale of one to ten?"

"Five. I'm waterlogged. I'm ready to burst."

"I can see that."

"Am I weird?"

Thomasina rubbed her hands and laid them on his abdomen. She was glad no other teachers were in the staff room. "Do you mind if I take you to Goose Bay to see Dr. Lioukras?"

"Is he Greek?"

"Guess what his first name is."

"I don't know."

"Apollo."

"It's not."

"It is. In Mexico there are all kinds of guys named Jesus. And in Greece there are Apollos and Athenas all over the place. I had a taxi driver called Hermes."

"Did he have wings on his feet?"

"Wayne, there are things I wish someone had told you when you were small. But they didn't. And it's not my place to tell you now. But you know what? It looks like no one else is going to. I'm going to take you to see Dr. Lioukras. If your father isn't going to deal with it, well, that's his problem. And your mother . . ."

The principal, Victoria Huskins, came in looking for her stash of coffee filters. Thomasina Baikie went silent and Wayne knew he and Thomasina had embarked on a clandestine adventure.

"Hi, Wayne." Miss Huskins thought children could not hear her unless her voice pierced their layers of dull incomprehension. How she had come to be principal Thomasina Baikie did not know. Rather, she knew and wished she didn't. Wayne was not scared of Miss Huskins like some of the younger students were, but he felt uncomfortable when she was in the room. The previous week, when she was checking the washrooms, she found excrement on the floor behind one of the toilets and announced her discovery over the school PA system. "Someone . . ." The speakers cracked and hissed over the heads of the kindergartens, grade ones, twos, threes, and fours. The grades fives, sixes, and sevens heard it too, though their bathroom was on the second floor. When Miss Huskins made an example of anyone, she wanted the lesson broadcast to all. "Some student has deliberately done their poo and left it on the floor against the wall in the first-floor bathroom. Who has done this?" She left a long pause. The students were silent. "I will find out. The person who has done this had better come to my office and own up now. It is filthy, and it is wrong, and whoever has done this will not get away with it."

Thomasina sighed, looked at her class, and said, "I hope that woman goes into treatment soon." Everyone but Donna Palliser and her attendants had felt sorry for the anonymous child who had obviously had an accident. Why did the principal not know it had been an accident? But no one discussed it. Everyone but Thomasina was afraid to speak up.

Victoria Huskins licked her thumb and blew on the coffee filters to separate one, and said, "So you're sick today, Wayne?"

He nodded.

"Stomach flu is going around."

"It is," Thomasina said.

"A couple of Gravol should keep you out of trouble till you get home. Have your parents been called?"

"We're trying to get hold of them now." Thomasina said nothing about driving Wayne to the hospital.

Miss Huskins got the coffee machine gurgling, then moved the pot aside and slipped her cup under the stream.

Drips hissed on the hot plate. "Hopefully the whole class will not get it. Hopefully the entire school will not come down with projectile vomiting. Try to come back before you miss too many math classes. What are you doing in math right now, Miss?"

"Decahedrons."

"Don't forget to have his parents sign the P-47." Miss Huskins went off with her mug that had a happy face on it from last year's winter carnival.

Thomasina said, "I'll take you in the truck."

"Are we allowed?" Wayne liked the idea of escaping in the middle of a school day. But he did not know what his parents would think. "I can walk home. I can tell my mom you looked at my stomach in gym class and thought I should go see Dr. Lioukras and she can take me tomorrow."

The coffee smell filled the staff room. Thomasina looked out the window at gold clouds. Everyone had such a small life it nearly drove her crazy. Perhaps it had driven her crazy.

"You told Miss Huskins I had the stomach flu?"

Thomasina looked at the floor and shoved her glasses up her nose. "I let her think it, didn't I."

Wayne thought Thomasina might stop the truck at his parents' and tell them she was taking him to see Dr. Lioukras. He thought they might go get a couple of Teenburgers and a root beer at the A&W in Goose Bay. But Thomasina drove fast down the main road and did not stop. The main road was featureless. Wayne hated it. It had a dark green stretch that went on forever between Croydon Harbour and Goose Bay. Thomasina did not speak and he wondered if she was making a mistake. What would happen when Miss Huskins realized they had taken off in her pickup without his mother and father signing that form?

"What does P-47 stand for?"

"Bureaucracy. Victoria Huskins's world. A world in which — do you know what a morgue is?"

"I saw one on TV."

"Every corpse has a ticket."

"Around its feet?"

"We're in a world where every person, or plant, or animal, or any entity whatsoever, has an explanatory ticket on it. P-47s are part of that."

"Do you think we should try to phone my mom again, when we get to the hospital?"

"Are you afraid of Miss Huskins?"

"She already freaked out about the poo."

"Do you feel like I'm kidnapping you?"

"Kind of."

"I guess it could seem like that."

"Yeah."

"You'll be thirteen next March the seventh."

"You know my birthday?"

"I do. So you're twelve. I'd call twelve the age of reason. So would every major civilization since the dawn of humanity. Twelve is when you wake up and you look around and you understand things. You know if your parents died that night you could figure out how to live in this world. I remember that about being twelve."

Thomasina had four vertical lines going down her face. Sometimes they were laugh lines and sometimes they weren't. Wayne found them serious and good. They made him trust her even though she was taking him from school in her truck in the middle of a Tuesday afternoon.

"I remember the clarity of being twelve. Do you feel it?" She put the radio on. With music in the cab, the road out of Croydon Harbour was not so lonely.

"I don't know." Wayne did not know whether he felt clarity or not, but he was glad Thomasina was addressing questions about his body, questions his clothes, his parents, his school had covered up. He had seen Dr. Lioukras not that long ago and the doctor had not explained anything. In fact, the doctor had put him to sleep.

"How do you know Dr. Lioukras? Did you see him in Greece?"

"I saw him before I went to Greece. I went to see him and asked him to give me a local's itinerary. I didn't want to take a bus tour. He's the one who told me how to get a pass to run the original Olympic track. He told me his favourite lunch counter in Athens and said to order the vine leaves stuffed with rice and mint, and some tiny lamb meatballs. He told me what kind of coffee to drink at what time of day, and he gave me the name of his daughter's bookstore. That's where I got the Greek bracelets and the music for our dance."

"I don't like lamb."

"I never met a child who did. I guess eating it seems like one of the more barbaric adult practices."

"It's sad."

"I guess it is, in a way."

Wayne liked that Thomasina could admit this. His father would not have done so, nor would his mother. They did not admit that it was sad to eat rabbits either. He wouldn't mind their eating these animals if part of them could admit, as Thomasina did now, that it was sad in some way. He didn't like that they pushed all sadness away.

"Why do you eat it, then?"

"There's something ancient about the flavour of lamb. People have been eating it for centuries. Grown-ups put the sadness out of their minds because to them, appetite is stronger."

"Being hungry makes you forget it's a lamb?"

"Appetite is king."

"Why?"

"I don't know. I need to think about it."

Wayne did not know any other grown-ups who would admit they needed to think about something. They all came up with some kind of answer, even if it didn't make sense.

They were on the wildest part of the road now. Wayne knew there were animals in the woods, and birds. Treadway would have found a story in the land that bordered this long, lonely road, and it might even be a story about meat, appetite, hunger. But daily meat, daily appetite, daily hunger. Not the kind Thomasina meant.

When Goose Bay appeared through the trees, there was nothing thrilling about it. The buildings were low and square, with no architecture. They were utilitarian and sat inert against the sky. The hospital had some feeling in it because it stood taller. It had many windows and a sense of mystery, but not an inviting mystery. Every time he had come with his mother, Wayne had sensed that something frightened her. He was not afraid of the hospital but he was afraid of what it did to his mother. It made her retreat from him in the days around his appointments. Thomasina was different.

The closer her truck got to the main gate, the more he felt she wanted to talk. Thomasina believed he was as sensible as she was herself. He could feel that. You can feel the degree to which anyone thinks she knows more than you do. Thomasina might know more facts than Wayne did, but her face told him she believed he was capable of understanding anything she understood. He felt something pop like ginger ale bubbles in his hands. Other parts of his body fizzed too: his scalp, and his cheekbones. His body fizzed like a wave. With Thomasina that was how you felt. You were riding somewhere, and it was exciting.

They parked under the pole with an M on it and walked across the lot.

"Everyone is a snake shedding its skin," she said. "We are different people all through our lives. You even more so. No one has told you this thing, and I'm going to ask you, do you want to know?"

A woman helped a child out of a van into a wheelchair. There were puddles, and Wayne smacked his sneaker sole into their edges. The hospital hummed and there was a smell of French fries and canned gravy.

"What?"

"If you had a choice between knowing a scary truth and a comforting lie, which would you choose?"

"About me?"

"Yes."

"What?"

"You'd want to know?"

"I'd want to know what?"

"I wish we weren't in a parking lot." Nurses and cashiers and candystripers smoked at the entrance, jiggling their feet and rubbing their bare arms. "I wish that inside there weren't puke green corridors with painted footprints."

"I know a really cool place inside."

"You do?"

He had found it the last time he was here, while he and Jacinta waited for tests. He had left his mother eating pea soup with salt beef and dumplings floating in it, which she had said was pretty good for soup in a Styrofoam bowl. He had gone exploring along the corridor with the green footprints, way into the west wing, to a place where a handpainted sign said SISTER ROSITA BON-NELL PALLIATIVE CARE WARD. At the end of the ward was a blue door. He led Thomasina to it now.

There were couches upholstered in material with blue fish. A window depicted a woman with a crescent moon and the earth under one foot, and a falcon on her arm. A candle burned. The window was gold and green. The colours were rich and not too hot.

"That's not even Mary," Thomasina said. "It's Isis. Sister Rosita Bonnell must have been a renegade."

"Is that like a bandit?"

"She must have gone to Bolivia and got herself a splendid education, then come back and done things the Pope would hang her for if he knew."

"What was the thing you wanted to tell me?"

"When you were born, Wayne, I was there. Did you know that?"

"No."

"Well I was. I was there, and I saw something."

"I was born in my house. Not here."

"I know."

"I came to the hospital after I was born."

"Do you know why?"

"Because of my blood disorder. That's why I have to take all the pills. It's some rare thing."

"I wouldn't call what you have a disorder. I'd call it a different order. A different order means a whole new way of being. It could be fantastic. It could be overwhelmingly beautiful, if people weren't scared."

"What was the thing you saw when I was born?"

Thomasina wanted to say, A daughter. You were a daughter as well as a son. But what would Wayne do with the truth? He would need more than the truth. He would need a world that understood. What had she been thinking?

"What was it?"

The door opened and a young woman came in wheeling a bearded man with a rose in his hand and an intravenous unit hooked up to his arm. They looked at Thomasina and Wayne for a second, then sat together in front of the candle. The man was dying. He looked as if he wanted the woman to love him, but she looked too tired to love anybody. She looked as if she might die before he did. The room turned into a container for weariness, and Thomasina took Wayne's shoulder and herded him out. They walked around a bucket full of water with a mop in it, then around a trolley with covered dishes smelling of fried ham and instant potatoes.

"What?" Wayne insisted.

"It's not the right time."

"You should have told me before those people came in."

"We'll go see Dr. Lioukras." Thomasina had lost her courage. Prudence. That was what everyone had been trying to exercise. That was the quality she herself lacked.

"What?" Wayne stopped under a pane of wobbly glass. There was no Isis, no nurse, no ham or potatoes. Just tiles with specks in them, and a corridor that led from the dying to the living. He could not hear the rest of the hospital from here.

"I'm not going to see Dr. Lioukras until you tell me." He put his hand on the sill, which was cold and bumpy and had been painted years ago. This place was like the root cellar his father had shown him at a house out near the Black Cliffs. They had gone in on one of the few hot Labrador days, when little orange moths clustered on thistles and there was a haze over the hay. The root cellar was cool as a plunge in the pond under the big overfall. If Thomasina wanted to tell him a thing, why didn't she just do it?

Wayne tried to see out the window. It had been made for adults to look out of. It had been made to shed light on this corridor from a height. The light cascaded and made you feel like you were about to realize something. Wayne closed his eyes and tried to discern if he could feel light on his head the way he could feel warmth, or the touch of a hand. Light felt like a thin layer of water. But the door at the end of the hallway clicked open and someone came through but did not walk towards them. Who was it? He realized Thomasina was staring at the person, who was in shadow, and that she looked guilty. Then the person opened the door again, a door with diagonal planks like a dungeon door, and the person went back out. When it

closed, the door echoed, and Wayne wanted to get back
to the modern part of the hospital. Whatever Thomasina
wanted to tell him, she could keep it to herself. He didn't
have to listen to her. He wouldn't mind a hot dog. He
wouldn't mind a plate of fries and gravy.

"My stomach doesn't hurt right now. I might be
better. I'm fine."

"It's not that you're ill." Thomasina looked defeated.
"Dr. Lioukras is the one who should talk to you. I'm no
good at the facts. I hate them, to tell you the truth"

Dr. Lioukras's hands felt warm on Wayne's belly. "That
fluid will have to come out." His hair had big loopy
curls that should have been cut, according to the nurses,
but they would have liked to get their hands in them. Dr.
Lioukras liked Labrador. There were berries and fat ducks
and there was wine, and there was more sunshine than
in many warmer places, because high-pressure systems
floated over the land here. Dr. Lioukras had a little camera
he was always using. He would interrupt an operation to
snap a shot of geese he heard honking past the window.
Thomasina sat under that window now, in a chair parents
normally sat in. Dr. Lioukras took pictures of the children
he saw in his surgery, and nobody minded, as he was such
an optimist. Nobody ever said, "Hey, Dr. Lioukras, make
sure you get the parents to sign a release form."

"How do you get the fluid out?" asked Wayne.

"I'll deaden the area and make a small incision and

drain it. You're going to lose that bloatedness." Dr. Lioukras managed to suggest that he deadened areas and drained fluid out of boys' abdomens every day, and that nothing could be more normal or upbeat.

"My stomach will be flat?"

"Flat as a pancake."

"What about my chest?"

"Let me see it."

Wayne lifted his Trans-Labrador Helicopters T-shirt. His breasts were like tinned apricots that have not broken the surface tension in a bowl of cream. No flicker of alarm or warning crossed the doctor's face. He looked at Wayne's chest as if it were the most ordinary boy's chest in the world. Thomasina loved him for it. She could not have looked directly at Wayne's chest without Wayne's knowing she felt there was a deep, sad problem. When Dr. Lioukras looked at Wayne's breasts, he saw beauty equal to that which he would have seen in the body of any youth, male or female. It was as if he saw the apricots growing on their own tree, right where they belonged.

15

Boreal Owl

FOR ALL HIS FATHERLY TALK about how Labrador boys had to be part of a pack, Treadway Blake was the most solitary man in Croydon Harbour. The families of solitary people don't always know they are living with someone unusual. They think maybe lots of families have someone quiet like this. A person who can go days without making any sound other than the scrape of a knife on sinew, the scrubbing of boots on the brush mat, the clink of a cup put back in its saucer. But then they go into someone else's house and realize other people have husbands, wives, children, who yell and laugh and wrestle with each other and cry out over a foolish thing the cat has done.

When Treadway had anything on his mind, he spoke not to Jacinta or Wayne, and not to any man. He did not go down to Roland Shiwack's shed to drink with the other men on a Friday night, and he did not hang around the door of the community centre talking to husbands who had come to walk their wives home from bingo. If he had to talk to anyone about what was on his mind, he went into the woods, far from the community, and he spoke there. He did not speak to a god in his mind like the god of the Old Testament, nor did he envision the young, long-haired Jesus from the *Child's Treasury of Bible Stories*, which had been the only book in his house, outside of the Bible itself, while he was growing up. When Treadway needed to speak his mind, he spoke it to a boreal owl he had met when he was seventeen. He and the boreal owl shared physical traits. Both were small for their species. Each had a compact, rounded shape, efficient and not outwardly graceful. The boreal owl was one of the quietest, most modest birds. It roosted in tall, shady thickets of black spruce and drew absolutely no attention to itself. Treadway had met the owl as he rested halfway between the Beaver River and the trail back home. He had been in the same spot more than half an hour when the tiny owl caught his eye, twenty feet over his head. He didn't know what had caused him to look up at that spot. A silent impulse of recognition. Treadway often discovered wildlife like that, as if an invisible bubble had burst and somehow it made you look in that spot.

The owl had made no sound and no movement. It looked like a piece of tree. He saw it, then he couldn't see it. Then he could. He started talking to it in his quietest voice, and he hummed a tune to it. Which he would not have done for any other living being; not his mother, not his father, not his brothers, not himself. He liked, about the owl, that it asked nothing from him, and he had spoken to it ever since as if it were listening to him, though he never saw it again. It calmed him to talk to the owl, and he spoke to it now about Wayne.

"Everyone thinks," he told it, "that I know what I'm doing. For God's sake, I don't have a clue what I'm doing. You know that."

The owl listened from wherever it was. Deep, deep in the woods, past Beaver River, past the pond, which was the pond in the interior where the waters changed direction and began to run magnetically north to Ungava Bay, the pond whose name was a secret.

"I should have let well enough alone," Treadway said. "I think that now. What would have happened if I had let Wayne become half little girl?"

The owl allowed Treadway to see Wayne as a girl child. So Treadway stood there in the woods and saw a vision of his daughter. She had dark hair and a grave face. She was an intelligent girl, and Treadway loved her.

"You're a beautiful child." But the child could not hear him as the owl could. The owl listened, and Treadway felt, for the first time since his wife had given birth, pain flow out of his heart and into the moss. It sank into the moss and became part of the woods. The owl took some of it. This had not happened to the pain before.

"I could stay here," Treadway said. "You're a brave little owl." He thought of the owl as alone. He thought of it, really, as himself, although he did not think he was brave at all. People call their friends admirable in this way or that way — brave, honest, loyal — but they do not see these qualities in themselves, even if they are present in greater quantity than in the friends. Treadway could not see the good in himself. His wife thought he could, but he could not. He knew he was not as self-contained or as brave as the owl, but he identified with how it had chosen to live. If only the world could live in here, deep in the forest, where there were no stores, roads, windows, and doors, no straight lines. The straight lines were the problem. Rulers and measurements and lines and no one to help you if you crossed them. His owl was not going to come out of the deep woods. It was not going to come near the fences and doorsteps of Croydon Harbour. It knew better than to try and live in that world.

"I wish," Treadway told the owl, "I could bring him in here with me for a good six months. Longer. Forget about the medicine that keeps him being a boy. Hospital medicine, no. The medicine in these trees. The turpentine. The smell of the blasty boughs. What would happen?"

Where was the owl?

"If I brought him here and never took him back? We could live here."

The owl had its back to the man.

Treadway stayed out until dark. He navigated home the way he always did, by knowing the contours of the land, by the moon, by parts of Orion and the Dog Star, which appeared in certain clearings. He came home to a note on the table and two plates of dried-up salt fish and congealed drawn butter. The stove had gone out. The phone rang and it was Thomasina.

"I've been trying to get you."

"Why?"

"We're in Goose Bay. Wayne had to have pressure taken off his belly. There was a lot of built-up fluid. You weren't home. But Treadway, I'm asking you to do something for me."

"What's that, Thomasina Baikie?"

"Tell Victoria Huskins I called you from the hospital and you gave me permission to bring Wayne in. She'll have my head on a plate if you don't."

There are degrees of trust and mistrust. Treadway mistrusted a woman like Victoria Huskins much more than he mistrusted Thomasina. When you have known someone thirty years, even if you have different personalities and even if you would approach the same problem differently, at least you know where you both came from. There is a bedrock of respect. Victoria Huskins was not, in Treadway's mind, basic. Thomasina was. There was a basic person in there to whom you could talk, in a worst-case scenario. Victoria Huskins, in a worst-case scenario, Treadway thought, would not be basic. Her concerns would be that the correct papers be filled out, that her skirt have its back seam running directly up the middle, that any stranger or pilgrim who sat in her pew be re-educated right away. He had seen this.

"What kind of built-up fluid?"

"Blood."

"Blood?"

"A lot of it, Treadway."

"Is he injured?"

"It's normal blood that flows out of a girl's body when she reaches Wayne's age. Menstrual blood trapped inside. And there is another thing, but I would have to tell you in person."

"Should Jacinta . . . ?" Treadway was not happy talking about menstrual blood. He did not know what to do. "She's out. With Eliza and Joan. Where's Wayne now?"

"He'll be home in the morning. I've been trying to call you. Visiting hours are over in five minutes. If you talk to the head nurse they will give me permission to stay here with Wayne. I can stay for the night, or you and Jacinta can come. He's asleep. If you talk to them now they'll let me stay. Otherwise I have to leave."

"I'll be there." He was not going to let anyone but himself or his wife stay by Wayne's bed overnight in the hospital. He did not phone Jacinta. He put his woods coat back on, though it was damp, and he got in his truck and went to get his wife.

One difference between Eliza Goudie and Joan Martin was that when they were drinking with the women for the night, Eliza bought piña coladas from the liquor store and Joan brought over a bottle of her husband's single malt Scotch. Eliza liked fizzing concoctions with pineapple and coconut flavouring and palm trees on the bottle, while Joan just liked to get quietly wrecked. Joan heaved herself onto the loveseat and Eliza sat in the big old rocking chair near the television, which was a big television because her husband had liked to sit watching it while she was out at all hours with the geography teacher, or with the lovers she had had before that. He had liked to watch Bob Barker on *The Price Is Right*, and after that, *Jeopardy*.

"He hums," Eliza told Joan and Jacinta, "the theme from *Jeopardy* while we're making love. Dum da da diddle dum da daaaaa, dum, dadumda dee dee diddle diddle . . . talk about unconscious. Could you have an orgasm with that going on? Could you? Because I can. And do you know why? Because I imagine he's gone to sleep on his surfboard and really I'm in bed with Dudley Moore and my hair is all in cornrows like, you know, what's her name?"

"I dunno," Joan drank from the bottle. "This is on the peaty side of single malts. It was made in a cave. Some tiny cave in the north of Scotland, more remote than we are here. My husband picked it out because of the cave. My husband, the caveman."

Jacinta had a bottle of Mateus that had been in the freezer for half an hour. She liked how frost steamed around the gold label, the *fffftz* and the puff of fruity scent. If she was going to drink, Jacinta wanted fizz. She wanted Spain. She wanted celebration and the word *rosé*.

Joan had made the sour cream and onion soup mix dip from the new Kraft commercial, and had brought a huge bag of rippled chips. Eliza had brought a plate of Cheez Whiz on celery sticks, and Jacinta had made marshmallow cookies with melted chocolate chips and Parawax.

"What's her name? Dolores?" Jacinta asked. "It's not Dolores, is it?"

Joan said, "I can't remember her name in the movie, but her real name's Bo Derek."

"I don't see how anyone can go to see movies in that ratty old cinema in Goose Bay," Jacinta said. "Half the time they put the last reel on first or the projector breaks down altogether."

Eliza said, "You know what really pisses me off about that movie?"

"Um," said Joan, "could it be the fact that the only thing that happens in it is they play Ravel's *Bolero* ninety-nine times and the women have no personality, just a number given to them by men like prize pigs at a county fair?" She took a swig of her Oban.

Jacinta said, "I want to ask you something." The third glass of wine was for her the magic glass. At a

Christmas party or an evening out with other families, she had two glasses. The third glass was the glass that floated her above. She did not have that glass as a rule, but this was not a night when the rule applied. "I know you're having sex with your husband again," she said to Eliza. "I know all about the leopard-skin boots and the Valium. What I want to know is you, Joan, you're not on Valium? You're not on anything that artificially enhances your sex drive?"

"My what?"

"I just want to know if anyone besides me here looks at an erect penis as a ludicrous object all of a sudden."

Joan looked at Jacinta as if she were finally seeing the light.

"I mean, I have no problem with Treadway. As you know, he is a good man."

"Yeah, he's that," Joan said.

"He's a really good man. I figure if I can't get along with him, I might as well go crawl off by myself into a little hole somewhere."

"But you don't want to have sex with him."

"It's menopause, right? I mean, one month I was 'Hello Mister Penis, how are you tonight, happy to see you in all your cheery Mister Penisness. Good job, Mister Penis, yes, I like you.' Then the next month, 'Whoa there, bucko, you most ludicrous of creatures, what in the name of God do you think you're trying to do? Go near my vagina? Get in it? Why would you want to do that? Oh, most ridiculous idea.' If it wouldn't have mortified Tread-way I'd have burst out laughing."

"Valium will fix all that."

Joan settled into the cushion with the needlepoint windmill on it. "I didn't need menopause. One night when I was twenty I looked at Harold and his cock was a nose, his nipples were eyes, and his little bush of hair was a woolly moustache."

Eliza spit pina colada on the floor. Harold walked around Croydon Harbour a neat little man. If you had to explain to an alien what a human man was like, if you wanted the straightest, neatest definition, you might pick Harold Martin as your example.

"From October to July," Joan said, "he never takes his insulation off." She had explained to them that Harold had made himself an undergarment out of house insulation, the silver kind that has a layer of bubble wrap between two layers of foil. Harold tied this around his torso with Velcro. "So the effect is enhanced."

"I don't mean to ridicule my husband," Jacinta said. "I'm just sorry that I seem to have gone through a gate and he's still on the other side."

"What's on your side?" Joan asked.

"I'm hanging around the gate looking back at my husband, waiting for him to even see the gate. He just thinks it's another part of the fence."

"Don't you go feeling sorry for him," Joan said. "You think he's puttering around there in the dandelions in the same old field, but he's not. You think he can't see where you are, but he can. He can see just fine. He just isn't talking about it. Rest assured, though, that if you passed away tomorrow, Treadway would suddenly become the liveliest man in Croydon Harbour. You would look down from your new home and be amazed. You'd say, 'How come he wasn't like that when I was with him?' He would suddenly become everything you've wished him to be for years."

"Why do you think that?"

"He would lose ten pounds. He would start eating vegetables. He would go to the Garden Club and offer to plant Persian rose bushes by the boardwalk. You'd want to descend right back down from heaven and go to bed with him on the spot."

By the time Treadway knocked on Eliza Goudie's door, Joan and Eliza had forgotten what a husband looked like. They had drunk so much that the sight of Treadway on the doorstep puzzled them. An alien creature had found its way to the house. Only Jacinta recognized him, and he knew, when he saw her, he did not want her to accompany him to the hospital in that state.

"I have to go in to Goose Bay, on an errand. In case you went home and found me not there. I didn't want you to worry."

"What errand?"

"Valves for my compressor." She was in no condition to hear about Wayne. Treadway did not want to drive

over the wilderness road to Goose Bay with a hysteri-
cal woman in the truck. So he lied. "Maynard White has
them and I need them before I go into the bush."

"What about Wayne?"

"Wayne is at a sleepover."

"Where?"

"He's at a sleepover with Roland Shiwack's kid."
The other two women were making a racket in the living
room. They had recovered from the feeling that a husband on the doorstep had elicited and were listing habits
their own husbands had not revealed until after a few
years of marriage.

"Harold refuses to eat chicken," Joan said, "because
he says they pee through their skin."

"Pee?"

"He says their skin is constantly bathed in pee and he
doesn't see how anyone can eat it. He says if you watch
the back end of a chicken you'll see chicken shit only."

"Is everything all right?" Jacinta asked Treadway.
Orion's Dog Star hung above his shoulder, and she
remembered she loved him, and he did not look his ordinary self. He looked as if he wanted to say something no
one in the world but herself could understand.

"My husband," said Eliza in the distance, "is a con-
noisseur of his own farts."

"What do you mean?" Joan asked.

"Everything's fine," Treadway said. "If you go home,
watch your step. There's not much of a moon."

"I might stay here."

"Better do that, then." And he gave Jacinta a formal little hug.

"Your coat is damp."

"It's only a bit of night dampness." Treadway left her in the lit-up doorway and climbed into his truck.

The northern lights were putting on a show of pink along with the turquoise and silver, which was unusual, and normally Treadway would have stopped the truck and got out on the side of the road. His parents, and his grandparents, had respected the mystery of those lights in a way people did not do now. The elders looked at them the way English children once lay in fields and picked dreams out of clouds. Sounds had come from the sky then. Only the old people heard them now. Treadway, though twenty years younger than most of the good listeners, had heard the moaning song. But he did not hear it tonight. In his childhood he had broken a leg in three places, and his mother had taken him to Goose Bay, and the anesthetic had been too strong. He had not woken at the right time. The doctors had told his mother this was all right. They had sent her home to wait for news. When she got home, Treadway's father asked her where Treadway was, and when she said, "I left him at the hospital," his father had driven his truck over two rivers after midnight instead of waiting for the morning ferry, and had brought Treadway home and laid him in a cot by the stove. Whenever

Treadway heard his father tell that story, it always ended with "I'll never know how she could leave him like that."

And it is true it is hard to know how much anesthetic to give a young person. Wayne's doctors had not been in agreement about it and had given him a measurement between the doses allotted a child and an adult. It put him in a state between waking and sleeping, and dulled the pain from the cut Dr. Lioukras made to open the vagina that had been hidden. The flesh was a centimetre deep, and when he cut it, Dr. Lioukras asked the nurse to get a stainless steel bowl from the trolley immediately.

Wayne had not seen the blood, which was copious, because the staff had erected a sheet the way they did with all gynecological operations. He saw the masked faces move in slow motion through a gelled lens, and heard their voices as a stretched, continuous murmur, with now and then a word plopping out whole. He heard blood and anomaly and *oh*. He heard *rush* and *no* and *never*. He heard Thomasina say, "No," and he heard the staff ask her to stand back, and he heard her cry out. But the sounds were muted. What came close, what rushed head-on at him, was the colour red. Red can be black-red, and this was. It can be scarlet, and it was this too. When you close your eyes in a field in the sun and you are young and the world has not imposed memories on you that can't be erased, there is a red-orange that sits against your closed eyes and contains the warmth of all future summers, and the red rushing headlong behind Wayne's closed eyes included this red too. It scared him, the swirling red world, yet it thrilled him too, and the anesthetic had pinned his arms and legs to a soft, soft cloud. He could not get up from the dizzy red world no matter what looked out from it at him, and, like the words rising from a murmur of sea-sound, there was something half-formed in the red world, looking at him, and he did not know what it was, though he felt it was drowning in blood and trying to speak, but the red whirl-pool was going too fast. In his anesthetized world, sound from the unconconscious rose up, a sound that normally comes to the waking world only through portholes like the northern lights, or the voice of an owl, or the ground whispering.

Wayne heard the sound become louder and drown the voices of the staff. The inchoate red world took form: a red trench, a tunnel, a map of the womb inside him and the passageway leading from it, which had all been closed and that he had no idea existed. The red world knew everything in him, and it showed him the map of his own feminine parts, and they were the most vivid, living, seductive red he had known in waking or in dreaming life. He heard the sound of himself falling into this tunnel, a long, low moan, then a shout. The staff heard it, and none of them had heard this before outside a birthing room. The youngest nurse ran out of the operating room, downstairs to the walk-in fridge in the back of the cafeteria, and drank a carton of Old South ruby red grapefruit juice mixed with crushed ice.

16

Falling Away

THERE IS A FALLING AWAY IN all little families: families having a mother, a father, and one child. There
is a new world for every child, sooner or later, no matter
what kind of love has lived in the home. Strong love, love
that has failed, complicated love, love that does its best to
keep a child warm through layers of fear or caution. One
day the layers begin to fall. Before his night in hospital,
Wayne had not broken from his mother, but he had begun
to yearn for the unnameable mystery young people want.

The morning after Wayne's operation, Jacinta had
woken on her own couch with a hangover. Why was the
house cold? It was cold in a way she remembered from
uninsulated houses of her friends, in winter, in St. John's.
A cold that pried into your joints and tormented you.
Treadway never let the house get like this. Five thirty

in the morning was late for him to rise. Every night he
made sure there were dry splits ready in the box beside
the stove. He twisted newspaper and set the splits in a
pyramid. Then came pieces of slab from Obadiah Blake's
sawmill, and junks of the same black spruce that sent
incense from every chimney in the cove. Jacinta rose, still
in her party clothes. She had stumbled uphill at three in
the morning and had noticed the truck was gone, but
Treadway was always leaving it with Maynard White for
one reason or another. He had said something at Eliza's
door about valves. And he had told her Wayne was sleeping over at Brent Shiwack's, which was unusual. Wayne
was not the most popular boy in Croydon Harbour, and
Brent Shiwack was not his friend.

Jacinta went down the basement stairs and lit the fire
herself. She cut soaked apricots into the little pot of oats
and made fruit porridge for herself, and tea with the bag
in the cup. When Treadway was in the bush for months
at a time, and Wayne at school, she got into a routine of
being alone. But this day she grew lonely, so when Treadway came in the door in the afternoon she was glad to see
him. But he was not glad. He did not light up at all when
she hugged him. His body felt like one of the cold logs out
by the fence. He told her what had happened: the blood,
the surgeon, the loss of their secret. But there was a new
part he did not mention.

"Thomasina Baikie," he said, "told Wayne everything. And told me more besides."

"Where is he?" Jacinta felt elation, even while she could see her husband's face might not recover from its careworn collapse. The life that had drained out of Treadway began filling her face. He saw it. Why was life coming into her when he felt this way?

"Goose Bay." He opened the fridge, took out his bread, made himself a Maple Leaf bologna sandwich with mustard, and put the kettle on. He sat at the kitchen table, ate the sandwich, and waited for his kettle to boil.

"Is he by himself?"

Treadway shrugged, his mouth full. "There were nurses."

Jacinta had slung her coat on Treadway's La-Z-Boy when she came in, and now she put it on. The keys were beside his saucer, and she grabbed them and shoved on the easiest shoes and went out with no scarf, which she never did. Even in summer Jacinta wore a silk scarf or a thin cotton one around her collarbones, but not this day.

When she reached the hospital, she went straight to Wayne's room and saw that he was so pale his freckles looked as if they were floating in cream. She hugged him and he clung to her, and it was the first time since he was a baby that she could allow love unimpeded to escape her heart and flow to her child. It buzzed like the power line on her old back lane in St. John's. She had not freely loved the girl part of Wayne, as the girl had not been acknowledged to exist. Jacinta kissed her child on the forehead. She rubbed her own tears into her face and they stung the nicks that the wind had chafed, and she brought her child home.

But the falling away had started. When the child separates from its parents to explore the new world, the parents can do one of two things. They can fight it with rules, pleading, tears, and anger: "Why do you want to go out in minus-fifteen-degree temperatures in that T-shirt when you could wear the wool I've warmed for you over the woodstove? It's so cosy." Or they can admit the new world exists, dangerous and irresistible. Cosy is not what awakening youth wants. Safety is not what it wants. The material world is not what it wants either.

"Why does Dad watch the stock market report every night?" Wayne asked his mother. She was peeling carrots and he had been writing a poem about Remembrance Day for the annual school contest. "You know what his slippers remind me of?"

The blade on the carrot peeler was loose and it rattled. Jacinta kept the tap running to rinse fluffs of peel off her knuckles.

"You know the holes in them? Dad's brown socks poke out right where a mole's nose would be. I pretend his slippers are moles."

Treadway ordered a supply of Torngat Heavy-Spun work socks from the Hudson's Bay Company every spring and fall. "You don't mind if you lose one," he said, "when they're all the same. I can never understand why people have socks in a dozen colours and sizes. People like to make work for themselves, I guess."

"Why does he, Mom?"

"What?"

"Watch the stock market every night."

"Your dad bought some gold and he likes to track it."

"Dad bought gold?"

"A little bit. Enough to get by if there's some sort of crisis in the world. Not for long. Just enough to pass through the crisis. So he likes to keep up on how the price fluctuates, and he likes knowing what's going on with prices of other things while he's at it. He's just interested in it. People can be interested in things."

But the moles, Wayne thought, were blind. He suspected they were dead. What was the good of having feet if all they did was act like dead moles?

"How come he does the same thing every night? He falls asleep in his chair and he snores. Doesn't he find it boring?"

"That's precisely why" — Jacinta flung a carrot in the sink — "your father goes on his trapline for six months of the year. He can't stand it in here either. Your father is more interesting than you think. I suppose you wonder the same thing about me."

Wayne looked at her guiltily. He had wanted to ask the night before, as Jacinta read Luke and then John through the stock market report, "Are you hoping God wrote something new in there since last night?" He had begun to wonder, as autumn darkness closed in, why both parents were satisfied with such quietness. With no brothers or sisters in the house, there was no one to share his restlessness.

"Anyway — oh, I hate this peeler." She threw it down. "Where's my little white knife? This makes the carrots fluffy. I hate fluffy carrots."

She searched in a drawer with her back to him. "You might think I'm boring as hell too, but that's what happens to people who get married and have a kid and buy carrot peelers and Mr. Clean and all the rest of it, and make sure everything goes okay for their kids at school, and go to the hospital in Goose Bay five times a week . . ." She grew louder. Medical follow-up had meant the two of them had been back and forth to see the doctors many times. Wayne got his stitches out and started a new regimen of hormones. They had to meet Dr. Lioukras and go over signs and symptoms: what to do if the abdominal swelling recurred.

"Women start out," Jacinta said, "with all kinds of passion. Every time I saw an ordinary old starling I'd look at the gold line around every one of its little feathers. Gold. I saw everything like that. Sharp. Edges of leaves. Sounds. Rain. I loved going downtown with all the streetlights, looking at shoes in shop windows. Portholes all lit up on a big boat from England. But you know what kills me? I'm too tired to do that now, even if I could. Even if St. John's Harbour was at the end of that fence where your father left his tent bag. Women don't have tent bags, Wayne. Not Labrador women. Men have the tents. I wouldn't mind my own tent. Mine would be different from your father's, I can tell you that."

"What would yours be like?"

Wayne was stuck on verse two of his Remembrance Day poem but didn't dare ask her for help. His mother hated the way the school made assignments out of every holiday: Remembrance Day, Christmas, St. Valentine's Day, even St. Patrick's. "It's the same every year," she complained. "I think they do it because no one in that place has a scrap of imagination. If it weren't for pumpkins and reindeer and bloody leprechauns all over the walls, they wouldn't have a clue what to be doing with the youngsters."

Remembrance Day nearly drove her insane: every child in the school trying to imagine what it was like in the trenches and asking their mothers what rhymes with poppy. Maybe, Wayne thought, that was what the matter was with her now.

"My tent? Well . . . it'd have a string of Chinese lanterns, for one thing, and I'd find a way to have music."

Wayne knew it didn't matter what rhymed with poppy. He knew the difference between real feeling and doggerel you wrote for homework. Why did there even have to be words? He sank more teeth-marks into his pencil and tasted the paint and wood. Names of things got in the way. What was a poppy if you didn't call it a poppy? If you just watched one and refused to give it a name. Thomasina was a good one for naming things in a way that still let you ask questions. That night in hospital, waiting for Treadway, she had tucked the cool sheet around Wayne's neck and talked about his operation. Thomasina had not called it an operation, or a surgery.

"Those waters rushed, didn't they." Her hand had cooled his forehead. "They rushed over the landwash. Our bodies are made mostly of water, Annabel."

"You're calling me that again."

"I am. Is it all right?"

"I liked it when I was little. I thought it was Amble." He remembered it had felt like a name you would call a newborn puppy or a child you loved. "But it wasn't Amble. It was your little girl. Annabel. I like that too."

"Your mother and I were good friends. There were things we both lost. Things that have to do with you and why you're here. But you have to wait for the doctor. And for your father. It's not my place."

"What did you call the rushing thing?" He had been half asleep. Treadway's voice was in the hall. Thomasina went out to him. "Rushing . . . what was it?" The hall grew louder. "Dad?" Was Treadway shouting? Treadway never shouted. Wayne had not discerned the words. Rushing. Landwash. Annabel. Lost. He slept.

Dr. Lioukras had done his best. He believed you could talk to any child over the age of eleven as if the fully realized person inside had begun to open, and he had tried to use words that were true. The limitations of medical language were no greater, in his mind, than those of language as a whole. Science, medicine, mythology, and even poetry shared a kind of grandeur, as far as he saw. He had two copies of Donald J. Borror's *Dictionary of Word Roots and Combining Forms*, which broke biological terms into their earliest known fragments, and he read it just for fun. But even Donald J. Borror was having a hard time helping him now.

"This is one time," he told Wayne, who sat propped up in bed balancing green Jell-O cubes on a knife and letting them melt on his tongue, "when medical science has given itself over entirely to mythical names. A true hermaphrodite" — he said it as if the state were an attainment — "is more rare than all the other forms. It means you have everything boys have, and girls too. An almost complete presence of each."

"Only my balls aren't the same as the other boys'. I saw in gym."

"Right. You have only one testicle. And your penis. If you weren't taking your pills . . ."

"My pills are about that?"

"Yes. Your penis wouldn't be as large as it is now."

"What would it be like?"

"Hermaphroditism is so rare. It's not certain. You would become more like a girl than you are now. You're already a girl inside."

"Inside?" How could he be a girl inside? What did that mean? He pictured girls from his class lying inside his body, hiding. What girl was inside him? He pictured Wally Michelin, smaller than her real self, lying quietly in the red world inside him, hiding.

"You've been menstruating. That's what the fluid was inside you. Menstrual blood that couldn't escape."

"Has it escaped now?"

"We let it out."

"But it happens again, right?"

"In girls, yes. Every month. But in your case we don't know how often."

"Can it get out now? New stuff?"

"We're hoping" — Dr. Lioukras had eyes you could see uneasiness in right away — "that with new medication, it will stop."

"But if it didn't stop, would it get trapped again?"

"You would have to come in again, like this time, if it happened. You would need another gynecological intervention."

So it was with names — suture, true hermaphrodite, menstrual blood, gynecological intervention — that the doctor had done his best to acquaint Wayne with the story of his male body and the female body inside it. Dr. Lioukras was not happy with the talk. He had wanted it to be about life, and possibility, not blood and stitching and cutting. He had to remind himself that the work of a surgeon is poetry of a kind, in which blood is the meaning and flesh is the text. Without his work, he told himself, many people would be buried early among the stones on Crow Hill, over the slow, cold inlet, and would feel no more joy, or life, or love.

Now, after the operation, Wayne felt the power of names in a new way. His father ate his evening toast, sometimes with a kipper. Jacinta crocheted. They did not look outside at the night. Wayne tried to remember a time before he knew the word for *sky*. You explained away the mystery of the night, he thought, by naming its parts: darkness, Little Dipper, silver birch.

His mother did not find her little white knife. Wayne wished he could find it for her. He was glad after supper when he saw her open her tin of crochet hooks. The tin was oval, and decorated with a woman in a white robe.

"How have you forgiven me?" She broke a piece of new green wool for the edge of a hat.

"For what?" Wayne liked watching her make something. Treadway was pouring a bucket of cement down three weasel holes he had found in the root cellar.

"Keeping the secret."

Though Dr. Lioukras had told Wayne the name of his condition, the family had not discussed it. They had come home and resumed their old life, as if everything was ordinary. "You let me order my bathing suit," Wayne said.

"The suit" — Jacinta laid her hook on the hat — "was such a small thing. That was nothing compared to not telling you."

"You gave me the Niblets box to hide the suit in. And now the suit's getting too small. Dad's the one who didn't say anything. The dog . . ." Wayne had never been able to love the dog Treadway brought home the day he dismantled the Ponte Vecchio. He wanted to love the dog but he couldn't, and he blamed his father. "The dog deserved love."

"I know. Love gets blocked if you dam it. Your father builds dams in his sleep. He doesn't know he's doing it." Wayne had a dog he could not love though he wanted to love it, and Treadway had a son he could not love though he wanted a son and he wanted to love that son. Father and son suffered from backed up, frozen love, and this ate Jacinta's heart.

"I'm going," Treadway had finally announced, "to give that dog to Roland Shiwack before I go trapping. Since no one here feeds it or gives it water besides myself. Roland offered me seventy-five dollars for it. You can use that while I'm gone."

Working the hat edge, Jacinta said, "If I'd told you all the times I knew you were my daughter . . ."

"Tell me now," Wayne said with such eagerness she lost her stitch count. It had not occurred to her that Wayne would want to hear about those times, as if they were beautiful stories. It had never entered her mind that the countless lost moments could be recovered by speaking about them.

"Tell me about when I was a baby."

"I don't know if I can remember individual times."

"Can you remember any? Even one?"

"Well, I used to rock you in my arms and you had a green blanket and you looked like a little baby girl for sure."

"I did?"

"And I sang you lullabies with the word *girl* in them."

"Like what?"

"I can't remember them, Wayne. Mothers forget things. Everybody expects them to remember everything. I guess I sang "Dance to Your Daddy." That was one my dad knew."

"Sing it."

"Well, it goes, 'Dance to your daddy, my little laddie, dance to your daddy, hear your mammy sing.' If you're singing it to a baby boy. And if you're singing it to a baby girl you sing, 'Dance to your daddy, my little lassie.' And the rest is the same."

"Did you sing *lassie*?"

"I couldn't sing *laddie*. That was the thing. You and I were alone and no one heard. I felt if I didn't sing to the part of you that was a baby girl she would feel so lonely she might get sick and die."

"Are there any more verses?"

"Well the rest is, 'You shall have a fishy on a little dishy. You shall have a kipper when the boat comes in.' First it's a kipper, then it's other kinds of fish, and you keep singing it until you run out of kinds of fish or the baby girl is asleep."

"What other kinds of fish?"

"You shall have a bloater. Then a mackerel. There were all kinds of fish, Wayne. I sang all kinds of fish you can't get here. Fish they had in England, where the song came from. Fish I heard from my dad."

"What other times was I almost a girl?"

Treadway came in then and said, "That should fix him." He meant the weasel. Wayne was shiny-eyed, waiting for his mother's next revelation, but he didn't get it that night. Memories of when Wayne was a girl became a secret conversation held while Treadway prepared for his winter on the trapline.

"Your feet were slender," Jacinta said as Treadway packed his World Famous bags and his caribou pouch in the yard.

"Are they still?" Wayne peeled his socks off.

"Certain parts of you were so feminine I used to think people were going to stop me on the road and tell me they knew you were a girl."

"Who?"

"I don't know, Wayne. Kate Davis for one, I guess. What mother can remember everything?"

"What parts, then?"

"What?"

"Parts. You said parts with an S on it. Other parts of me that were like a girl."

"Before you started taking all the pills."

"Then I wasn't like a girl any more?"

"Not as much."

"But before then, what parts?"

"Your face. Your whole face. I don't know why the whole town couldn't see what I could."

"Because you were my mother and they weren't."

"I guess."

"And they weren't looking."

"Maybe."

"My clothes were boy's. And everyone called me Wayne, except for one person."

"Thomasina was the only one."

"Annabel." It was the first time Wayne had said the name out loud to anyone but Thomasina. "Mom?"

"What?"

"Are they going to let Thomasina come back and teach us?"

"I don't know if she wants to come back, Wayne."

"How long did Miss Huskins suspend her for?"

"Miss Huskins didn't suspend her, Wayne. The Labrador East School Board did."

"How long for?"

"A month."

"That'll be over soon."

"But sometimes when there's a break, a change in the way things are, even for a little while, it's really a chasm."

"Like the Gulch?"

"Yes. The change is only for a month, or even a week or a day, but it breaks something. It breaks the pattern and things aren't the same."

"I love Thomasina."

"I know you do, Wayne."

"I hope she comes back."

"I know."

"Mom — could you call me my girl name?"

"Annabel?"

"Yeah."

"I don't know."

"Mom?"

"I can't — what?"

"Do you remember anything else?"

"Your dad might hear."

"Dad's taking his Ski-Doo apart. We've got lots of time."

"I thought he was packing."

"I heard him laying out his wrenches." Wayne's ear was attuned to the clinking of metal on cement, and to all the sounds Treadway made inside and outside the house.

"When you were in kindergarten you cut a tarantula out of a *National Geographic*. Its legs were as slender as my hair. The teacher said no other boy could do that."

Attuned though his hearing was, there was one thing Wayne did not hear Treadway do, one thing his father had vowed to do before his months on the trapline. It happened while Wayne was in school and Jacinta was buying sugar cubes, which Treadway preferred to loose sugar. Cubes cost more per weight, and it was not like Treadway to prefer a less economical choice. She had asked him, long ago, "Why do you want me to buy cubes?"

"I like cubes," he said. "I like the way they fit together in the box. One cube is exactly the right amount in my tea, every time. You can't spill them. If a rat puts a hole in a bag of sugar, you lose whatever spills out. Humidity will ruin a bag of sugar, but to ruin cubes you'd have to drop them in the river." He had gone on like this, outlining the advantages of sugar cubes, astonishing Jacinta with his seriousness regarding such a small thing.

So Jacinta was buying sugar cubes, and this gave Treadway a chance to look at the phone book, which was difficult for him to do. Treadway could read Voltaire. He could wait eight hours in silence for a lynx and read the tracks of a dozen duck species and know each by name. He could find them in Roger Tory Peterson's guidebook, and had read the journals of James Audubon, but the phone book was a torment to him, as were government documents, tax forms, insurance policies, bank statements, and telephone or hydro bills, all of which Jacinta dealt with. She looked things up for him in the phone book when she was at home, but he wanted to do this thing without anyone knowing.

He phoned the library in Goose Bay first. They told him to phone the A. C. Hunter Library in St. John's, and A. C. Hunter said his best bet was to call Memorial University. By the time he found a woman named Augusta Furey in the office of the dean of music, almost an hour had gone by, and he was worn out as he wrote down the New York address she gave him out of the Albert J. Breton Catalogue of Sheet Music for Soprano, Alto, Tenor, and Bass Voices.

"The price might have changed," she warned him. "This is last year's catalogue. We keep asking them to send us the new one as soon as it comes out. But we can't control everything."

Treadway wrote Albert J. Breton a letter ordering a copy of "Cantique de Jean Racine" by Gabriel Fauré. He phoned the Croydon Harbour post office and got the number of Gerald and Ann Michelin's mailbox.

Over the next week Treadway cleaned and reassembled his Ski-Doo. He filled his sled box and his reading case. He packed his *Collected Works of Robert Frost*.

"Sometimes," Jacinta told Wayne, "you looked at me like you knew."

"But I didn't!"

"I imagined you did. People think all kinds of things when they are alone with a secret. They think what they want to think. Maybe I imagined the whole look."

Treadway wrapped fourteen extra pounds of flour and cornmeal, and he hoped the woods would be lovely, dark and deep.

There was a tiny travel agency on the main road in Goose Bay. Thomasina thought of it as a hidden gate. The agent, Miriam Penashue, had spent all her summers in the bush near the Quebec border and had not finished high school. Miriam had not even finished grade six, and she had no plans of ever going to school again until she found out that if you took the travel agent course at the community college in Goose Bay, the government would pay for you to see six travel destinations. Once she had seen them, Miriam Penashue was no ordinary travel agent. She did not put up posters of Dominican Republic resorts or offer deals to Disney World. Her shop had one handbill on the door; Miriam Penashue had made it herself. It read, COME IN AND TALK TO MIRIAM PENASHUE ABOUT WHERE YOU WANT TO GO.

After the Labrador East School Board sent Thomasina its letter of suspension, something about Miriam Penashue's sign appeared so unpretentious and so promising, she went in. She was carrying a bag from Happy Valley Northmart with six grapefruit in it that she wished were better grapefruit. They would be all right once she had sliced their membranes down to the drupes, but in their trip from California a layer of air had developed between the rinds and the fruit. When you have received a letter that says you have not acted in the best interests of the children you are teaching, it is hard not to feel ashamed. Thomasina felt ashamed and angry at the same time: ashamed because she should have done things differently. She could have been more discreet, more patient, instead of getting all righteous and hauling Wayne to the hospital in a way that attracted the attention of people who had no sympathy. People like Mr. Henry, who had caught wind of the hospital trip and had made a point of inquiring about it at the school office. The principal herself, Victoria Huskins, with her white pants and her intercom.

"There are two reasons I have no choice but to have you disciplined," Victoria Huskins had said. "Taking a child off school property without adherence to a single one of the regulations we have in place. And lesser, but pretty important to me as someone who has to keep a semblance of order here, publicly ridiculing my reprimand of the child who wilfully left poo on the washroom floor. Filth. You should know better, Thomasina Baikie. For the children's sake. People are going to think we don't care about the children. I can't have that at my school."

Shame was what Thomasina felt the day she noticed Miriam Penashue's handbill. It was undeserved shame, but it did its job nevertheless. It dampened her heart, then burnt its edges so she was left with a mess of charcoal and saddened fire. From Miriam Penashue's handbill came a puff of freedom: COME IN AND TALK TO MIRIAM PENASHUE ABOUT WHERE YOU WANT TO GO.

Miriam Penashue was halfway between the ages of Thomasina and her grade seven students. She wore her hair in a bob and kept bubblegum in her mouth and had a coffee mug that said GRENFELL HUSKIES. She hired no one and her office was painted with turquoise paint left over from the fish plant where her boyfriend worked. The thing Thomasina liked about her was that she really did want to talk to you about where you wanted to go, and not where she wanted to send you. It appeared that she did not care whether or not she sold you a ticket to anything.

"Some places," Thomasina said, "you go and you just feel like sighing and sitting down in an armchair like the one you've put right here."

"Watch out for the spring at the back."

"Its lumps are in the right places."

"How are you doing?"

"You've probably heard."

"When a hundred kids are going around with the news, you don't need a story in the *Labradorian*. 'Specially if it's about poo. And what's wrong with taking a kid to hospital? Didn't he have appendicitis? Maybe it would've ruptured if you hadn't brought him in. Maybe you saved his life."

"I should have done it differently. Victoria Huskins is not a well woman."

"None of the parents blame you one little bit. They should go down to that school board and have you reinstated. But they aren't going to. They talk about it but they won't do it. What kind of a trip do you want to take?"

"When I sold my house, I got twenty thousand."

"That's the house the Michelins live in now, right? How come you sold it?"

"I paid my way through teachers' college with four thousand. And I travelled on my own with another four."

"Did you ever regret selling it?"

"I had no intention of selling it at first."

Thomasina had begun, right after the drowning of her husband, Graham Montague, and their daughter Annabel, to clear out everything that might trap sorrow within the walls. For weeks she worked in the yard with a bucket of soapy water and a sponge, washing clamps, wrenches, sockets, and hammers, feeling them carefully with her hands the way her blind husband must have done, but knowing her hands could never interpret their shapes the way his had done. Part of her wanted to keep certain tools: his staple gun, his spirit level, the sixty-yard measuring tape in its leather case. But she had not kept them.

"Just like I had no intention of coming in here today."

Thomasina had gone into her drowned daughter's room and collected the dolls, the lavender sachets, the books. She had smelled Annabel's clothes, then given them to Isabel Palliser for children along the coast. She had not kept the salmon pink cardigan with dog buttons.

"It was a house I couldn't empty. I thought if I got rid of it . . . You'd think a grown woman would know better."

"I wouldn't think that. I think a lot of grown women hide a lot of different kinds of sadness."

Thomasina Baikie found it hard to accept consolation. "I have twelve thousand left and I heard there's a kind of ticket you can get where you can go around the world. You go to Heathrow and you can fly to Portugal and from there you can go where you want."

"But you have to decide your route. You can't backtrack. And you have to complete your trip within twelve months. It sounds to me like you might not want that."

"I don't know what I want."

"You might want to sit in public squares and people-watch for an hour in one place and a month in another. I can tell by the way you're peeling that grapefruit. You want to get lost. Somewhere where they have ordinary life you can join in. Slip right in there and have a bowl of soup in the clothes you have on now. Go hear a concert you read about stapled to a telephone pole. There are lots of places like that in the world."

17

A Real Little Man

"YOU CAN'T TELL ANYONE," Jacinta said.

"Not even Wally Michelin?" Wally stayed to herself. She got the highest marks in the school and went around with her chemistry text against her chest the way she had once carried Fauré's "Cantique."

"Not a soul."

Jacinta was thinking of Wayne's safety. Part of him knew this, but the new-found part, Annabel, wanted to tell someone. Wayne closed his eyes in bed and saw the hidden part of himself in the schoolyard, in a dress with a green sash and shoes of red leather with a little heel like Gwen Matchem's. There were lots of things that changed if you were a girl: not just your heels or the way you put your hair, but things you talked about and the way you looked at the world. Wayne felt this in waves.

By grade eight his sequined bathing suit was far too small; its straps cut his shoulders and the crotch was tight, and the time had passed in which he had enough innocence to order another in a larger size. He longed to wear it, but he left it crumpled in its box under his bed. He missed Wally, and he wondered what would happen if he could tell her they were both girls, at least in part. He wished he could ask Wally to call him Annabel. They could be best friends like Carol Rich and Ashley Chalk, who passed battleships-and-cruisers paper to each other in Mr. Wigglesworth's class and ate hickory sticks on the fire escape. Wally and Annabel.

But Annabel ran away.

Where did she go? She was inside his body but she escaped him. Maybe she gets out through my eyes, he thought, when I open them. Or my ears. He lay in bed and waited. Annabel was close enough to touch; she was himself, yet unattainable.

There was a piece of information about Wayne's night in the hospital that Treadway had not told Jacinta.

When Treadway went on the trapline, his family did not hear from him, nor he from them. Some men made themselves reachable. Before Graham Montague had died, he had always told Thomasina how she could find him if she needed to get a message to him in the woods. Eliza Goudie's husband could radio in and out from his cabin. Even Harold Martin, despite his Innu woman, had come out of the woods in two days the time Joan got third-degree burns on her foot from tipping her canning pot as it came to a boil around her winter's supply of bottled rabbit. Jacinta had never tried to get in touch with Treadway.

"I thought," Dr. Lioukras told her on a follow-up visit, while Wayne was in the hematology lab having two vials of blood drawn from his arm, "you knew."

"No."

"Your husband knew. The woman who was here that night — Wayne's teacher, I believe — she knew."

"Thomasina. She's not Wayne's mother. I'm his mother."

"And it's true I never spoke to you about it."

"I wasn't here. I was at a stupid party getting drunk with my friends."

"I assumed you knew. But I shouldn't have assumed it."

"A normal husband would have told me."

"Perhaps when you go home now, you can discuss it."

"Treadway won't discuss anything with me until spring." Jacinta assessed the Greek doctor. He was a man who could love a woman. Not a closed, cold, unreadable machine. She slumped in the chair. He put a hand on her back and his hand felt warm.

"I know it was drastic."

"No one told Wayne?"

"Not to my knowledge."

"Will I tell him?"

"No."

"I'm so sick of not telling him things."

"I can't stop you. But in my experience — I know my experience is limited — he isn't mature enough to understand."

"How could anyone understand a thing like that? Moses couldn't understand that. I'd like to see you understand it if it happened to you."

"He might not get as big a shock if he were older."

Jacinta did not think Treadway had an Innu woman like Harold Martin did. But she thought he had begun to think like the animals he trapped. He had begun to walk like them, and sleep like them. He had become wild, and there was no way you could send a message to him if you did not know the wild language. So Jacinta was alone with the new piece of information.

What Jacinta spoke about, alone for the winter with Wayne, was not the mystery of his body. Treadway had told her, before he left, he wanted her to begin training Wayne to make and use money wisely. "It's time," he said, "Wayne started learning how to keep body and soul together. For his own good. How much does he make with those cod ears?"

"I'm not sure," Jacinta said, though she knew the exact amount. In the summer before grade eight, Wayne had learned how to make twenty-five dollars a week. He peeled shrimp for Roland Shiwack and he cut out cod tongues at the Croydon Harbour wharf and sold them for fifty cents a dozen door-to-door. While he was at it, he cut out the pretty white, shell-like bone in the cod's head that people called the ear, and soaked these in a pot of water with a few drops of Javex. He sold them to the craft co-op at the new museum in North West River, where they made earrings out of them.

"I'd say he's saving twenty-five dollars a week." Treadway was a good judge of how much work a person did, and how much it was worth. "Let him save half. But let him contribute the other fifty dollars a month to the household."

"You want me to charge him for the electricity he uses listening to his record player?"

"He can start helping pay his own expenses. His books and clothes. He can put a bit on the household bills after Christmas. It's the principle. It won't hurt him one little bit. I might stay out longer this spring. I might do the whole spring hunt up the river. Now he's older he can give you more of a hand."

When Wayne brought home the school bill for his new chemistry book, Jacinta gave him the money but said, "Your father wanted me to ask you to pay for part of it."

"Pay for my books?"

"He said keep half your money and give me the other half for books and clothes and the household."

All his life Wayne had deferred to Treadway's pronouncements, and he did so now. As far as he knew, other boys' fathers gave them more money as they grew older, not less. Brent Shiwack's father bought him an Arctic Cat, and Mark Thevenet's dad was ordering Mark his own Sea-Doo, which cost more than a car. Wayne did not expect Treadway to act like the other fathers, and he didn't protest. There was a restrained economy under Treadway's roof, part self-denial and part moral exercise, and Wayne had been trained into it. There were things he wanted, but a Sea-Doo was not one of them.

"Do you need more money, Mom? The co-op is always after me for more cod ears."

"Your father just wants you to be self-sufficient. It's his way of —"

"It's okay, Mom. I can get more money. Roland Shiwack wants me to work more hours. He doesn't like giving work to Brent. I could make eighty-five a week easy right now."

"You don't have to make that much. Your school work —"

"I'm fine, Mom. My school work is fine."

Wayne did extra work for Roland and his feet began to peel again, as they had done the summer before grade seven. He told Roland, who said it was because of the shrimp.

"That's why I can't do it myself. That and the fact it takes too long and I have a million other things to do. There's a substance in there that causes my hands to peel red raw. Funny it affects your feet. I guess it migrates. Can I have a look?"

Wayne shoved off his sneaker. The skin on his soles had broken into sheets and curled at the edges. He peeled off a sheet of skin.

"That's it. That exact same thing, only on my hands."

"It doesn't hurt."

"My hands sure hurt."

"Well, my feet don't. But I'm glad to know the cause."

Wayne had always associated his peeling feet with the day Thomasina rushed him to hospital. He had thought it had something to do with his swelling abdomen. This time, he had been afraid the whole thing was starting again.

"It's a relief to know what it is. That it'll pass when I get the shrimp done."

"If you want to stop, I'll certainly understand. I can get you to shave the ends of that pile of fenceposts instead."

Jacinta did not tell Wayne that Treadway might stay all spring in the interior. She forced herself to peel potatoes, boil them, then cut and fry them with egg and moose sausage, the way she would have done for the three of them as a family. But when the doctor visits died down and November came, when the clocks turned back and nights grew long, she stayed up later at night. Wayne had to get himself up in the mornings in time for school. At first Jacinta dragged herself out of bed and made a family breakfast. Then she made easier things: toast and jam or peanut butter, and milk; then she let Wayne get his own breakfast. She woke at ten, then eleven, then noon.

She ate store-bought jam, bread, and tea. A boiled egg once in a while. Treadway had cut three months' worth of wood junks into stove lengths. When it was gone, she used the bucksaw and cut a few lengths each day. One day Wayne came home and the stove was out, and after that he sawed enough wood on Saturday mornings to last the week. The household had always run, as did all households in the harbour, on stored supplies gathered in season and used economically over time. Now the house began to run in a fashion that Jacinta's mother would have called hand-to-mouth. Wayne made toast and ate rabbit meat out of the jar. He washed his own shirts, pants, gym clothes, and underwear in the little machine on wheels, and he watched his mother become as unreachable as his father had been. One day he found her lying on the couch with something pink all over her face.

"What is that stuff?"

"Mashed strawberries. Out of the freezer."

"Why is it on your face?"

"It softens your skin."

There were more strawberries on the kitchen table. Later in the evening he watched as his mother poured Carnation milk on them and ate them. She did not watch television but sat in the chair in front of the set and cro-cheted cotton dishcloths: green and white, or blue and white. She did this night after night as Wayne conjugated *avoir* and deciphered his slide rule and worried about her. He worried that it was his fault his father went on the trapline earlier than other dads and came home later. He worried that Jacinta was sad because no matter what he did, he would never be a normal son. A son with two testicles, not one. A son whose father did not have to sell his dog to a man he didn't like.

"Crochet," Jacinta announced, "is like drawing. You have one line, and you can make it go anywhere. It doesn't have to be a stupid dishcloth."

"You said those dishcloths work better than J-Cloths."

"I don't need a hundred of them. If you know the basic stitch and a few variations, you can crochet any shape you want. You can crochet a rose, if you have a mind. That wild dog rose by the kitchen door? You can crochet the whole bush if you feel like it. All you have to do is make a chain of three, close it, and go around the ring and make a gathered petal in each stitch, using rows of half-double crochet." There was yarn all over the house: rose, mustard, green.

"Can you crochet a cup and saucer?"

She studied a cup on the table. "I could try." When Wayne laid his bookbag on the table the next day, she had done it.

"Can you crochet a horse's head?"

"If I can figure out how to draw one."

That school year she lined the shelves, the TV, windowsills, and armoire with replicas of razor-clam and mussel shells, a conch, a trout, a smelt, a salmon, seven sea urchins, three cups and saucers, and twenty-eight starfish. She loved starfish.

Jacinta used up her Briggs and Little wool, then went on to linen yarn and a kind of yarn made with silk and seaweed that she had been saving for booties for the next baby born in the cove. In Treadway's shed she found his twine and made pots out of it. They stood on their own. She filled them with stones and pieces of juniper, and she crocheted tiny birds and perched them in the juniper. She crocheted a roll of snare wire into a bowl like bowls in the catalogue, into which people in big country homes put their brown eggs, and she bought eggs from Esther Shiwack to put in it. She began to crochet abstractions. A green and brown wool spiral fortified with snare wire. A blue river strung with beads. Extreme close-ups of leaves.

"I let the yarn talk to me," she told Eliza Goudie on the phone. "I can't explain all the shapes." She stayed up all night and made more, and the shapes were not recognizable.

Had Jacinta been in a city this might have been all right. Someone might have understood what she was making. They might have bought one from her and hung it in the lobby of the Bank of Montreal. Wayne would think this later in his life. But at fourteen, fifteen, and sixteen he wished his mother would go back to starfish. His father lived outside the house longer than he lived in it. He brought home wood, caribou, salmon and smelt, and money from his furs. Before he left for the trapline or his cabin on Bear Island, he drove Wayne to Goose Bay for his medical check-ups.

They stopped on the way for burgers and root beer at the A&W in Goose Bay, and agreed that a burger was no good without bacon. Treadway never asked how Jacinta fared in the months he was away. They discussed the beaver house at Thevenet's Bend, thirty miles in; whether the beavers had vacated it or were in there, with steam coming out of the hole. Treadway gave Wayne beaver teeth when he could get them. The co-op paid two dollars a set, for necklaces. They discussed money, and Treadway made sure Wayne remembered how to find the key to his private box in case the family should need the gold while he was gone, or in case Wayne had to consult his checklist of medications, which Treadway kept under his will, which was under the gold.

"You can't run out," he warned, "and you can't let it slide."

"Fine, Dad."

"And Wayne, don't worry about how much the medication costs."

"I wasn't worried, Dad." It had not occurred to Wayne that his parents had to pay for his drugs.

"You'll have time enough to worry about that when you're older."

"How much do they cost?"

"Hundreds of dollars, son. But MCP covers ninety percent of it until you're eighteen. Then they cover forty percent until you're twenty-one, unless you're in university. Then they keep covering the forty percent until you're twenty-five."

"Hundreds of dollars?"

"They're pretty strong drugs, I guess, son. And I guess they don't have them in great supply for a whole lot of people."

Wayne took his pills but was always on the lookout for symptoms: swelling abdomen, abdominal pain of any kind, the appearance of breast tissue. Any change in facial or pubic hair. If any of these things happened he was to get Jacinta to drive him to Goose Bay and see Dr. Lioukras right away. Almost every day Wayne imagined such changes had occurred. It was hard to know if he had a real or an imagined ache. He was so relieved that his peeling feet came from the shrimp and not from some new health crisis, he was able to gulp more air.

As his father grew more distant, Wayne cleaned fish and cut staves for Roland and for other men in the cove whose sons had got part-time service jobs or work with the military base in Goose Bay and did not want to do the traditional work of Labrador sons. He sold cod ears, earring bones, and beaver teeth.

Now and then tourists came from Maine or Newfoundland, and Wayne took them hiking or snowshoeing on trails along Beaver River, or he helped them hook half a dozen trout using flies Treadway had left neatly labelled on a strip of sheep's wool nailed to the shed wall.

"Wayne is a great help to you, isn't he?" Eliza Goudie asked Jacinta. "Never stops thinking of ways to add to the household. Getting to be a real little man."

18

Prom Night

AT SEVENTEEN WAYNE TOOK DOWN the wallpaper border in his bedroom and persuaded his mother to let him buy a gallon of maroon paint. He spent a lot of time alone in there fooling around on a mandolin he had bought from a guy named James Welland, who had hoped to take it in his kayak on a trip he was doing for *National Geographic* up the old Mina Hubbard route. Outdoors journalists were forever trying to follow in the footsteps of Hubbard and George Elson, and they all had to get rid of half their gear as soon as they realized what Labrador was really about.

"You can paint three walls," Jacinta told him. "Leave the other one white."

"Why three? What's so big a deal about the fourth wall?"

"It's too dark. And will you put that Spirograph away if you're not using it?"

"Fine."

"There's another wheel in the vacuum cleaner hose. Just clear them up off of your closet carpet. As a matter of fact there's a whole pile of stuff on the floor of that closet that you never look at anymore. All your drawings, for one thing."

"Don't go in my room with the vacuum cleaner."

"Two saucers of cheese and pickles under the bed. The cheese had fur on it. If I don't go in there . . ."

"Fine."

"Do you want that Spirograph? You used to love it."

He had loved its purple and green pens and flat wheels with holes and cogs for drawing circles that whorled and intersected in an infinite number of symmetrical designs.

"The ink dried up a long time ago, Mom."

He had bought his mandolin for seventy-five dollars, and as soon as he started playing it he threw away the old Elizaveta Kirilovna swimsuit. You could do the same thing with mandolin notes without making a fool of yourself. He plucked notes and left a space around each one. He made patterns with the notes. A note was like a synchronized swimmer: elegant on its own, part of an exquisite language when it floated with the others. No one would know, as you tried out sounds, that you had a girl's body inside you. No one would think there was anything weird about playing a musical instrument. Brent

Shiwack and Mark Thevenet practised guitar in the Shi-wacks' shed every Friday night. They knew how to play everything on side one of Jackson Browne's *Running on Empty* and were working on side two. A mandolin was unusual for Croydon Harbour, but its first owner, James Welland, had been in the paper, and people thought he was a normal guy. Donna Palliser's sister had made him poppyseed muffins for his trip.

Wayne could play the mandolin alone in his room and no one would suspect the things that were going on in his mind. No one would know he lay awake imagining what would happen to his body if he stopped taking the pills: bones of his hands rearranged, longer, thinner; his shoulders slight instead of looking like the framework of a big kite. His waist longer and his breasts the shape they had wanted to begin a few years earlier, before the extra hormones. His Adam's apple no longer riding an elevator up and down his neck whenever he swallowed. His feet inside Gwen Matchem's Cuban heels and no one saying anything if he wanted to dance.

Wayne danced in his room in the light from one street lamp. If he looked at his shadow in the pool of gold the street lamp spilled on his wall, and if he turned his body certain ways, it could be the body of a woman.

No one in Croydon Harbour knew he had his mother's eyeliner on, or that if he turned his face a certain way his cheekbones looked almost like the cheekbones of Wally Michelin, still easily the most beautiful girl in the school, in Wayne's mind. At seventeen he could have fallen in love with her easily. It didn't matter if you were a girl or a boy. You could fall in love with her either way.

But Wally had not come back to him. She had not told him when the new edition of Gabriel Fauré came for her at the post office, and she did not appear to miss Wayne, though he missed her so terribly that when he saw her now, his chest felt like his mother's pincushion with a darning needle lodged in it.

Wally Michelin had floated into her own new universe. There was a tall boy, Tim McPhail, whose father had become the new minister at St. Mark's Anglican Church when the old reverend, Julian Taft, had gone back to Kent to grow champion roses. Wally was the only one, had always been the only one, with whom Wayne wanted to spend time. Wally stood in front of Tim McPhail's locker, a copy of D. H. Lawrence's *The Rainbow* in her hand. As far as Wayne could tell, Tim McPhail wouldn't know it from *The Password to Larkspur Lane* by Carolyn Keene, which Wayne had seen Gracie Watts reading on the bus. Wayne had read *The Rainbow*. He had read *Sons and Lovers*. Wally Michelin reminded him of Gudrun. She wore the same bright stockings; Wayne was sure Tim McPhail had no idea. Tim got hundreds in physics and he played chess. He was almost good enough for Wally Michelin if Wayne compared him with everyone else, but he was far less than she deserved. He might not hang around the smoking entrance with Brent Shiwack plotting to get his skin on grad night, but he thought about it all the same. Wayne heard boys talking. Grad night, for the boys of Croydon Harbour, was about beer, hot knives, parking, figuring out how to unhook bra straps, and getting girls drunk enough to have sex. He heard girls talking too. For the girls it was about falling in love, and before that, finding the right dress.

Gracie Watts asked Wayne to the graduation dance.

Every second day she asked him if he promised he would have a boutonniere to match her gown. He was sick of hearing about it and wished he had told her he was not going. But you had to go. This year Donna Palliser had announced they had to call it a prom, like in the States.

The dresses came to the Hudson's Bay store as soon as Christmas was over. Old Eunice White, who had a purple birthmark covering half her face, hung them from circular racks in the back section used to store seasonal merchandise. Every year there was something new in dresses. One year it was greens: all the dresses were shades of lime, chartreuse, forest, mint, and emerald. Another year it had been sequins sewn under layers of net so they glimmered like scales on dream fish or glitter on dragonfly wings. In '84 the dresses had been cut on the bias, with asymmetrical hemlines that had made Wayne uneasy. This year he watched, in a way that other boys did not, to see what Eunice would wheel into the back section once she had cleared out the last of the Christmas garlands and New Year's Eve streamers.

He knew what he would wear. Each grade twelve boy in Croydon Harbour rented a tux from sliding flats in Eunice's back section. The only thing that changed each year for boys was the colour of the cummerbund; they had been purple the year before, a great disappointment to Brent Shiwack's older brother and all his friends. A real pansy colour. This year they were scarlet, and you could get them in matte linen with a black stripe, which everyone wanted, or in satin. If you had a whole dress the colour and feel of the satin cummerbunds, Wayne thought, then you would have a dress worth talking about.

He tried not to let Eunice see him examining the dresses on the racks, one by one, to find the dress he would choose for himself in a perfect world. If Eunice came near him with her long pole that had a nail on it, to snag a World Famous bag or a reflective vest off the top shelf, he pretended he was looking at the fly-tying gear. One minute he was looking at gauze and lace, the next at feathers and glass beads. You could hook some of the fly-tying stuff onto the dresses and it would look pretty good.

There had been a revolution somewhere in middle America, where the heart of prom-land lay waiting for its prince, and the dresses this year were short. The girls felt cheated.

"Actually," Donna Palliser announced in the school-yard, "short dresses were in two years ago. It has taken them this long to reach Labrador. My mother has ordered me the latest: a lemon gown from California. It's the exact colour of lemons in the lemon grove south of San Francisco where the designer has her summer home. It sweeps the floor. You have to wear four-inch heels if you don't want to trip over it. Short dresses are actually from 1983."

But Wayne liked the short dresses. Not only were they short, one in particular was restrained in its line, fabric, and colour. It had no gauze and no sequins or beads. The dress was brown and had a green satin ribbon in the hem, which could be seen only if you turned up the edge and looked. The green was a muted, shimmering green that had brown in it. The dress had a fitted bodice, and it was different too from the other dresses in that it was sleeveless, without caps, bells, or any of the shoulder details that puffed and spoiled the other dresses' shapes. The brown dress with the hidden green hem was elegant. The cloth felt cold, and you could crumple it in your hand and hide it there, the material was so pliant.

"Are you interested in that dress, Wayne?" Eunice said, the third time he visited it. "For your date?"

"I might be."

Eunice shook out the crumples Wayne had lovingly made it suffer. She laid down her pole and hung the dress over her wrist. "It's a nice dress."

"Yeah."

"It has a hint of the twenties about it."

Eunice's birthmark was shaped like Africa, and it

was about the size of Africa on the globe in Mr. Ollerhead's class. Her hair was brown and white and had thin patches.

"Did you ever wear one like that?"

"I'm not that old, Wayne. I was thinking of my mother. My mother would have worn a dress something like this one when she went to dances with my father, before I was born. Only hers wouldn't have had the satin. She wouldn't have had the money. What's this one?" She looked for the tag.

"A hundred and ninety-nine ninety-nine."

"Pretty expensive. Your girlfriend could get this one," she fingered a rose polyester dress with a lace belt, "for only one nineteen. You don't like it, do you?"

"No."

"The truth of the matter is, you get what you pay for. Who are you taking?"

"The person I'm taking isn't really the one I was thinking of. For the dress."

"Ah." Eunice held the elegant dress against her body. "There's someone you wish you were taking."

Wayne was glad there were shadows in the store. He wanted the part of him that was Annabel to try the dress on. He longed to take it home and let her dance in it, just one night.

"Well, don't go breaking the heart of the one who wants to go with you, all for the sake of the one who never will." Eunice looked at him as if her whole life had been about that very tale. "Do you want me to put this away?"

Had Eunice seen him hide the dress the other times he had been in to see it? He had hooked it inside a winter coat on the sale rack.

"So you can tell the girl you're thinking of to come in and look at it?"

"Not really."

"Who are you going with? If you don't mind my asking."

"Gracie Watts."

"Gracie Watts." Eunice held out the dress and stared at it. "I can't see Gracie Watts in this."

Wayne couldn't either. He could see Gracie in the rose-coloured dress with the lace, or the mint green one identical to it.

"The truth of the matter is . . ." Eunice was always saying that. The truth of the matter is, no-name peas are made in the same factory as Aylmer peas. The truth of the matter is, by the time fresh milk makes it up here there's no more than two days left before it turns sour. The truth of the matter is, Quebec blueberries might be twice the size of ours but they don't have half the flavour. Now she finished. "I can't see this dress on anyone in your class. The girl who could wear this dress would have to have what I'd call her own style. Someone who didn't mind not going with the crowd. Someone elegant herself. An artist, one who acts in plays. You'd have to be what they call striking to pull this dress off. On Gracie Watts it would look like she was wearing a mushroom. Not that I don't think Gracie's a nice girl. The truth of the matter is, she's my grand-second-niece. She'd do well in nursing school. Too bad her father is an alcoholic. You know who would look nice in this dress? Wally Michelin. Wally Michelin could carry it off in a heartbeat. But the truth of the matter is, she already has this other one over here on layaway." Eunice opened the cabinet behind her counter and took out an armload of red satin, glimmering in the shadows like the cummerbunds.

Wayne was not prepared for the transformation that took place among the girls on prom night. The girls, of course, had prepared for months, slathering their chests with self-tanning lotion and experimenting with curling irons, rhinestone combs, and baby's breath. There was a dinner of stuffed chicken breast, mashed potatoes, and green beans in the gym, followed by Donna Palliser's valedictorian speech, then the lights went down and Rodney Montague fooled around with his disco equipment for half an hour before blasting Joe Cocker and Jennifer Warnes, singing the song from which Donna Palliser had extracted this year's prom theme: Donna and her prom committee had festooned the gym with banners that read, CLASS OF 85: WHERE EAGLES FLY.

Gracie led him onto the floor. She placed his arms around her where she wanted them and she snaked her own hand inside his jacket and let a chilled lump slip into the pocket that had the TURINA SUPERIOR MENSWEAR MADE IN ROMANIA label on it. He knew it was the flask of brandy she had told him she would bring. He was surprised how papery her dress felt, how rough its stitches were, like seams in one of the meal sacks his father bought for the trapline. Her body pressed the material like the flour: solid, yet her waist was small. His own hands felt big, holding her. Gracie's hand, after it slipped him the flask, slid under his jacket and warmed his kidneys. He felt her against his crotch. Because of her dress, with its layers of material, no one could see how close they were; he felt her heat and became aroused, which puzzled him, because he had not thought about Gracie as having to do with sex. He had come here with her because she had asked him to; everyone came to the dance, and Gracie had asked him unsentimentally in the corridor, her little face composed, in case he said no. Could you become aroused just by touching a girl, even if you felt nothing special towards her? It troubled him, but he was heated and excited just the same, and did not think of moving his body away. He could smell her perfume. The whole gym was thick with a scent like that of the sickly lilies a family had brought the boy next to him the night he had spent in hospital. Gracie moved her other hand on his chest and played with the flowers in his boutonniere. His heart beat under the flowers and she found it and put her hand on it; she knew exactly where to touch him. Her hand on his heart almost made him cry. He had not realized how much his heart had waited for someone to touch it, physically, with a hand as strong as Gracie's. It was as if someone had given her a booklet on how to melt a boy. He had been worried about the night: what to do, how to dance. With Gracie, all he had to do was stand there and move naturally to the music, and she carried the whole problem of how to hold each other and what to talk about.

"It's cry," she said now. She raised her cheek so it grazed his neck.

"Cry?"

"It's where eagles cry. Not fly. No one even notices. The grad committee decided the real words were too sad for the theme, so they changed them. Cry. She plagiarized half the song in her speech."

"She did?"

"The road is long, there are mountains in our way, but we climb steps every day." Blah blah blah. You didn't notice that?" Gracie said this as if being slightly stupid were a lovable trait in Wayne. She touched his jawline and moved her hand across it; he felt the pad of flesh between his testicle and anus tighten and loosen. He remembered she had told him, during spin the bottle in grade seven, how she had been kissing lots of boys since she was four. The peaks at the top of her lips were still sharp, and the scoop between them still had three little freckles, stars behind the mountains.

"You have aftershave on." She took a hungry little

sniff. "Let's go out behind the school and drink the brandy."

Parents and some teachers had volunteered as chaperones, but they weren't in gear yet. They were still talking to each other, eating date squares, and fixing balloons that had come unmoored from their Scotch tape. Some male teachers were dancing with bolder girls who were on the volleyball team or the grad committee and who had been teasing the teachers about this dance for months.

"How did she get her hair like that?" Wayne asked, as Donna Palliser twirled past in the arms of Mr. Ollerhead, who looked flattered and dazed. Donna's hair had new platinum curls, lifted above a sheen of combed hair that followed her head like the pelt of a seal. "How do the curls stay there, and what makes them so fat?"

"It's a hairpiece. She got it done at Details and Designs in Goose Bay. She had to sleep in it last night."

"How?"

"You use two pillows and an empty Javex bottle. You have to make a kind of mould and sleep in it, and you can't move all night."

Wayne looked at Gracie's home-styled curls, pulled on top of her head too, but without the mould, the lacquer, or the Sun-In spray.

"Do you like hers better?"

"It's pretty artificial looking."

"But do you like it?"

Wayne admired it because it was the pinnacle of what

all the girls in the room were trying to achieve, but his admiration held no affection, no desire, no longing. "It looks a bit like something out of a fifties movie."

"She'd love to hear you say that. Which one? Elvis, Gidget, or the Beach Boys . . . what?"

Wally Michelin had entered the gym with Tim McPhail, in her satin gown. Wayne saw now that it was longer than the short dresses, but shorter than the lemon meringue confection of Donna Palliser. Wally's dress came just past her knees, and on its sleeveless shoulder she wore one white rose. Tim McPhail had not ordered his tux from Eunice, Wayne saw that right away. His had thin satin lapels, and his cummerbund matched Wally's rose.

"Oh." Gracie stood deflated, looking at Wayne watching the couple, who appeared to float though they were not yet dancing. Joe Cocker ended and Rodney Montague segued into Kenny Loggins and Stevie Wonder. Gracie danced half-heartedly, then told Wayne she had to go to the washroom. When she came back out, she looked fiercer. She led him out the fire exit, which was propped open with a chair. They stood among thistles. She swigged the brandy and handed it to him. What was Rodney playing now? The bass thumped under the muffled melody and a voice wailed out. Bowie. Wayne sat in the thistles. The air was fresh out here, the stars familiar yet distant.

"What's so interesting about Wally Michelin anyway? She never so much as opens her mouth. Are you going to put your jacket down for me?"

"My jacket?"

"So I can sit too. Why would you want her?"

He took the jacket off and she arranged her dress so it fell inside the jacket's lining and not on the ground. He leaned against the wall. He had not realized how rough bricks are. They snagged his shirt every time he lifted the flask. What he wanted, though he did not say this to Gracie, was to talk to Wally, for ever and ever.

"I don't want her."

"You sure looked like you wanted her. You looked like you wanted to run over there like a little dog and sit in her lap and lick her hand."

"I didn't want that."

"Do you want to slow dance with her?"

Maybe that would be the thing. Not to feel Wally Michelin's body heat the way he'd felt with Gracie. Not that. But if he could have one slow dance with Wally Michelin, it would break the silence. He knew now, from dancing with Gracie, you could say anything you wanted when you were that close. The normal restraint that made you keep things private was gone for the few minutes of the song; that's what music did, with the darkness and the closeness. If he could get that close to Wally Michelin, for one dance: that's what a dance was, he saw. It was to get the two of you in your own world. You could make that world anything you wanted. You could make it as far from here as possible, yet to the rest of the room you would look as if you were still here. They would have no idea where the two of you had gone.

He could hear Black River now, closer than the sound of Bowie or Billy Ocean or Joan Jett and the Blackhearts. Black River flowed behind the school and along the base of the Mealy Mountains. It went miles through birches and black spruce, and stayed small the whole way. He had often seen a leaf float down Black River without breaking the surface tension, and his mind had floated with it until the leaf went out of sight. Now the river's sound was enticing: moving away from here on a journey, small and intimate, never-ending. That's what the dance with Wally Michelin would be like, only shorter, unfortunately. A feeling of mystery and going forward with more than just your body. Underground streams feeding your mind. You'd ask questions and get lost together.

"What are you hoping to get with her? That you couldn't have with me."

"I don't know."

"You must know something or you wouldn't be thinking it. I can feel you thinking it." She undid his top buttons and laid her hand on that place over his heart that calmed everything. It was amazing how her hand knew the spot. She gave him more brandy. He swallowed a mouthful and its heat flowed to where her hand stayed, so he was warmed from inside and out.

He tried to explain. "Remember the last poem we did in English?"

"The one nobody had a clue what it meant?"

"By John Donne." Brent Shiwack had complained that the word *sublunary* wasn't even in the dictionary. But it had been. Wayne had looked it up. "Dull, sublunary lovers' love, whose soul is sense . . ."

"Wayne?"

"Yeah?"

"Those are words, right? A poem."

"Yeah?"

"By some dead guy. Can't you feel my hand?"

"Yeah."

"Can you feel this?" She touched his jaw, his hipbone. She didn't go for the centre of him right away but found places she knew would call to that centre and wake it. He resisted and she said, "I don't want to go all the way, you know. If that's what you're worried about. I'm not stupid."

It was June and there was still snow on the Mealy Mountains. The wind blew over the snow before it came down here, and his shirt was thin. The alcohol had got to him too. This whole thing wasn't what he wanted. The cold, the thistles. His teeth started to chatter.

"I have to pee."

"Here." She took something out of her dress and he was terrified it was a condom, but it was a pack of Sen-Sens. "Don't let Mr. Ollerhead smell your breath. I'm going to use the bathroom too."

Wayne did not have to pee. He noticed Wally

Michelin's date, Tim McPhail, at the canteen buying a Sprite and a Pepsi. He made sure his buttons were fastened and put a Sen-Sen under his tongue before asking Wally Michelin to dance. It wasn't a slow dance; it was Cyndi Lauper singing "Girls Just Wanna Have Fun." It did not create the moment he wanted to create at all, and he felt stupid. He realized Wally knew he was drunk. The music was loud, and instead of saying she would dance with him, Wally stood against the wall and said something he couldn't hear, so he shouted.

"It's okay," he shouted, "if you don't want to dance with me. I just wanted to say hi." She opened her mouth again but there was no way he could hear her, and it reminded him of a terrible summer afternoon the June after she had lost her voice.

Wayne had walked beyond the apple tree blossoming behind Treadway's shed to read *My Darling, My Hamburger* in the long grass. But the apple blossom had lured him back under the tree. He lay with the book on his chest, listening to bees, then to the rustling of beetles in the grass, then the robin who had her nest in the shed's broken window, then the songbirds over the whole village. Once you tuned into a sound it led you to other sounds a place was making. Distant gulls, which usually sounded harsh, were softened that day, a Saturday, just as everything about gulls is softened on a blue, high day. The gull that is raucous and starved on a sleety November day becomes a different bird in the sun: wheeling white and gold, floating in ascending spirals — you can't believe how high — and transparent, sun shining through its wings. Then, under the tree, Wayne had heard another sound: something injured, an animal hurt, or maddened. A hermit thrush rang its high, tumbling bells over the tree-tops, then the harsh sound came again, almost human. Wayne left his book under the tree and carefully, silently walked to where the sound came from. There was a clearing. Wally Michelin stood alone, opening her mouth with the awful sound coming out. The sound dropped as soon as it left her, and fell on the ground. She's singing, Wayne had realized. She's trying to remember Fauré. He had flushed in shame and embarrassment. He backed up, forgetting his book, which was a library book that would get rained on the next day, and he would have to pay the librarian eight dollars to order a new copy. He backed up and hoped Wally Michelin had not seen him. Wally had had her back to him, but with Wally you never knew.

Now here he was, saying something inane to her. Just wanted to say hi? Stupid. He didn't want to say anything remotely like hi. He wanted to ask her if she had seen him in the clearing that day. He wanted to hear her voice again, even if it couldn't sing. He wanted to hear her speak, to him alone, even if *hi* was all they could manage. Maybe *hi* could be the key to their old world. Keys were smaller than the things they opened, and some keys did not look like keys. To lock his shed Treadway had a stone he kept on a string threaded behind a skinny hole in the boards. If you slotted a stick through the hole and pulled down, the stone undid the latch. Where was the stone Wayne could hand to Wally Michelin now? Tim McPhail wound his way through the crowd balancing Wally's Sprite and his own Pepsi, his elbows managing to stick out awkwardly and gallantly at the same time. The crazy thought came to Wayne that he could give Wally Michelin his cummerbund. He unhooked the back, crumpled the material into a smashed satin rose, and slipped it into her hand.

19

Hope Chest

"How," Wayne asked his mother, "can a postcard take five months to get here?"

"A postcard is such a scrap of a thing," Jacinta said. "It's a miracle any arrive at all, especially from across the sea."

The bridge on Thomasina's card from Bucharest was only half a bridge. It started in the middle of a field and ended in mid-air. It was not beautiful, and it could not be completed because there was not enough money, or the engineers had failed to consider that the height would interfere with power lines on the far side, or some combination of these things, along with other factors that made the city such a mix of grandeur and chaos.

Thomasina could see how a person could become addicted to moving all over the earth. You started in a new place and the whole city, in this case Bucharest, was a spiritual opening. The people were beautiful. It did not matter that you had been so lonely in Paris you began talking to cedars in the parks. You were out of Paris now, with its smell of Gitanes and violets, and you were in Bucharest. "I have never seen," she wrote to Wayne, "so many interesting shoes in my life. People rushing, rushing, rushing."

After Paris, with every street corner and balcony curated, Bucharest felt random and wild.

"I like the ugly parts," Thomasina wrote, "the old concrete-block buildings, the noise and the dirt, and half the place dug up for repairs. I like that as well as the main boulevard with its cobblestones and very old, grand row houses."

There had been a stack of books on the sidewalk that she tripped over as she was looking at pieces of sculpture on the lintels.

"I thought it was wonderful," she wrote to Wayne. "A book sale. Of course I realized I could read none of them. Books started at the door and came down over the steps, filled the little yard, tumbled out the gate, and spread themselves along the sidewalk . . . it looked as if someone opened the door in the morning and the books marched themselves out and plopped down comfortably wherever they felt like it. I had started to pick through them when I saw, slouched against the fence, a thin man smoking a cigarette. Not only was he surrounded by books, he was face and eyes into a book. You could not distinguish him from the books. I nearly stood on him. I laughed out loud and he never moved. I imagined him getting up at dusk, going up the steps, and saying, 'Time to come in for the night,' and the books would sleepily find their way back into the house for a nap . . . and burst happily out the door the next morning to do it all over again."

Four months was the length of time Thomasina could stay in a new place and feel the euphoria that comes with exploring streets you have not seen before, hearing a new language, and eating new food. The curiosities of Bucharest would last this long but then other things would take over. She would not write a second postcard when this happened. She would not tell Wayne Bucharest was full of people wearing the same clothes you could buy at the Avalon Mall in St. John's, or that the same fast-food chains were there, with the same seagulls cramming pieces of fried potato down their throats in the parking lots. She would not talk about the overweight people, the poverty, the sun damage to people's skin: everyone with gigantic moles. When Thomasina grew weary of a place, when she had absorbed all the surface beauty there was to drink in, she packed her small suitcase and got on a train to elsewhere. There were times she longed to do something simple with her hands that a person who had a home on this earth would do, even if that person's blind husband and red-haired daughter Annabel had been drowned long ago. Something simple like mixing flour, fat, and ice-cold water in a bowl with a wooden spoon, then rolling it out to make pie dough, and filling the dough with sliced apples.

Wayne wished he could write back to Thomasina. He wished her postcards did not come with no return address, and that they did not take so long to get here. The card from Bucharest was dated in April, and it was September now. What was the good of having someone for a friend, no matter how much they cared about you, if you couldn't reach them? He could not reach any of the people he should have been close to. His father spent more time than ever in the bush. His mother sat for hours at a time in her kitchen, crocheting or doing nothing at all. The one person for whom he would have given up all other friends, Wally Michelin, was farther from him than ever. Her parents had sent her to stay with her cousin in Boston and work in her aunt's shop. Boston in those days was where a lot of people went. There was excitement connected with the place. If you went there you would be in America, but it was the elegant and sedate part of America. So it was a place of new beginnings but it was not like the Wild West. If you went to Boston, the people back home in St. Anthony or Croydon Harbour knew you were serious about your future.

Young people had fallen from Croydon Harbour like leaves from the birches along the inlet, especially the young men, now that there were other opportunities besides trapping and hunting. A lot of boys went to military college in New Brunswick, lured by the shine on the soldiers at the American base in Goose Bay. Tim McPhail, the boy with whom Wally Michelin had gone to the prom, went to St. Francis Xavier to study engineering. His yearbook entry said his first love was physics, but any boy knew you had to have something practical to fall back on, though not hunting or trapping. The old ways of earning a living had been enough for the fathers and grandfathers, who considered them a kind of freedom and did not understand what would make a son want to wear work clothes you had to buy in a Goose Bay department store instead of coats and boots of seal and caribou. Treadway was not the only father who did not understand the new sons of Labrador, but he was the only one who did not lament about the subject with the other men. If he lamented he did so in solitude, on his trapline, or he consulted with the wild animals there. The only real friend Wayne had in Croydon Harbour was Gracie Watts, and he worried about this friendship.

Gracie's father was the kind of alcoholic who gets nasty and red in the face and whose cruelty is matched only by his cowardice and self-loathing when not drunk. Gracie's mother kept their house spotless. It had next to no furniture, because anything with legs or spindles, Geoffrey Watts broke. To look at Gracie's mother you would think her pious and stern. You would think she had decided to approach life as a parsimonious woman, joyless by choice.

She looked religious but she was not so much pious as she was scoured: all joy stripped from her by marriage. Gracie had seen this happen and intended to get out. She had asked Wayne to make her a hope chest and he had made it for her. He often went over to her house after her father had passed out on his daybed in the room beyond the kitchen and her mother had closed the door behind her in the little room she used as a sewing room. Their house was so quiet at these times you would think Mr. and Mrs. Watts were paper outlines, or shadows.

Wayne worried about the hope chest. There were young couples in Croydon Harbour, people his and Gracie's age, who appeared to gravitate together by some tidal pull rather than by desire or by any conscious decision. They went to a few dances together, and before you knew it one of their fathers was clearing space at the back of the family land for a new bungalow. Then before you knew it again, the men of Croydon Harbour were digging a foundation and laying down cement, and the girl was pregnant, and in what felt like an instant the new little family was ensconced in their brand-new bungalow.

Now Gracie sat and circled the order number on a Panasonic sandwich griddle on sale for $16.99 in the Canadian Tire catalogue. "It says here it corrugates the bread and increases its surface area so a sandwich grills in half the normal time."

"I don't want," Wayne said, "to be like Archie Broomfield and Carol Rich." He had been looking at the undersides of moths that had alighted on the window outside, armoured and malevolent. The wings looked delicate but the mechanism that nourished and propelled the wings was ugly.

Wayne had dovetailed the edges of Gracie's hope chest and made its floor of cedar to keep moths away from her pillowcases and a tablecloth her mother had edged in satin stitch. The hope chest was small, and the things in it were small, but he feared they held some sort of power he needed to guard against. He knew Gracie was buying silverware, one place setting at a time, from the Eaton's catalogue, and that the name of the design was Sambonet.

There were times Gracie made him feel desire, like the time she had melted him and made him feel protective of her with one touch of her hand at the prom. The latest pills Dr. Lioukras had given him were cumulative: over time they had increased his muscle mass and succeeded in making him look like any other son of Croydon Harbour. His voice sounded like a young man's voice, and he was stronger than a girl. He and Gracie looked, from the outside, like a couple.

Because Gracie wanted a home more than anything else, she came to his house when he was not working. She took him out for walks and she kissed him in the bushes. She had kissed many boys before, and she believed Wayne's kisses were the kisses of a normal young man. There was nothing to tell her otherwise, but she had no choice but to sense that he was holding back.

"Don't you want to make love to me?"

"Yes." He did. When Gracie got close to him and he smelled her Evening in Paris perfume and felt how soft the skin was inside her wrists, and when she touched him with the hungry way she had, yes. It was when he was alone in his room, thinking about his life and where he wanted it to go, that he knew he did not love Gracie. She did not ignite him, though his physical body responded to the fact that she wanted him. This was not the same as being ignited through your electric and imaginative bodies, but a long time can go by in which two people remain together because of the fierce longing of one of them. A lifetime can go by, and he worried about this.

"I don't want to be like Carol Rich and Archie Broom-field either," Gracie said. "I don't want to get pregnant, for one thing. And I'm going to make my own money. I'm going to take the paramedic course in Goose Bay. I'm going to do something useful. I'm going to drive a hundred miles an hour in an ambulance and carry people on stretchers and give emergency blood transfusions. I'm going to have my own job, my own paycheque, my own bank account."

Was she telling him this so he would not be afraid of having to make enough money for both of them? While his classmates had chosen normal career paths, Wayne had continued to sell cod tongues, some fillets, and pack-ages of Roland Shiwack's shrimp. He sold these, gave tours, and cut wood for women whose husbands were on the trapline and whose sons had gone away to work. He knew this was a haphazard way to make a living. He did not know what else to do. How had his classmates been so certain about what they wanted to do after high school? To him the world seemed big and small at the same time. There was Croydon Harbour, with everything he knew, then there was the world outside Croydon Harbour, about which he knew nothing. How did you get to know anything?

"I didn't know Carol Rich was pregnant."

"Well, she is. She's five months. That's why her father and his brothers have her and Archie's house half built behind the marsh. They have to have it done by the time the baby gets born next January. What did you think they were building it for?"

"I didn't know is all."

"And don't think Carol Rich got pregnant by accident. And don't think for a second that that's what I want. I told you, I'm going to earn my own money, and I'm not going to have a baby until I'm at least twenty-five. That's not for another six years."

But how, he wondered, did she plan to spend those six years? He had noticed she kept the lid of her hope chest open. He could not help thinking it looked like an open mouth, hungry. He responded to her physical touch but it was her mental hunger that frightened him, and he did not know how he was going to escape from it. He felt compassion every time he looked at Gracie, with her fierce little statements about how she would staunch blood and bandage trauma victims in her ambulance. She would have a transmitter that announced urgencies in the night: wounds, heart failure, poisoning. Gracie had told him she would love this. She would love triage, emergency cauterization, administering oxygen. She wanted to be the capable one amid panic or crisis: the one needed, the one who saved. That would be her work and then she would come home, where there would be peace and quiet. This idea of peace and quiet bothered Wayne. In his fear of domestic stasis he was more like his father than he knew.

Now he watched Gracie turn to page seventeen and underline electric carving knife number A00C94. Why did the moths have to be so loathsome? The darkness around their orange bodies pressed against the window. Gracie turned the pages slowly and underlined an iron and a little vacuum cleaner with a canister you could snap in and out.

"You know what I like? That there are no bags in this model. I hate vacuum cleaner bags. You can never find the right one. My mother has been looking for an Electrolux size four bag for fifteen years, and she hasn't found it yet. There's no way I intend to let that happen to me."

20

Willow Ptarmigan

THOMASINA'S POSTCARD FROM LONDON took only two weeks to arrive.

"I guess there comes a point," it said, "when your feet just say they don't care to do it any more. They don't want to do the lonesome trek. I had to go to a Boots chemist shop and buy myself a couple of donuts. You put them in the heel of your shoes. London is my favourite of all the places I've been, Wayne, as a place to live. But very expensive. I can't get over the fact that when you sit on a bench in Kensington Gardens, a man in a uniform comes and asks you for ten pence. You have to pay to sit in the park. It looks like I've got to make a bit more money if I don't want to be like George Orwell, living on tea and bread and margarine. The school board has told me I can substitute at Goose High. I arrive in Goose Bay on September sixteenth, and Nelson Meese is on the lookout for an apartment I can rent for the winter. Did your father get the letter I sent him from Bucharest? When I gave it to the postmistress, she threw it in a container that looked like it came out of the Dark Ages."

It was already September thirtieth. The Labrador telephone book was six by eight inches and less than half an inch thick, including the yellow pages. Wayne decided to phone Nelson Meese Junior. but he should have phoned the other Nelson Meese.

"It's my father," said Nelson Meese Junior. "But I know who you're talking about. He took her over there on Thursday. She's over at Daniel Lavallee's apartments on Michelin Street."

Wayne got in his father's truck. He was supposed to be packing bait and supplies for three members of the House of Assembly to go fishing in Rigolet. They liked locally cured meat and they did not like to run out of alcohol. He needed to go to Roland Shiwack's to buy caribou sausage, but he needed to go to Goose Bay for rum as well. He would visit Thomasina and then go get the rum.

But she was not at her apartment. He stood on the landing of the four-unit building and looked out at the small parking lot, where Kit Kat wrappers and Hostess chip bags blew against the chain-link fence that bordered the shortcut between Goose High and the main road. The three other doors had nameplates but the door to apartment four did not. He knocked on the other doors but no one answered. The building had a dead feeling, and he was disappointed. He went to the liquor store and bought a case of El Dorado for the members of the House of Assembly. It was three o'clock. He decided to go over to the school and wait in the parking lot. At three ten he watched all the high school students pour out the main doors. He felt much older than them though he had been in high school only a year ago. He waited until they had filed into their school buses then he continued to watch the door. But maybe she would come out another door. He stopped idling the truck and he went in. The office was at the head of the corridor, near the wall with the hockey and basketball trophies, and he went in.

"Is Thomasina Baikie teaching here today?"

"Who?" the secretary said. But a man, a young teacher, had seen her.

"She was in yesterday. She's a substitute. I didn't see her today." He was trying to get jammed paper out of the photocopier. The principal's office door was open but no one was inside. Teachers rushed in and out looking for staplers and the new grade eleven map of the world. Had his own high school felt this disorganized? Wayne felt he had walked into a world where people barely noticed each other. They sped around, resentful that they had to be there at all, and could not find the simplest things, like the three-hole punch that was supposed to be fixed to the front desk by a chain.

"Can I use the phone?" Wayne asked the secretary.

"There's a pay phone in the lobby."

"Have you got change for this?"

"The lunch money's gone down to Beaver Foods and I've been asking for Pay Records to set up petty cash for six days now." She handed him the receiver from a fixed telephone. The cord was short but he pulled at it. "What number?"

Wayne gave her Nelson Meese Junior's number and she dialled it, but it kept ringing. When he got back to his truck, someone had broken the window and the case of El Dorado was gone. A hundred and thirty-seven dollars. I should have stopped looking before now, he thought. I should have known in the apartment building that I wasn't going to find her today.

He went on the Rigolet trip with the members of the House of Assembly and almost lost one of them in the marsh. The men liked to think they had gone into the wilderness without Wayne. They liked to ignore everything he told them, so that when they returned to the House of Assembly they could tell their colleagues they had caught the fish by their own ingenuity. This time there was a story in the St. John's *Telegram* about how one of them had had a brush with death. There was no mention that Wayne had saved his life. If the life had been lost, Wayne would certainly have been mentioned. He had built a web of black spruce boughs and flattened himself on it and hauled the member of the House of Assembly to safety, but the

Telegram article implied that the member had called upon the same resources that made him such a wonderful minister of fisheries. Everyone said wilderness outfitting was one of the big new Labrador jobs. A real opportunity for anyone who wanted it. Wayne wasn't so sure.

When he got back to Croydon Harbour, the utility bills lay stacked against the toaster. Among them was a letter from Thomasina, from Bucharest, but it was not for Wayne. The letter was addressed to Treadway.

"You don't want to open it?" Wayne asked his mother. She had not opened the bills either. Wayne opened bills and he dealt with them in the months his father was in the bush. His mother would not look at the letter. She did not want to look at anything these days except *As the World Turns* on channel six, which she had always told him was pathetic.

"Watching daytime television is a kind of death," she had said. "I don't know how anyone can stand it who calls themselves alive." But now she kept watching it, and she said, "Your father can open that letter and read it himself, if ever he decides to come home."

Every night after the six o'clock news there was an ad for Minute Auto Glass that promised same-day service, but Wayne had never heard of anyone getting a truck window fixed at the Goose Bay franchise in less than five days. There was always some factor that made your glass a special order. He had to visit Goose Bay three times before his truck was ready, and on the third time, which they had promised would be the last or he would get the work done for half price, they asked him to wait two more hours. He went across the road to the A&W and sat by the window with his onion rings and Teenburger special, and that was when he saw Thomasina Baikie walking along the main road carrying two ShopRite bags.

In grade eight Wayne had believed Thomasina strong. Now she was smaller. In her late forties when he had last seen her, she had now entered menopause, and the thing that happens to a lot of women had happened to Thomasina. You might as well call her a different person. What happened to women, Wayne wondered, and why did it happen to some but not others? If you did not know Jacinta, for instance, and you looked at a picture of her the day she married Treadway and another one of her now, you would not be able to match the two. If you entered a contest and could win a million dollars by picking out the old and young Jacintas, you could win only through random luck. Thomasina was more recognizable than that, but still there was a shift when Wayne looked at her face. The shift between Who is this stranger? and, Now I see my friend inside this stranger. The direction her hair grows is the same. The temperature of her eyes. But the background has shifted. What, Wayne wondered, did Thomasina see when she looked at him?

There were two Teenburgers in a Teenburger special, and Thomasina accepted Wayne's offer of his second one. He bought her a root beer. They heard Mark Thevenet's sister on her drive-through microphone asking if some-one wanted fries with that.

Wayne saw things in Thomasina's face he had not seen in grade seven. He saw the day blind Graham Montague went out in his white canoe with their red-haired daughter. He saw the silver undersides of new leaves on the aspens overhanging Beaver River.

"Did you get my postcards?"

"They were great. I don't know if I got them all yet. Some took a long time to get here."

He knew it was stupid to call a burger a Teenburger. Anyone could eat it, not just a teenager. But he couldn't help thinking Thomasina should not be eating something called a Teenburger. He wished he had bought something else to give her, like one of the warm apple tarts.

"Did my letter arrive?"

"There's a letter from you for my father."

"Has he read it?"

"He's on his trapline. He's always there now."

"Has anyone read it?"

"It only came the other day. My mother didn't want to open it."

"Did you open it?"

"No."

"Do you think I could have it back?"

The last time Wayne had gone over the road between Goose Bay and Croydon Harbour with Thomasina, she had been driving, and he had thought she had all the answers. It was not so now. His new window was tight and clear. He realized the other windows needed a wash. He put the radio on to cover the silence. Why would anyone want a letter back after they had sent it? The postcards Thomasina had sent him spoke of the bridges and cities she had seen, but hearsay had given him pieces of her personal life, though the pieces were as fragmented as any postcard.

"She went too far," Treadway had told his wife in bed after the school board fired Thomasina. "It's not like she's twenty-one and straight out of college."

"She was only trying to help Wayne."

"If Thomasina Baikie had her way we'd all be driven around the bend. Wayne wouldn't be fit for anything but the fourth floor."

"Ssh. His door is open."

"I'm just saying the woman doesn't know when to stop."

Now, on the truck radio, a voice streamed: a mercurial line. It was a sound that pulled you to itself.

"You don't often hear a voice like that," Thomasina said.

The voice was high but golden. It was hard to do that, Wayne knew. Wally Michelin had told him. You could rise high but lose the body of sound. "Remember Wally Michelin?" he said now.

"Maybe it's a measure of how long I have been away that you can ask me that, Wayne. I don't think of it as remembering her. She has her own chair in my heart, just like you do. Are the two of you still in touch?"

"No."

"Do you know there's a clinic in London, the Harley Street Clinic, where they repair all kinds of voice injuries? Wally Michelin is saving up every cent she can make in her aunt's shop in Boston to go there."

"You heard from her?"

"We've talked on the phone, Wayne, and I've written to her, the same way I've written to you."

Wayne thought of the postcards that had come across the Atlantic Ocean from Thomasina to himself, and other postcards going from Thomasina, in England and Paris and Bucharest, to Wally Michelin in Boston. He saw the two lines across the ocean, like pencil lines, one each leading to Wally Michelin and to himself. He tried to draw a third line in his imagination, a line that connected Wally Michelin and himself, but there was only Boston, and the eastern seaboard, and the Gulf of St. Lawrence stretching past Newfoundland's west coast, then Blanc-Sablon and Pinware and Battle Harbour, and the land between these Labrador settlements and Croydon Harbour: land he saw at this moment, for the first time, as a place of emptiness. And he was in this land now.

The song on his truck radio persisted, and its beauty connected with the stark treeline moving past the windows, the way music becomes a soundtrack when you are moving with it across a landscape.

"The letter, Wayne, I know it seems odd to want it back. The thing is, I wrote it after I had three glasses of wine."

"It's okay."

"And really, though I wrote it to your father, it contained something I wanted to say to you. Now I'm looking at you here, I can see . . . you're older. It's not like I need to talk to your father anymore."

They were approaching a part of the road that looked out on the sandy flats of Hamilton River and a stretch of the Mealy Mountains almost as transparent as the sky, painted with snow. It was the only part of this road that held a feeling of height and perspective, and Wayne stopped the truck so they could look at it.

"I asked him," she said. "I asked your father in the letter to tell you this thing. I wrote that if he didn't tell you I wanted to tell you myself."

"What thing?" He turned off the engine.

"The hospital, that night I took you. What do you remember, Wayne?"

"I don't know."

"Anything at all? The colour of the walls?"

"Green."

"Any other thing?"

"There was a boy in the next bed with a plate of fish in batter. I could smell it."

"Then what?"

"The doctor became afraid. His face. He didn't like

getting my blood on him. He ran to the sink and washed his cuffs. I thought doctors got blood on their clothes all the time. I thought they were used to it. I thought they had a big supply of extra clothes in the cupboard and it didn't matter."

"It doesn't."

"Look over by that birch." Wayne did not like remembering that night in the hospital. A willow ptarmigan had been sitting on a low branch, and now it had descended and walked on the ground. "He's looking for insects. He must have a late hatching of young."

"Isn't it a she?"

"It's the male. They're vegetarian except when they feed the babies, and male willows are the only kind of ptarmigan where the father looks after the young." Treadway had taught him this, along with thousands of other pieces of information on Labrador birds and mammals and fish. He remembered more than his father thought, but something about the knowledge made Wayne feel lonely now.

"What else do you remember, Wayne?"

"The word *hermaphrodite*. One of the doctors saying it. Me thinking, Why is he talking about the Greek myths we learned in your class? Me not knowing what he was talking about until Dr. Lioukras explained it to me. Even after that, not really knowing. Long after."

He meant now. He meant things had not fallen into place even now. He looked at his hand on the steering wheel. His arm. With the last round of hormones it had become more like other young men's arms, but in school his arms had been thin, his body lanky. He had tried to conceal his slightness from his father, who had wanted him to have breadth. Wayne had walked as if covering a smaller boy with his arms, protecting him. He had walked with his arms away from his body, as if they encircled the smaller boy. You don't need to keep doing that, he thought now. You can walk like a man. But he had to keep reminding himself. He was always the smaller boy, the girl-boy, in his mind.

"Do you remember your father came to the hospital, and we had a fight?"

"You argued. In the corridor. Not like arguments between my mother and father. Your voice is a lot lower than my mother's. Dad was meaner than at home. Then you left."

"I did."

"My father sat under the window on a radiator with slits in it and paint that had dried in drips down the side. He didn't talk. You never said goodbye. After being with me the whole time. I never saw you after." Wayne looked for the female willow ptarmigan. She should be somewhere in the undergrowth.

"What I'm going to say might horrify you, Wayne. It might give you terrible dreams. I know it has given me dreams. And I want you to know I'm sorry. I'm sorry it happened, and I'm sorry I've known for years and not told you. I wrote to your father that I wanted him to tell you. I'm going to tell you now because it could happen again and it might be different. You might have to do something."

Ptarmigans stayed in pairs. They roosted on adjacent branches, and when one foraged, the other was always somewhere near. But Wayne could not see the female. Had a hunter killed her?

"When I took you to the hospital, there was menstrual blood. You knew that."

"I figured it out. It doesn't sink in at first. What something like that really is. Even when they tell you, it doesn't sink in. I know the medical terms. I know I'm supposed to take the white pills and the yellow pills and now one big green pill. There's lots I don't know though. It seems like no one knows. Not even the doctors."

"There was menstrual blood, yes. But also, trapped in a Fallopian tube . . . it would never have lived. Wayne, there was a fetus."

The ptarmigan cackled and shouted in short, angry barks, like a man shouting, "Get out!" over and over again to the silent woods.

"It can happen internally, Wayne. When the male and female reproductive organs are adjacent in the same body. It was nothing you thought or did. It has nothing to do with masturbation or ejaculating or anything people might think. The fetus could never have grown because of its location. Dr. Lioukras removed it with the rest of the lining and the fluid and blood. I asked him what the chances were of it happening again, and he said he didn't know. He said it shouldn't have happened. I asked if it did happen again, would the fetus always die? Or could it grow?"

There was the female ptarmigan, in the blackness under low spruce boughs. The male joined her and they walked into the darkness with their jerky little henlike movements, their fat bodies that made them so easy to shoot. But for now the couple was all right. Off they went to feed their young. The white on their bellies had already started to spread against their brown upper bodies. In winter they would be indistinguishable from the snow.

"Dr. Lioukras couldn't answer me, Wayne. He couldn't say yes or no."

Wayne turned the radio on and started the truck. He took Thomasina to his parents' house and gave her the unopened letter. He did not tell his mother he was giving back the letter. He told his mother Thomasina had come to have a look around old haunts, and after he gave her the letter he took her outside and drove her around Croydon Harbour. He slowed as they passed her old house, where Wally Michelin's parents still lived, then he took her down to the beach where he kept his canoe for his outfitting jobs, as if this were an ordinary occasion of showing someone around the place, but he was thinking about that fetus.

"Why," Gracie said that night, "do I always feel like you're not here even when you're sitting right there?"

They were playing cribbage. He knew she had the seven of hearts because a corner was torn off it. He knew she had the queen of spades as well. Her little nephew had scribbled Magic Marker on it. She had borrowed three books from her cousin whose boyfriend had taken the paramedic course she wanted to take, and these were stacked on the windowsill. He had read the titles and marvelled that Gracie really meant to know everything in these books. *Hollinshead's Textbook of Anatomy.* A big, expensive book on medical physiology by someone named Arthur Guyton, who Gracie said had polio and wrote the book after he realized the polio meant he could not become a surgeon. *Basic and Clinical Pharmacology* by Bertram G. Katzung. Wayne looked at the books, and he watched Gracie put down her queen of spades for two points, and he remembered what the willow ptarmigan had shouted. Get out! Get out! He wondered if there was anything in those textbooks that outlined his own physiology, his own anatomy. Would Gracie get to page 217 or page 499 and see a diagram of a person who had female and male reproductive organs in the same body? Would there be a cross-section diagram of a man who had a womb, or a Fallopian tube with a fetus trapped in it? Get out! Get out!

In his own bed he remembered the red world. The way the hospital room, the sheets and utensils and surgeons, had receded under the redness inside his eyelids. He remembered the masked faces, the gelled lens, the word *blood.* Then red, black-red, red-orange. Then dizziness; a red pool, whirling, and he was in it underwater, and something had been in there with him. He remembered that. Something had been in there looking at him, drowning and trying to speak, and he had not known what it was. It dawned on him that his father had known. His father had known all along that the doctors had found a fetus. Where was Treadway Blake now? He had disappeared into the same woods as the ptarmigan. Where was the fetus now? It had had eyes, and the eyes had watched him. He had been in the red world and the fetus and he had looked at each other. Had it wanted him to save it? If he had not lost it, if it had grown into a person, who would that little person be now?

"What I'm going to say might horrify you," Thomasina had said. But it did not horrify him. He found it the saddest thing in the world. She had said it might give him terrible dreams. But he did not dream about it, because he did not sleep.

By morning he had made a decision to take the ptarmigan's advice and get out of Labrador.

It would not be hard to tell Gracie. Gracie had her textbooks. She had her fierce little fist full of cards she was determined to play even if they were marked and torn. His mother would be the hard one. Wayne did not like to leave Jacinta alone. But he would leave her all the same, and his sadness over this was not bottomless like his sadness about the fetus.

Wayne's sadness over Jacinta was the sadness all sons and daughters feel when their ferry starts moving and the parent stands on the dock, waving and growing tiny. A sadness that stings, then melts in a fresh wind.

PART FOUR

21

Caines Grocery

IF THOMASINA HAD SPENT THE WINTER in Croydon Harbour instead of Goose Bay, she could have gone up the hill, climbed Jacinta's three steps, knocked on the door with an apple pie in her hands, and stayed on the step until Jacinta answered the door. Thomasina would have seen, immediately, that things were not right. She would have touched Jacinta about the shoulders, turned her around, stuck the soiled teacups in hot suds, and opened some windows. Thomasina would have done a load of laundry and she would have lifted the tangled sea of yarn that covered the living room floor. She would have helped Jacinta wash her hair and she would have brushed it for her, and she would have held her in her arms and listened.

A lot of things can go out of order in a lonely house over a lonely autumn and the start of winter, without other people in the village knowing, especially if that village prides itself on an independent spirit. Jacinta's neighbours could not see, on her windowsill, a doll the size of a thumb that Jacinta had made from clay out of her root cellar, clay she had mixed with water and a dinner spoon. Nor could they see the housedress and cardigan she wore all day and all night throughout the winter. Bread pudding was a thing Jacinta had eaten as a child. Her mother had kept a kitchen drawer especially for bread crusts. The crusts were what the family had left on their plates. Some had jam on them. You broke the crusts into a pan with milk and butter, nutmeg and an egg, and some sugar, and you baked the pudding. If you were a child and your mother was not looking and you were hungry between meals, you would open the drawer and steal a dried crust that had jam on it. There was never mould, because the drawer was airy, and a dry crust with jam on it tasted crispy and delicious between meals. This was what Jacinta ate now, and there was comfort in eating a childhood treat. You could live for a long time on crusts and tea, and you had a lot of hours to think about your son who had a girl hidden inside him.

Did boys not have moments of softness, moments of more incredible tenderness than girls did? Who was to say which moments were which? Many times during Wayne's childhood a wind had whipped through Jacinta's mouth. The world had breathed through her and told her that her son was also a daughter. Why had she questioned it? This wind had whipped through her mouth when it wished. One morning Wayne had blown through the door in his hockey gear and that wind had blown in with him. It blew in Jacinta's mouth and she saw that Wayne's skin and hair were made of girl material, girl molecules, girl translucence. She gave him Kool-Aid and a hot dog and told him to do his homework. Jacinta had let the blast blow through her and had not responded, but she felt sadder for the lost girl than if the lost girl had been herself.

Had Wayne grown up as a daughter and not as a son, Jacinta would have told him about her own girlhood in St. John's. She'd have confided the little places to go: Snow's, at the east end of Duckworth, crammed with violet pastilles and crinolines from the time Jacinta's own mother was a child. Lar's, all strung with lights at the bottom of Barters Hill, pyramids of candy apples — how did Lar get them to shine so hard? Caines Grocery, where Lee's Snowballs were five cents. All of it changing, Jacinta had known, maybe gone, but she would have told Wayne of it, had he lived the life of Annabel. These were the things Jacinta thought in Croydon Harbour, on her own in the lonesome house with Treadway away on his winter trapline.

And it was true, St. John's was not now the way it had been when Jacinta was a girl. On his first day there Wayne followed the advice of a woman on the ferry and went to the train station on Water Street to look at a bulletin board that had boarding houses and apartments listed on it, but he did not know any of the street names or where they were. He walked to Duckworth Street hoping to find a shop that would have a map, but all he passed were lawyers' offices, and a shop that sold beans and grain in big glass jars, and the courthouse. He passed some little cafés, and it was not until he had got almost all the way to the Newfoundland Hotel and the Battery that he saw Caines Grocery, which was the kind of place where a person might find the map he needed. By this time he was dying to go to the toilet and he would have liked to sit down and rest, because his bag was heavy and he was tired from looking at everything intensely because it was all so new.

He could smell the ocean in a different way than he had smelled it in Labrador. Sewage ran into the harbour here, and there was a lot of it, with gulls circling over the outlet down below Caines Grocery, and you could smell it. There were also smells of seaweed, and fish and chips and vinegar from a van on the street. The houses were much brighter yellows, reds, and greens than in Labrador, and they were tall and narrow and stuck together. The houses looked bright but stern, and the air was so clear the colours shouted out loud at him, and he felt weary from the force of all the corners and the sharp lines of the clapboard.

There was a news rack with the *Evening Telegram* and the *Newfoundland Herald*, some real estate listings, and other brochures, and there were road maps of the entire highway system of Newfoundland and Labrador, but he could not see a map that was only of St. John's. There was a man talking to a woman who had come to the cash register with two boxes of macaroni and cheese and a bag of apples. He was handing her something, a cheque. He did not address her by name.

"I think," he said, "you must have mistakenly written this cheque the last time you came in here, not realizing it would bounce." He said this kindly. He wore a shop apron stained with fingerprints and with blood from the meat counter, but Wayne felt that he was not a clerk. He had white hair and said everything to the woman in a gentle voice. There was no way the woman could argue. She took money out of her purse and was about to put the apples and the macaroni back, but the man told her it was all right. "You can take those," he said, "and settle with us the next time you come in." He let her go out feeling that he believed she had not written his store a bad cheque on purpose. Now the man turned to Wayne, and Wayne felt he could ask him for what he needed.

"I'm looking for a place to stay, and I need a map. And I would also like to use the toilet if you have one."

The toilet was up the narrowest set of stairs Wayne had ever seen. When he came down again, the man, who said he was Mr. Caines, told him the stairs were a hundred years old, and two men were coming the next day to tear every one of them down and put up a new set that did not sag or creak and that would be six inches wider.

"You've just seen a relic that is about to be no more. I'm curious to know how they'll do it." Mr. Caines opened a new box of Caramel Log bars and set them beside the licorice. "I'd like to see how they dismantle that."

He did not have a map for sale but he had his own map of downtown St. John's behind the counter, and he opened it and showed Wayne how King's Bridge Road opened onto a road called Forest Road behind the New-foundland Hotel. "The Forest Road Apartments," he said, "are the best place for someone like you to go. Someone new in town. You'll get a clean apartment and it won't be too expensive, and it's only a twenty-minute walk from downtown . . . Steve!"

A boy who had been putting egg sandwiches in a cooler came over. Mr. Caines marked the route three times with a pencil, trying to be sure Wayne knew how to get there, then he said, "Steve, walk up the rest of the east end of Duckworth Street with this man here and show him how you get to Forest Road." Mr. Caines looked up the phone number of Chesley Outerbridge. He said Chesley Outer-bridge owned the Forest Road Apartments and would help Wayne if he told him Mr. Caines had directed him.

Steve was about fifteen years old and Wayne won-dered why he was not in school. "Forest Road is useless," he told Wayne. "You should go to the Battery, where I live. I know at least four places for rent over there, and you'll get them a lot cheaper and it's way more interest-ing. Katie Twomey's place has no one living in it, and one wall is bare rock where water comes down into a little pool on the floor that you can drink out of."

"Steve," Mr. Caines said, "I've told Wayne about the Forest Road Apartments because lots of people new in town go there. They are good apartment buildings for anyone new." To Wayne he said, "The Battery is all right if you were born into it, or if you're a teacher at the university and you tear down one of the old houses and build your own new house. But half those houses have no water or sewer, and it's a rough place." He wrote down Chesley Outerbridge's phone number and gave it to Wayne and asked Steve to do what he said and show Wayne the way, then come back and finish stocking the cooler.

Wayne bought a couple of pepperoni sticks and a box of chocolate graham squares and thanked Mr. Caines. The boy, Steve, came out with him.

"I can find it by myself."

Wayne wondered if there was something about him that had made Mr. Caines think he could not find Forest Road by himself from a map that had been perfectly clear. He worried that Mr. Caines had thought he looked unintelligent. But when they got to the traffic circle on King's Bridge Road, Wayne was glad of Steve, because the road turned crazy. It went five ways: down King's Bridge Road, Military Road, Gower Street, Ordnance Street, and Fort William Place, leading to the hotel. Forest Road was just beyond this circle to the right, but without Steve, Wayne would not have found it. Steve told him his last name was Keating, and he wasn't in school because it was after three o'clock. He couldn't wait to be out of school for good though, because school was torture, and furthermore it was useless. Steve Keating said these things but Wayne could tell he was a smart kid. He could tell from the way Steve gave him his final directions, and because enthusiasm bubbled out of Steve Keating though he was only going back to Caines Grocery to stock Mr. Caines's cooler with sandwiches and apple flips.

22

Fabric and Notions

THOMASINA HAD WRITTEN Wally Michelin a different kind of postcard from Bucharest than the one she had written to Wayne. By the time she wrote Wally's card she had been in Bucharest for months. She no longer liked the chaos, the noise and dirt, or the old concrete-block buildings, and had decided to book a train and a boat to England.

"I want to go and sit in the park in London," she wrote. "I can stay at the Cale Street Hostel for August and half of September for practically nothing, and when I get sick of the young Australian backpackers I intend to try and get room 118 at the Cadogan Hotel on Sloane Street. It will cost nearly a hundred pounds a night but I want to spend at least one night in the room where Oscar Wilde was arrested, and then I might go to another hotel near Poet's Corner and go visit the monuments to my old friends the Brontë sisters, and Wordsworth. I wish they had a monument to Wordsworth's sister, Dorothy. If no one is looking I might leave a small memorial to her in some old crevice or another. A petal from one of the Queen's roses, or a violet from one of the gypsies in Trafalgar Square. Someone needs to leave something in memory of Dorothy."

Wally Michelin had not loved Tim McPhail, the boy who had taken her to her high school prom. She had loved the French composer Gabriel Fauré, and she had loved her music studies. When she arrived in Boston to work in her aunt's shop after graduation, her aunt had been kind. She gave Wally a room that had belonged to her grown daughter, and she had bought Wally her own record player and told her she could go down to the Berklee College of Music bookstore on Boylston Street if she wanted to buy books or records. It was at that bookstore, on the bulletin board, that Wally read about the Harley Street Voice Clinic in London.

Her aunt Doreen's shop was a fabric and notions store on Brattle Street, and Wally liked it. She liked the precision with which she learned to cut yards of linen and jersey from big rolls, using a yardstick on the long counter. She loved it when her aunt taught her how to pull a single thread from the weave so that the line marking its absence became your guideline for cutting. That seemed like a neat, graceful trick to her. She also liked the wall on which hung a collection of mysterious tools: bobbins for Singer sewing machines, long pins, and pearl-handled awls for punching holes in paper to transfer patterns. She liked Boston itself, so sedate and shadowed. It would have been sombre, she thought, were it not for the students who spilled into its streets in late August, enlivening the red brick and sharp angles of the sun as they swarmed Harvard Square and the surrounding streets with their armloads of textbooks and their young, intense faces that held adventure and studiousness alike.

In her years of high school, Wally Michelin's teachers and the guidance counsellor had tried to show her university calendars and had given her tests that showed she had academic aptitude in all kinds of directions. They had not done this for every student but they had done it for the ones they felt had the intelligence and the money to go places. She had resented this, and wondered why they had singled out her and a few others such as Tim McPhail when students like Wayne Blake were ignored and left to fend for themselves. One of the teachers had asked Wally to write a list of the relatives she had in Boston, as if they were part of the qualifications that gave her special academic ability. She had replied that she had no relatives in Boston, just to shut the teacher up, and it had worked that day: the teacher had walked away disappointed. What the teacher had not known, and what Wally had not told the guidance counsellor or anyone else, was that if she could not study music she was not going to study anything at all. She would work in her aunt's shop and would learn how to tell the difference between French and American ribbon, and to discern which buttons were long lasting and valuable and which were cheap, and in her spare time she would turn on her record player or go to free student concerts and listen to the music other people made.

Wally's mother and her aunt Doreen were sisters, but Wally thought her aunt looked happier than her mother. She had her hair done more often, and she had pedicures too. Her toenails were painted a warm pink. It was nothing for her to go out to a restaurant three times a week. Wally had heard her mother say that Doreen's shop and her husband together made more money than Doreen knew how to spend, and now Wally wondered if it were just that Aunt Doreen was more prosperous or whether she was happier by nature. The living room had a bay window, and in the bay part was a basket lined in satin, and on the satin lay a white mother poodle and five puppies. There was a piano in the living room, and on a shelf Doreen had a collection of dolls that were not toys but were dressed in elaborate garments. Wally knew from a catalogue her aunt kept in a drawer of her china cabinet that the dolls cost more than a hundred dollars each, some up to three hundred and beyond. Their shoes alone were little works of art.

But it was not just that her aunt had a piano and purebred puppies and her shop and the dolls; her aunt Doreen was interested in things. She knew when an operatic star was coming to town or when a new Italian film was on at the repertory cinema, and she loved to get any kind of news, and to think about it and talk about it in a lively way. After the quietness of Croydon Harbour, Wally loved the bustle and activity of Boston, as well as this lively way her aunt Doreen had of making every ordinary thing in life an event. When the mail brought a postcard for Wally from Thomasina in Paris, then another from Bucharest, Doreen made an event of standing it on the table in the hall, against the vase she kept filled with carnations and white iris. There was music in the house, and there were books, and there was always a cake in a box from the Modern Pastry shop on Hanover Street.

Aunt Doreen was a person to whom you could mention things, and the day Wally saw the notice about the Harley Street Voice Clinic at the college bookshop, she told her aunt about it. The cake in that day's box was a Swiss roll spread with jam and studded with coconut, and Wally marvelled at its sponginess as her aunt cut them each a piece to have with tea in English teacups.

If you did not know that Wally had had an injury to her voice in junior high school, you would think she was a girl with a slightly softer than normal voice. You might think her voice had a beauty, that it crumbled in a way that sounded inviting to the ear. In a world of harsh voices Wally's injured voice was quiet, but this was no blessing to Wally herself, and her aunt knew it.

The Harley Street Voice Clinic, Wally said, was not on Harley Street at all, but on a street called Wimpole Street. It had a team of doctors who did nothing else on this earth except repair vocal cords that had nodules on them or that had been strained or torn or otherwise injured. They did it for people who had devoted their lives to singing but who could not sing because something had injured their instrument. Their voices were their instrument. Wally told her aunt this, and her aunt — who had wanted to play piano but who had not been taught it when she was young enough — this aunt understood what Wally was telling her. Her aunt knew all about Wally's injury, about what had happened to her at Donna Palliser's party years ago. Everyone in the family did.

"I suppose," Wally said, "it's expensive to go have that done. And it's so far away. Maybe there's a place in Boston."

"If there were a place in Boston, the Berklee College of Music would not have information about the place in London on the bulletin board in the bookstore. They have it there because they know that is the place to go."

"I wish it wasn't all the way to London. If there was something like that here, I could get on a bus and go visit it and see for myself."

"If we knew anyone in London we could ask them to go and have a look. Then you would know. You would know what kind of feel the Harley Street Voice Clinic has. If they have a serious atmosphere, if they are able to do what they say they can do."

"Thomasina Baikie said she was going to London in her last postcard, remember? She was tired of Bucharest and looking forward to going to her favourite part of London and eating fish and chips and staying in that hostel and that other place."

"Get her postcard off the table."

They read the postcard again.

"She's there now," Aunt Doreen said. "If she did what she said she was going to do, she's still there. She's at that hostel or one of the hotels. We can phone them and leave a message for her to call us."

"Call us from England?" Wally could not imagine imposing on Thomasina by asking her to make a telephone call over thousands of miles of ocean. But her aunt was excited. She was a woman who became enthusiastic about things, and now she took three of the puppies in her arms and fed them pieces of cake.

"Collect, silly," she said. "We'll leave a message asking her to call us collect, and we can ask her to go visit Harley Street."

"Wimpole Street. The Harley Street Voice Clinic is at number thirty-five Wimpole Street."

"Wimpole Street then. And she'll go. This woman will do that for you. She'll go and check it out. We'll talk to her and give her the exact information that is on the records your doctor sent when you came here from home, and she can show it to those doctors on Wimpole Street and they can tell her what they think. And then you'll know."

23

Franchise King

FOREST ROAD STARTED OUT ELEGANTLY, though it bordered the penitentiary and the defunct stadium. It was lined with three-storey houses that had dormers, stained-glass porches, and dragon door knockers; fall crocuses, winterberries, and Bell Island slate. It had railings, old yews, and silence. But it opened out; it spread downhill towards Quidi Vidi Lake, and on this disappointing bare stretch Chesley Outerbridge had built his apartments of featureless brick, where call-centre employees lived and many apartments were vacant or used for spaces that were anything but homes. In the parking lot Wayne noticed a for-sale sign on a white van whose door read STOCKLEY'S: EXCELLENCE IN PEST CONTROL SINCE 1971. Behind the building ran the lake trail, supporting earnest joggers, disheartening algae, and geese maimed by fish hooks and road salt. On Wayne's third night in the building, a pizza he had not ordered came to his door.

"Echoes?" The man from Venice looked at his notebook and squinted at Wayne.

"No."

"What's the name?"

"Wayne Blake."

"Could I take a look at that?" Wayne's telephone book lay on the floor. "Yellow Pages," said the man. "Under Escorts."

Though he shared Echoes' landing, Wayne never saw anyone emerge. He heard men come up the stairs, and wondered about them. He spent days sitting on his carpet beside his open suitcase. In the suitcase was everything he had brought from Labrador: his jeans, a couple of favourite shirts, a binder into which he had put his bridge sketches and Thomasina's postcards, and some work socks from the Hudson's Bay store.

"Make all your socks the same colour," Treadway had said. "Then you won't have to fool around with pairs in your laundry." This was the sole piece of advice his father had given him on leaving home.

In the binder with his postcards and sketches he had put a black-and-white photo of Wally Michelin from his high school yearbook. The caption, chosen by Donna Palliser and her yearbook committee, read, "They say love hides behind every corner. Well, then, I must be walking in circles!" He sat near the suitcase and looked out the window at blueberry bushes on the hills.

The hills were an example of how brutal something can be when you do nothing to make it softer or more beautiful. This apartment, Wayne's mother would have told a daughter, was just about the worst apartment a girl could have if she were living in St. John's for the first time. To a daughter Jacinta would have said, "You might as well check yourself into the Waterford." But she would not have said this to a son. A son might stare at the hills but he would buy boots with felt linings and see what he could do about buying that van in the parking lot. He knew he had been right to leave Gracie Watts behind, but he wondered if it would be all right to call her now, just to see what she thought about the idea of him buying that van, and to cut through the loneliness. If he had brought Gracie with him she would have helped him find something to hang at his windows. She would do something about getting a few dishes. Cheerful ones with wheat on the rims. Red cups. A salt shaker instead of pouring salt into his hand out of a box the old tenant had left behind and throwing half the handful down the sink. He knew he could not have brought Gracie, but he wished he could talk to her now.

Every morning a bird's voice came through the Forest Road window like a needle. At night the carpet chafed Wayne's face and moonlight blared through his eyelids. Why hadn't he just walked the streets when he reached St. John's and found an apartment on Gower Street, or above the Tan Tan takeout on Colonial Street? Somewhere with cats on doorsteps, and window boxes. Even if the boxes contained straggly lobelia and daisies strayed from vacant lots. At least daisies were something. Each day he rose from his floor, poured himself a glass of milk, and ate a few of the chocolate graham squares he had bought at Caines. Mr. Caines might know the corner grocery business but he did not know how to direct someone to an apartment that felt anything like a home.

He did not want to phone his mother and make her worry, but he had to talk to someone, and finally he called Gracie. He called her at night, when he knew she would be studying her paramedic books and her mother and father would be out of the kitchen.

"Gracie?"

"Wayne? How are you doing?"

"I'm thinking of buying a van."

"Have you got a job yet?"

"You can work for yourself if you've got a van."

"So you haven't got a job?"

"People who don't have vans don't realize the potential. Is it all right if we talk on the phone for a few minutes?"

"I have to study, Wayne."

"What are you studying tonight?"

"I'm studying how some bacteria have their own minds."

"They have minds?"

"They can think independently. They can start new ideas on their own. They have brains."

"That's something."

"Wayne?"

"Yeah?"

"I have to study. Really hard. I can't be on the phone just chatting, you know?"

"Okay."

"And I have to protect myself. I have to act like I'm a person in charge of taking care of Gracie Watts, and do things that will make sure she's okay. Do you understand what I mean?"

"I guess."

"Are you all right?"

"Yeah."

"You don't sound all right. Have you made any friends? And what about money?"

"That's what I'm saying. I'm hoping to work with the van."

"I can't talk about vans, Wayne. Not right now. Did you call your mother?"

"Not yet."

"Well, you should. She phoned my mother at one o'clock in the morning looking for your address. My mother says she didn't realize what time it was."

"I sent her my address."

"Well, she must have lost it. My mother said she shouldn't be left alone, Wayne. She said she was carrying a bag of potatoes from the store on Saturday in her summer dress. It was freezing and she had no coat on."

"My mother doesn't need potatoes. She has a whole root cellar full of blue potatoes for boiling and Yukon Golds for French fries."

"Well, she bought a twenty-pound bag on Saturday and carried it home in her bare arms. Maybe you had better call her."

Wayne called his mother's number but there was no answer. He ate a Mars bar and looked out the window at the van. He thought about it some more on one of his walks to the edge of the city. By the fifth mile of a walk like that you forgot where you were and how you had got there. If you had the right boots and clothes, it could rain and you could still walk and think and work out where your life should go, now that you had left things behind that confused you, that defined you as a man when you weren't a man. Not the son your dad wanted. Not a son who kept up family traditions. Not a Labrador trapper, strong mettled and well read, solitary but knowing how to lead a pack. Instead you were ambiguous, feminine, undecided. You had even had a baby beginning to grow inside you, and you kept wondering to what size it had grown before it died, and thinking about its eyes. Wayne was glad Gracie had not tried to stay on the phone. Glad she was stronger than him, though he suspected she had forced herself to say she did not want to talk to him.

Walking miles through the city, past the downtown neighbourhoods, beyond Rennies Mill River, up Kenmount Road to the neon signs, the car dealerships, the sound barriers, the chain restaurants selling ribs by the bucket and coleslaw by the pound, you could decide how to make a living in a new town where no one knew you. This was one of the ways in which he thought like his father. Treadway had influenced him early with the idea that you had to be self-sufficient. Wayne passed lines hung with blue and silver flags snapping in the wind. Chevrolet, GM, Ford. Used or new. You were independent if you had a van. You could sell something out of it.

Wayne ended up in places no walker should attempt. This drainage ditch between the Wonder Bread factory on O'Leary Avenue and the Avalon Mall. This was more than a ditch, it was a whole system of wasteland, chain-link fences, yards filled with lumber awaiting construction, unidentifiable boxes, Quonset huts, coils of insulated wire, landfill, piles of asphalt, and sinister-looking rubble. Wayne walked through this waste-scape and into Donovan's Industrial Park, where he found Frank King, who was looking for a driver to sell hams, ground beef, pork roasts, racks of lamb, and a scattered cod fillet door to door among the big houses downtown. Frank's warehouse door was open; Frank shouted through it at men lifting pallets of chocolate-covered cherries. A poster on the door advertised Tunnock's Teacakes. Puddles all over the parking lot reflected a robin's-egg sky with puffy clouds moving fast. A couple of tractor trailers idled and the air stank of diesel.

"Wayne Blake. You have your own vehicle?" Frank King's office was the colour of ballpark mustard.

"Yeah."

"Where?" Frank looked at Wayne's head, shirt, pants, and boots. He looked closely at Wayne's face, as if it were odd, and Wayne wondered what Frank King saw. Frank King did not appear to be the most observant of men, but sometimes an unobservant person could surprise you with a piece of startling insight.

"I'm in the process of buying it."

"Clean?"

"I'm getting it repainted this week."

"Inside and out? You want a spotless vehicle, Wayne." Frank King was egg-shaped. His skin was glossy and his hands jewelled. He had a moustache whose ends he kept clipped. He wore a gold chain, and when he wanted to make a point, he pointed. "I'm not putting any of my refrigeration units in a less than hygienic situation. They don't call me the Franchise King for nothing. I regard each of my drivers as a franchisee. All franchises, my friend, have standards. That is what makes a franchise a franchise, Wayne. Standards."

Wayne took the number seven bus home. Six Ethiopian men got off at the *Evening Telegram* building. A woman in the front seat held a pink comb with half its teeth missing. She combed the first few inches of her hair. The rest looked as if it had not been combed since she was a child. When the bus got to Empire Avenue, she pulled a cap over the combed part of her hair, covering it completely.

The pest-control van was fourteen years old and had three flat tires. Its sign said INQUIRE AT TONY'S AUTO TECH BEHIND ELIZABETH DRUGS.

Tony rolled out from under a Buick on a set of mechanic's wheels. "That Vandura," he told Wayne, "belongs to my brother-in-law. I can tow her into the shop. You're going to need at least a new floor in her and a timing belt, and brake pads and probably a couple of ball joints if you're going to pass inspection. It's liable to cost you five to seven hundred to get her roadworthy."

"I need 'Pest Control' painted over. I'm thinking of using it for meat."

"You need the whole body done?" Tony looked as if he thought painting over "Pest Control" was frivolous.

"How about you do whatever you can for this." Wayne fished in his jeans and handed Tony half a dozen hundred-dollar bills.

Tony sat up and looked them over. "Where did you get these?"

"Bank of Montreal, Goose Bay."

Tony held one against the caged bulb that lit up the Buick's transmission. He looked Wayne in the eye. It was a look no woman normally gets to see. "You seem like a decent enough fellow but I had to ask." He shoved the bills in his jeans. "I know guys who have garbage bags full of hundreds that are worth no more than twenty each."

Wayne took the time to learn about the meat he sold from the van. Ribs were his most popular item, and after that pork roasts and lamb shoulder chops. Old women rattling around by themselves in the biggest houses on Circular Road wanted lights, hearts, tongues, and livers, and Wayne convinced Frank King to let him sell those instead of sending them to Morrison's factory on the Southside to be mixed with fish offal for pet food.

It grew colder, and Wayne had to carry ribs, chops, and hearts along paths the householders had shovelled, carry them in his arms like children, only they were not children, they were slabs of flesh and blood: red, marbled with fat. He wondered if anyone besides himself saw the meat as he saw it, raw and powerful, having the power to keep living bodies hot in the wind and ice. He carried meat past black railings, past a wreath on a door, past lights strung across a bay window. Women took the meat out of his arms; they embraced it and took it down hallways to the lit hearts of their houses. He wondered what it was like to be such a woman. They roasted it and ate it and gave it to their husbands and babies — did they think of the meat as powerful and important? From their faces Wayne thought they did not, and he felt more alone than ever, so he went to Water Street.

He walked to Bowrings and bought a stainless steel food mill, like the one through which Jacinta had milled cooked apples to separate the applesauce from the seeds and core. He visited Woolworth's, past the sad-eyed man with his sooty *Telegram* bag slung on his shoulder, past the bubble-gum machines where children begged their mothers for nickels so they could win the black gumball, past the orange booths and Formica tables where you could get fish, chips, and coleslaw or a Woolworth's Special Steak-Umm Sandwich. He reached the place where you bought dishes and Tupperware bowls and graters and egg whisks, and he bought himself a small glass salt shaker made in France.

24

Sugar Plum

THE WIND IN ST. JOHN'S was not like Labrador wind.
Here it was damp. It sneaked under Wayne's jacket
and unnerved him until he had got a hot coffee in him at
Shelley's. Forest Road was not a home, and as the winter
progressed he regretted having rented it. Home, when he
had finished making his deliveries for the day, became
Shelley's All-Day Breakfast, between George Street and
William's Lane; or the Ship Inn, where he heard old unac-
companied songs on Wednesday nights; or Afterwords
Books, across from the courthouse, where nag champa
incense mixed with the aromas of free coffee and musty
editions of *How Green Was My Valley* and *By Grand
Central Station I Sat Down and Wept*. Home was the
alleys through which Wayne walked back to Forest Road,
looking in other people's lit windows where there were

children, sunflowers in vases on the floor, and fireplaces that had once burnt coal but now had sheets of tin screwed over them and little electric heaters on the hearths.

Spring aches on Forest Road, once you get past the gingerbread houses. There isn't one piece of softness through March or April. Oh Henry wrappers in the gutter. Black snowbanks with bubbling holes. Every dog turd excreted over the winter has found its way to the edge of the sidewalk, and these too have the bubbles. Everything melting has the bubbles. You don't want to stand on the bubbling crust, but the town does not clean the sidewalks. Wayne had no choice but to crunch the mess as he walked back and forth between Forest Road and the harbourfront, where at least there were boats, cranes, women with high heels, men with briefcases, and street people sitting in the doorways of coffee shops, begging, their dogs wearing cowboy scarves.

He saw a reflection of his loneliness on the street, where regulars wove in with the people who worked in the shops and banks and law offices. He watched who gave panhandlers and buskers money and who did not. He watched the constabulary clear corners where men played busted harmonicas. He learned names. Caroline Yetman stood playing a Sears guitar at the bottom of the courthouse steps. Paul Twomey sat on his parka in front of the Gypsy Tearoom making portraits with broken pastels. Betty Flanagan pushed her shopping cart from the east-end post office to the old Woolworth's building in a pair of silver platforms.

"Have you been to Corner Brook?" Betty asked Wayne. "I used to teach school in Corner Brook. I taught at Broadway School for seventeen years."

Hobo Bill sat on George Street reading Dostoevsky. "I have never," he told Wayne after asking for a quarter, "asked a woman for spare change. And I never will."

Joanne Dohaney, the oldest waitress at Shelley's, daily gave Hobo Bill three coffees, a BLT, and a tub of vegetable barley soup.

"That Bill," Joanne told Wayne, "has not had a bath for the past however many years I've seen him around Water Street. I don't know how you can stand out there talking to him."

"I don't have all that many people to talk to."

"You got no friends? A fine-looking fellow like you — if you combed your hair and tucked in that shirt. You look like you could talk about anything you wanted. More intelligent than a lot of them out there. How come you don't make more of yourself? You could get a nice smart girl up at the university."

"There was only ever one girl I liked talking to."

"That's what you put me in mind of. Someone up at the university. You're not though, are you? What girl?" Joanne Dohaney didn't mind asking a customer anything. This one would be out of her hair after his second refill. It wasn't like she had to sit and listen to him all day.

"When we were kids. Her name was Wally Michelin. She wanted to be an opera singer."

"Yeah, well, I wanted to be the sugar plum fairy." Joanne hoisted a tray filled with stainless steel teapots through the swinging doors. She was in her fifties but there was something expressive in the turn of her wrist. Wayne did not remember ever hearing people talk about the beauty of wrists. The little bone like an ankle bone. He noticed it again when she came out.

"Did you really want to be a dancer?"

Joanne rolled her eyes, took the empty Heinz bottle, opened it, squirted in new ketchup from the kitchen's generic mother bottle, and wiped the Heinz cap with a dishrag. "I dance by myself in the kitchen when no one's around. If you could see into houses all over St. John's, and all over Newfoundland for that matter, and while we're at it, all over the whole world, I suppose, you'd see women dancing by themselves. Men don't know that. Now you're one of probably three or four dozen men in the world who do know. Because I've told you. But you're still only a boy. You'll forget." Wayne smelled Javex, perspiration, and Ivory soap escaping from under Joanne's uniform. "I really did want to be the sugar plum fairy. You thought I was joking about that, didn't you."

He did not tell her that he had always danced alone in his room to music on the radio, and that he still did it now, in the apartment on Forest Road. That he danced, and watched the shadows of his body on the wall, and tried to connect the music's beauty with those shadows. Street lamps soaked through the window from Forest

Road. Their light soaked into his shirt, and in the dark you could not see it was a man's shirt. You saw that it folded, that it was cotton, that it draped.

What was beauty? Not frailness, not smallness. Wayne looked at his arms and tried to imagine them holding Joanne, with her expressive wrists circled around him. That was how lovers' limbs were. Years of hormones had made him angular, and it occurred to him that he wished he could stop taking them. He wanted to stop swallowing them every day and having them alter his body from what it wanted to be into what the world desired from it. He wanted to throw the pills down a toilet here in Shelley's All-Day Breakfast, where no one knew him anyway, unless you counted Joanne, and she did not really know anything about him. He wanted to throw the pills away and wait and see what would happen to his body. How much of his body image was accurate and how much was a construct he had come to believe? He tried to see his body objectively.

If he squinted it could look softer. If he stopped taking the pills might his breasts bud, as they had done at puberty? He was afraid of having breasts. But were breasts beautiful? Could anyone tell him? At night when he danced alone, his body wanted to be water, but it was not water. It was a man's body, and a man's body was frozen. Wayne was frozen, and the girl-self trapped inside him was cold. He did not know what he could do to melt the frozen man.

He did not tell Joanne at Shelley's All-Day Breakfast any of this. He had no one to whom he could tell anything. There was a funny old woman on Circular Road who, when he made his deliveries, often asked him to come in and do tasks for her that had nothing to do with delivering meat. She had him fix a broken rail in her banisters, and she asked him to change the water in a font under her staircase. He had to clean the font with a rag she had for that purpose and pour in new holy water the priest had brought her in a Harvey's Bristol Cream bottle. He had a few customers like that, who turned his meat deliveries into something more like doctors' appointments or some sort of gentle social services call. It slowed him down and meant he was earning less money per hour than he should have been, but he let these customers hold him up because they were the closest thing he had to friends. They talked to him, and they were something to look forward to in his week of lonely deliveries. People had family, didn't they? People had someone who remembered them from one week to another.

To walk home from Shelley's All-Day Breakfast, Wayne had to pass the Anglican graveyard, where massive beeches had knots the size of faces, and the knots grew malevolent. He knew this was a trick of his mind, but they did; they flew alive, became malicious spirits, and as he walked past them he had to look away, for fear they would snatch his mind. Wayne knew this was a dangerous way to think, and he thought instead about the way Joanne's wrist had insinuated itself around the swinging door. As he passed the cemetery trees, the tree he found most malevolent faced him: angry sinew with an eye rimmed in gold bark and studded with a pupil of cracked wood. The loneliness doled out to each of us in different quantities, hidden or diluted, was unmasked. It had the power to grab the backs of Wayne's eyeballs and pluck them inward.

He heard a Metrobus stop on Chalker's Hill, the shout of a three-year-old boy running over the graves, his mother shouting, "Ashton! Ashton! Get out of that, come over here!" The whirr and scree of starlings. Houses petered out and bald grass banked the lake, studded with Coffee Crisp and Aero wrappers and Pepsi ring tops. There was the parking lot of Wayne's building, feature-less brick with its flat roof and rust stains running from the eavestroughs. There was a letter in his mailbox. His feet clacked on the plastic edges of the stairs. To open his door Wayne had to force it over the carpet. There was a bowl of egg congealing on his little half-table with its Formica top. He had intended to make an omelette. He put the letter on the table. His sheet and pillow lay under the living room window.

Wayne warmed his small glass salt shaker on the stove and lay down with it and pretended it was part of his lover's body. But who was his lover? He closed his eyes and pushed the warm glass against the deeply hidden vagina that belonged to Annabel. This created an orgasm,

deep inside, deeper by far than anything he had experi-
enced with Gracie Watts. He shuddered and cried out
for the lover who had done this to him, who had found
Annabel's body inside him, but he was alone. His phone
was flashing. It was the previous tenant's phone and had
been flashing since he moved in. He looked out the kitchen
window at the vinyl siding of a bungalow next door. The
bit of sky over the bungalow roof was a piece of endless-
ness. Wayne felt he had randomly superimposed himself
on a city that could have done equally well for itself with
or without him. He lifted the receiver, pressed a couple of
buttons, and listened. A man wanted Lucinda to pick up
Clorets and reading glasses at Lawtons. The man had sat
on his old ones in the car and broken them. Wayne erased
the message and remembered the letter.

25

Economics

PEOPLE WILL NOTICE WHEN A neighbour is not herself but for a long time they will not intervene. Time is so sneaky that one minute you are thinking you have not seen such-and-such a person for a few days, perhaps you should phone them, and the next time you think that thought, spring has come. During the winter that Jacinta was alone, Joan Martin and Eliza Goudie had thought about her many times. Eliza clipped an article from January's *Chatelaine* that described exactly how a woman could view her middle-aged husband with renewed romantic vigour, and she put it under the brass dolphin on her hall side table to give to Jacinta, but by spring it was still there. Joan phoned Jacinta's number several times to say they had the old, traditional kind of sweet william in Vesey's seed catalogue, because Jacinta had told her that was one flower she would take the trouble to send for by mail, but Jacinta had not answered the phone. Joan ordered an extra packet of seeds for Jacinta, but by April they had not arrived.

Treadway Blake did not often write a letter. His address, in ballpoint, was shaky and intimate but his letter was short and to the point. With it inside the envelope were two more letters: one from the department of motor vehicle registration and the other from MCP, which was the provincial medicare plan. The second one had been neatly opened with a knife. That was how Treadway opened letters.

Dear Wayne, Treadway had written. Here is your driver's licence renewal. You need to get that done. I've also had a letter from the government about the insurance for your medication. I'm not sure what to do about it and there are some parts I cannot make head nor tail out of, so I am sending it to you and maybe you can have someone look at it down there. There must be someone at the confederation building who knows what it is all about. Your mother and I are fine, but I came home from the trapline to find her a bit confused. I am going to try to have someone look in on her when I go out again in a week or so. Love, Dad.

Wayne looked at the government letter. It contained forms and columns, and it asked Treadway to fill out the forms and the government would arrive at a decision about the amount Treadway would have to pay for Wayne's medications between now and the time he turned twenty-one; then there was another form concerning the years beyond that date. They seemed to want to know whether Wayne was going to a university, and there were so many numbered lists he could not figure out the form any better than his father had done. But there was one thing he could discern, and it was that his hormone medication cost a lot more than he had imagined. There was a figure for the MCP contribution over the past year and another one for parental contribution.

The only time to get his father on the phone, Wayne knew, was at five in the morning. That was when Treadway ate breakfast, and it was the only time he could be relied on to be inside the house. Wayne was awake half the night thinking of what he would say to his father.

"Dad?"

Treadway was a man who did not like talking on the phone. The phone was for getting information across that could not be exchanged in any other way. It was the new form of telegrams.

"Did you figure it out, son? Were you able to see exactly what MCP was getting at?"

"I'm calling to say you might as well save yourself some money."

"What's that now, Wayne?"

"I've been thinking for a while about being on all these drugs, and not liking it."

Wayne had been watching people. He watched men and women who passed him on their way to get pea soup at

Shelley's at lunchtime or croissants at the new bakery across from the Bank of Montreal. The street smelled of cigarettes, perfume, and coffee, and Wayne saw that the faces, bodies, clothes, and shoes of the men and women who passed him had been divided and thinned. The male or female in them had been both diluted and exaggerated. They were one, extremely so, or they were the other. The women trailed tapered gloves behind them and walked in ludicrous heels, while the men, with their fuzzy sideburns and brown brief-cases, looked boring as little beagles out for the same rabbit. You define a tree and you do not see what it is; it becomes its name. It is the same with woman and man. Everywhere Wayne looked there was one or the other, male or female, abandoned by the other. The loneliness of this cracked the street in half. Could the two halves of the street bear to see Wayne walk the fissure and not name him a beast?

His father did not know Thomasina Baikie had told Wayne about the fetus, and Wayne did not want to talk about that now. He did not want to explain himself to his father at all. He did not want to talk about the beast, or the fissure, or anything that he felt. His father had known things and had not told him. His father had kept secrets he had no business keeping, secrets that were not Tread-way's own.

"What are you saying, son?"

"I'm saying I've been thinking about letting the drugs go gradually. I was thinking about it anyway, before they sent you the forms."

"Going off them?"

"Yes. And now I see how much they cost —"

"You don't want to stop taking those, son, regardless of the cost." Treadway was definite, as if he had some kind of authority over this subject that Wayne did not have.

"I didn't call to have a debate about it, Dad. I'm only telling you because I've decided already." He had not decided, not for sure. He was scared of the decision. But he needed to be definite with Treadway. He did not want to explain his complicated feelings and he did not want his father paying that amount of money and he did not want his father to be the one who had authority over this subject any longer.

There was silence, and it gave Wayne a worse feeling than if his father had argued.

"I wouldn't have said anything to you, Dad, if it wasn't for the fact that you're the one paying."

"I'm glad you're talking about economics, Wayne. That's an important subject. I'm glad you've thought of it. If you like, I can send you the money directly that I will be saving when you no longer take the drugs." There was something so deliberate in the way Treadway said this that Wayne sensed his father did not mean it. He sensed that what his father was really trying to do was scare him in some way.

"Dad, no. I don't want you to do that."

"The world is full of the dire results of economics. You must have seen some of that in St. John's."

Wayne was not sure what his father meant. "Are you talking about different kinds of neighbourhoods and people?" Wayne was very aware of the difference between Circular Road and a place like Livingstone Street, where he had seen a woman with a black eye and a baby in each arm. Did his father mean that, or had Treadway Blake understood something else?

"I mean, you must have thought about all the economic implications of your decision. You must have seen people who don't match society's expectations, and you must have thought about how you are going to deal with that."

How did his father do this? Treadway had said nothing about specific difficulties yet had evoked in Wayne's mind the beast he was afraid of becoming.

The beast was vicious. She hurtled and would not back up. If she got hit in the chest with brutality erected by the street, she kept going. Her pain threshold was high. She was not pretty. She prowled, animal-like, uncivilized. She walked all night.

She was without language. She watched how everyone else was doing. How tame they were, living in the same wind, night, and wilderness in which she hunted and was hunted.

"Dad?"

"Yes, son?"

"Nothing I do with economics is going to change what I am."

"No, it's not going to change who you are. But it is going to directly affect how hard your life will be. People who have a hard life — you must have seen them. That's what I mean. In St. John's. I'm talking about misery. I'm talking about being haggard while you're still young. Not being able to afford a meal, losing your teeth, and, Wayne, getting into the criminal side of life. It's all waiting for people who haven't thought of economics. You need to get some training if you're going to live in the city. You need to think about economics, and you need to look ahead. You need to plan your actions carefully." Something about this speech made Wayne think of home: the smell of woodsmoke over Croydon Harbour, feeling a sting off the waves.

"Do you think I should come back home?"

"Not if you go off those pills. You're looking for trouble if you stop taking those, Wayne. And it won't be any easier in a tiny place like home."

Again Wayne wondered if his father was saying what he really meant. He wondered if some part of Treadway Blake simply could not handle having a son in the house who was openly changing into someone Treadway could not explain to himself or to anyone in the community.

"It won't be easy in St. John's either. You're paying for an apartment. And feeding yourself. You need that job you've got. You're going to lose it if you're not careful."

"What do you think I should do?"

"I don't know, Wayne."

"Dad, going off the medications might not be that bad. I just don't know exactly what I'm going to look like to other people."

"That's one of the things I'm worried about, son."

"If I start to look too strange I can work after the sun goes down. I can walk up people's driveways at dusk and put up my hood and wear a big jacket and no one has to notice."

There was another silence and Wayne felt sorrow flow through the phone. His father's sorrow. He did not want it. He wanted to see something happy. He had not wanted to start explaining his feelings to his father but he had begun to do so anyway, and now wished he had not. When he got off the telephone, he went to the bathroom cabinet and took the remainder of his green pills and flushed them down the toilet. He did this because they were the biggest. He was supposed to take one of the green pills each day, and if he did not cut them in half they got stuck in his throat. He hated the green pills. The other pills, the yellow ones and the white capsules, were smaller. The yellow ones were tiny. He would take one a day of each of these instead of two, until they ran out. He had enough left that he could do this over a month or six weeks, and if that was not gradual enough he would just have to live with whatever happened.

26

The Battery

THE CITY GREW OPPRESSIVE. If it was not formal wear in the Model Shop that disturbed Wayne, with its bridesmaid gowns and tuxedos that reminded him of the travesty of his own prom, it was the homeless people. He felt quizzical gazes from them, as if they recognized something in him. He had expected to have more time than he had to get used to the changes in his body. But his body jumped at the chance to become less like a man and more like a woman. When he had been reducing the pills for just one week, he felt tenderness in his breasts and he felt them start to swell, as if they had been constrained but were now able to expand. In the course of a normal day he had little cause to speak to anyone, except to pass a quick hello to a customer or answer Frank King a simple yes or no about the sale of a box of sausages, but he became conscious of a change in his voice. It cracked the way it had done when he was fourteen, and sometimes when he tried to speak, it was a false start and no voice came, then he had to take a breath and speak with what seemed like unnatural force for his voice to come out at all.

Wayne looked into the polished marble of the Bank of Montreal and saw a soft shadow with hair that blew around his face like a girl's hair. He could be a girl in a mirror like that, a surface of polished stone. But in a real mirror what was he?

Part of him wished for the safety of Croydon Harbour, but was it safety? His father had intimated that it was not. Yet St. John's was all angles. It was corners and intersections and panes of glass, and every time he passed through one of its clearly defined spaces he felt he did not fit into it. His body, or the idea of his body, had grown amorphous and huge.

There was one place in St. John's whose wildness did something good for Wayne: the Battery. He visited it because he remembered that kid in Caines Grocery, Steve Keating, saying he would like it. You could walk between its higgledy-piggledy houses and through the outer Battery and around the Signal Hill trail. Or you could stay in the middle Battery and look at the houses that were built like boats, and you could look down on the water and see the ships and the harbour-pilot tugs leading them in. The Battery was, like himself, part one thing and part another. It was pure city, shambling from the downtown core into the main chambers of the heart, the harbour, of St. John's, its houses part of the lining of the womb of the port city. But it was also like a tiny coastal community. It was unregulated, much of it without plumbing, as Mr. Caines had said; full of kittens and youngsters that no one claimed to own much of the time. A garden, or more likely a scrap of vetch and boulder, was as likely to be festooned with the week's sheets and long johns as with strings of lanterns or beer bottles lined up in the sun. The Battery was the domain of pigeons and gulls, and the houses and fish sheds nearest the harbour stood on half-rotted stilts awash with weeds. At night, no one in the imposing merchants' quarter of St. John's had the enchanted view owned by the youths who hung around the wharf drinking: lights of ships from Portugal, Poland, Spain, and Russia floated like a sparkling dream. If a ship had a rusting hulk or held a starving stowaway, none of that mattered in the night. The night on the Battery was a necklace of floating light, a world of dreams, part city and part ocean, a hybrid, like Wayne himself, between the ordinary world and that place in the margins where the mysterious and undefined breathes and lives.

Wayne walked there at night just to look at the lights and did not talk to the youths who drank on the wharf under the lower Battery. There was a store called Jack's Corner Shop on the corner of Duckworth Street and the lower Battery, where old men loitered smoking their cigarettes. It was in that shop, as he bought two hot dogs for eighty-nine cents from the machine with silver rollers that made the wieners look more delicious than they were, that Wayne met Steve Keating fetching a tin of Carnation milk for his mother.

"Hey! You're that guy I met in Caines. Are you?" Steve Keating peered into Wayne's sweatshirt hood.

At work Frank King had already expressed doubt about Wayne's changing appearance. In fact he had told Wayne he had better clean himself up in the next week or Frank would have to take him aside. "You're preoccupied," Frank had bellowed. "You're not energetic. A person can hardly hear you." Frank had stepped back to get a better perspective. Wayne's eyes held something that looked to Frank King as if it had gone through the end of wrong or right and come out another side. "You are not projecting an air of confidence, my friend. I don't know how you have sold any meat at all." It was true that some of Wayne's customers had stopped ordering from him. He had begun making deliveries later in the day so that the bulk of them would happen in darkness, just as he had told his father he might have to do.

"You look different," Steve Keating said now. "But you've got the same boots on and the same jacket, and the way you walk is just the same. Do you want to go look in Katie Twomey's front window? I can show you the waterfall in her house."

They walked the lower Battery and Steve went in his own house and gave his mother the tin of milk while

Wayne waited outside. Steve's house was a cream-coloured bungalow with two tiny windows, and below it was scraggly rock that led down to the wharf where the youths hung around. Wayne saw them look at him, sodium vapour lights from the harbourfront lighting their faces orange. They were older than Steve. When Steve came back out, one called up, "Hey! Keating! Who you got there?"

"Never mind him," Steve said. "That's only Derek Warford. Come on." He started back up the hill. "I'll show you Katie Twomey's private waterfall."

"Hey!" Derek Warford shouted. "Keating! Answer me when I ask you something, you little fucker."

"Wait here," Steve told Wayne, and he went down to where Derek Warford had started walking uphill. Wayne waited. He did not want to go down there and have Derek Warford look too closely at him. He saw Steve talk to Derek Warford, then hand him money, and Warford went to the wharf and took three beer out of a case and gave them to Steve.

"Here." Steve handed Wayne a bottle.

"What did you tell him?"

"I told him you were looking for Archibald White's house."

"Who's Archibald White?"

"Archibald White is an English professor who built that blue mansion up by the Battery Hotel. I told Warford you were lost and I was showing you how to get there."

"Why did you tell him that?"

"So he wouldn't bother us. Come on."

They went up a staircase and behind some gardens until they came to a house with no lights on. There was a scrap of bare veranda and Steve sat on it, opened a beer, and began to drink it. He made no effort to look in the window or try to show Wayne what was inside. It was one of the first nights when the wind was not cold enough to cut through you. Wayne sat down and the wood was not warm, but cold did not creep through his jeans. They had the whole night harbour down below them. The sodium vapour lit up the undersides of gulls circling over a Belgian research vessel and a rusted hulk from Russia. If you had binoculars you could look right into the portholes, and even without binoculars Wayne thought how exciting the round, lit-up portholes always looked, no matter how derelict a vessel appeared in daylight.

Steve popped the top off his second beer and said he was sorry, he only had enough money for three. Derek Warford charged him three dollars apiece and there was no way they would even look at him down at the store. Steve kept glancing at Wayne, and finally he said, "How come your face is like that now, puffy?"

If Steve Keating had asked this in an aggressive way, or with a drop of ill humour or insult, Wayne would not have answered him, but Steve had no ill humour in him. He was merely curious, and with a kind of good humour that Wayne liked. He had not met anyone in St. John's to whom he could tell anything. He could not talk to any of his customers, not even the ones who asked him to fix their stair rails or remove caulking with a chisel so they could open their pantry windows after the winter, and he certainly could not talk to his employer, Frank King.

Spring had tortured coltsfoot out of the ground in vacant lots all over St. John's. There was a tiny railed landing between Church Hill and Cathedral Street where hyacinth bulbs had newly burst and he had smelled them. He knew all the world was about to open up because of summer, but he had to remain closed. He had to keep secrets and he had to keep his body covered because of what people like Frank King and his customers and Derek Warford's crowd on the wharf might think. He did not know Steve Keating, and Steve Keating was not his friend, but Wayne felt he wanted to tell him things. It was not just Wayne's face that looked puffy, as Steve had said. His abdomen was filled with fluid, as it had been at puberty. He wore loose shirts to cover it and kept the button on his jeans undone, but he was starting to feel afraid. He was afraid that what had happened before inside his body might have happened again.

"As a matter of fact," Wayne said, "I should probably go see a doctor."

"Are you sick?"

Wayne had a feeling you could present Steve Keating with any problem and he would look at it without moral or social judgement.

"Steve, do you know what a hermaphrodite is?"

"Yeah. Black sea bass are hermaphrodites. Me and my dad catch them every fall. They don't come this far north any other time. But that's what black sea bass are. Half male, half female."

"Did you ever hear of a person being that?"

"No." Steve took a mouthful of beer and lifted his eyebrows and made great big eyes at the sky as if to say to the clouds, Here's a good one. But there was no judgement or ridicule in him. He looked at Wayne with real interest, dying to see what he would say next.

"Well, I am. I was born like that. And I didn't know for a long time because no one told me and they did surgery and I was on a lot of pills. But now I'm off the pills. And the one thing I'm worried about is something you wouldn't believe."

"I'd believe it if it was true. I'd have to, wouldn't I?"

"The one thing I'm worried about is, my body apparently has everything it needs inside itself to make itself pregnant. I bet you never heard a guy say that before."

Steve looked at him, impressed. There was a sound coming from down on the docks. Night crane workers were lifting containers off a ship that had come down the St. Lawrence from Quebec. There were two cranes. Wayne loved seeing their lattice booms lit against the dark, and he loved how slowly but surely they moved, lowering the containers on their hoist lines. The lattice design was like the bridges he had loved and sketched as a child; there was something about the sight of the cranes that reminded him of the beauty of bridges, and of the slow music Wally Michelin had wanted to sing. Sitting here, now, on the makeshift veranda with Steve Keating, reminded him too of the summer he and Wally had spent on the bridge that he had made with his father. It was intimate, and there were lights strung nearby, and the world was held back a little bit, so it did not encroach on the two people who sat together, set back from ordinary things such as Jack's Corner Shop and the van and Frank King, and everything to do with loneliness and with selling meat.

"We have a fake baby in human dynamics class," Steve said. "You want me to see if I can borrow it? It's supposed to show us how bad it is having to get up at night and look after it. It's supposed to scare us to death."

"I'm scared without the fake baby, Steve."

"Moira Carew was five months pregnant and she didn't even know. Want me to buy you a pregnancy test? Mr. Caines has them hidden in his shop, down under the pork chops in the back freezer. When Moira had her baby, Miss Tavernor — she's the human dynamics teacher and the gym teacher too — she made Moira take the fake baby home even though she already had a real baby."

"That's cruel."

"Well, she made her. And Moira killed it. It registers dead if you don't treat it right. It's electronic. Would you keep yours?"

"My what?"

"Your baby, if you had one. Would you keep it?"

"Jesus." Wayne began to regret telling Steve Keating what he had told him. Steve was too young, and once he got excited it seemed as if he could not stop talking.

"Would you give it up for adoption? Do you get periods?"

"I don't have a place for the blood to run out. I had surgery, which I think I've got to get undone. I'm petrified, if you want to know the truth."

"So she's all backed up in there." Steve touched Wayne's abdomen. It was the first time anyone had touched his body since he had come to St. John's.

"Yeah."

"Plus you could be pregnant."

"I'm hoping that's not the case. But that is what I'm afraid of."

"I can take you to the hospital. I take my mother's car all the time when she's down the shore at her sister's. You know what you do? You put chalk marks on the driveway smack up against her back tires. Park her in that same spot when you get back. Right to the molecule."

"I have my own van, Steve."

"You do? I'm your man, then. Pass 'em over."

"What?"

"Your keys."

"I don't think so."

"Come on."

"I wish you were a bit older."

"How come?"

"So I could talk to you sensibly."

"You know what you should do?"

"What?"

"You should take down that hood. Take it down and clean up your face and get some new clothes that fit. It's weird — you had the same jacket on that other time I saw you, and now you look fatter but that jacket is way too big. It's like you got bigger and smaller at the same time."

"It's muscle mass, Steve. The hormones gave me muscle mass like a man, and now it's going away and everything is softer."

"Take the hood down off you so I can have a look at your face."

Wayne did not want to take the hood down, so Steve took it down for him. Wayne was glad there was darkness, though he knew Steve could see his face because he could see Steve's, in the light from the ships and the dock lamps. Steve looked at him and frowned with the effort of trying to examine his face objectively.

Wayne had delivered a duck on Old Topsail Road earlier and a little girl had looked up at him from the doorway while her mother went to get the money. The little girl had stared at him, then shouted along the corridor, "Mommy, is that a lady or a man?"

Now he felt the fluid in his abdomen, accompanied by an ongoing ache, and he remembered the fetus that had formed in him before. He imagined its eyes and he easily imagined its face looking at him now. If it had happened before, what was to stop it from happening again? What was to stop him being haunted by one pair of eyes after another, just the same as that first pair?

"The thing I'm most worried about right now," he told Steve Keating, "is not how my face looks."

27

Lotus

WAYNE DID NOT EXPECT, when he went to the Grace General Hospital, that the doctors would treat him as a model on which to train their students. He understood it in retrospect, but that did not make it any easier.

The Grace General was close to downtown. It was on a part of Military Road that sat on the descent to the harbour. It had black railings like the churches and it had impressive smokestacks with white smoke belching out, and a thousand blank, dark windows, narrow and small like the windows in a castle a child would draw, but not a beautiful castle. There was a Subway restaurant across the road, and a taxi stand, and a corner store and other one-storey businesses that looked hovel-like next to the big cream-and-soot-coloured building. What was the hospital burning, Wayne wondered, that caused all the white smoke?

Gracie Watts had once told him that hospitals were constantly getting rid of dangerous waste, and he wondered if that was what was going up in smoke now over the traffic lights and the hamburger stand with broken clapboard. He wondered what kind of dangers were in the smoke.

He had a lot of explaining to do when he tried to tell the receptionist and the nurses why he had come in. He had to make not one but seven trips to the hospital before they understood his case, or thought they understood it. He brought in the forms his father had forwarded to him, outlining the medications he was supposed to take and their cost, and he gave the names of the doctors who had treated him in Goose Bay, or at least those whose names he remembered. Several times during this process he lost his courage and thought, These people are never going to be able to help me. He watched other patients in the corridors, and that made him want to run away. There was a man whose mouth sat perpetually open lying in a cot next to a bucket of grey water that had a mop standing in it. From a cafeteria somewhere in the bowels of the building came the smell of alphabet soup and meat pies. When doctors finally did listen to Wayne, sitting in an admission room holding clipboards, he realized they were not doctors but people who interviewed you before a doctor did. They interviewed him at length, then left him to wait a long time alone in the room.

He went through with all this because he feared the swelling and the tenderness in his belly. When, after several visits, his records finally arrived from Goose Bay, a doctor named Haldor Carr came in with two more doctors and seven interns. These observers all watched carefully, hoping to learn a great deal from Haldor Carr about a kind of case most interns never got to see.

His first real appointment involved the doctors telling Wayne he should not have done what he had done. They were unhappy that he had stopped taking the green pills, the white capsules, and the tiny yellow pills. He should at least, they said, have consulted with them first and agreed upon a timetable. He should not have taken matters into his own hands. Now they could guarantee nothing. They could not guarantee the safety of any medical intervention from now on, and had Wayne considered this before he had acted so rashly, they would not now all be in a position of risk. It was not just the patient's own health that was at risk here, Haldor Carr said.

Wayne realized the doctor had stopped talking to him and was addressing his interns. Haldor Carr was a teaching physician, and he was teaching now. Wayne was an exhibit. He wanted to leave the room, but if he did that there would be no way to find out if his body had again become pregnant. He was terrified it had, so he stayed in the room with this crowd of people, none of whom looked at him directly except for one girl, an Asian intern, small and serious.

Wayne did not know what Dr. Haldor Carr was ready to do in the name of teaching and of medicine. He might

remove Wayne's penis, or his womb. Wayne heard him
talk about these possibilities. Or Haldor Carr might do
nothing but reopen Wayne's vagina and ask each intern
to insert a gloved hand and feel the cervix, the placement
of it and its distance from the vaginal opening.

Wayne listened to all of this and felt helpless and
angry. He realized the doctor did not know any right or
wrong thing to do, and that his motives for deciding were
not the same as his own. Haldor Carr had power and
Wayne felt powerless. He was lying down, but he forced
himself to sit up and use the only thing of influence that
he owned: his voice. His voice did not want to come out
of hiding, but he knew he had to exercise it or Haldor
Carr would choose one of the surgeries and perform it.

"When you open my body this time," Wayne said,
"and let the fluid out, I don't want my vagina closed up
again. I want it left open. And I don't want you to remove
anything."

This way, Wayne thought, he would become who he
had been when he was born. At least he would have that.
The truth of himself, who he really was.

The doctor did not want to hear about it.

"If you can't agree to that," Wayne said, "I'm going
to walk out of the hospital." He did not want to walk out
of the hospital at all. But he said this as if he possessed
great certainty.

Wayne had spoken up, and now he had done so, he
knew he had spoken with his whole self: with the voice

of Annabel and not only that of Wayne. If Haldor Carr wanted to teach those interns, he had no choice but to do what Wayne asked.

As Haldor Carr let out the trapped blood with its stench of iron and fermentation, all Wayne could think about was whether there had been a second fetus trapped inside him. But Haldor Carr did not speak to him. When the interns had cleaned up the blood, the doctor resumed teaching them.

"Here" — he touched Wayne with an ice-cold wand of metal — "latent and manifest tissues share the same characteristics. This penis has presented as ambiguous. In the absence of the medications this client was meant to take, it has reverted to what we might consider to be an elongated clitoris. But we might equally consider it still to be a penis, though a truncated one. This is the kind of thing that happens when a patient refuses compliance."

Wayne tried to interrupt. "What about in the Fallopian tube?"

Haldor Carr wrote in his notepad as if Wayne had not spoken, and his interns crowded in to learn what he thought. They had their backs to Wayne. But the small, serious girl heard.

"What did you say?"

"Last time this happened, in the Fallopian tube there was a fetus."

She laid her hands on Wayne's abdomen and pressed down, but not hard. She touched him carefully. The other interns listened to Haldor Carr tell them all he knew about hermaphroditism. About phalometers and undescended testicles. About charting levels of testosterone, estrogen, and progesterone. About how, twenty years ago, there had been no surgical removal of Wayne's lone ovary or the womb, and look at the mess this patient was in now. They moved in a pod to the other side of the room. The gentle intern inserted gloved fingers carefully into Wayne and did an internal exam. She was a good student and she did this conscientiously.

"You have a womb. You have a cervix. You have one ovary. You have one Fallopian tube. Everything is clear and there is no fetus. Everything is okay."

The doctor and the other interns kept their backs to Wayne. They were looking at a chart.

While the gentle intern removed her gloves and washed her hands in the sink, Wayne touched the opening behind his penis and felt hunger leap from inside the pain. The hunger was an old memory. Not his own memory but a memory belonging to women and their latent passion, ready to flare.

The gentle intern had come back, and she said, "Before everything heals, it's better not to touch."

But he had ignited the centre of his body, which no one had done: not Gracie Watts, and not himself. He remembered Wally Michelin, who had somehow touched this centre but in a way that belonged to the mind, the heart, and the imagination. There was a lotus inside a person, and another person could share its atmosphere, its fragrance, even if those two people were not touching. Wayne did not understand why he should think of Wally Michelin at this moment, except that there was bliss in knowing this centre of the world, and it had to do with deep connection with another person.

"Do you wonder," the gentle intern asked him, "what your life would have been like if you had been brought up female?"

"My name would have been Annabel."

"Annabel. That's beautiful."

"But look at me."

"I see you. I see there was a baby born, and her name is Annabel, and no one knows her."

The intern said this, and Annabel, inside Wayne, had been waiting for it. She heard it from her hiding place.

"You can use her name," the intern said. "Haven't you got a friend you can tell it to?"

"I did." Wayne longed for Wally Michelin. "But I lost her." The incision Haldor Carr had made began to hurt. It hurt a lot, and now all Wayne wanted to do was sleep.

"You have no one?"

Steve Keating had begged to drive Wayne to the hospital. He had badgered him about it until the last minute. Steve had been very interested in the whole story of the part of Wayne that was really a girl.

"I guess I do have one friend," Wayne said.

But the name, Annabel, was a spell that altered Steve Keating.

Steve had kept the scientific information about Wayne in confidence — there was enough fascination in it for him that he had not needed anyone else to know. But when Wayne came back from hospital and told Steve Keating the new name, Steve could not assimilate it as he could the other facts. It was not as if Wayne had asked Steve to call him the new name. Wayne simply told it to him, and the sound, Annabel, floated like a water lily in Steve's mind. It bobbed, surprising him in the night as he walked towards Derek Warford and his friends on the wharf.

"Keating," Derek Warford said. "Where's your friend tonight? Your new buddy. You and him pretty close or what?"

"Get lost."

"What's his name, anyway?"

Steve paid for a bottle out of Warford's six-pack. He bought a couple more. When he had drunk them, he said, "His name's Wayne Blake. And guess what."

"What the fuck, Keating."

"He just had a sex-change operation." Steve did not know what else to call it.

"Fuck off."

"He changed his name to Annabel."

"Get lost."

"Look at him up close next time you get the chance."

"You're full of it, Keating. You need your balls kicked in. That'd be a perfect sex-change operation for you, wouldn't it, boys?"

Jack's Corner Shop had a shelf of Hunt's tomatoes and
Chef Boyardee ravioli and Carnation evaporated milk. A
shelf of paper towels and toilet paper and maxi-pads and
tampons and garbage bags. A rack of chips and Cheezies,
and a shelf of batteries and iron-on patches and WD-40,
and a shelf of paper plates and plastic knives, forks, and
spoons and birthday candles in the shapes of numbers.
Beside the hot dog machine stood beef jerky and apple
flips from Janes's Bakery and one jar of pickled eggs and
another of pickled weiners, and lotto tickets, and behind
the counter there was a meat slicer on which Jack's wife,
Josephine, and his daughter Margaret Skaines sliced three
hundred dollars a week's worth of turkey roll and bologna. The boys of the Battery went there for smokes and
slices of Maple Leaf bologna, and this was what Derek
Warford was doing the night he saw Wayne, who had
spent a half-hour after work up in the place Steve had
shown him — Katie Twomey's verandah — watching
the lights on the water. Wayne had parked his van across
from Jack's Corner Shop and walked up the hill. For the
past couple of nights he had not seen Steve. But he did not
mind quietly watching the lights alone. Steve had been
inclined to talk on and on.

Derek leaned against the counter as Margaret Skaines
wrapped his slices in waxed paper, and he took a good
look at Wayne.

"How's it going?"

"Not bad."

"That's nice to hear."

Margaret Skaines gave Derek his meat and he paid a dollar forty-nine for it, and he bought himself a couple of Sweet Marie bars that Jack's had on sale for sixty-nine cents. He unwrapped his first bologna slice, peeled off the plastic rind with its red and blue letters, threw it on the floor, and bit into the pink, then moved closer. Wayne saw his teeth-marks in the bologna and the brown ridges in the skin over his Adam's apple, and he felt a finger of fear. Derek Warford sized up Wayne's chest, noticing it in a new light.

"Sorry for your troubles there, Wayne."

"Pardon?"

"I heard you had to go in for an operation. Hope it wasn't too serious. Hope it wasn't prostate cancer or nothing."

Wayne saw that Steve had told Derek something.

"No one likes to go under the knife." Derek looked at both sides of his slice. He was particular about flies and specks of dust. "Myself, now, you wouldn't catch me near anything like that. What was it you had done? You didn't lose nothing, did you?"

Derek leaned close enough to escape the earshot of Margaret Skaines, who was wiping the meat machine with a paper towel and lemon spray. Wayne smelled the lemon mist and the bologna on Derek's breath as Derek whispered, "You didn't lose your balls, I hope."

Wayne headed out of there and got in his van. He did not feel like going back up to Katie Twomey's veranda now, but he did not want to go home. He wanted to watch the lights on the water because they calmed him, so he drove the van up Signal Hill Road and he parked it in the parking lot beneath Cabot Tower where lovers and tourists parked. On the ocean side you could see nothing because there was so much fog. You would not know an ocean was even there, just a smoky haze that blocked your view. But on the harbour side the fog tapered and trailed in torn fingers, and the green and red and orange ships' lights and the lights of the cranes and of the arterial road and the churches and the whole city lay spread out, and Wayne looked at those. He did not know Derek Warford had watched him drive up Signal Hill Road, and when six people opened his van doors and got in, it took him a minute to realize it was Derek Warford and his crowd.

"Hey, little girl," Warford said. He held a beer bottle and waved it in Wayne's face, and Wayne realized the bottom was broken out of it.

"Come on now, little girl. Take us for a ride down to Deadman's Pond."

"Where?"

"Guys. Little girl don't know where Deadman's Pond is located."

The bottle hovered over his face and Wayne thought about beauty, and how he had never had it, and he realized he had been hoping for it to come. He didn't want a lot of it but he was hoping for some. Just once to look in the mirror and see a beautiful face, even if the beauty was subdued. Even if no one could see it but himself. It didn't even have to be beauty; it only had to be a fair face. Without the big pores. With creamy skin. Without the remnant of Adam's apple. With ordinary beauty, the same as Margaret Skaines at Jack's Corner Shop, or the woman on Old Topsail Road whose little girl had asked if Wayne was a man or a lady. No, that woman had been really pretty. Wayne didn't need that much beauty. That would be greedy.

"No one took you to Deadman's Pond before, little girl?"

Derek Warford held the broken bottle over Wayne's face. "Sure, you just drove right past it on your way up Signal Hill. Most little girls round here, time they get to half your age, know where Deadman's Pond is. You start her up, that's right, turn her around, drive down there where you came up, right on, and when you get — no, steady there now — down on the left, that's it; you need good tires here, I'll tell you that. Right in here, in behind, keep going, keep going, that's it, folks, in this nice little hideaway. Park further in, behind there. Turn the radio on now. What the fuck station you got on here? What kind of fuckery is that sound?"

The broken beer bottle had beauty. It had a stag on it, with antlers, and the label had a border of gold and a green part like a ribbon unfurling. Warford held the bottle close enough that Wayne could read the small golden words under the stag. VERITAS VINCIT. Veritas, he

thought, must mean truth. What was vincit? Was it anything to do with the word invincible? Was it strength?

"Put her on KIXX Country for fuck's sake." Warford
said. "Put on some Conway Twitty. Some Cunny Titty.
Boys, we got ourselves a little girl who's never been down
here before. I heard she got a real nice set of tits on her.
A real interesting cunt too. Someone want to touch her
hair? Most times a little girl who comes down here, someone plays with her hair a little bit, gets her going. Girls
like it. Hey, Broderick, you check out her hair. Play with
it a little bit. Get the little girl going."

"Fuck off, man. I'm not touching its hair."

"Fuck you, Broderick." Derek Warford pulled down
Wayne's hood. "See that hair?" Derek took a handful of
Wayne's hair and twisted it. "Nice head of hair if only a
little girl would comb it once in a while." Derek took a
flask out of his jean jacket and handed it around. "Like
vodka, little girl? Don't show up on your breath at all.
When you get home to your boyfriend, Steve. Hey, don't
want him to know you were out with us, do you? Where
is he tonight? Know what? I think I saw him over by
Katie Twomey's place just after you left. I think he's over
there waiting on her veranda for you come spend another
evening with him. Sweet, hey? Isn't that sweet, boys?
You fuck Steve, little girl? You and him give it to her on
Twomey's old planks? Good thing she's gone out west to
visit Brian and doesn't see what you and Stevie are up to
on her property. Take off your bra for us now, little girl.

Some of those snaps on them new bras are hard to get off unless you're the owner. What, you don't have a bra on? Okay, boys, we need a volunteer. Fifield, what's wrong with you? Get your — yeah, get the little girl's shirt off. Yeah. Holy shit, what have we got here? I wonder, is there any hair on the fucking tits? Holy fucking Jesus snapping fucking fucked arseholes. Fifield, undo its belt. Give me a report on what you find."

Beauty is gone, Wayne thought. Beauty is gone and beauty is never coming back and it has not even been here yet. Just like Wally Michelin wanting to sing the "Cantique de Jean Racine" when they were little more than children. A thing could depart before it reached you in the first place. There were things like that. The "Cantique" was one, and beauty was another.

"Fuck, Warford, headlights."

The lights arced across the bushes and glinted on Warford's jagged bottle over Wayne's closed eyes. If he opened his eyes he would have to stop thinking about beauty and start thinking about sight. Whether he wanted to lose that or not. Warford could do it in one lurch. Then it wouldn't matter if beauty was gone forever. Wayne's own eyelids, then air the thickness of one more set of eyelids, lay between the broken bottle and his eyeballs.

"Fuckin headlights."

"Fuck, man, what's wrong with you? That's only Jesus Graham fucking Morrisey what does he know? He's got his head so far up Tina Payne's cunt he don't care about no little girl we got here. No little monster fucking girl with hairy tits and — what has she got down there, Fifield? A cunt or what? Too bad we haven't got a camera. See, what I'm interested in is which one of us has the guts to fuck this here little girl."

"Don't go looking at me."

"What about you, Broderick? Come on. Get your fingers ready. You can go at it with your fingers first, then unpack your cock. Come on."

"Fuck off, man."

"Or one of these Sweet Marie bars. What about that? Come on, Fifield, what's wrong with you? Too bad we didn't get one of those black corncobs off Mary Fifield's front door — that'd be just like a big nigger cock we could use. Go get it, Fifield; it's your aunt's door. Big fucking Jesus nigger cock."

"Come off it, Warford."

"That's what she wants."

"Give it up."

"I mean, why would anybody want to be a little girl when they didn't have to, unless they wanted to get fucked?"

"Come off it."

"That's what it's all about, folks. That's the name of the game. See here, boys, what you got here is a real, once-in-a-lifetime opportunity."

28

The Costume Bank

ARK GREEN VELVET, almost black, caught light from
the costume-bank ceiling, and there was muslin
too, and lace, some of it handmade. Wally Michelin
had learned the different kinds of fabric in her aunt's
shop, and she liked knowing their names and their quality. Before she had come to work in Boston she had not
thought about whether her own clothing, or that of her
mother, her neighbours and classmates, had been made
well or thrown together cheaply. Even the dress she had
worn to her prom, with its tailoring and its red satin, was
not, she saw now, like the satin dresses here. These had
more weight and felt colder against her skin. She still had
her satin dress from the prom. It hung in her closet in
Croydon Harbour under a dry-cleaning bag. She still had
the white rose too, dried and pinned to its piece of fern, in

the top drawer of her bureau, beside the red cummerbund Wayne Blake had given her that night. She knew why he had given it to her. She felt it was his way of saying he was sorry for everything that had happened. He was sorry his father had destroyed the Ponte Vecchio, and mortified that Donna Palliser had destroyed Wally's voice and her dreams, and he did not know how to bring any of it back, though he wanted to bring it all back with a longing that was beyond words. But now the cummerbund was stored away in a drawer full of past things, and here, in this many-textured room, hung the present.

The costume bank was not big but it contained all the dresses and trappings for stage performances put on by the Berklee College of Music's theatre and music performance sections. The room was too small, really, and as she made her way through the costumes, which hung from racks strung from the ceiling, the velvet and lace brushed Wally's face, her shoulders, and her hands, and she felt like someone in a story from the Arabian Nights, passing through the doorway of a veiled tent, magical and starlit. She had begun working here in April, two hours a week on Saturdays, doing an inventory of the costumes in time for school to start in the fall. She had to find worn elbows and hems, torn seams, and anything else that would require mending, and she also had to pull out any garments that were too far gone and label them for discarding. Her aunt had got her this job because she knew the school's costume mistress, who regularly came into the shop looking for trimmings and tailoring supplies. Wally had learned quickly in her aunt's shop, and the costume mistress liked her. There would be no pay but Wally would earn tuition credits so that if she wanted to take Berklee courses when they started up in September, she could do so at a fraction of what it would normally cost.

"You don't have to do it," her aunt said. "If you want to take courses without doing the work, we can get you into some courses. If we got you as far as Wimpole Street in London we can get you to Boylston Street."

"I want to," Wally said. She knew singers had worn the costumes onstage. Musical notes would have fallen into the cloth, and the musicians' bodies had touched the dresses and had left their shape in the shoulders and bodices. There was a nearness, touching the velvet and lace, to what she herself had wanted to be, and she could not resist a chance to handle the garments that had been worn by students who sang, even if she could not sing herself.

Thomasina Baikie had gone, in the first week of the previous September, to visit the Harley Street Voice Clinic as Wally and her aunt had requested. They had found Thomasina not at the Cale Street Hostel nor at the Cadogan Hotel, but at the other hotel, the one near Poets' Corner in Westminster Abbey, a hotel Thomasina had not named. Wally's aunt had inquired on the telephone and found out the names of a dozen hotels near Poets' Corner and had phoned seven of them. At the George Hotel the concierge had promised to give Thomasina their message on her arrival on August twenty-ninth, and he had done this.

Thomasina visited the Harley Street Voice Clinic, which was a private clinic and immaculate, she reported to Wally and her aunt. There was an original painting by J. M. W. Turner on the wall of the reception hall, and a sculpture by Henry Moore under a skylight. The doctor who looked at the information Thomasina presented to him on Wally's behalf had not promised he could repair Wally's voice. There was not enough information, he said, on the exact damage done to her vocal cords, and a lot of time had passed. He would need magnetic resonance imaging and he would need to see Wally for himself.

Wally and her aunt had made an appointment for February. From the week she had begun working in her aunt's shop Wally had saved her wages, and by February she had the fare to England and the fee for a consultation, but not for any treatment.

"You let us worry about that," her aunt had said, and Wally remembered how her mother always said Aunt Doreen and her husband had more money between the two of them than they knew what to do with. They had accounts and investments up to their ears, Ann Michelin had said; Doreen did not even have to run that shop if she didn't want to. She could quit the shop tomorrow and live out the rest of her days with a mouth full of caviar. Wally had not seen her aunt eat caviar and she had not seen her uncle at all. But there was a maid who came on Wednesdays. Wally had seen her in the doorway of her aunt's bedroom changing the linen, a new blue-white sheet billowing in a breeze from the open window.

The discards from the costume bank had trimmings that needed to be kept, and to salvage them the costume mistress had given Wally a tool box containing a pearl-handled stitch ripper, some razor blades, and a pair of scissors from Finland. She had a box with partitions for buttons, silver fastenings, brass fittings, rivets, hooks and eyes, tassels and cords, and pieces of pocket or wristband or waistband embellished with needlework. These things could be reused, and so could squares of fabric from parts of the garments that were not threadbare. Wally sat on an arrow-back chair under a lamp and cut these and folded them and arranged them by colour and fabric type so they could be used in new pieces that were always being tailored downstairs. It was satisfying work and she loved the beauty of it, and at times she thought she might look in the Berklee College calendar and see what other courses they had besides singing. At those times she thought it would be good to put these hours of work to use, to let them pay for courses as the costume mistress had offered. But at other times she remembered her old resolve: if she could not study singing, she did not want to study anything.

The doctor at the Harley Street Voice Clinic had told her there was not much of a chance he could restore her voice to what it would have been had Donna Palliser not thrown shards of that glass ball. The wait between the injury and his attention had been long, he said, and even had it not been years, even if Wally had come to see him immediately, there was probably not much more he could have done than that which he offered to do now. He could perhaps restore her speaking voice, he said. He could make it stronger, and she could even sing. Perhaps she could sing in a choir, though he could not guarantee it. She could certainly sing for her own pleasure, and if she had any ear for music she would be able to sing according to the tunefulness of that ear. But as for the strength of her singing voice or anything approaching a professional solo career, he could not see that as a reasonable outcome.

"Well, I don't want you to do anything," Wally had told him. She did not want her aunt and uncle paying thousands of American dollars for her to sing for her own pleasure. She told her aunt this on the phone.

"But your own pleasure," her aunt said, "is sometimes the only pleasure you have in this life. You're over there now. You're in England. Get the most out of it that you can."

The doctor did the best work he could and told Wally to rest her voice for six weeks. Then, if she wanted to sing for her own pleasure, she could gently begin with voice exercises he set for her. He told her again that it was possible she could sing in a choir if she chose.

"You don't have to have a solo voice to be in a choir," he said. "In fact, there is something about a choir that brings together imperfections in the voices and uses them to make something new, like an infusion of different kinds of tea leaves. It can be quite beautiful."

He had been a kind man, and Wally had felt his kindness, though he had not done what she wanted him to do and had not said what she had hoped with all her heart he would say.

29

Seed Potatoes

JACINTA BLAKE APPEARED TO SOME people to have retreated from the vigour she had possessed when her son lived in the house and when her husband spent more time with her. She walked less often the road to the Hudson's Bay store, and she had not been to church through the winter, not even for the funeral of Kate Davis, who had been the nursing administrator at the hospital in Goose Bay and whose funeral was attended by everybody, even the lieutenant-governor of Newfoundland, who had flown up from Government House in St. John's. It was true that, over the fall, winter, and spring when her son was away, Jacinta had not eaten enough and had lost sight of what day it was, but from her point of view it was not she who had retreated from living.

She remembered, or thought she remembered, a time when her husband had stayed at home for more than a week or two at a stretch, and had looked at her when they spoke instead of looking at the stove, or out the door towards the kindling, or farther, to the sky and to gulls and scoters and other birds that moved in that sky. She tried to remember that intimacy. Had it been an illusion? She was sure it had not. And it was no illusion either that she now floated in an existence in which she remained untouched. No one touched her body, and now that Wayne had gone away, no one touched her soul. She had become unreal, she thought, to anyone outside herself. And as a result she was losing a sense of her own effect on the world. She had an effect on the kettle if she put it on the stove. It boiled. She made tea. If she drew the curtains the curtains remained closed. She had no problem having an effect on the curtains. Her slippers lay where she had placed them after their last use, as did her glasses, her cup, and her saucer. But as for an effect on the larger world, which she had had as a mother and did not now feel she had as a woman living practically alone, that effect had lost its power.

When Treadway came home in the spring, he saw that she was not sure whether it was a Wednesday or a Saturday, and that was when he wrote to Wayne that he thought she was confused. But she was not confused, not in her own mind. She watched Treadway tidy the house and open the curtains and doors and windows. He even washed the windows, which surprised her. He washed them with Windex and did it in the methodical way he had with every task, using a system that included three types of cloth. When they went to bed, he kissed her goodnight on the cheek as if he were kissing a niece or a nephew goodbye at the train station, then he turned his back to her and began his soft snoring almost instantly. She had never been bothered by his snoring, which was a kind of music to her, but she was sure she remembered a time in their marriage when being with Treadway while he was sleeping did not feel the same as being with him while he was awake.

Now he did other tasks that belonged to the month of May. He climbed a ladder to the roof and cleaned the chimney, and he descended into the root cellar and brought up last year's old, soft potatoes to use as this year's seed potatoes in the garden. He did not know she had bought potatoes at the store while he was on his trapline. She had done this because it was nicer to walk outside in the daylight and buy clean, unsprouted potatoes than it was to go down the cellar steps and carry up potatoes that had to be washed and that had sprouted long white tentacles and developed wrinkly skins. So there were plenty of seed potatoes remaining, and Treadway laid them in a pile on the front path and began to cut them in pieces so he could plant them before he left. In the past it had been normal for him to stay at home in the summer. His new pattern, his wish to be away in the wilderness all the time, went unacknowledged.

He sat on the chopping block, a chunk of birch he had rolled over from the woodpile. Sun shone through its loose bark and turned it red gold, and when he cut the potatoes with his small knife, the task looked inviting to Jacinta. The fact that Treadway had carried the seed potatoes up from the dark, that he had poured them into a neat pile, and that he had made a little seat to sit on while he cut them, made Jacinta feel she wished she could cut them herself. The pile of seed potatoes had gained human care and attention from Treadway, and now the sun shone and warmed them even more. Treadway filled one bucket with the cut potatoes and went to his shed to fetch another bucket, and she took his spot on the chopping block and began cutting the potatoes herself. When he came back with the bucket, he set it at her feet and stood looking at her for a minute. This felt like the longest they had spoken to each other in a long time, though neither said anything out loud; then he went to tidy the woodpile, which had dwindled over the winter, so that he could replenish it on a solid base.

When she had finished cutting the seed potatoes, she left them in the sun to dry their surfaces so mould could not attack them before they began to grow, then she went to the sink to wash the ingrained dirt out of her hands and wrists and nails. She scrubbed until her skin tingled and then she decided to take a bath and change her clothes. Treadway had to go in the truck to Goose Bay to replace some of his drill bits in order to repair his Ski-Doo, and she asked if she could go with him. She stood in the Mealy Mountain Outfitters' Co-op while he spoke with the owner. She smelled the oakum and canvas and metal dust from the key-cutting machine, and she asked him how he felt about going in to Mom's Home Cooking for some fries and a couple of hot dogs and a cup of coffee. Treadway liked onions on his hot dogs, and Mom's Home Cooking was the only place in Goose Bay where they had a bowl of chopped onions on the counter beside the ketchup, mustard, and relish, because that was what Americans working on the base liked, and Georgina Hounsell had paid attention.

Treadway said, "I haven't been in there for a long time." He saw she had been looking at fancy gardening gloves hanging on a display rack with a sale price on them, left over from Mothers' Day. He had his drill bits in his hand along with a box of cotton work gloves and a packet of sandpaper. "Do you want me to buy you a pair of those?"

"No."

"They have nice flowers on them."

"I don't like flowers on gardening gloves. If I'm going to work in the garden I want plain work gloves like those you've got there." His work gloves were white cotton and a box of twenty pairs cost the same as one pair of the ladies' gardening gloves. He had known this about Jacinta, that she liked using his plain white gloves, and he had always liked the fact, but it was one of the things he had forgotten.

"I don't need all these," he said. "You can take half."
He remembered as he said this that sharing a box of gloves
was a thing they had done often, but not in recent years.
Another thing they had done was eat in a restaurant on
an outing to Goose Bay but ask the waitress to give them
their coffee in paper cups after they had eaten. They would
take the coffees in the truck and drive to the lookout on the
highway back to Croydon Harbour and stop the truck and
drink their coffee while looking out at the Mealy Mountains. Today after their hot dogs at Mom's Home Cooking
they did this again, and it felt very good to them both, so
that when they arrived home, Treadway said, "I don't have
to go into the bush yet. The shingles on the old part of the
house are gone, and while I'm up on the roof I might as
well have a look at the flashing."

Jacinta put on the work gloves, got her small-bladed
shovel out of the shed, and turned the garden over to get
it ready for the potatoes. She brushed her hair and put
on a red dress and her green wool coat and her shoes
instead of her winter boots, and she walked to the Hudson's Bay store to buy carrot and parsnip seeds and snow
peas and, while she was at it, sweet peas, which she grew
not for any pea but for their frilled flowers that grew
six feet high if you knew where to put them. None of
this could be planted for another two weeks, but it was
nice to spend that fortnight with the seed packets on the
kitchen windowsill, imagining the shoots coming up out
of the ground.

Roland Shiwack had borrowed Treadway's wheelbarrow the previous autumn and had not returned it. Now, when Treadway went to ask for it back, Roland mentioned that he had noticed Jacinta out turning over soil to prepare the garden.

"Now that is something," Roland said, "my own wife will never do. I admire that you have a woman who can work hard like that and still look nice." Roland had seen Jacinta in her green coat and shoes. He did not know where the wheelbarrow was, and Treadway could not understand that. He could not understand why a grown man would borrow another man's wheelbarrow in the first place instead of getting one of his own, and he could understand less how anyone could lose a whole wheelbarrow and not know where it had gone. There was something, moreover, in the way that Roland Shiwack had said Treadway's wife looked nice that Treadway did not like. It was as if Roland had voiced something Treadway felt too shy to say out loud himself, and Jacinta was his own wife. If Treadway was married to her and could not say it, how did Roland Shiwack summon the nerve to pass a comment on Jacinta's looks? And what was wrong with Roland's own wife's looks? Melba Shiwack looked like a normal woman. There was nothing bad looking about her. She was unremarkable, as far as Treadway could see, and he did not know why Roland had now decided to remark on Treadway's own wife.

Treadway would not have called these passing thoughts jealousy, but he did think, on his return home, that it was a good thing he had decided not to go back into the bush just yet.

Jacinta did a laundry in which she washed as many of her filmy nightdresses as she could fit in the washing machine, the ones that had unconsciously reminded Treadway of misty stars while he was reading the book of Job in his hunting cabin. She hung them on the line, where the late May breeze made them dance over the mix of newly dug garden and what was left of the snow.

3o

The Makeup Artist

STEVE KEATING SHOWED UP at Wayne's apartment door on Forest Road, the picture of remorse. He looked, Wayne thought, like someone who was twelve years old instead of fifteen, and he presented Wayne with a lunch from Caines Grocery.

"It's a cold plate." Steve handed Wayne the bag and Wayne took out a paper plate covered in plastic wrap and laden with the kind of food Mr. Caines's regular customers bought for their husbands on Saturdays before they left their kitchens for the bingo hall. Two slices of boiled ham, two of turkey, some coleslaw and macaroni salad, a bread roll, and potato salad dyed purple with pickled beet juice and triggered out of an ice cream scoop.

"I told you," Steve said.

"You told me what?"

"That if you really got to know me you wouldn't like me."

"You never told me that."

"I did."

"I don't think you did, Steve."

"Well, I thought it then. If only I had kept my mouth shut. I never meant to blab about you to Warford, honest to God I didn't. My mother says I can't keep my mouth shut, and she said she wouldn't be surprised if you tore the head off me after what I done."

Wayne had not gone to work in the days that had passed since his attack. He had a cut near his eye and he had injuries that Derek Warford and his gang had inflicted when they were experimenting with his body, but he had not gone to a doctor and he had not told anyone what had happened. At the drugstore he bought ointment whose label said it was cooling and healing and you could use it on babies' skin, and he put that on himself in all the places that were hurt and that he could reach. When Steve came to the door with the lunch, Wayne was hungry. He had nothing in his fridge but half a tin of beans and some bread. When he called in sick, Frank King had told him not to stay off the job too long or he would be replaced, and now he was afraid to go in because he knew he did not look well, and he also knew Frank King would soon say something about his appearance. On Signal Hill Derek Warford had kept referring to his breasts and mocking them, and Wayne realized, when he took a long look in the mirror, that if Frank King had not already noticed, he would surely do so soon.

"I wouldn't blame you," Steve said, "if you hated me now."

"I don't hate you, Steve."

"You can if you want."

"Once I like someone, no matter what they do, I keep liking them."

"That's what Miss Cramm used to say. She was my teacher before she went away. She let me make top hats for the school play and I didn't have to be in the play, and that was a good thing because I can't remember any lines. But now I have Miss Fiander and she doesn't like me one little bit. Are you working today?"

Wayne had been devising a way to go in and load up his truck without Frank King seeing the cut on his face. He knew Frank took the same lunch break every day and ate at Wendy's. He wanted to make his deliveries after dusk, but it was nearly June, and every evening the light lasted longer.

"I'm having a problem," he told Steve, "with the thing I told you about. How I want to go after dark to deliver the meat. Last night it was still light at almost nine o'clock, and no one wants a delivery man coming later than that."

"I can do it!" Steve looked overjoyed to be able to make it up to Wayne. "My mom has my supper ready at five thirty, after I come home from Caines, and at six o'clock I can come here and we can go in the van and I can go up all the driveways and you can stay in the van. Anyway, you don't look that bad, if you went and bought yourself some clothes that weren't so baggy on you."

Wayne let Steve make the deliveries. He let him go up the driveways with the meat and come back down to the van with the money. And he went to Frank King's warehouse to load up between 12:40 and 1:30 every day, when he knew Frank was down Thorburn Road eating a double cheeseburger and a baked potato with grated cheese and cheese sauce at Wendy's, so that Frank would not see him.

But one day Frank came back early because Wendy's had run out of cheese sauce, and he spied Wayne.

"You definitely need," he said, "to become more image conscious." Frank looked at Wayne's jeans, his shirt and boots. "Clean, clean, clean." Frank circled around Wayne, and Wayne knew it was his body, not his clothes, that unnerved Frank.

"There's something about your image," Frank said, "that doesn't quite . . . I can't put my finger on it. Go to Tony the Tailor and get him to fit that shirt for you. He only charges seven dollars. Customers want a cleaner look than what you've got here. They're going to take one look at you and they're going to shut their doors."

At night, after his deliveries, Wayne dropped Steve off and drove down to the waterfront and watched the cranes. Sometimes he watched them from his van, but police were always on the lookout for people loitering on the docks, and he did not want to have to answer as to what he was doing down there at midnight. So he went, in the June nights, to sit on the ground under the Southside bridge, and he watched the cranes from there, the lattice booms lit yellow and orange, and the sounds of seawater smacking the dock, and up above, on Water Street, the howls of drunk people on George Street, and honking taxis, and the hum of cars driving between the hotels and steak restaurants and late night bars.

He sat there and he saw men drinking across the road behind the Murray Premises, and he saw other things too, things that reminded him of what his father had said on the phone about what happened to people who did not plan their actions carefully, who lived in the city and had no training, who had not thought of economics and had not looked ahead, and had gained entry to the criminal side of life that was waiting for them. He looked up at the bridge above him, the Southside bridge, and he thought of all the bridges he had once sketched and studied, and he thought how this bridge was not like any of those. It was utilitarian and did not have the beauty of an Italian bridge, and it did not even have the ugliness of London Bridge. It had its own ugliness that came from the fact that nobody cared how it was designed as long as it got cars from the west end of Water Street onto Southside Road. There were beer bottles under it, and condoms and

Coke cans, and the bridge itself had a galvanized guard-rail with rusty bolts, and it was without spans or any design whatsoever.

The world, evidently, Wayne thought now, was a place that did not care about much in the way of beauty. Derek Warford and his gang had treated him like a piece of garbage they wanted to use and discard. They had cut his face with a broken bottle. They had talked of killing him and tossing his body over the cliff at the top of Signal Hill. But he had escaped. Now the only beauty he knew was in the symmetry of these cranes, their lattice booms and their slow movement, and the way their hoist lines and heavy hook blocks lowered the containers in a slow, straight line the same as a plumb line. There was both engineering and beauty in this, and he spent hours watching it, and in the afternoons before he made his deliveries he did a lot of walking, noticing as he walked that he enjoyed hidden and slanted streets, like Nunnery Hill, and streets with names that were paradoxes, like Long Street, which was the shortest street in St. John's, or Road de Luxe, which had nothing deluxe about it at all.

Road de Luxe was a funny, steep little road that took you from Waterford Bridge Road to the Village Mall on Topsail Road. It was just a poky little hill with a name that raised your expectations. What it had on it was a shop called Valu Best Convenience, which looked as if it could have been there from a time before the street had acquired its name. Envelopes sat next to matches and emergency candles and ladies' dress gloves. He noticed a box of loose combs and thought about the length of his hair. He had not had it cut lately because he did not want to go into a barber shop and have the barber look at him closely and ask what kind of back and sides he preferred. With his body's new softness, the breasts and the new shape of Annabel, a man's haircut would have looked stranger than hair that had some freedom in it. He had never needed to shave as his father shaved, faithfully every morning, and he had never possessed stubble or what people called five-o'clock shadow. His face had always been smooth, though had he not shaved there would have been some downy facial hair, gold and soft. He bought a razor and a comb. But if he was going to grow into the softness of Annabel, he did not want to have a man's barbered head or face. He did not know what he wanted, but he knew he did not want to continue to pretend to be a man. At the top of Road de Luxe he decided to cross Topsail Road to the mall. He took his new comb and razor into the men's washroom near the food court and shaved the almost invisible down from beneath his ears: no more than exists on the faces of many girls. The soap from the dispenser had a chemical scent. His hair, as he used the new comb, reminded him of the soft ferns that would, at this time of year, be sending up feathery heads along the creek behind his parents' house. Had his face ever been a man's face?

He checked his Adam's apple by swallowing. Was it as big as a man's? He could imagine the answer being either yes or no. Wayne wished he could tell, but his own face was too familiar. A man came in to use the urinals and looked at him suspiciously. The man carried his wallet in his back pocket and there was a faded square of denim around it. The man zippered his fly and shot Wayne a look that had disgust and fear in it. Maybe Frank King had not been far off the mark.

The mall always felt to Wayne as if it were trying to convince him of an illusion that he was not quite getting. That the world was a place with glittering lights. That you could show you loved someone by giving her a new mug with a little white bear inside it. He had once come in to find socks and realized that, in all the mall's 116 stores, there was not one pair of socks his father would have worn. He looked now in the windows of those stores and tried to catch sight of himself as if he were looking at a stranger. He tried to see, in the transparent reflections of himself walking against racks of blazers and halter tops and Italian-style dinnerware, what other people saw when they looked at him. Were his shoulders hunched? He tried to straighten them, but this thrust his chest out in a way that disquieted him. In the window of Fairweather hung a sweater that looked as if it was the colour it had been when it lived on the sheep. It was a woman's sweater, but what made it a woman's? He went into the store to touch it. He pulled the neck to see the size. It was size eight. A salesgirl asked him if she could help. He felt embarrassed. He wanted to know what the sweater would look like on him.

"Have you got this in a larger size?"

"What size would you like?"

"How do the sizes work?"

"Well an eight is about my size."

"I need it for someone bigger."

"Are they big-boned or are they tall?"

"Tall." Wayne was guessing now. He suspected the salesgirl did not want to say the word *fat*. He was not fat.

"You can bring it back if it doesn't suit. You have to return it within fourteen days, unworn and with the tags attached. Would you like to try a twelve or a fourteen?"

"Fourteen."

Wayne wondered how the salesgirl would know if a garment had been worn. He wondered how long you had to wear something before the fact of your having worn it would show. He paid for the sweater and went into a shoe store. Women's shoes were small. But it was not just that they were small. They had insubstantial soles. He picked up a black pump. It was light as a piece of toast. He couldn't imagine standing in it without the whole thing crumbling. He was five feet nine and weighed 150 pounds, and he knew there were women of that height and weight who were considered normal women. But these shoes did not seem to him to be able to support his weight. Were male pounds denser than female pounds?

A clerk saw him standing with the shoe in his hand. He saw a woman's lace-up walking shoe on a bottom shelf. It looked more promising, but still, the toe was tapered.

"Do you have this shoe," he asked, "in a size ten?" Wayne remembered that when they were children, Wally Michelin's feet had been the same size as his own, but the sizes on their shoes had been different.

"We have up to forty-one in European sizes. That's about a ten. It depends on the make."

"Can I see it?"

She brought the shoe and with it a green shoe Wayne liked. It was the colour of birch leaves, and he bought the pair. In Suzy Shier there were plain skirts with a back slit that came just past the knee, but he could not bring himself to buy a skirt. Behind the skirts were pants made of the same material: women's slacks. What made them women's? He held a pair and regarded its seams. They were flatter than men's seams. Women's slacks were held together much more lightly. He paid twenty-nine dollars and hoped they would not fall apart. A sign proclaimed a three-for-ten-dollar special on ladies' trouser socks. It said they were a staple in any woman's wardrobe, and Wayne bought some.

He wanted to change in the washroom but knew he couldn't go in the men's toilets to do this. There was a washroom whose door had a blue wheelchair painted on it, and when he opened the door he saw this was just one

room, with a toilet, sink and mirror, and he went in. He
put the sweater on, and the slacks and the green shoes.
He put his old shirt and jeans and work boots in the Fairweather bag and the shoe store bag. He stayed in there
for a long time and checked that the door was locked. He
looked at himself in the mirror. He was shaven and wearing the slacks and the shoes, but it was still impossible for
him to tell whether he looked anything like a woman. He
suspected he did not. The only way he could see how the
shoes looked on him was if he raised his knee very high
and rested one foot on the platform in front of the mirror.
There was a small heel on the shoe, half an inch, and it
did look like a convincing slope, his foot sloping into the
green leather the way women's feet sloped. He kept his
eye on the door handle, and when the handle moved, he
tried to put his foot back on the floor and he lost his bal-
ance and wrenched his leg. He took the slacks off and put
his jeans back on, with the new socks still on under them.
But then he changed his mind again. He put the slacks
back on, and the shoes. The shoes were tight. He wished
they had had the next size up. He wished he could see
himself from the back. If he saw himself from the back he
might get a fresh perspective. He might know whether or
not his body had anything like a feminine air. The mall
was a place with hundreds of people in it, maybe a thousand people, and none of them knew him. He could walk
through it once and see how it felt. He decided to go to
the drugstore and buy himself a hand mirror so he could

look at the back of his body in the mirror. He could not remember the last time he had seen the back of his body, or if he had ever seen it.

It was hard to find something as small as a hand mirror among the multitudes of products in the drugstore. As he searched he came across the hosiery rack, and decided to buy a pair of extra-sheer stockings for a five-foot-nine person weighing between 145 and 160 pounds. The shoes might feel more comfortable with stockings instead of the socks. As he carried the stockings past an island stacked with pots of makeup, a man spoke. The man was bigger than Wayne, with hair that came to his shoulders. He had a kind face. He held a brush with a gold handle.

"Would you like to have a consultation?"

"What?"

"I am here for Lancôme. If you would like, I can show you how to apply colours that are best for your face. You have no obligation to buy anything. If you do not have time I understand completely."

The man had the kind face of Robin Williams. He looked like the kind of man who would be riding on a motorcycle through the hills with a little boy, his son, in a movie. The movie would be all about how he tried to take care of his son through heartbreaking circumstances. He was looking at Wayne now and offering him a makeup consultation with no trace of irony. There was nothing quizzical in his face. Either he believed Wayne was a woman or he had chosen to treat him with dignity.

Wayne could not tell which. There was a stool under a lamp and Wayne sat on it.

"Women's beauty goes beyond appearances," said the man who looked like Robin Williams. "It is an emotion on the very surface of your skin."

"I've never worn makeup."

"We believe every woman is beautiful. I am not going to do anything to your face that will be harsh or look unnatural."

"I wouldn't know the first place to start."

"We start with a coat of foundation." The makeup artist dabbed a dot on Wayne's face. It was hard for Wayne not to laugh at the idea of foundation coated on his face. The procedure reminded him of painting walls. But the makeup artist had such a sympathetic face, and was so careful with his touch, Wayne did not want to hurt him.

"I am going to blend the foundation on one half of your face and show you." Wayne closed his eyes and let the makeup artist brush the paint on his cheek and eyelid, his forehead and chin. He wondered what the artist's real name was. He was afraid he might accidentally call him Robin. There was something incredibly relaxing about sitting in the stool under the white light and having your face brushed so gently. Wayne wondered if the makeup artist had any idea how it felt to receive his work.

"If you go out," the artist said, "and it rains, even if you swim, it will be all right. It will not run or smear. Even if you cry. Life is life after all, and maybe you will cry."

He said this with kindness, and Wayne had a sense of the world being a place where everyone had the sorrows he had, whereas, before sitting here with Robin Williams, the world had been a place where most people coped much better than Wayne did. Wayne pictured everyone in the rain with their sorrows, which were quiet, personal sorrows of every kind, and Robin Williams had studied them all. Did every woman feel this way once she had accepted the offer of a makeup consultation, or was this artist unique? Wayne had no idea. He thought of the name Robin, how blue the egg of a robin was in spring and how a robin meant certain hope.

The artist told Wayne that you wear colours on your face that are the opposite of the colours in your eyes. He showed him how to create a lifetime supply of lipstick by using a pot of face powder for pigment and mixing it with any clear lip gloss.

"If you take this face powder meant for women with dark skin, you can push it into your lash line with a brush and one pot will last you for years."

"Thank you," Wayne said when Robin Williams showed him his new face in the mirror. He wondered if the colour around his eyes made him look harrowed. He was not sure. He decided to have faith for now, and bought the pots. He did not feel that Robin Williams was unscrupulous, or that he was there purely to sell.

"I applied these with a Lancôme brush, but you can use any brush. You do not have to buy Lancôme brushes, which are twenty-four dollars."

The makeup artist was there to sell pots of makeup, to be sure, but Wayne felt he cared about what he did. Robin Williams felt that life was something in which maybe you would cry, and he gave every woman dignity by tracing her mouth, her eyes, her skin, with kind hands.

When he went back out into the mall, Wayne was glad there were crowds. He thought he might like to come back here in future and just walk or sit in the food court and know no one was interested in him. There was no Frank King, and no Derek Warford. He did not like the mall or find anything in it beautiful. It was ugly, really, as featureless and anonymous as any mall in North America, but this gave him a feeling that he was hiding, just for a while, from daylight and from scrutiny. St. John's had a hard daylight sharpened by the shale of Signal Hill and the Southside hills. There was no retreating from it downtown or in the Battery. But here in the mall you were anonymous, and you could rest.

But he was sitting in the food court with a hot chocolate in a paper cup, thinking about whether to get noodles from China Hut or some teriyaki chicken from Koya Japan, when he saw someone he knew. At first he hoped it was not the person he thought it was. He did not want that person to see him in the clothes he had bought from Fairweather. Several times now he had thought he saw people he knew from Labrador. It was a thing that happened when you went to a new place. People from your old home seemed to appear, but it was an illusion of place, and when you got close to them, you realized they were not that person at all. This had happened to Wayne a few times. Once he even thought he saw his father, but of course he had not. But this woman looked more and more, the closer she got to Wayne, like his old school principal, Victoria Huskins, the woman who had berated a child in kindergarten for having an accident in the school washroom. The woman responsible for suspending Thomasina Baikie the time she took Wayne to the hospital when he was in grade seven. She had come out of the drugstore where he had just had his face made up by Robin Williams, and she had entered the food court and was now looking around at the different stalls as he had done, trying to decide what she was going to eat, and he was still waiting for the moment when he could tell himself it was certainly not Victoria Huskins, but a stranger, when she recognized him.

31

My Dear Companion

WHAT HAPPENED, WAYNE WONDERED, to make a person like Victoria Huskins appear younger after her retirement? Without saying anything about his appearance, she greeted him with what felt like genuine warmth, asked if he was free to chat with her while she had her lunch, and left her bags at his table while she went to get herself a Dairy Queen cheeseburger and a caramel sundae. When she came back to the table, she did not unwrap the burger but began eating the sundae.

"I'm having dessert first." Her hair was straight instead of being held in a controlled helmet style as it had been when she was his principal, and she had grown it so that it framed her face in a way that was pretty. "How are you, Wayne?"

He felt exposed and had to tell himself it was not like it had been when she was his principal. He had left grade seven long ago. She had faded out of his life, and in senior high there was a new principal. But he felt now that if he did not control his feelings, he would turn into thirteen-year-old Wayne Blake here in front of her, and she would have a principal's authority over him.

He told himself silently that he had grown up and had left school, had in fact left Croydon Harbour behind, and did not need to feel ashamed that he now sat before Victoria Huskins looking like a young woman instead of a young man. Did he even look feminine? The lights in the food court were not bright. And even if they were, did he look like Annabel or did he look like Wayne? The only people who had given him any idea had been the man he saw earlier in the washroom, who had looked at him strangely, but had Wayne imagined that look? That man, and the makeup artist who looked like Robin Williams, and he had been so kind, so non-judgemental that Wayne still did not know how he appeared, at this moment, to someone like Victoria Huskins. And even if he did look more like Annabel than like Wayne, why should he feel ashamed in front of Victoria Huskins? He wished at that moment that his whole life had not been a secret, that lots of people were like him, instead of his being alone in a world where everyone was secure in their place as either woman or man. His aloneness was what made him feel ashamed, and he did not know why it had to be so. Now he looked at Victoria Huskins as she collected the last of her caramel sauce on the end of a plastic spoon, and he knew she was not what he had thought. There was nothing in her face that matched the idea he had of her when he was younger. She appeared to him to be much more human.

"I'm all right," Wayne said. "How about you?"

"Retirement is wonderful. I spent most of June in the vegetable garden, and I come down here to see my sisters and my old friends from university and we cackle a lot and talk about living wills and planning for when we get old and feeble, and between that and some painting I've always wanted to do, there's hardly any time left for belly dancing or getting on my stationary bike. In fact I think I might have to sell the bike and just concentrate on the dancing."

Wayne remembered that Joanne, the waitress in Shelley's All-Day Breakfast, had told him that women all over the world danced. They danced by themselves, in ways no one knew about. He wanted to ask Victoria Huskins now, Where was the belly dancing when you were the principal of grades kindergarten through seven in Croydon Harbour? But he did not. He could see in her face that she had found a freedom he did not have. Somehow this inflexible woman had become flexible, and she was beautiful in a way that he could not attain, though she was old. He wondered if he was imagining her new flexibility. He wondered if she was the same hard person she had appeared to be in his childhood, and if he was the one who had frozen or petrified, so that even Victoria Huskins was now softer and more human than he was. He did not know who he had become, and now here was Victoria Huskins asking him to tell her what he was doing in St. John's.

"Are you in university, Wayne? Are you up at Memorial? Tell me what you're studying. You were always so good at math and science, and art too. I remember when we put the class diagrams of ocean life up on the walls, you had the best drawing in the school. Some kind of anemone, wasn't it?"

"It was a Tealia anemone." Wayne was surprised Victoria Huskins remembered his drawing. He had spent a lot of time working out the symmetry of it.

"I always loved the grade six science projects. Are you studying any science now?"

"No."

"Really? I thought for sure you would do something in science or engineering. But you were good at art too. Are you doing some kind of design or drafting?"

"I'm not at Memorial."

"Are you at one of the technical colleges?"

"I'm not at any kind of college. I'm working."

Victoria Huskins had unwrapped her burger but now she looked at it, wrapped it again, and put it in her purse. "People don't know this," she said, "but you can reheat a burger and it is every bit as good as it was fresh. What kind of work, Wayne?"

"I'm working for one of the wholesalers on Thorburn Road."

"What kind of wholesaler?"

"Food. I have my own refrigerated van. I make deliveries all over St. John's and part of Mount Pearl."

"What do you deliver, Wayne?"

"Meat. Fish. Different kinds of sausages."

Victoria Huskins looked him in the eye. She did not linger on his hair or his clothing or his makeup. "So you are selling meat from a van."

She had not asked him about his appearance. They were a thousand miles from Croydon Harbour. She waited for him to tell her more but did not appear to be curious about his maleness or femaleness.

"I never thought of going to Memorial," he said. "I'm working on figuring out a lot of other things."

Now her face changed. "What kind of things?"

Wayne felt his own story amass as a cloud. He could not be coherent about it. He wanted to talk to someone but he did not know how, because somehow the facts, with their tidy labels and medical terms, reduced his whole being to something that he did not want it to be. How could he sit here and tell Victoria Huskins what the doctors had labelled him without reducing himself to the status of a diagram like the one she had mentioned: his grade six diagram of the North Atlantic Tealia anemone? He could not begin to explain, so he sat without words. He did not know if he could trust her, and even if he could have trusted her he could not explain his whole being with words. The cloud rose in him and reached his throat, where it amassed as a blockage that felt leaden and sorrowful. He felt it as a lump that threatened to silence him.

"You are sitting here," Victoria Huskins said, "the picture of misery. I know what happened at the hospital, Wayne. When you were with me in junior high. Did you know that?"

Wayne had not thought of himself as "with" Victoria Huskins in junior high. He had not thought of her as knowing anything. His father had always made it plain that he should not say a word about his condition to anyone in Croydon Harbour.

"I know everything that happened that day and night, because I made it my business to know. My job meant I needed to be on top of what was going on. It was all confidential, but I do know what happened and I know how it has led to where you are now."

"How did you know?"

"I asked a friend, Wayne. A friend who had a long history of working at the hospital. I asked Kate Davis. She was the nursing administrator there her whole life, and a very close friend before she died last winter. Kate was my dear companion, and I asked her to get a copy of your file because I needed to know what was going on. I needed it to help me know how to deal with you as a student, and with Thomasina Baikie too."

"But you fired Thomasina."

"I didn't fire her, Wayne. The Labrador East School

Board wanted to fire her, because someone saw her in the hospital with you during school hours and she had not notified your parents or followed any of the correct procedures."

The lip gloss that had been applied by the man who resembled Robin Williams had begun to bother Wayne.

"I convinced them to temporarily suspend her. I told them that while she had broken rules she had done it because it was an emergency situation, and I couldn't have told them that if I had not believed it in my own mind."

The lip gloss felt gooey on his mouth. He took a napkin and wiped it off, and he thought about the other makeup that the artist had applied to his face and his eyes. He could feel it on his skin.

"That's the reason I needed to see your file. But Wayne, that's not important now. What's important now is why you aren't at the university, or at college, or doing anything at all with your mind and your talents."

Over Wayne's face were two layers of makeup: the foundation and the daubed powder. He began to feel as if his face was smothering under the paint.

"Youth has carried you so far. That's what I say about all the children passing through my school."

Wayne remembered how he had not been sure what to think about the eye makeup when the artist had shown it to him in the mirror. He had wondered if it gave him a harrowed look, a kind of false vulnerability that invited people to look at his face in a way different than anyone had looked at it when he presented himself as male. He had these thoughts now as Victoria Huskins questioned him about his mind and his talents, and he did not know what to tell her or what to tell himself. All he knew was that he had to get to a sink and some water and wash the makeup off his face. Why was it called makeup? Did it claim to make up for some deep failing inside a person, and if it did claim to do so, how could the claim be anything other than a façade and a lie? The makeup exaggerated something. Wayne was not sure what it exaggerated. It exaggerated something and diminished something at the same time, and the green shoes had begun to pinch his feet. He felt as if his feet were growing larger with every moment, and his body too, pressed against the seams of the new pants. He knew his body was not really growing, but he knew too that it did not want to be confined in the new outer casing he had found for it at this mall, and it did not want to listen any more to Victoria Huskins, whose voice surrounded him like a third layer of something clammy and alien, on top of the makeup and the clothes. He knew she meant him no harm, and neither had the makeup artist or the salesgirl at Fairweather. But he remembered a cotton shirt and his favourite jeans at home, if you could call it a home, on Forest Road, and he ached to go there and wash the mask off his face and put cotton next to his skin and let it breathe.

"You start out with all the potential," Victoria Huskins said, "and you're young. But what happens is, one day you wake up, Wayne, and potential is a thing of the past."

He did not want to hear this because he already knew it. What was more, he felt that if potential had existed in Victoria Huskins's other students, it had perhaps not had a chance to exist in himself. Had it? He felt his father had never believed in him. His mother had hoped but had lived under a layer of sorrow throughout his childhood. The only person who knew whether he had ever had potential of any kind, the only one who had ever told him the truth, was Thomasina Baikie. He did not want to sit here talking to Victoria Huskins. He wanted to see Thomasina.

32

Treadway's Gold

"Dad?"

"Wayne, I'm going to describe to you where I am and I'm hoping you'll know where that is."

"Dad?"

"I'm not lost but I'm in a situation where I can't figure out where to go."

Wayne heard car horns behind his father. He heard the engine of a truck and he heard a siren and someone shouting, "Gary! Meet me over at the Fountain Spray."

Treadway Blake had been in the Labrador woods all his life and had not become lost. He could go to a place in the woods that he had never before visited and could travel deep into the new mystery of it, encountering streams that criss-crossed and turned back on themselves. He could turn back on his own path and follow such streams, and it did not matter how many figure eights his path took or how many miles he ventured from territory he had known — he could always find his way home. He had only to look at the tops of the trees to see how they had been shaped by the prevailing wind, or at the direction in which a stream flowed, or the sky above the trees and the sun's path in it, or the paths of the moon and stars. The wilderness of Labrador was home to him, and he could have explored thousands of miles there and not worried about losing his way. But the seven square miles of downtown St. John's were a different tale.

He knew the downtown was small because he had seen most of it from the terrace on Military Road below the basilica. It dropped down like a pop-up card full of steeples and coloured houses leading down to the ships' masts and the harbour. But the fact that it was small did not help Treadway find his way around in what felt like a maze. The only part of it that did not fill Treadway with a sense of claustrophobia was the hourglass exit to the harbour, whose little piece of horizon he gazed at to get his bearings, and when he gazed at it he felt he could breathe again. There were shorebirds out there, some related to shorebirds he knew at home. There was also a hawk: he had seen it from Military Road, circling the top of Signal Hill. Was it a red-tailed or a rough-legged hawk? He had watched its flight pattern but from that distance he had been unable to discern. Then he had looked back at the street, and his own path on it, which he had hoped would lead to the Forest Road address where he knew his son rented an apartment.

Treadway Blake had received two visits: one from Wayne's old principal Victoria Huskins, the other from Thomasina. He did not know what to make of the first visit. He could not imagine his son looking the way Victoria Huskins had said he looked, and he did not know whether Victoria Huskins's view of anything was a view he could trust. Thomasina Baikie was a different story. She came to him after a phone call from Wayne.

Wayne had asked her to come down to see him; he had a job and he offered to pay her fare down. There was a place in the cliffs, he said, called Ladies' Lookout. On it was a giant slab of stone in a patch of grass, surrounded by rock that opened onto the sea. He told Thomasina he watched the cranes on the harbourfront every night after work, then he walked to Ladies' Lookout and sat there alone. He told her what had happened on Signal Hill with Derek Warford in the van, and he said that sometimes he wondered what would happen if, instead of sitting on the stone at Ladies' Lookout and watching the ocean, he stood and relaxed into the darkness and let his body drop over the edge. He did not think anything worse could happen than what had already happened.

Thomasina asked him specific questions about what Derek Warford had done and he answered them directly. He was telling her all this, he said, not because he wanted to upset her but because she had asked, and because she was the only person he could think of who might know what to do. He was sorry for telling her about it, and he apologized.

"And I'm sorry for telling you," Thomasina told Treadway. "But I didn't know what else to do."

She had not wanted to go into every detail, but Treadway had not permitted her to leave out anything. He was silent then, and she did not know what he could be thinking.

"I could go," she said. "I told him I could be down there in three days. But I went for a walk in the bush and thought about it and I realized you should know about it. And maybe you want to go down instead of me. I didn't want it to be like the other time."

She meant the time that had led, when Wayne was in junior high, to her taking him to hospital. She did not know if she had interfered too much then, and she did not want to risk doing so again. She would go if Treadway would not. But if Treadway wanted to go and help his son, then she felt it was his place to do so and not hers.

In bed Treadway could not sleep. He could not tell Jacinta what had happened; he was alone with the images in his mind. The images came into his mind again and again and he could not make them go away, or change, or turn into other, less harrowing images. He kept seeing that van door opening and six young men invading the van and holding broken glass over his son's face and humiliating him. In his mind, over and over again, Treadway saw the shadowy figure of one of them tearing the buttons of Wayne's shirt and undoing his pants and seeing Wayne's body underneath, the body of Treadway's own daughter, or son, it did not matter. What mattered was that no one had been there to help Wayne. Treadway had not been there, and he was not there now.

He closed his eyes but the scene played out again and again and he could not stop it. Everyone was nameless in the scene, and Treadway could not see their faces. If he had a name or a face he could have held on to that. It would have been a piece of information he could have used to get a handle on the scene, to stop it, to say wait a minute, to pause the scene and perhaps change it. Treadway lay in bed and knew he would never be able to change that scene. He knew it had passed, and that the only thing he could do now was go to St. John's and take time in his hands, time that had not yet irrevocably passed as the scene he now saw over and over again had passed.

There was future time, and Treadway could enter only that. It was all he could do, and he did not know what it would mean, but he had a few thoughts about what a father could do to someone who was on the loose and able to do this to his child, or to someone else's child in the future. There would be no future for that person and his actions if Treadway Blake had anything to do with it. This was the only thought that could stop the scene from playing over again and again, the only thought that could break the pattern of the thing that his mind was playing over and over. It did not break the pattern entirely, but it made it jump. It made a father's agony hesitate.

What mystified Treadway Blake about downtown streets in St. John's was the dead ends. You could start down a street that began in a perfectly ordinary fashion, but then you met stairs, and the stairs led into what looked like a lane between back gardens, and before you knew it you had come into an enclosure surrounded by tall fences, and you were met by the headlamps of a black cat on a grassy mound, and there was no way out but the way in which you had come. Then there was the strange way in which the houses, because they were all different — crimson, blue, purple with yellow trim, or brown with a window box of geraniums — began after a while to look the same as each other, so that you did not know whether you had encountered a new box of geraniums or travelled in a circle to meet the same one twice. The togetherness of the houses, the way they were so much more densely crowded than any house in Labrador, made him feel the houses were crowding him. It was as if they had shoulders and eyes and were closing in on him, so that he felt St. John's had swallowed him and he was lost in its guts, and the guts were the streets that twined around and through each other exactly like the intestines of moose and caribou he had hunted and cleaned, except that here in downtown St. John's, Treadway was no great hunter. He was not even able to find his own son, whose address he carried written on the inside cover of the bank book in his pocket. He kept taking the bank book out and looking at the address anew, but it did not help him find Forest Road. Why, Treadway wondered, had they called it Forest Road when there was no forest in sight? If there had been even the vestige of a forest, Treadway might have known what to do. But there were only the lurid houses on their interlocking tangle of avenues.

He looked at the bank book repeatedly, then stuffed it away again, afraid of losing it. In it was a figure that both pleased and disappointed him. It was the total amount of money that the Labrador Credit Union in Goose Bay had agreed to trade him for his gold. The figure pleased him because it was a lot higher than the amount he had originally paid for the gold, but it disappointed him because he knew that now, converted into money, that figure would no longer increase.

The word was *liquidation*. Treadway had liquidated the gold, and now it would get smaller, because you spent money, you did not save it. The regret he felt was not on his own behalf.

Treadway was going to give the bank book, and the money it represented, to his son. He regretted only that the figure could not grow and that its power was uncertain: when it was spent, his son might be in a position to make a good living in this world, but he might not. Treadway regretted that he could not see into the future and know for certain whether giving this money to Wayne would be fruitful or not. Fruitfulness might be an old-fashioned concept, Treadway thought. It might be something he had read in his hunting cabin in the books of Genesis and

Matthew. It might be something the land and the animals of a place like Labrador understood while a city like St. John's might not. Fruitfulness was a thing that came from seeds and plants and animal life. It was a thing that happened naturally in the wilderness. But it might be forgotten here, in this place where his son now lived. Selling the gold and turning it into money was not fruitfulness, and Treadway knew this, and was aware, on this day in which he was lost in the city, that mere gold could be like many of these streets. It could be a dead end, when what his son really needed was life.

"Dad? Are you near the Fountain Spray?" Wayne had heard someone shout about the Fountain Spray in the background noise. The Fountain Spray was a shop on Military Road, near Bannerman Park.

"I don't know, son. I'm across the road from a grey and white church."

"Is it St. Thomas's Church?"

"I can't see from here. I'm in a phone booth and there are five roads going in all different directions."

"Dad, can you see the Newfoundland Hotel?"

"There is a pretty big hotel to my right."

"It sounds like you're at the traffic circle on King's Bridge Road. Can you see any street signs? Can you see Military Road or Ordnance Street?"

"I can't see the signs from here, but yes, I just walked along Military Road."

"Okay, stay there and I'll meet you."

"Just give me directions, son."

"It's okay, Dad. It's not far, and it's confusing. I was confused myself by that intersection when I first got here. It would confuse anyone."

Wayne could not bear to think of his father lost in a telephone booth at the King's Bridge Road traffic circle. He put the phone down and ran down Forest Road and King's Bridge Road, and when he saw the telephone booth in the distance with cars and trucks and traffic lights and the hotel all buzzing around his father, who stood in front of the phone booth carrying a rolled-up sleeping bag, he thought how lost his father looked, how small and round and like a wild owl or a shore duck that had been blown a thousand miles off course, far from its own habitat.

When Treadway saw Wayne's apartment, how bare it was, he said, "It's a good thing I brought my sleeping bag." But he did not dwell on this or make Wayne feel as if the apartment was not good. Treadway had slept in harder conditions than this, and he made do with the floor as his son did. There was a bedroom, and Treadway rolled his jacket into a pillow and said the floor was palatial. Hearing his father say this made Wayne realize Treadway had the capacity in him to be funny, which Wayne had not known. Treadway unrolled his sleeping bag and took out of it another bag, one of the woven fertilizer bags he normally used to bring sawdust from Goudie's sawmill to pack around his carrots in the winter shed. From that bag Treadway took a coil of snare wire and his toothbrush and three pairs of socks and three pairs of underwear, which Wayne realized was the sum of his luggage.

"Let's go to Ches's for fish and chips." Treadway folded the fertilizer bag flat and tucked it into his waistband. Wayne was surprised his father knew about Ches's.

"It's famous," Treadway said. "Everyone has read about Ches's."

In fact, Wayne told him, Leo's was better than Ches's. Leo's was not as famous but they fried the fish twice and the batter puffed like a cloud, and the fish was better too. Treadway said he was starving, so they walked together back to Military Road and up to the end of Long's Hill, where all the fish and chip shops were. As they walked, Treadway kept surprising Wayne with things he knew about the local roads and architecture and details of the city.

"They got the stones for that from Galway," Treadway said as they passed the basilica. "The limestone anyway. The granite they brought over from Dublin." He looked at everything and seemed interested in it. When they reached Leo's, Treadway sat down and scuffed his feet over the floor and said, "You don't get many terrazzo floors anymore."

Wayne had been in Leo's many times and had not noticed the floor. Now he looked at it.

"It's old. Cracked," Treadway said. "They can't get anybody to fix it in this day and age. But beautiful."

There were a few things Treadway wanted to do, he told Wayne, while he was in St. John's. He was staying for three days, and he wanted to see the exhibit of Beothuk and Inuit tools and household artifacts and hunting clothes in the Newfoundland Museum on Duckworth Street. There was a carving knife he particularly wanted to see, and a child's fur coat with part of the tail of the animal intact.

"And I'd like you to tell me," Treadway said, "the name of the person who attacked you. And if there is a grocery store nearby, there is something I'd like to buy in it."

It was the first mention Treadway made of why he had really come: the misery and sadness of his son. He had not said anything about Wayne's appearance but he had taken it in, and he did not appear to be shocked or upset by it. Wayne had always appeared more graceful than other boys as far as Treadway was concerned. He had always had an air of gentleness about his face, and his shape had not been very much different from what it was now, though there had been muscle where there was now litheness. Wayne wore a plain shirt and jeans that were the kind he had always worn, and Treadway had noticed the girl's breasts on his son before. They were not new to him, and they were small. You could miss them if you were not looking carefully. But Treadway was looking carefully.

He took his pocketknife out and used it to cut his fish, and he noticed everything around him, including the type of engine on the city bus that passed by Leo's window, and the German make of the clock on the fire hall across Harvey Road.

"Dad, I didn't know you knew so much about St. John's."

"I don't know anything about St. John's."

"You do. You know what kind of stone is in the churches and where it came from, and you know about the floor here and the bus engines, and you know what exhibits are down at the museum. I didn't even know there was a museum."

"You would have noticed it sooner or later. And I don't know about the stone in all the churches, just the basilica and the Anglican cathedral, and some of the churches and castles in England and Scotland, because I read about them. Anything I know about I've usually read, even a lot of what I know about trapping. I get a lot from books."

Wayne realized how often he had seen his father reading. He knew there were books in his trapping hut, and there were always books beside his bed at home. He had not thought about the books as having the ability to help his father orient himself in St. John's, or in any strange city. The thought was new to Wayne. His father might have become lost on the way to the Forest Road Apartments, but he was not lost in the world of terrazzo flooring or German clocks, or the history of his ancestors, and it was because he read.

"I've had a lot more time than you have had to read. And I've had a lot less to contend with in my life than you have had in yours. What I'd like to know now, Wayne, is the name of the person who attacked you."

"Derek Warford. Why?"

"Because I might like to have a word with him. And I would like to see the place where it happened. This Deadman's Pond that Thomasina told me about."

"Dad."

"As a matter of fact, I'd like you to show it to me now. But before we go up Signal Hill I'd like to go to a grocery store and I'd like to buy a really nice orange."

Wayne took his father to the Parade Street Dominion and then they walked down Harvey Road and took the steps to Long's Hill. They walked along Gower Street, and while they were walking in front of the chain-link fence outside Powers' Salvage on the east end of Duckworth Street, Treadway handed Wayne the bank book. There was no one to witness this but the gulls that circled the city's sewage outlet. They stood near the giant pyramid of salt that the city was storing to put on the roads next winter, and there was a smell of seaweed. The fog was coming in but had not come in yet, and the sounds were gulls and cranes and containers echoing as they landed down on the docks, with the squeaking of pulleys and now and then a man shouting. The men were tiny in the distance in their hard hats. Wayne watched them through the fence, and he did not know why his father

had handed him a bank book until his father explained
— it was the gold.

"The gold you always had in your closet?"

"I want you to have it. Put it in your pocket and we'll
go to the credit union tomorrow and I'm going to sign
that account over to you. And you, I want you to use it
to do something with yourself. I don't care what it is but
I want you to think about it. Go and visit different places
if you want, places where they can teach you something
you want to know how to do. It has to be something
you have an interest in. And this thing here" — he gave
Wayne an envelope — "is a ticket Thomasina Baikie gave
me to give you."

Wayne put the bank book in his pocket and unwrapped
the ticket. It was a ticket for a performance of American
folk songs by the Boston Downtown Community Choir.
The ticket had cost five dollars and the date on it was
August the twenty-fifth, which was in six weeks' time.

"Thomasina wants you to see your old friend. The
trip won't cost much, and even if it did, what else is
money for?"

"Dad, I don't want to take your gold."

"As I said, son, you've had a lot more to contend
with than I have ever had. I want you to take that. Your
mother and I want you to have it and we want you to do
something with it that will mean we don't have to worry
about how you are going to make a living. It's pure selfishness on our part."

"Does my mother know?"

"Does she know what, son?"

"Does she know I've gone off the drugs? And what about what Derek Warford did? She doesn't know about that?"

"No. I didn't say a word about Derek Warford. Your mother would not have been able to stand hearing that."

"I know."

"But she knows about the drugs. Your mother has always — part of her — wanted you to be who you are now. She has always been the one who felt the drugs might not be the right thing. Ever since you were little. So yes, I told her about that. And she was happy."

They were at the intersection that led up Signal Hill and, to the east, along the Battery.

"She was happy?"

"Well she cried, but she said she was happy. And I almost forgot to give you this. I hope to God it's not bent. She'll kill me if I've bent it." Treadway took a small square out of his pocket. It was two pieces of cardboard measuring no more than two by three inches and held together by a rubber band, and when Wayne took the band off, he saw it was a photograph. There had been a newspaper clipping that showed the moment Elizaveta Kirilovna had won her gold medal for synchronized swimming, when Wayne was eight years old. Jacinta had clipped it at the time, and they had looked at it together and felt Elizaveta Kirilovna's joy.

"But this is not newsprint," Wayne said. "It's a real photograph." Elizaveta Kirilovna was waving and her face was wet. You could see a drop of swimming pool water on her mouth. Wayne had, when he was eight, told Jacinta he could almost imagine that Elizaveta Kirilovna was waving to him personally.

"Your mother took it to Sooter's in Goose Bay and asked them to reprint it on photo paper. They do that now. They can make a poster if you want it. But your mother wanted it small. She asked me to go into S. O. Steele on Water Street and have it put in a sterling silver frame for you, but I didn't get around to it. Could you do that yourself, son? Your mother doesn't need to know. I don't tell her everything, and I sometimes have the feeling there are details she keeps from me."

They walked past the convent and past the coloured houses that straggled up the hill and petered out before you got to the Battery Hotel, the front all white on the hillside like a cruise ship, though it was dilapidated at the back. Then came the hill's steepest bend and around it emerged Cabot Tower.

"Deadman's Pond is in here," Wayne pointed into the bushes. There were blueberry bushes that had flowers on them: modest pink bells and new green and white and pale purple berries, and on a few, one or two berries that had turned blue. Water peeped through the bushes and they saw the worn-down shrubs where people had driven vehicles to get closer to the pond. Wayne did not know why his father wanted to come here, and he felt uneasy. He had not walked up here since his attack, and he did not want to see the pond.

"I want you to leave me here."

"Why?" Wayne was afraid someone might come and challenge his father. He knew Derek Warford was unlikely to come here in the daytime but he pictured it anyway. He did not know what his father planned to do and he did not like leaving him here alone.

"I want to have a careful look at the place and I have something I want to do here by myself. I've got the key you gave me and I'll use it to get back in the apartment when I'm done."

He knew Wayne had to go to work. It was late afternoon. Wayne stood on the side of the road and watched his father walk into the bushes and stoop down and eat a few blueberries as he would have done in the blueberry bushes around home. He saw that his father's hands were big around the berries, but his thumb and finger had no problem aiming for the delicate berry and picking it.

"All right, Dad." Wayne did not move.

"Go on, son."

Once Wayne had turned to go back down into the city he did not look back at his father, though he wanted to, and his back felt exposed and sensitive as if it were a naked screen and the image of his father alone at Deadman's Pond was projected on it.

33

Red Hawk

THE GROUND UNDER THE BLUEBERRY bushes was, Treadway thought, drier than ground under similar bushes in Labrador, and the berries had a different perfume. But the pond was like a pond he knew back home called Bottomless Pond. This one was called Deadman's Pond, he figured, because a dead man could disappear in it for a good long time. Of course Bottomless Pond at home had a bottom, and so did this pond, but it was a deep bottom. Treadway could tell how deep from the contours of the pond, from the sediments he saw between the shrub roots and the surface, and from its colour.

He had not been able to stop seeing what Thomasina told him had happened here to his son. But now that he was here the scene changed, as scenes always do when we visit their real setting in person. He had pictured the trampled bushes where vehicles came as being on the pond's other side, and he had not thought the terrain would be this steep. He walked around the pond looking for the place where it plunged most abruptly to its greatest depth, and he found it next to some boulders on the north side. He dislodged a small boulder from the nest in which it had sat for perhaps hundreds of years and rolled it over the lip of the pond, and it disappeared. He sat on one of the bigger boulders and thought about what he had planned to do.

He had hunted countless times in terrain that was not much different from this terrain. He looked at the path, the twigs on the path, their dryness and how they cracked. He looked at the available boulders and their sizes, and at the diameter of the shrubs and the hiding places underneath the shrubs. He felt the direction of the wind and was glad it was a cold wind, and that it had a sound and a deep loneliness. He was glad this place was as lonesome as he had imagined it might be. He saw evidence of several kinds of small animals and he saw moose droppings.

Treadway did not want to go over in his mind the conversation Thomasina had had with him, but it was the kind of conversation that haunted a father. Though Treadway had never called Wayne anything but his son, he knew and had always known that within his son lay hidden a daughter. He had seen this daughter in the past day here in St. John's. He had seen Annabel in Wayne's face, and he had wanted to come to Deadman's Pond to see if coming here, where this thing had happened, would change his mind or confirm in his mind that he wanted

to remove the possibility that Derek Warford could ever
do this again to his son, or daughter, or to anyone else's
daughter. He could remove that possibility, he saw now,
looking at the landscape. There was little difference in a
wilderness like this between trapping a wild animal and
hunting a man. There were several ways Treadway could
do it. He could use a trap like those he used at home,
but that would mean he would have to go buy the trap,
and he did not want to go to Wilson's outfitting shop on
Water Street and meet any of the Wilsons or have them
remember him. What he had thought about doing, the
possibility that seemed most careful to him now, was a
thing he had done one winter when he came across a live
lynx caught in a trap belonging to Roland Shiwack.

The fertilizer bag in which he had brought his socks,
underwear, and toothbrush was a multi-purpose bag. It
was light and portable, which made it good for trans-
porting sawdust, yet it was strong enough to carry fifty
pounds of fifteen-thirty-fifteen fertilizer, and it could carry
more weight than that if need be. Treadway saved fertilizer bags the way he saved wire and any kind of rope, and
he had brought this one to St. John's because it fit easily
into his sleeping bag with his clothing in it and because he
knew what else he could do with it.

It would not be hard to find Derek Warford and
appeal to his vanity and to his wallet.

"They told me at the shop on the corner," he imagined himself saying, "that of the young fellows around

here, you'd be the one who best knows your way around. I'd like to see what all visitors come for: Cabot Tower and the trail down over the cliffs, but I can find those myself. What I want is to get off the main road."

What this reconnaissance trip was for was to see if everything he had thought of doing was in fact feasible, and it was. Treadway took the fertilizer bag out of the waistband of his trousers. At the pond's deepest shore he found a large stone. He put the stone in the bag and hid it under the bushes, marking the location in his mind. He had to use the steeple of St. Andrew's Church in the distance down below as one of his markers, and for the other he used the tip of a transmitter tower on the South-side hills. He was not used to using manmade markers for trapping, and he kept thinking this would work only as long as the same men who had built the steeple and the tower did not decide to come and remove them, which could not happen with a mountain or a river bend or any of the markers he used when hunting in Labrador.

He hid the stone and the bag and he remembered the lynx. Roland Shiwack was a man who was not careful enough with his traps, in Treadway's opinion. Treadway had trapped many a lynx but he had rarely trapped one that remained alive in the trap. He had used the right kind of trap in the right terrain, whereas Roland Shiwack made do with substitutes for the best trap, and that was why Roland's lynx had been going crazy when Treadway found it. Treadway had not had his gun at the time, but he did have snare wire, and he had a bag like this one, and he was in a part of the land where there were boulders and a river with rapids that contained a deep pool. Any kind of cat will instantly calm down when you haul a bag over its head, even a wounded lynx, and then you can tie the bag with wire at the animal's neck, and if you are lucky enough to be beside deep water you can carry the lynx to the pool, and as long as you have tied the snare wire properly and the stone inside the bag is the right stone, you can drown the lynx, and thus end one of the little pieces of torture that plague the secret corners of this earth.

This is what Treadway had in mind to do with Derek Warford. He had doubts, as he had done when he drowned Roland Shiwack's lynx. What if the bag did not calm the lynx? What if the lynx clawed through the bag before the stone plunged him deep enough? What if the lynx, or Derek Warford, was stronger, or smarter, than Treadway knew?

But Treadway knew instinctively that Derek Warford did not have a lynx's intelligence, and he knew that while he was almost sixty, his own strength still came when he needed it, and that someone like Derek Warford, who had not trapped in Labrador and had not been alone in the wilderness for months and years and decades of his life, did not know how to fight the way Treadway knew, and would not be expecting Treadway to do the thing he had planned. Still, Treadway knew it was possible that Derek Warford, because he was younger, could overpower him.

He thought a lot about that possibility, and he also thought about the question of malice: was there malice in himself, directed at this person, Derek Warford? He thought about it and he knew there was no malice. He did not want to punish Derek Warford as much as he wanted to simply remove him. A person like that, a person who would do such a thing as Derek Warford had done to Wayne, needed to be removed from the scene. That was all. It was a question of ridding this little place in the world, the Battery, of someone who had done this crime and who would probably do it again to someone else. It was not a crime about which Treadway Blake wanted to consult the police, or anyone like the police. That thought did not rest in his mind at all, the thought of police stations and forms and explaining what had happened to his son, and having to explain the femaleness of his son. But there was someone at the top of Signal Hill with whom Treadway did want to consult.

Treadway had seen a hawk from Military Road and had watched it circle the top of Signal Hill and plummet for prey, then rise and circle again. He had watched it until he knew where it lived, and now he climbed Signal Hill and took the orange he had bought at the Parade Street Dominion out of his pocket and placed it in the grass on a remote tuft of the hill.

He sat for several hours, and the orange was the only bright thing in the grass. When the hawk came, it did not alight. It was a red-tailed hawk whose body glowed red-brown. It hovered, and Treadway spoke to it in the same way he spoke to the boreal owl and to other wild animals in Labrador. He did not have to speak out loud but had only to silently present his idea about ridding the world of Derek Warford. Treadway knew a hawk is a merciless animal. He knew that if a woman happened to be up here on Signal Hill picking blueberries or partridge-berries with a baby, especially a newborn, she had better watch out or the hawk could take that baby. It had hap-pened before, perhaps with this red hawk, and it would happen again: a hawk was a carnivore and it could take a large bird or a baby away and kill it. Treadway had seen a hawk carry off Graham Montague's biggest rooster. He did not expect a hawk to have mercy for a person like Derek Warford.

But Treadway had read Pascal, and the Bible, and the essays of philosphers, and he had read poets, and against his own will the hawk reminded him of things he had read. It did not speak to him out of its own wildness, perhaps, he thought, because it had spent too much time circling above steeples and libraries and museums that held the thoughts of civilized men. He had not thought a hawk would do this. Now, as it dipped and circled close to him on its flight path between the crags of Signal Hill and the ocean below where its own prey lay — capelin and young cod and sea urchins with peach-coloured roe — this hawk told him something old, the same thing over and over again. It was not what Treadway wanted to hear.

"I would dearly love," Treadway told the hawk, "to finish off Derek Warford in the manner I have planned."

The sun was setting and the orange glowed in the grass. The hawk still did not say what Treadway wanted it to say. He had been hoping for a blessing. He had thought the hawk would understand carnage and vengeance. He thought if anyone understood how he felt in his heart at the thought of what Derek Warford had done to his son, his daughter, in that van, the hawk would understand. The hawk had possibly seen with its own eyes what had happened and knew better than Treadway how much Derek Warford deserved to be sunk with a stone to the bottom of a bottomless body of water. But the hawk did not recognize any of this. It did not swoop down and take the orange or land near Treadway. But it hovered. It hovered in front of him and it reminded him of the same words over and over again, from the books of Deuteronomy and Romans and also the book of Hebrews in the bible Treadway kept in his trapper's hut: Vengeance is mine, I will repay, says the Lord.

"When?" asked Treadway. "When is the Lord planning on getting around to it? Because I can have it done by this time tomorrow."

But the hawk used an argument Treadway had used many times himself when Jacinta had asked him to explain or justify a decision he had made. The hawk used the argument of one lone proclamation followed by silence, and in that silence, Treadway knew, he could protest all he liked, but he would not win the argument.

34

The Fire of Your Grace

WHEN HE GOT ON THE TRAIN from Portland to Boston,
Wayne felt what his father had promised he would feel.

"Don't go in the van," Treadway had said. "Leave
your van and get on the bus to Port-aux-Basques. Get the
ferry to North Sydney but don't get on the train there. Go
to Yarmouth and get the Yarmouth ferry to Portland, and
then you'll be almost in Boston. You don't want to be in
the van, navigating."

Treadway had carefully studied a map he had bought
in the gift shop at the Newfoundland Hotel. "You want
to sit back and look out the windows at everything. You
don't want the trip to be one road sign after another and a
maze of overpasses. Trains and ferries will give you a real
journey to Boston. Your van is a responsibility. Navigating
is a chore. A train will take the weight of the world away."

The train went through what seemed to Wayne to be private sections of ordinary people's lives: balconies and backyards where shovels had been left against fences, and clothes hung in a damp wind that made them tremulous, so that the clothes appeared intimate. The balconies had chairs on them: wooden chairs and a few upholstered chairs that no one minded leaving in the rain. Some balconies held small tables and the people who lived there had left pitchers and coffeepots on them, and had done so recently, so that the balconies, as Wayne passed them on the train, felt as if remnants of conversation hung inside them. There was a tumbledown feel to the flowers that clung to trellises at the backs of American towns, and in blue clematis or scarlet runner beans against red brick lay a feeling of peace Wayne found unaccountable, yet he felt it as he looked out the train window. His father had been right.

Wally Michelin's aunt Doreen had answered the phone and told Wayne to come down. She had a small spare room. Wally was excited about having been accepted into the Boston Downtown Community Choir. Yes, the ticket had been for Thomasina, and no, Wally would not mind that Thomasina had given it to Wayne.

"Thomasina wrote and told us," Doreen said. "She told us to look after you."

In the weeks following Treadway's visit, summer had turned. No leaf had changed colour but the sky had changed. It was silver and leaden and it brought out the colours beneath it in a way the summer sky did not. Summer sky swallowed colour, but the sky of late August made colour ricochet back to earth, and there were sharp edges on all the buildings and curbs and even on the leaves of the trees and on the impatiens in the flowerbeds of all the towns through which Wayne travelled to reach Wally Michelin. The closer he got to Boston, the sharper this light grew, and the more he feared he had done the wrong thing in coming. It was one thing to have a ticket in your pocket for a choir performance. That gave you permission to go into the theatre and take your seat. But did it give you permission to re-enter the life of a beloved friend after you and she had left each other behind?

Wally's aunt Doreen had told him that Wally was happy he was coming, but as the train approached Boston Wayne worried about meeting her again. He looked again at the light wool coat he wore, and the thin scarf and the corduroy pants, which were the colour of malted milk and caught light from the train window so that there were pale and dark stripes. No one looked at him twice on the train. He had a haircut that made him look like any young person. He had gone to a salon on Duckworth Street that cut both men's and women's hair and had asked the girl to give him a haircut that suited his face. There were students on the Boston train, and he looked like one of them.

His train was delayed for an hour outside the city because something had gone wrong with the switches. A conductor announced that the switches had to be done by hand. By the time the taxi brought him to Wally's address her aunt Doreen welcomed Wayne alone.

"She's gone to choir practice. Are you hungry?"

"I had a sandwich on the train."

"I've got a cup of broth for you. Have that and I'll take you to watch the rest of her practice, then when you both come back, we'll have a real supper."

Wally's aunt, Wayne discovered, was a gracious woman who looked through your eyes and into whoever was in there. Certain things were visible to her that were not visible to other people. He felt at home with her, and he felt nervous when they pulled up to the building where Wally was practising and her aunt told him to go in alone.

The place had been a church hall but was no longer affiliated with a church. The whole church and the buildings with it were rundown, but a group called the Appleton Street Neighbourhood Association was working to revitalize it. Wayne read this on a plaque in the hallway. He could hear chairs dragging across the floor inside double doors that each had a tiny pane, and he looked through the panes and saw the choir on a stage, and he saw the conductor and a piano player. They were between songs and the conductor was talking about the purity of consonants. Wayne waited until the choir resumed singing so that there was a wall of sound. There was not much light and he was glad of this as he quietly entered. The choir director kept starting and stopping the music. He told the choir to skip pages, and sometimes they skipped ahead to an entirely different song that they began singing but did not complete. It appeared to Wayne that the entire practice was all about ripping the songs into pieces and working on those pieces as if they would never again belong to the original song, as if fragments of music were all the conductor hoped for. He saw Wally Michelin in the back row, second to last. He recognized her not so much from her features, which he could not see, but from the way she stood, and had always stood, and from the rippling hair and the shape of her face. It occurred to him that Wally Michelin was singing, though she had been told she would not sing again, and he marvelled at that though he did not know if he should believe it, as her voice was not alone but was part of the choir's sound.

When the practice was over, she came to his seat as if she had known he would be there, and as if it were ordinary that he should be in Boston with her. She sat beside him, and there was so much activity around them — people taking date squares and deli sandwiches out of purses and unwrapping them and eating them and talking about Linda's new grandson and George's holiday in Florida, which meant George would not be here for the concert — that Wayne felt he and Wally were alone in a sea of sound.

"You came."

"You don't mind?"

"No. I'm glad you came."

He was not alone with her but he felt as if they were alone. He felt they recognized each other in a way that no one else recognized either of them. Other people could look at him but they did not see what Wally Michelin saw, and perhaps others saw in her the same thing he did, but he did not think they saw it. What it was was limitlessness. When you were with an ordinary person, you could draw a line around the territory the two of you covered, and Wayne had found that the territory was usually quite small. It was smaller than a country and smaller than a town and sometimes smaller than a room. But this room, the room they were in, did not really exist. Boston did not necessarily exist either, although Wayne could sense it, fizzing with the unfamiliarity of its lights, its parks and streets, beyond the practice-room doors. The way he responded to Wally's presence was that he felt as if life at this minute was blossoming inside him instead of lying dormant. He felt the electric presence of his own life, and he did not want that feeling to end, although he knew it had ended in the past and that it would end again. She whispered into his ear and the piece of her breath was warm with cool edges.

"I won't get a chance to use what your father sent me yet," she said. "Not in this week's concert. But I asked Jeremy if he had ever conducted it and if we could do it in another concert, and he said it is one of his favourite pieces of music too and we might do it next spring."

"What my father sent you?"

Wayne knew nothing about the time Treadway Blake had ordered a replacement for Wally's lost copy of Gabriel Fauré's "Cantique de Jean Racine." But Wally Michelin had not forgotten it, and she took it out of her black folder now. It had the imprint of Albert J. Breton on it and Wayne could see that the paper was now old and that Wally had bookmarked it in many places with green tags. She flipped it open and he saw she had highlighted many passages throughout and had written in the margins in exactly the same way she had done on the original version, the one Treadway had lost when they were both twelve years old.

"It was never meant as a solo piece," Wally said, "It was always a piece for four parts, for a choir, and that's only one of the things I didn't realize."

"My father gave you that?" All this time Wayne had thought his father had not been at all sorry. About the bridge, about the music, about anything.

"Remember how you used to sing the alto part to help me practise?"

"Yes."

She leaned over and hummed into his ear. She was humming the alto part, the part that he had sung with her on the bridge. Wayne saw she still had her freckles. She was the same now to him as she had been when they were twelve years old, on the bridge, looking through its spans at the sky. She hummed the tune quietly at first. Around them blared the choir members dispersing and clicking their folders shut and someone fooling around on the piano: a din that began to contain echoing spaces as members of the crowd went out to their cars. Under it, Wally's voice occupied a different wavelength. It did not have strength but it possessed warmth, and she sang some of the words.

"*Répand sur nous le feu de ta grâce* . . . I can't sing the soprano part yet, but they told me I might never be able to sing anything, and I can already do the alto . . . *De la paisible nuit nous rompons le silence* . . ."

The sound insinuated itself underneath all the other sounds, and this sound, alone in the room, entered Wayne's body. Wally Michelin was singing the tune she had always told Wayne she would one day sing.

The thing about Wally's life in Boston, Wayne saw the next day and the day after as they approached the night of her concert, was that it was full of movement. She was forever in motion, between breakfast and registration and showing him around the campus she would attend, and the costume bank where she had salvaged yards of satin and linen and given it a new life, and two dress rehearsals and then the concert itself. He had thought before he came to Boston that the concert would be the most exciting thing Wally Michelin was doing, but it was not. On the day following, she showed him where she would be taking a course in music history, two in theory, and a fourth that was an introduction to formal voice training.

Wayne had a feeling, as she took him around the quadrangle and through the first and second floors of the library and out to the garden, where students sat on the grass studying maps of the campus and drawing circles around course numbers, that he was in a kind of wilderness; it was similar in some ways to being in the bush with his father. There was a sense that the sun was strong and there was no domesticity for miles. Any venture you made was because you were setting out on a kind of exploration that was the same as a hunt. The students around him were beginning a journey that was openended, like his father's journeys away from the curtains of his mother's kitchen and into a vastness of territory that remained unnamed. If anyone named it, you could unname it. There were no walls around the terrain. It occurred to him that his father would have liked such a place as this, and he wished his father had come with him so he could see it.

The other thing Wayne noticed was that among the students he did not feel out of place because of his body's ambiguity, as he had felt on the streets of downtown St. John's. Many of these students looked to Wayne as if they could be the same as him: either male or female. There was not the same striation of sexuality that there was in the ordinary world outside a campus. There were girls who looked like he did, and there were boys who did too, and there were certainly students who wore no makeup and had a plain beauty that was made of insight and intelligence and did not have a gender. He felt he was in some kind of a free world to which he wanted to belong, and he wondered if all campuses were like this.

In the train on his way back from Boston he kept thinking about this. His father had given him money. He had not known what to do with it when Treadway had handed him that bank book near the salt pile for the roads of St. John's. But he knew what to do with it now. Wally Michelin had helped him see it, and so had his father, and so had Thomasina Baikie, and now, on the train, he did not travel the route by which he had come. Between the Vermont border and the Newfoundland ferry were five schools that Wally Michelin and her aunt had helped Wayne find in brochures and university calendars. He intended to stop at them all. He did not yet know which world he wanted to be in, but he had begun to glimpse the worlds.

Again as his train passed the backs of towns, Wayne noticed intimate pieces of domestic life like those that had touched him on his way to visit Wally Michelin. Washing lines with plaintive little pulleys; men and women who lived near the track and had watched a thousand trains pass. It was a beautiful world, the one inside the houses where kettles boiled on blue gas flowers, but he was glad he was not in it, and in this respect he was the same as his father.

He thought about the bridges the train would cross, and bridges that had not yet been envisioned. He knew now that there were schools where you learned how to design bridges that would be built, bridges that were beautiful. This was what he wanted to do. In his pocket lay the Labrador Credit Union bank book containing the record of his father's gold. He knew on the train that in his thinking he was not so different from his father. His father would, this coming winter, walk his trapline towards unnamed places, and Wayne would finally be on his way to a landscape that was for him as magnetic and as big as Labrador.

Epilogue

L E THÉÂTRE CAPITOLE IN QUEBEC CITY was a relic from the twenties, when you did not watch a show, you attended a spectacle. The seating was not in little English rows but in sweeping arcs upon which rested chairs that swivelled around black tables with room enough for one martini each. By intermission, cigarette smoke hung in blue swirls so thick you were lucky to see the performer's face rising over it like a mythical demigod. Thomasina loved it. She had bought the tickets and had asked for them to be held at the box office, and they were good tickets, in the first row of the second-highest tier. She had told Wally Michelin that she and Wayne would arrive together.

Thomasina had decked herself out with a good little car. When you were forty and fifty, it was all right to take buses and trains. But when you were over sixty, it was important to go where you needed to go. You did not have to stop in Bridgewater if what you wanted was Spring Garden Road in Halifax, where Wayne had completed his fourth year at the Technical University of Nova Scotia. He was studying not only the design of bridges but also the architecture, design, and planning of whole cities, and as he and Thomasina drove into Quebec City he saw it from the point of view of someone who had begun to understand not just the surfaces but also the underpinnings of a city's character: its ugliness or, in the case of this place, its beauty and grandeur.

The Théâtre Capitole had been renovated. Everything was fire red, blue, and gold. Wayne and Thomasina sat in cabaret chairs that had been covered in velvet. There was a scent of blackened steak, which patrons ate with two-pronged forks, and the smell of Gitanes and expensive soap mingled with this. The evening was a program of Schubert presented by the Berklee College of Music in Boston and the Juilliard School in New York.

"Wallis," Wayne read in the program. "Wallis Michelin."

Wally Michelin wore a headpiece that winked and flung stars across the theatre. She wore a gown that billowed at the sleeve and a breastplate that made her look, Wayne felt, ready for a battle under the waves, with Poseidon and an array of glorious fishes. When her voice began, Wayne knew it did not come from the girl he had heard under the Croydon Harbour apple tree. It came from a different person, a person who had learned how to build a voice from the ruins up, a person who had lost everything and had begun from having worse than nothing. A person who had not given up believing she sang, that music would come to her because she wanted it to come, and it had to come, and she would use everything in her power to encourage it to do so.

"You go down to the green room," Thomasina said at the end of the program. "I'll wait for you here."

Wayne stood against the tide of audience members as they left the theatre, then descended the stairs, passed the pillars, and took a corridor to Wally's dressing room. He knocked on her door, holding flowers.

There were lights around a mirror and pots of makeup. Wally had taken her costume off and stood in her camisole and slip, taking makeup off her face with a sponge. She had peeled her stockings and hung them over the back of an unpainted chair. People had given her other flowers: yellow and red roses, and cream coloured roses, and lemon roses with blushing edges. There was a bird of paradise surrounded by freesias. But the flowers Wayne gave Wally Michelin were Labrador plants that Thomasina had kept alive in a piece of soaked caribou moss: Labrador tea with its orange furze under the leaf and its misty white bloom; wild rhododendron's asymmetrical purple on a woody stem; sundew and pitcher plants, carnivorous and threatening and beautiful in a way only someone from Labrador would know. The first thing Wally did with the flowers was break a leaf of the Labrador tea so that its scent, which is the scent of the whole of Labrador, broke over the two of them.

The pitcher plant's leaves, exactly like little jugs, still held ants and a few tiny flies caught in the sticky substance the plant produced as a trap. With pitcher plants, some creatures got away and others did not. The pitchers caught other things too. They caught the changing light of Labrador mornings and springtimes and snow light, and they caught the sounds of the harlequin and eider ducks and hermit thrushes, and some of the sounds were considered beautiful and others were not, but the pitchers caught them.

Labrador tea with the same scent grew undisturbed around the shore of that central lake in Labrador, the unnamed lake from which the rivers run both north and south. The same insects visited lethal pitcher plants and a sky looked down; some might call it a merciless sky. And now and then in the pitchers' water a cloud journeyed, and so did patterns of ducks on their spring flight.

Treadway Blake came to this place as he had always done, this birthplace of the seasons, of smelt and of the white caribou, and of deep knowledge that a person did not find in manmade things. Only in wind over the land did Treadway find the freedom his son would seek elsewhere. Treadway was a man of Labrador, but his son had left home as daughters and sons do, to seek freedom their fathers do not need to inhabit, for it inhabits the fathers.

Acknowledgements

I THANK MY BELOVED FAMILY and friends, especially my husband, Jean Dandenault. Thank you to my writing group: enginistas Danielle Devereaux, Lina Gordaneer, Julie Paul, and Alice Zorn. Thank you to Agnes Hutchings. Thank you to my wonderful agent, Shaun Bradley. Thank you to Sarah MacLachlan and the staff of House of Anansi Press. Thank you to Lynn Verge and the kind staff of Montreal's Atwater Library. Special thanks to my editor, Lynn Henry, for her profound expertise and dedication. And thank you, dear reader.

ANNABEL

. . .

KATHLEEN WINTER

QUESTIONS FOR DISCUSSION
ANNABEL BY KATHLEEN WINTER

• • •

1. How is Wayne a litmus test for the humanity of others in the novel? How does he challenge their preconceptions?

2. What is Thomasina's role in the book? How do other people react to her?

3. How does Jacinta foster Wayne's love of art, music, and fantasy?

4. What does the practical Treadway hope to instill in his son? Is there a spiritual element to this Labrador trapper? How is this world part of the legacy he hopes to leave Wayne?

5. How do Treadway and Wayne treat each other? Do you recall Treadway trying to understand the boy?

6. Do you think marriage is extolled in this book? Whose? Is it seen by any of the married people as a full salvation? Does Wayne cement or fragment his parents' marriage?

7. "Wally Michelin had stomped through kindergarten and grades one and two with a certainty Wayne found fascinating . . . Wayne was in love with her from the moment he heard her crumbly voice. So in love he wished he could become her. If there was a way he could make himself into a ghost without a body — a shadow — or transparent like the lures his father used to catch Arctic char, he would have done it. He would have transformed into his father's lure, slipped under Wally Michelin's divinely freckled skin, and lived inside her, looking through her eyes." Describe the relationship between Wayne and Wally.

8. The flowers that begin to bloom in Wayne are not only sexual. Through Wally, Thomasina, and Jacinta, how does he, nose twitching, get a scent of a world larger than his own home?

9. Discuss the significance of Gabriel Fauré and "Cantique de Jean Racine." How are they important to the story?

10. "To Thomasina people were rivers, always ready to move from one state of being into another . . . Everyone was always becoming and unbecoming." Do you think this philosophy helps Thomasina come to terms with the loss of members of her own family, Graham and Annabel?

11. How do music and dancing expand Wayne's sense of possibility?

12. Near the end of the novel, why does Treadway leave an orange in the grass? What is the outcome? Is it possible to relate the journeys of father and son in the novel?

AUTHOR PHOTOGRAPH: JULIETTE DANDENAULT

About the Author

KATHLEEN WINTER has written dramatic and documentary scripts for CBC Television. Her first collection of stories, *boYs*, was the winner of both the Winterset Award and the Metcalf–Rooke Award. A longtime resident of St. John's, Newfoundland, she now lives in Montreal.

www.twitter.com/supremetronic
www.kathleenwinter.livejournal.com